Did God Die on the Way to Houston? A Queer Tale

Did God Die on the Way to Houston? A Queer Tale

A Work of Theological Fiction

DAVID B. MYERS

RESOURCE *Publications* · Eugene, Oregon

Resource Publications
An Imprint of Wipf and Stock Publishers
199 W. 8th Ave., Suite 3
Eugene, OR 97401

www.wipfandstock.com

PAPERBACK ISBN: 978-1-7252-5950-8
HARDCOVER ISBN: 978-1-7252-5951-5
EBOOK ISBN: 978-1-7252-5952-2

Manufactured in the U.S.A.   07/21/20

Contents

1

An Extraordinary Invitation and the Appearance of Shekhinah

Is God hiding? Is God afraid of us? Has God gone on a voyage? Emigrated?

—Friedrich Nietzsche, "The Parable of the Madman," in *Thus Spoke Zarathustra*

August 2018. How open are you, dear reader? How open am I? The encounter I am about to describe certainly tested my willingness to listen. Recently, earlier this month, I received a request to meet from a woman who claimed she had been God. *This book is not another in the vein of "A Conversation with God." There is even a mediocre movie by that name. And of course there is a TV series called* God Friended Me. *These various dialogues with the deity are works of fiction that pretend to be conversations with a being Who is actually God. The woman with whom I conversed never claimed to be God. No, she claimed she had been God. Notice the language: "had been"—was—no longer is. I am not claiming that I had a conversation with God. I call it theological fiction because I did not believe this woman's story, but the conversation is not fiction. How could I make this up? I am sharing with you an actual conversation with an actual person who asserts that she abandoned heaven for earth.*

The woman in question asked me to keep an open mind, but doesn't that have limits? Most of you reading this will probably agree that this outrageous claim would be reason enough not to listen, not to be open, indeed not to meet. Her claim to have been God is of course an absurd claim. I was not sure what to make of the storyteller: someone with a theological sense of humor, a large-scale liar, or a person suffering from a delusion of grandeur and thus profoundly mentally ill?

Imagine, on a Sunday afternoon, just waking up from a nap, opening up your laptop to see an email with this terse invitation: "Professor James Friedman: Would you please meet me for coffee? I want to tell you about a decision to terminate my existence as God and to become a human being. Please keep an open mind. I'm looking for someone to hear me out. Given your theological views, I think you will be especially receptive to the story I have to tell. Are you free next Sunday? If so, could you please meet me at 8:00 a.m.? I will be at the Starbucks in Sugar Land Town Square (a large shopping center). This is in walking distance of my apartment. I don't drive. With appreciation, Shekhinah."

She gave no last name. Was someone luring me to this location for some nefarious reason? Maybe an anti-Semite who heard me, a Jew, speak on "Why God Hates the Ideology of White Nationalism"? I ruled that out. Shekhinah emailed this invitation, as you can see, the Sunday prior to her requested meeting date. With such short notice, I could have used this as a reason to decline, but what if she proposed another date? I gave it a lot of thought for a couple of days. After wrestling with this perplexing invitation, and against my better judgment, I reluctantly said yes. She was not aware of my reluctance—or was she? Could even an ex-deity know the thoughts of others? She would in fact answer this question.

To be honest, prior to the meeting, I continued to have a difficult time persuading myself that her story was worth hearing. Did I really want to waste a Sunday hearing something so bogus? Let me repeat: against my better judgment, I agreed to sit down with her. You might reasonably ask why she chose me. As she stated in her email, it had to do with theology, my view of God, one that, as you will see, was in many ways similar to the God Shekhinah said she had been. As you will also see, I was not her first choice, but I suppose I would have to do. Now long retired, for thirty-two years I was a professor of philosophy at Texas State University in San Marcos—where I taught, among other courses, World Religions; Reason, God, & Nature; Philosophy of Judaism, Christianity, and Islam; Ethics; and The Holocaust.

I am still, at least for a few months more as I write this, the executive director of an interfaith organization in Houston, one I founded in 2008: The Center for Interfaith Action and Dialogue. So I have more than a passing knowledge of and interest in religion and theology. As a person who is the face of an interfaith nonprofit, one that promotes respect for diverse beliefs, I have had to maintain at least the appearance of being open—even to the strangest religious stories and worldviews. The Center organizes opportunities for people of different faiths—and persons who identify as spiritual but not religious, as well as atheists and skeptics—to come together for respectful dialogue, so that they can better understand each other. People of different faiths and world-views invariably find the beliefs of the Other strange, maybe even baffling. Strangeness, like beauty, seems, however, to be in the eye of the beholder. Jews and Muslims find strange the Christian claim that Jesus was fully divine and fully human, God in human flesh; many Christians find the denial of this claim strange. Many Jews, Christians, and Muslims find it strange that there are religions, such as Buddhism, that lack the idea of a Creator.

I am a very unorthodox Jew. I have long appreciated the fact that liberal Judaism, as I understand and live it, values questions over answers, affirms that deed is more important than creed, and emphasizes this life over the next. I also love Torah study: gathering with fellow Jews to argue about the meaning of a sacred text, trying out creative interpretations to make a text more accept-able, and sometimes even arguing with and rejecting what the text says, when it purports to be the word of God. I like exercising my freedom to raise ethical objections to the behavior of the mythical God of the Torah (understood here as the first five books of the Hebrew Bible/Old Testament), such as when this God in the Noah story spared one family and a select group of animals while drowning the rest of humankind—countless human beings, including infants and children—and of course all other animals. This is not a bedtime story for children or, in my opinion, a morally redeemable tale. Surprisingly, very few rabbis or pastors call this terrible story into moral question. Their silence is deafening. Some fundamentalist pro-life Christians, feeling no horror at this story of divinely ordained global mass murder of millions of creatures, created a replica of the Ark you can visit in Kentucky. Do pious visitors ever raise moral questions about the story of the Ark?

Although a member of a Reform synagogue, Temple Shir Shalom (the name means "Song of Peace"), I am by rational inclination a skeptic who, when uttering words about God from the Jewish prayer book, may not literally believe every word I say or sing. I'm one of only a few who attend services on a regular basis. In many liberal religious congregations, fewer people are showing up to worship. Often, I'm more drawn to the music—prayers sung or chanted in Hebrew—than to anything else that happens in a synagogue service. At home I recite Jewish prayers in Hebrew each morning. (Truly ob-servant Jews pray three times a day.) Is my prayer practice just a habit? Maybe, but there are days when I can actually believe there may be a God listening.

I humbly confess that I don't know whether Judaism is true, but, when I am able to suspend my natural state of doubt, I can, at least on some days, live as if Judaism is true and there is a God. In Judaism, as I interpret it, belief is not as important as action: one could even say that belief in God is not a requirement. For me, Judaism is a religion of orthopraxis (correct practice) *rather than a religion of orthodoxy (correct belief). By the way, Judaism does not claim to be the only path to the world to come (heaven?), assuming there is life after death. Again, most religious Jews I know, including Orthodox Jews who regularly attend synagogue services and observe Jewish rituals, don't have a great deal of interest in life after death: their focus is on living a good life in this world.*

My struggle with belief in God began in junior high after I read nine-teenth-century agnostic Robert Green Ingersoll's blistering moral attack on the God of the Bible. Belief in God, apart from problems with the morally problematic God described in the Hebrew Bible/Old Testament, sometimes portrayed as a God of war who from time to time commands acts of genocide, was also made difficult by my awareness of such evils as the Holocaust. The existence of unjust suffering struck me as the biggest obstacle to belief in the God of traditional theism, which affirms a Creator Who is perfectly good and all-powerful. The solution I found to the problem of evil is one that connects me to Shekhinah. To see that connection, I ask, dear reader, for your patience.

When I attended the University of Houston during the late 1960s, as an undergraduate philosophy major, I learned that one of the most important questions in the philosophy of religion is the problem of evil, sometimes also called the problem of suffering. The suffering in question is not all suffering—because one can imagine suffering that might bring something truly good for the sufferer: for example the pain of childbirth—but rather undeserved, point-less, or degrading suffering. An attempt to solve the problem of evil is called a theodicy, a term that means the vindication of God in the face of evil. It was this philosophical problem with which I became academically and personally obsessed.

It remains for me the problem that makes belief in God difficult. As a Jew, my detailed knowledge of the horrors of the Holocaust (a subject I researched and, as already mentioned, taught at Texas State University) gave this prob-lem a special meaning. Although I never want to privilege Nazi genocide by in any way diminishing how terrible the genocides were that happened else-where—for example, Turkey, Cambodia, Darfur, Rwanda, Bosnia, and the United States against Native Americans—I think it is fair to say that in terms of the number of persons murdered, the cruelty of the agents, and the system-atic, factory-like nature of the killing, the Shoah (a Hebrew word meaning "catastrophe," which some Jews prefer to the word "Holocaust," which literally means "sacrificial burnt offering") was in fact shocking.

Aware that during the Shoah Jewish children were sometimes thrown alive into crematory fires at Auschwitz, I remember, over the years, reading and rereading Orthodox Rabbi Irving Greenberg's sober and disturbing warn-ing to those who seek to explain this theologically: "No statement, theological or otherwise, should be made that would not be credible in the presence of burning children. To talk of love and of a God who cares in the presence of burning children is obscene and incredible." It shook me. Could the whole project of theodicy be obscene? Maybe, but I could not leave it alone. I thought of Greenberg's statement recently when I read about Buddhist Myanmar soldiers throwing screaming Rohingya Muslim children into burning houses. It appears we can now add Myanmar to the list of genocides.

When I studied philosophy as a PhD candidate at the University of Texas, the Austin campus, I continued to think about the problem of evil and in fact completed my dissertation in 1974 on this topic, giving it the title "Undeserved Suffering and a God of Love: Toward a Credible Theodicy." My dissertation director, Charles Hartshorne, then still in his youthful mid-eighties, lived to 103. Hartshorne was a creative metaphysician and a theological pioneer in a movement called process thought, which is now a longstanding if minor philosophical and theological tradition in the United States.

Hartshorne had studied under the brilliant philosopher-mathematician-logician Alfred North Whitehead (1861–1947), the thinker who wrote some of the first works developing the process viewpoint, including Process and Reality, an abstruse and groundbreaking book full of neologisms, a book that became the bible of those philosophy graduate students at UT who fancied themselves process thinkers. My copy, now lost, was full of underlinings, paper clips attached to key pages, and copious notes in the margins.

The process view of God, especially as developed by Hartshorne, in such books as Omnipotence and Other Theological Mistakes, offers a solution to the problem of evil. The basic question raised by the problem of evil is whether we can reconcile the existence of unjust suffering with belief in God, especially if God is conceived as perfectly good and all-powerful. Hartshorne, drawing from Whitehead's ideas, had developed a new way of thinking about God that gave up the attribute of omnipotence while retaining the notion that God is perfectly loving. Hartshorne's God is a dynamic Subject who influences but is also changed and enriched by an evolving cosmos, a God who also remains in some aspects changeless (for example, in goodness and in not being subject to death). I found the process view of God a way to make belief in God more plausible: indeed, it enabled me to utter the word "God" meaningfully when I engaged in Jewish prayer. You will see soon enough how my interest in the problem of evil and Hartshorne's God are connected with my encounter with the woman making the amazingly bizarre claim.

In retirement I returned to the place I had spent my youth, Houston, the city severely damaged by Hurricane Harvey in late August of 2017, a year ago as I write this. The destruction caused by Harvey's winds, which was considerable in coastal towns such as Rockport, Texas, was in the Houston area minor compared to the damage done by what felt like endless days and nights of rain generated by the storm. The rain, adding up to fifty inches of water, twenty-seven trillion gallons, brought about widespread catastrophic flooding in residential areas throughout Houston and surrounding cities. Another effect of the hurricane was the generation of tornadoes, very frightening in their destructive power, really a form of natural terrorism.

Harvey was the kind of natural disaster about which one wants to ask believers who see God's will at work everywhere, whether, as the insurance companies would have it, this was "an act of God." When only a week later mammoth Hurricane Irma—after leaving a trail of destruction in the Caribbean Islands (which would be assaulted again a week after Irma by Hurricane Maria that devastated Puerto Rico, causing, we learned only recently, close to five thousand deaths!)—hit the southern Atlantic coast, with major damage to Florida while also causing significant flooding in states such as Georgia and South Carolina, executives of insurance companies may have wished they could blame it all on the Creator and not have to pay out enormous sums to the victims. Maybe they should have sued God.

About the same time Harvey, Irma, and Maria were hitting the United States, half way around the world, a flood, largely ignored by Western media, did far greater damage to parts of Bangladesh, Nepal, and India, bringing the worst destruction seen in years. Over twelve hundred people were killed and twenty-four million were affected. Compare that to up to eighty-four killed by Hurricane Harvey and about seven million people affected directly or indirectly. The national media that could not take their eyes off of Texas said very little about that catastrophe, not to mention the devastation in Puerto Rico. Are Asian and Puerto Rican lives worth less? We need to try to avoid, if possible, an "America first" mentality in reporting natural disasters. Of course after Harvey, Maria, and Irma, Mr. America First, Donald Trump, was overseeing the recovery process. Trump, who I still have a difficult time believing was elected president, has mastered the art, not of the deal, but of vindictiveness and childishness, and, as I write this, is in process of dismantling all the progressive components of American government.

One way the interfaith organization I direct promotes understanding across lines of difference is to provide opportunities for religious and secular individuals to work together on projects beneficial to the Houston community, such as organizing interfaith rescue and cleanup crews during natural disasters, as we did when Hurricane Harvey struck August 25, 2017. This kind of cooperative humanitarian work creates interfaith solidarity, solidarity that comes from joint action for the common good. This is probably the best way to introduce people of different faiths to each other and to create respect between those who hold very different, indeed conflicting, worldviews. After working *together on a humanitarian project, team members then engage in interfaith conversations about what in their spiritual or secular worldview motivated them to engage in this kind of humanitarian work and how it felt to work with others representing different faiths and secular viewpoints.*

I will focus on Harvey because I experienced this hurricane firsthand. Our various interfaith humanitarian working groups, drawn from different religious and secular communities (including Humanists of Houston), supplemented the work of local first responders, the National Guard, and other U.S. military organizations. Our interfaith teams did their best to help as waters rose in Houston neighborhoods, sometimes using their own boats to rescue people from flooded homes and apartments. Some joined in to help even after losing their homes to flooding. We worked in what were often unsafe conditions—with E. coli bacteria at dangerously high levels in floodwater that was often thick and oily, also infested with angry clusters of fire ants.

While performing such humanitarian work, members of our interfaith teams tend to avoid tough theological questions. In response to Hurricane Harvey, Hindus, Jews, Christians, Muslims, Sikhs, and Baha'is worked well together, never stopping to ask out loud: Why, God? Also joining in our work were Buddhists and atheists; having no belief in a Creator, they did not need to raise that question. No doubt there were some traditional Buddhists who explained the disaster to themselves in terms of the law of karma. Of course our task was not to debate theology, but to join cooperatively together to help those in need and engage in the compassionate action our religious or humanistic value-systems demanded of us. It is amazing how much good a disaster can bring out in people of all faiths and, for that matter, those of no faith.

From a Jewish perspective, performing compassionate acts that relieve suffering is much more important than discovering theological beliefs that will explain suffering. So, in a sense, silence about God was fine with me. Indeed, it was my view that God is most present in compassionate human behavior—or so I told myself since God seemed otherwise not present at all. And the truth is that those of us involved in providing immediate help to people hurt by Harvey did not have much time to talk theology. After the floodwaters receded, it was then urgent for us to organize interfaith cleanup teams to help residents tear out soggy drywalls that were quickly becoming moldy. Risky work. We had to wear protective masks so we would not have to breathe in the toxic mold that can make one acutely ill. Our focus was on helping flood victims restore their homes without endangering our own health. Theological questions were not in the forefront of our brains as we worked to help people make their homes livable again, where that was possible.

No member of any interfaith humanitarian team I was part of even spontaneously raised any hard theological questions. I am sure, however, that at least some of the Hindus, Jews, Christians, Muslims, Sikhs, and Baha'is who belonged to our disaster working groups must have been wrestling with how to reconcile what they saw during and after this natural disaster with what they believed about "their" God, and some atheists were probably thinking, "This is why belief in God makes no sense." Still, despite all the devastation we had seen, there was an implicit understanding that we would not discuss together any difficult questions, such as, "Why would God will or allow this?"

Even after we finished the sometimes exhausting work of helping home-owners clean up and restore their flood-damaged property, after we had a better sense of the devastating effects of Harvey, when we met for interfaith dinners to talk about what we had done, we mainly discussed, following our guidelines for conversations across lines of difference, as already mentioned above, the values in our religious or secular worldviews that motivated us to help others in need. In interfaith dialogue, this is a safe thing to do. It is best, in interfaith conversations, to avoid theological debate or questions about God's purpose or the law of karma, even when one has the time for it. Religious doctrine is where we live in tension, in profound disagreement, often occupying radically different worlds. For example, God and Nirvana are very different takes on Ultimate Reality. Even if one restricts oneself to the Abrahamic religions—Judaism, Christianity, Islam, and the Baha'i Faith—God is understood in very different ways in these traditions. Three of these religions embrace a unitarian theology, with of course Christianity the odd faith out, affirming a Trinitarian view of God. And although both Judaism and Islam want nothing to do with the idea of a God Who is Three-in-One, they radically disagree about whether it is defensible to challenge God. Jews have a history of arguing with God; Muslims traditionally believe submission is the most appropriate attitude toward the Creator.

On the other hand, we can always find common ground when we discuss our fundamental values and how they lead us to work together for the benefit of a community in crisis. Despite different metaphysical worldviews, most faiths affirm the need to live in a way that is compassionate and generous. On the basic question of how we should treat each other and the need to render aid to those in need in a natural disaster like Harvey, there was fundamental agreement among members of our humanitarian working teams. This was safe territory compared to the issues such as the existence of God and why, if God exists, there is so much suffering in the world. Questions about the reality of God and whether God is just were, in a sense, taboo.

I am not so restricted in what I say here: I feel no need to refrain from asking tough theological questions. By the time this is published, I will, because of my wife's needs, no longer be the director of the interfaith organization and will no longer have to keep up the appearance of neutrality. If Harvey was not an act of God, my skeptical self wants to ask those who believe in an all-powerful Creator Who oversees the world, "Where was God?" Did God will Harvey or just permit it? If either, why? What, if any, is the moral difference between willing and permitting mass destruction, especially if one thinks of God as a caring parent? In both Judaism and Christianity, God is conceived as a loving Father. If God causes hurricanes, tornadoes, floods, tsunamis, and other destructive natural phenomena, God appears to be an extremely abusive parent; if God could intervene but lets these disasters happen, God appears to be a grossly neglectful parent.

I was personally monitoring how local pastors were responding to Harvey. A nondenominational minister of a megachurch in Houston, a preacher of the prosperity gospel and the power of positive thinking, said when interviewed about Hurricane Harvey: "God won't allow it unless He has a purpose for it. We may not see it at the time, but that's what faith is about. We should praise God for providing a purpose for every event, even if we don't understand it." Should we praise God for having a hidden purpose for ruining, or allowing to be ruined, so many lives? I felt like screaming.

What could possibly be the divine purpose for the death of the four small children and their great-grandparents who experienced the horror of being trapped in a van swept away by floodwaters, dying by drowning in their submerged vehicle? What was the divine purpose for hundreds of people made homeless because there was no salvageable home or habitable apartment to which to return? The notion of a hidden purpose seems an all-to-easy way of letting an omnipotent God off the hook.

Another Houston pastor, a fundamentalist Lutheran, speaking to a Houston Chronicle reporter, tried to explain the hurricane by actually blaming it on human beings. Now if he wanted to argue that humanly caused climate change contributes to the intensity of hurricanes that would be plausible, but that's not what this climate change denier had in mind. Instead, his account invoked what was for many centuries the orthodox Christian solution to the problem of suffering, especially when the causes are natural events. Basically, he said this: when Adam and Eve disobeyed God in the garden of Eden they destroyed what was then a perfect natural order, bringing about a defective world marked by such phenomena as earthquakes, hurricanes, floods, tornadoes, and disease. This view can be traced back to St. Augustine's major theological work, The City of God. The Lutheran pastor's implausible claim is that all of us were somehow there in Eden, participating in the sin of Adam and Eve and thus we all carry guilt in our souls: we possessed this sin even in the womb. This is the heart of the doctrine of original sin.

As the pastor put it: "We are the ones who brought the hurricane about. The truth is we all deserve death and destruction." An amazing claim! In other words, because of our mysterious complicity in the sin of Adam and Eve, we deserve to suffer terrible things in this world and in the next. On this view, because of original sin, we all deserve not only to suffer in this life, but to be eternally punished in the next. Only by the grace of God, through faith in Jesus Christ, do any of us avoid the everlasting punishment all of us deserve. My liberal Christian friends will have none of this, but obviously this theodicy survives for those crude enough to repeat it as an explanation of natural disasters.

This solution to the problem of evil creates more problems than it solves. After all, does it make it sense to say that people deserve hurricanes because of what the first two human beings did? In what sense can we be held culpable for Adam and Eve's sin? Is sin an inherited condition? Do children also deserve death and destruction, including death by drowning in floodwaters? Are children so tainted by original sin that they deserve whatever suffering they experience in this world, and, if they die without being saved, do they deserve to go to hell? The reader will discover that the woman who said she was God finds the suffering of children to be a paradigm case of undeserved suffering, an evil that makes God's existence questionable, even to God. You will see shortly what she means by this. Please bear with me.

Back to the Houston disaster: Rivers and bayous in Houston overflowed as the heavy rains continued for days. When the waters rose in some flooded neighborhoods, becoming higher by the hour, authorities recommended that residents write their Social Security numbers on their forearms in waterproof ink, so they could be identified in case their dead bodies floated away! A religious skeptic, easily dismissing both the "we will know God's reasons someday, just have faith" and" the original sin theodicy," could reasonably ask an omnipotent providential God, perhaps somewhat sarcastically: "Was there really some good that was supposed to come out of devastated lives, the newly homeless, the terror of rising waters in homes, causing some residents to move to their attics and, once the water reached there, to break through the roof with a pickaxe, for those lucky enough to have one?" That would be an excellent question to put to the Creator if one had the opportunity to ask Him/Her/It face-to-face. In theory, that would be my privilege.

Does the reader still wonder why the woman who claimed to have been the Creator chose me to hear her story? Although I may not have been her first choice, you can see why, given my preoccupation with the problem of evil and my openness to new ways of thinking about the nature of God, I was at least a logical conversation partner for her. I assume she found me on our interfaith website—which contained, along with my email address, my bio, copies of talks I have given, and interfaith podcasts hosted by me, including an interview with Elie Wiesel I did just before he died. Shekhinah had invited me in her email to meet her at the Starbucks just off the Sugar Land exit of

Highway 59. Sugar Land, a large, prosperous, fast-growing city just southwest of Houston, was also hit hard by floodwaters caused by Hurricane Harvey, and some neighborhoods were still recovering from the disaster at the time I met with the woman making the odd claim.

I traveled to Sugar Land in my still dependable 2000 Prius (liberal, absent-minded old professor, battered briefcase by his side, a living stereotype with thinning white beard and hair, driving old, battered Toyota hybrid, the first model sold in U.S.) by way of the Sam Houston Freeway, also known as Beltway 8, which I entered near the George W. Bush Airport, close to where I live. I treat places like Sugar Land as part of Houston, although legally they are independent cities near Houston. Houston and the surrounding areas are a maze of freeways with cars traveling at high rates of speed, some ready to run over me for keeping to the speed limit. I am finding freeways more challenging this late in my life as my eyesight worsens and my reaction time becomes slower. It was, however, an easy trip this day because on an early Sunday morning the traffic is relatively light.

That morning, after rising at 6:00 a.m. to bathe, dress, and have a bagel and orange juice, I did not have the time, as was my habit, to read the Sunday New York Times. I needed to be on the road by 7:00 a.m.—so I only had time to look at the headlines. I was waiting for a close friend of my wife who had agreed to stay with Beth as long as I wished and to fix lunch and dinner for her. Beth is in an advanced stage of Parkinson's and cannot be left alone. Because of her condition we recently moved into an assisted living apartment at a senior complex that, luckily, because it is on high ground, remained dry during Hurricane Harvey. Many assisted living places and nursing homes had to be evacuated. There is very sad photograph I saw that shows very elderly individuals in a nursing facility sitting in their wheelchairs or on couches, with floodwater up to their waists.

Our senior living complex is probably the last place we will live, the place where my wife and I will die, with a plan to die under hospice care. More than likely, Beth will transition to a room in the nursing unit down the hall when I, even with help, can no longer care for her. My wife was once a very successful Houston business executive; now the executive function of her brain—which would normally warn her not to try to walk without her walker—has atrophied. She has broken both hips, both wrists, her left shoulder, and knocked out her upper front teeth (now replaced with a bridge)—all from falls due to her disease. Although she can still surprise me with her insights about politics and people, she rarely knows what day of the week it is, even after I repeatedly tell her. I have to help her dress, eat, use the bathroom (including wiping her), and bathe. It has been difficult watching *her rapid mental and physical decline—something God needs to answer for, even a retired deity.*

The Sunday of the scheduled meeting was a typical oppressively hot and humid August day in Houston, with a forecast high of 103. In the early morning I could already feel the heat and humidity. When it is that hot, I always crack the car windows a bit and put a shade cover on my steering wheel so that it will not be too hot to touch when I return to my vehicle after leaving it in the sun for hours. This day was certainly no exception. Such heat seems inhuman and brutal, making one wonder what God had in mind. Maybe humans were not supposed to spend summers in places like Houston. The air-conditioning in Starbucks felt refreshing after the hot walk from my car. I arrived thirty minutes early for the 8:00 a.m. meeting, bought a small black coffee from an overly cheerful barista, and, though it was a bustling place, managed to find a table for two because a couple was just leaving. It was one of the high tables with two high chairs, next to a window.

I always like to arrive before the individual or individuals I'm meeting, so I will not feel rushed and also have time to think about what I want to say or ask, especially if there is an agenda. In this case no preparation was possible. Still I wanted get myself in a receptive state of mind for whatever was coming. After all, I was about to meet a person who claimed to have been God and wanted to discuss her reasons for exiting heaven.

As the time for her arrival passed, I was increasingly of the opinion that this was probably a joke, some kind of prank, but I also thought, if this person shows up, it might an interesting experience. In my old age, I am game to talk with anyone about anything. I had met recently with a young White Nationalist (who said he was not a White Supremacist), maybe in his early twenties—whose greatest concern was what he called "White genocide," the extinction of the White Race—just to understand how he had arrived at his point of view, which was also anti-Semitic. I thought it might be instructive if he met and talked with an actual Jew, to compare a flesh and blood Jew with his bloodless stereotype of "the Jews," considered by his ideology to be a mongrel race. The conversation was surprisingly civil, but of course that is one of my skills: creating peaceful exchanges between individuals whose views are worlds apart. I have known Jews and Christians who brought with them a negative view of Muslims and Islam—although they had never met a Muslim—who, after engaging in directed interfaith dialogue with a Muslim, hearing about the joys and sorrows of this person, walked away with a different view. Whether the young White Nationalist left our conversation with a more positive view of Jews I don't have a clue, but he left with an image of a person who respectfully listened to his views, who truly heard what he had to say. I made clear to him why I was committed to progressive causes and why I reject his claim that Jews are a race, mongrel or otherwise. He seemed surprised to learn that there are Chinese, Japanese, Indian, Ethiopian, etc. Jews—and that one can be a Jew by choice (a convert), something that contradicted his view of Jews as a race.

From my photo on the website and on my email, Shekhinah would be able to recognize me. Would she really need a picture to know what I look like if she had truly been God? So, again, I wanted to ask: Shouldn't she, if once the Creator, remember my face, or was her divine memory lost or impaired when she became a human being? There was no photographic image on her email so I had no idea what she looked like. She evidently did not have a Facebook page for understandable reasons; I have one that I rarely visit. I am old-fashioned in preferring actual face-to-face exchanges and do not use the word "friend" loosely. Now, I was about to meet face-to-face with a person who said she had been God. I did have her name and sometimes I think, even if irrationally, a person can look like her or his name. Shekhinah is a Hebrew name, and in Judaism names in Hebrew can be revealing: in some cases, they are thought to have a kind of reality themselves.

When you're meeting someone for coffee you haven't met before, and you arrive first, you tend to think every person (more specifically, in this case, every woman) who enters the door may be the one you're meeting. I kept asking myself, as different women entered: Does she look like a "Shekhinah"? I had never known anyone by that name. Although Shekhinah is a female Hebrew name, it is not a traditional name Jewish parents would give a daughter. Interestingly, in recent years, it has been increasingly adopted as a girl's name by conservative evangelical couples.

As a scholar of Judaism I knew of course that Shekhinah is the postbiblical Hebrew name Jewish mystics first used for the immanent dimension of God, conceived as a female presence. It is the name for the presence of God in the world, as opposed to God as a Transcendent Sovereign, depicted as a Male Ruler, Avinu Malkeinu ("our Father, our King"), to use the traditional liturgical language for God we repeat during the Jewish High Holy Days, the time Jews suddenly show up in great numbers at synagogues to confess their sins collectively and seek forgiveness. This kind of God language—God pictured as a royal male sovereign—always makes me squirm. During Rosh Hashanah (New Year) and Yom Kippur (Day of Atonement) we very liberal Reform Jews have to utter these words for God a lot, and you can be sure that I'm not the only Jew squirming in my seat. Fortunately, our new Reform prayer books for Rosh Hashanah and Yom Kippur contain defiant poetry. One title is "Avinu Malkeinu: A Prayer of Protest." If God really is such a powerful Father-King, the author (not identified) has, in the long Jewish tradition of arguing with God, some questions for Him:

Avinu Malkeinu, why?
Avinu Malkeinu, are you there? Do you care?
Don't make us bow or grovel for your favor.

After a while, I stopped checking to see who came in the frequently opening and closing door of Starbucks and looked down at the journal I take everywhere. I write down daily what I am doing, copy from books sentences that seem worth noting, and record random thoughts. I printed the date at the top of a new page entry with the heading "August 26, 2018, Meeting with Shekhinah." I then wrote down, "Waiting for the mystery woman to arrive, strangely nervous." The time was 8:25. Would a former deity be late for a meeting? Maybe this was a joke after all, and no one was going to show up claiming to be Shekhinah. I had almost concluded that. Just in case, I wanted to make sure I would have an accurate word for word record of our conversation, not something I could do in my journal. So I brought a recorder. My Olympus DM-720 4GB Digital Voice Recorder—with fifty-two hours of battery power— would give me a digital record of everything we said. Indeed, what you are about to read is a transcription from this lengthy recording. I used Google's dictation software called Voice Typing to do the transcription, with relatively accurate spelling and punctuation. I did of course have to make corrections.

As I was focusing on my recorder, making sure it was ready to go, I suddenly heard a voice. A very young voice! What did she look like? Like a young Tracy Chapman (a politically and socially active African-American singer-songwriter younger readers may never have heard of), interesting because I will quote from one of Chapman's powerful songs in the course of my conversation with Shekhinah. Shekhinah (if that is really her name) had very short, kinky hair on the top of her head marked by a red streak, with one side buzzed close to the scalp, contrasting with longer hair on the other side: a bit of a Lesbian look (if I'm permitted a stereotype). She was Very Black. I'm Very White. I should point out that Shekhinah—who appeared to be over six feet tall, with an athletic build—was using crutches because she had only one leg. She wore a white t-shirt, with bold letters in black, on both sides, that said "Black Lives Matter," and she was also wearing shorts, so brief that her stump was sticking out the left cuff, something that caused a few customers in Starbucks to gawk.

Looking shaken, indeed trembling, she asked if I was Professor James Friedman. I asked her to please call me Jim, to dispense with the title that as someone retired I now felt uneasy about. I invited her to sit down across from me, which, despite the height of the chair and her having only one leg, Shekhinah did gracefully while standing her crutches in the corner right next to our table.

The following is a record of her tale, occasionally interrupted by my questions, comments in parenthesis directed to the reader, and my occasional challenges to Shekhinah's claims. Shekhinah spoke in a voice that could be either masculine or feminine for someone who could not see her. She talked in a quiet way, although her voice did seem to carry to some nearby tables if their occupants strained to hear what she had to say. In preparing this manuscript based on the transcript of our conversation (including also the words of others who interrupted us), I had to frequently insert quotation marks because Shekhinah often quoted, even extensively, from works of literature, scripture, popular songs, religion, and philosophy. She frequently quoted from the New York Times *because she obviously knew it was my favorite newspaper. My questions, comments, and thoughts are always in italics. As you may have noticed, I also sometimes capitalize words that are not usually capitalized, such as, when referring to skin pigment: Black and White. My peculiar style, inspired by the style of Neo-Marxist philosopher Herman Marcuse, someone I admired. I had been a Marxist in my early teaching career—but, over time, becoming more interested in getting people elected than political purity, I became a Liberal Democrat. Or should I say Progressive Democrat because of my support for Bernie Sanders?*

Even if you don't believe Shekhinah's story—and of course you will not— she provides us with much to think about when it comes to God's relationship to suffering in the world. Indeed, she questions most of our fundamental assumptions about the nature of God, not just the assumption that God is omnipotent and has perfect knowledge of the future, but also an assumption that I, who questioned the traditional concept of God in so many ways, had never doubted: namely that God cannot die. Don't assume that because I do not continually challenge her story I bought what she was selling. You will see I made it clear to Shekhinah that I found her tale unbelievable, and, in the end, called into question her claim that God needed to cease being God.

You could say that some of my questions and comments reveal I was playing along with her conceit, for the sake of argument, as philosophers sometimes say. As in: for the sake of argument, let's say you are telling the truth. Although I was honest in telling her up front that I found her claim to have been God incredible, which she expected, I still wanted to try to practice the art of genuine listening that I had been teaching others who wanted to participate in interfaith dialogue.

It can be a fine line—that is, between trying to be open while not seriously entertaining incredible claims. I wanted to truly listen to what she had to say without, as she was talking, always thinking about how I might trip her up. Once, you will see, I warned her that she was making a questionable factual claim about the origin of the cosmos that could be undercut by new discoveries. *The fully informed reader will catch some of Shekhinah's factual errors, but of course she could explain this away by saying that her memory was no longer perfect. Although I tried to stay in a listening mode, it was difficult for me, as a Jew and a philosopher, someone programmed to argue, to stay silent when I thought Shekhinah should be challenged. And so, a few times throughout our conversation, I argued with her.*

On the other hand, I sometimes, in my role as receptive listener, pretended to be open to Shehkinah's claim that she possessed a memory of her life as God, that she could recall events in the evolution of universe and the history of the earth. Thus, phrases such as "as you must know," deferring provisionally (ironically?) to her claim to remember everything since the beginning of time, are used as prefaces to something I really wanted the reader to know. You will see that Shekhinah and I agreed about a lot of things, theologically speaking, but she also, as I've already indicated, took ideas in a direction completely alien to my thinking about God.

When I look back, maybe I—in violation of my own interfaith dialogue code that requires one to listen receptively even to what may appear to be absurd claims without trying to refute your interlocutor—was too often needlessly argumentative. Mainly, however, I let her have her say even if I could not, in all honesty, view her story as in any way credible. Still, I have to admit there were times during our conversation when I almost believed her and, to this very day, sometimes have doubts about my doubts. The reader will of course have to reach her or his own conclusion about Shekhinah's strange tale. By the time this book appears, it may be several years after my encounter with this extraordinary young woman. Before our conversation began, I told Shekhinah that I planned to publish a transcript of it on our interfaith website and eventually in book form. That is what she wanted. Her view: it would be God's final revelation?

2

The Arrival of Shekhinah

Shekhinah is the aspect of G*d that suffers with us and
is spoken of as walking out into exile as a mourner
with Her people.

—RABBI GOLDIE MILGRAM, *RECLAIMING JUDAISM*

(Her voice and demeanor suggested someone shaken by something.) Forgive
me for arriving late. Two young White Nationalists in a huge black pickup
with enormous, intimidating tires, which easily could have crushed me,
came close to doing precisely that. They drove by me slowly at first with
their vehicle facing me; a confederate flag and a miniature white shield with
a large black X on it decorated the hood of the truck *(a symbol of the League
of the South, a far-right Southern Nationalist group)*. I also saw in large white
letters "White Lives Matter" on the on the side of the door as the vehicle
passed me. The driver and his buddy, in their late twenties, both in baseball
caps turned backwards, glared at me. They were probably provoked not only
by my Black Skin and what they perceived to be my "Queer" appearance,
but also by what they saw printed on my t-shirt. They were clearly enraged.

Evidently the driver, after passing me, quickly turned the truck around,
stepped on the accelerator, and, driving onto the curb, came within a few
inches of me. As they were driving away, I could hear one of them yelling at
the top of his lungs, "nigger bitch filthy dyke cripple." I was so rattled that I
ducked into the bathroom of a 7-Eleven to regain my composure and to feel
safe. I also called the police to report this. I gave a detailed description of the

vehicle and occupants. I'm meeting with the police tomorrow morning. The Sugar Land police know me, as you'll soon find out.

The more I think about it, the more I'm convinced that these young men wanted me dead. After the near miss, I immediately thought of Heather Heyer, only thirty-two when she died, one of the anti-racist counter-protestors at the Unite the Right Rally in Charlottesville, Virginia—August of 2017. She was hit and killed by a car driven by James Alex Fields, Jr.—a twenty-year-old Neo-Nazi sympathizer—when he drove his vehicle into the crowd protesting the rally, injuring nineteen other protestors. I wouldn't be surprised to learn that the guys in the pickup had attended this rally and had praised Fields. I entered the world before this rally. So, I don't know whether they were there.

They may also have attended the "White Lives Matter" rally in Shelbyville, Tennessee, in late October of 2017: an event at which White Nationalists and Neo-Nazis, the extreme faction of the alt-right movement, again met heavy resistance from counter-protestors and police. As you know, White Nationalists are angered by what they perceive to be the diminishing power of White males in American society. Indeed they sometimes describe it as White genocide.

Yes, I know. I recently met with one. They blame the Jews for White genocide.

Of course. At the Shelbyville rally young males like the two I encountered were literally following in the footsteps of Mike Tubbs, the large former Green Beret who spent time in prison for plotting to bomb Black and Jewish businesses and who was largely responsible for the violence at the White power march that took place in Charlottesville, Virginia. In Shelbyville, he led some two hundred White Nationalist demonstrators into their designated rally area and told the media they were in the city to defend their White Heritage against the forces of darkness. Members of the *League of the South* were the main organizers of the "White Lives Matter" rally. Michael Hill, president of the *League*, yelled "Hail Dixie" and "Hail Victory" over a loudspeaker before he led the usual "Blood and Soil" chants *(originally a slogan in Nazi Germany)*. Also, they yelled, as you must know, the slogan, "Jews will not replace us."

Yes, they blame Jews for replacing Whites with Immigrants. One of the Jewish organizations they hate—HIAS (Hebrew Immigrant Aid Society)—has since 1881 been helping refugees rebuild their lives in safety, work inspired by the biblical command to welcome the stranger, meaning the refugee and the immigrant. (My conversation with Shekhinah occurred before Robert Bowers, a White Nationalist, murdered 11 Jews on October 27, 2018 while they were worshiping at the Tree of Life Synagogue in Pittsburgh. In his social media posts prior to the attack, Bowers blamed HIAS for genocide of Whites. He knew that this synagogue supported the work of HIAS.)

Many White Nationalists of course also despise Blacks. You can see why the two guys who came close to killing me were probably provoked by my "Black Lives Matter" t-shirt as much as anything else. As I think about it, I'm now certain that these two young zealots felt such hatred toward what I symbolized that they wanted me dead. That's just sinking in and gives me a sinking feeling. It's the second physical attack I've suffered since I immigrated to Houston.

I'm sorry.

No need to apologize. Two young White males, while demeaning me with racial epithets, attempted to rape me shortly after I arrived in Houston, something I will say more about later. But let me give credit where it is due. Houston has come a long way. Despite such hateful acts, I think Houston is a much more tolerant place than it was when you grew up here. After all, Houston voters elected a Same-Gender-Loving-Woman, Annise Parker, to the office of mayor, giving her two terms. She was the second female mayor in the city's history.

If you had told me when I was young man growing up in Houston that voters would one day elect as mayor a woman who was openly Lesbian, I would have thought you were crazy. Right-wing Christians waged a mighty battle against her election and were surprised when they failed to defeat her— twice. Many fundamentalist Christians have not been able to forgive Houston voters for this grave sin. A conservative Christian pastor said recently that this is why Houston was hit with Hurricane Harvey. Just out of curiosity, why do you use the term Same-Gender-Loving instead of Gay or Lesbian or, what has become acceptable in many circles as a self-description: Queer?

I'm okay with "Queer." The term "Same-Gender-Loving" was created by Cleo Manago, an African American activist, columnist, blogger, and founder of Black Men's Xchange, a community-based movement committed to promoting a healthy self-concept for Same-Sex oriented men of African descent. Manago rejects the terms Gay and Lesbian because they are linked to people of European descent, to Eurocentric constructed identities that don't affirm the culture and history of African Americans. The term "Gay," appropriated as term of identification by White Same-Gender-Loving Men in the fifties, was, as Manago sees it, cultivated in an exclusively White male environment. By the sixties, the predominantly White Gay Liberation Movement emerged in an atmosphere that seemed to exclude Blacks and Women. In response to this, White Same-Gender-Loving Women coined the term Lesbian, a word derived from the name of the Greek Island Lesbos, the place where the sixth-century poet Sappho wrote about the daily lives of women and proclaimed her love for women.

My reason for preferring the term Same-Gender-Loving is less complicated than Manago's and unconnected with race. Although I do think it's important that African Americans who engage in Same-Sex relations be able to name themselves in a way that is not dependent on the dominant White culture, I prefer Same-Gender-Loving because it is a description that indicates the relationship is about more than sex alone—which too many so-called "Straight People" associate with Same-Sex couples. The term I have chosen emphasizes a relationship in which two individuals of the same sex interact with each other in a caring and affectionate way. The terms Gay, Lesbian, and Queer fail to convey this. Same-Gender-Loving is for me an aspiration because I have not yet found a lover.

So you identify as Same-Gender-Loving.

Yes.

I can see this will be a very strange conversation and maybe a disturbing one for readers who are religious conservatives. And I do want to talk about that before we're done. For the time being, I want to return to your choice of a place to live.

Houston is in many ways a progressive city. In addition to electing a Same-Gender-Loving Woman to two terms, it has elected a Black mayor twice, two different men. The current mayor is Black. Houston is one of the most diverse cities in the United States, the fourth largest city in the country, with 145 languages spoken, as you probably well know. Signs of religious diversity are everywhere. Houston is a place with Sikh gudwaras, Hindu, Jain, and Buddhist temples, one of the largest mosques in the United States, an Ismaili Center *(a branch of Shia Islam)* right here in Sugar Land, a Baha'i Center, and synagogues of all kinds, not to mention hundreds of Christian churches of all denominations, a respectable number of Unitarian Universalist churches, and many Humanist groups. It is, however, still a mixed bag when it comes to prejudice of all kinds. Racism and homophobia remain an ugly but a significantly diminished reality here, with occasional hateful acts like the one I just experienced. Clearly, bigotry has radically declined in Houston.

Still, I do puzzle over why you—claiming to have left heaven—decided to make Houston your home. That will be as puzzling to some as your decision to embody yourself as Black, Same-Gender-Loving, and Female.

I will talk more about God's choice of Houston in due time. More important, I want you and your readers to know why God deliberately chose to incarnate as a Black Same-Gender-Loving Woman. I realize that my claim that God elected this form of human embodiment will be a scandal to some—many?—who read this. Occupying these identities with pride, I plan to fight for a different world against long-standing forms of prejudice: racism, homophobia, transphobia, and misogyny, just to mention a few. I chose three often denigrated identities as a way of affirming them. So, before leaving my life as God, I freely decided I would enter the world embodied as you see me—as a way of making a statement. I'm hoping, through my meeting with you, the word will spread that God is not—to be accurate, I should say "was not"—racist, misogynistic, transphobic, or homophobic.

I do have atheist friends, including many Jews, who openly say this about the God many people worship, namely that He seems to be a bigot.

As you know, to be Black meant for centuries in too many majority White societies—and this has been reinforced by those who told us that the God of the Bible said yes to this—to be *denigrated*: a term which itself means both to blacken and to belittle. I chose to incarnate in the darkest of dark skin because, as you are aware, there is another prejudice known as *Colorism*, a term coined in 1982 by Pulitzer Prize winner Alice Walker for the privileging of light skin over dark: the darker the skin, the greater the prejudice, including among some in the Black community.

Even many Asian women in American society spend their adolescence wishing they were White. Kelly Marie Tran, whose heritage is Vietnamese—she was the first Woman of Color to have a leading role in a Star Wars movie and was the first Asian woman to appear on the cover of *Vanity Fair*—reports that, growing up in the United States, she felt devalued and doubted her own worth simply because her skin tone was not White. After being subjected to sexist and racist online abuse for her role as Rose Tico in Star Wars VIII, Tran was bothered by the fact that she started to believe the words she read. She wrote: "Their words seemed to confirm what growing up as a Woman of Color had taught me: that I belonged in the margins and spaces, valid only as a minor character in their lives and stories."

Prejudice in favor of lighter skin is prevalent in countries as distant as Brazil and India. In Africa, India, and China—home to over 50 percent of the world's population—countless women aren't comfortable in their own skin. In Africa today many women—who continue to be affected by colonialist skin color ideology—use skin-whitening creams. Indeed, lighter complexioned women in many parts of Africa are considered more beautiful. Thus, the preference for whiter skin is a global prejudice. If you doubt my word, look at the research of Kimberly Jade Norwood writing in the Washington University *Global Studies Law Review*. Since skin color bias is often unconscious, many people are unaware that they practice *Colorism*. That's why the movie *Black Panther* is counter-cultural and indeed revolutionary. Cultural critic and African American Clarkisha Kent observes that its director, Ryan Kyle Coogler, "went out of his way to cast dark-skinned women in every single role that calls for a woman—including the love interest." When I decided to leave heaven for earth to become a human being, I wanted to say yes to the darkest of dark skinned human beings.

Incarnating as a Woman was another act of affirmation. Given the continued devaluation of women in the world, even in countries as advanced as this one, I wanted to say yes to being a woman. There is a long history of religions devaluing women while also sanctioning, indeed making holy, male domination of them. Women were for too long viewed as essentially inferior to men, only gaining the right to vote in this country in the early 20th century. Misogyny remains a serious problem globally. That's why the #MeToo movement is so important. I will talk about this in detail later.

And I will be saying more about the need to fight for the rights of those in what I will call the Queer community. Just so you have a sense of the complexity this word signifies, I could, to be more precise, refer to the LGBPTTQQIA+2 community. Let me briefly give my take on this alphabet soup—which many of your readers may see as unwieldy—and why I think it is important to keep expanding it. Some may dispute my definition of each letter, but I'm open to amending the meaning of as well as adding to these letters. Everyone knows that the first two letters refer to those who are Lesbian and Gay, to people whose sexual and/or romantic attraction is to people of the same gender. Individuals can of course be romantically attracted to those to whom they are not sexually attracted, and vice versa. This makes classifications more complicated, but we are dealing with differences that are very complex and difficult to categorize. Our language may not be up to the task of fully capturing the complexity of sexual and gender diversity.

The third letter of course refers to those who are Bisexual. Although usually defined as individuals who are sexually and/or romantically attracted to people of more than one gender identity (but not all), many who so identify want you to know their attraction is not, despite the name, limited to the binary: male or female. For example, there are some Bisexuals who are attracted to individuals with female breasts and male genitals, sometimes called "SheMales"—a term some consider derogatory. The problem is that language some consider offensive others want to positively claim: consider the history of the word "Queer."

P, often omitted but needs to be added, refers to persons who are Pansexual: those who can be romantically and/or sexually attracted to people of any gender identity. (Facebook provides its users with nearly sixty options.)

The first T refers to Transgender Persons, those who experience a gender identity or express a gender different from that assigned at birth—including, in addition to self-described Trans Men and Trans Women, the often neglected and excluded Non-binary Trans People: those who do not identify as only male or only female. In an oppressive society, Trans Persons may not choose to openly express their felt gender identity. The second T refers to Transsexual Persons. Like Transgender People, they experience an identity different from the gender assigned at birth, but they also desire to permanently transition to their felt identity, many even seeking medical help to achieve this (through hormone replacement therapy and/or surgery).

The first Q refers to those who are Questioning: people who, because of their uncertainty, are in the process of exploring their sexual orientation, gender identity, gender expression, or some combination thereof. The other Q refers to people who self-describe as Queer—transforming what was once a pejorative term into a positive self-description—really, an umbrella term referring to a variety of sexual orientations, gender identities, and gender expressions, excluding heterosexuality.

Four other symbols are often omitted: I, A, +, and 2. Intersex refers to persons whose variations in sex characteristics—including chromosomes, gonads, or genitals—do not fit the typical definitions of male or female. Asexual individuals are those who experience little or no sexual attraction (or may even be sex-repulsed) toward others, but this does not mean that they cannot have romantic relationships with other people. Intersexual and Asexual individuals often feel they have been made invisible—that they have been ignored, even by other members of the Queer community. I see the + as applying to all those other Queer identities that aren't captured by the letters I have mentioned; some take + to mean simply an invitation to love, accept, and embrace all those outside dominant sexual or gender norms. There are readers who will of course object that there are important identities I've left out or that I have mischaracterized what a particular letter stands for. To repeat: I'm open to additions and corrections. This is simply my current provisional list.

There is in fact a digit I've added to the letters, also frequently omitted: 2. This refers to Two-Spirit, a term adopted by consensus in 1990 at what was described as an "Indigenous Lesbian and Gay International Gathering" in Winnipeg, Canada, the mission of which was to recognize the various sexual orientations, gender identities, and gender expressions within Native American/First Nation/Indigenous communities. It is a complex term that can narrowly refer to Native (North) American individuals who identify as having both a masculine and a feminine spirit. Or, more broadly, it can refer to an Indigenous non-heterosexual way of living or being, embracing a wide variety of gender and sexual variance, including people who in Western culture might be described as Gay, Lesbian, Bisexual, Pansexual, Trans-sexual, Transgender, Intersexed, or Gender Queer. Very important: the use of the term "Two-Spirit" by people who are not Indigenous is considered a cultural appropriation and thus unacceptable. The digit 2 refers exclusively to the First Nation People who choose to use it, marking them as part of an Indigenous Community: thus, 2 is about more than gender or sexual labels. It is especially troubling when White People without a Native lineage steal words or ideas from Native American tribes and people—because it brings up a painful history of theft, not just of words, but also of land and resources.

Let me repeat: no set of letters can capture the full complexity of all those who do not fit rigid sexual or gender norms that have dominated far too long. LGBPTTQQIA+2 serves as a name for people so diverse that no group of letters can do justice to the reality of differences. In the act of creating a cosmos independent of divine control, with the potential for the emergence of diverse life forms, while also denying myself foreknowledge, I could not know that this complexity would one day emerge and cause so much suffering to those perceived as "Queer." Individuals who believe in an all-powerful God completely in charge of things from the beginning of creation to the present moment—and who morally condemn the Queer community—must explain why God would create a world in which so many individuals are powerfully drawn to what these "Straight" pious individuals consider a deviant life. The claim that every Queer Life is the free choice of a person who could have easily chosen otherwise is not plausible.

My personal choice to incarnate in a body of a woman erotically drawn to the same gender was a way of divinely affirming this form of sexuality. One reason I became a human being was to join in the fight for the rights of the entire Queer community. By the way, if I sometimes use only the letters LGBPTTQQ, LGBTQ, or some other truncated list, that's because I'll be referring only to those persons who fit under one of these letters and not to those who belong to the omitted letters.

One more thing: Although sexuality and gender identification can be fluid—with individuals changing over a lifetime how they identify or express themselves—maybe we need to be careful about accepting the current trend, strong in the academy under the heading of gender and feminist studies. It is the trend toward claiming that all sexuality is fluid, and that persons should be free to gender identify as they please. I would advise those who say this to at least listen openly to the concerns of Pippa Fleming, an African American performance artist, writer, and spiritual practitioner who has committed her life to chronicling and preserving the art, culture, and achievements of Black Same-Gender-Loving Women.

She warns us that the now ascendant idea that all persons can identify as they please is leading to the erasure of Lesbian Identity, something that Fleming takes pride in and thinks is distinctive. She fears that her Lesbian Identity is being blotted out, and that is for her a profound loss. Fleming reminds us that every letter in LGBPTTQQIA+2 represents a community of individuals who "fought tirelessly to be recognized as vital members of a community that is expanding," and that "it is our responsibility to educate each generation about the torchbearers that preceded them and to name their unique identities."

We should listen to this woman who sees the trend toward asserting that sexuality and gender identity are completely fluid as something that renders Black Lesbians invisible. According to Fleming, to regard gender identity as interchangeable with sex—and abolish biological distinctions between men and women—threatens Lesbian Identity because it calls into question who is actually a woman. Andrew Sullivan, a thoughtful Gay conservative political commentator seems fully aware of her concern, even if he does not mention her name in an important article, "The Nature of Sex," in *New York Magazine*. He quotes Sky Gilbert, a drag queen: "If there is no such thing as 'male' and 'female,' the entire self-definition of Gay Identity, which we have spent generations seeking to validate and protect from bigots, collapses."

God's decision to become a Same-Gender-Loving Woman was and is an affirmation of this distinct identity. Clearly there are those in the Queer Community who will say I need to recognize that "female" and "male" are constructs, identities that anyone, regardless of genitalia, can claim. They may interpret my resistance to this as evidence that I was not really God, because a former Creator would know better! And they might also say that, if truly courageous, I would have chosen another, maybe more risky, form of human embodiment. I could have incarnated as an openly Trans Woman, an identity that of course also needs affirmation and protection in a world where those so recognized daily encounter prejudice, ridicule, discrimination, hatred, and even violence. That would have been supremely transfirmative, but I decided otherwise. I of course knew, before departing from heaven, that, statistically, openly Trans Persons are more likely to be targets of deadly violence than those who openly identify as Same-Gender-Loving. Despite what happened this morning, I know that I am, as an SGL Woman, a less frequent target of hateful acts than a Trans Human Being. And of course there was an element of arbitrariness—and maybe even self-protection—in God's choice of how to embody Herself. What would Christians say about their God's choice to incarnate as a celibate—on their view, either an asexual or abstinent—Jewish male? Christians of course give biblical reasons for God's choice that I will talk about later.

Also, but not by choice, I now experience the world from the perspective of someone missing a leg. Now I experience being called a "cripple" by those who use this as a term of disdain, and I now personally know what it feels like to be belittled because I lack a body part. Just as many in the non-heterosexual community have positively reclaimed the word "Queer," so a number of those outside the non-disabled community have positively appropriated the term "Crip," to describe themselves. Thus I accidentally became a member of another historically disrespected community. I am now, in the eyes of some hate-filled Houstonians, even if small in number, a *nigger bitch filthy dyke cripple*, quite a mouthful, said venomously. I positively claim this intersectional identity: I proudly own it. Apparently, for many adherents of White Male Identity politics, all my identities render me worthy of contempt—and evidently, in the eyes of some of these haters, unworthy of life.

(Noticing that her body continued to tremble, and that she was shivering as she talked, her teeth slightly chattering like someone whose body was freezing, I needed to recognize this): You still seem disturbed.

Obviously my fear is palpable. Being afraid of being killed is a relatively new experience for me, after eons of being indestructible. Well, not entirely new: a couple of years ago I lost my leg and was nearly killed because I mindlessly walked in front of a car while crossing a busy Houston intersection. During my early life on earth, there were too many stimuli entering my very human brain—an overwhelming flow of sense data: a dizzying and chaotic mixture of sounds and sights surrounded me. I no longer had the all-encompassing awareness I possessed when I was God. At the time of the accident, lost in thought, I had not yet learned to make full use of my eyes and ears before walking in this or that direction. What could be more heedless—and less mindful—than walking in front of a moving car? You could say it was an accident, but you could also say it was my fault. That's why this recent scare with the pickup truck was so traumatic. The pickup's near miss this morning brought back memories of the disorientation and panic I felt when the car literally blind-sided me. To be medically precise, it was my PTSD kicking in.

I remember the feeling of shock, not to mention pain, when the car hit me. Couldn't even tell you its make or color because I didn't see it coming. I now have one less leg thanks to my failure to look both ways. Of course I should have known better. On the other hand: let's face it, I'm no longer God and, like other human beings, I sometimes do stupid things.

So, if I understand you correctly, you didn't plan, before your exit from heaven, to lose a leg, maybe as a way of witnessing personally to a life of disability.

I had intended to be what most people call normal: namely a bipedal human being. I certainly don't want to lose the other leg. After the amputation, I could see that people perceived me differently, seemed to find me less attractive. Why wouldn't they? After all I had a stump where my left leg used to be. In addition to the prejudice against my extremely dark skin, I knew, once I became an amputee, there would be those who would see my one-legged body as shameful. It is one thing to observe this on high as God and another to directly experience it. I've become acutely aware that some people, when they see my stump, which has finally become natural to me and not something I feel the need to hide, seem embarrassed by it, really uncomfortable in my presence. And there are people who visibly cringe and look disgusted. Amputees have to transcend the socially implanted idea that there is something inherently ugly about their condition, about their stump—about them.

That reminds me of a character in a book by my favorite novelist, Nobel Prize–winning author J. M. Coetzee. By the way, he was on a Fulbright finishing his PhD in English at the University of Texas at Austin when I was beginning my doctoral program there; we must have passed each other on campus a few times. In Coetzee's novel, Slow Man, *the central character, Paul Rayment, is also hit by a car, and also undergoes the amputation of his leg. He feels the shame you describe. Rayment, reflecting on the statue Venus of Milo, observes that, despite her lack of arms, she is held up as an ideal of feminine beauty. As the story goes, the statue once had arms but somehow they were broken off. Rayment perceptively comments that if it were discovered tomorrow that the statue was really modeled on an amputee, it would immediately be placed in basement storage. Rayment asks, and these words have stuck in my mind: "Why can the fragmentary image of a woman be admired but not the image of a fragmentary woman, no matter how neatly sewn up the stumps?" My answer, and probably yours, is because our culture has created—and many businesses make huge profits from this—an unreal ideal of physical perfection, treating people with missing body parts as seriously flawed, incomplete, and less than fully human.*

You're right about that. I learned a lot about how to deal with my physical loss from a woman I will be mentioning many times: Audre Lorde (1934–1992), a Caribbean-American, daughter of immigrants, who describes herself as "Black-Feminist-Lesbian." She broke new ground on many fronts. I appreciated her *Cancer Journals (published in 1980)* where she models a different way a woman can respond to a mastectomy, refusing to feel any shame because she has a missing breast, refusing to conceal her new shape. In the late 1970s, to the local medical establishment's horror, she refuses to wear a prosthetic breast. Her refusal is a way of affirming her new one-breasted body.

Some contemporary feminists judge her view to be dated because we are now supposedly living in a post-human age when nothing is alien to the body, and nothing is inherently human, an age when all bodies are seen as constructed, just as gender is constructed. We are all potentially cyborgs. Later I'll respond to this criticism and say more about what I perceive to be Lorde's still relevant view of prostheses. I personally am not opposed to wearing a prosthesis—I in fact often use a prosthetic leg—but in my case I can only use a prosthesis for a limited period. The important point is that I no longer feel shame about my stump, about my new body. Lorde's example helped me to become comfortable with my altered physique.

To return to your original question: yes, being able to walk on two legs was my original plan, perhaps a selfish one, for reasons I will make clear later. After being hit by a car, and losing my left leg, I got a valuable lesson in a form of loss that I only knew from afar. And yes, it *was* an accident: there really are accidents in the world, despite what some believers may think who imagine that God's invisible hand is behind every event. This includes "the everything happens for a reason" crowd. It has always been amazing to me how believers in a providential God can so easily rationalize the most terrible things that occur in this world, including even natural disasters like the one from which Houston is still recovering. I know you share my views on this.

Correct. In my theology, God does not control the course of things or even intervene from time to time to perform miracles.

Many believers in an omnipotent God conclude that God causes natural disasters or fails to intervene to prevent them for a good reason. Of course these believers would say that God, being all-powerful, could easily stop a hurricane if He wished, maybe if enough people prayed hard enough. I ask you: Is there any evidence God has ever intervened to extinguish a single hurricane? Have people's prayers to stop a hurricane in its tracks ever been demonstrated? The right-wing televangelist Pat Robertson once prayed for a hurricane to move north toward New York rather than hit Virginia where his Christian Broadcast Network was located. It did turn toward New York, but there is no evidence that Robertson's selfish prayer had anything to do with this. The fact is this: we have no credible account of prayer actually causing a hurricane to change direction or, more dramatically, extinguishing a hurricane in some miraculous way so that it suddenly disappeared from weather radar, stopped in its tracks by divine intervention.

I obviously share your view that God does not intervene to prevent natural disasters. This view of course makes the world seem more frightening, namely the idea that God cannot intervene to save us from natural or human evil. You were almost killed by a couple of guys who hated your appearance, hated your body—even your t-shirt—hated everything you represented in their minds. Yours could have been another pointless death. And then your exit from heaven would have been for nothing, assuming your plan was to live a long life as a human being.

With the recent truck incident, I have now quickly learned another hard lesson. In my previous existence as God, I, as I just mentioned, never had to fear for my life, worry about bigots running me over, beating me up, or shooting me. Now, one of my greatest fears is being murdered by people who hate something that they think I stand for. The idea that this life I recently acquired, the only one I now have, might be cut short, deeply troubles me. To be honest, I'm now afraid of an untimely death. In fact I cannot seem to stop thinking about what happened earlier: as you can see, I'm still shaking—and remain profoundly shaken. In fear and trembling, I now fully understand that my life might, at any moment, be suddenly ended by a hate-filled racist, homophobe, or misogynist—maybe by someone who is all three. Or extinguished by another accident.

Still, to be honest, what most frightens me is bigotry. Prejudice, even when it is not physically threatening, can take its toll. Blacks encounter it everywhere, even in places like this. It wasn't too long ago that two young Black men sitting in a Starbucks in Philadelphia—waiting for a third man to arrive for a talk about real estate—were asked to leave by an employee, allegedly because they were not buying anything. Loitering? The store manager called 911, and the police arrived and took the two away in handcuffs. Isn't this a clear case of racial profiling? This miscarriage of justice led the CEO of Starbucks to close more than eight thousand stores for one afternoon last May for racial bias training of employees. Racial profiling, as we now know, happened at other Starbucks stores prior to this incident. It happens in this country all the time in all kinds of stores. I've had security follow me around stores, even as I hobbled on my crutches down different aisles to find something I needed. It's degrading to be targeted only because of your Dark Skin.

The stress of constantly having to deal with bigotry can be toxic. I'm now feeling that. If racists don't kill me, it's possible that stress from repeated acts of belittlement may. I'm not exaggerating. This is something I saw as God: I could literally see deteriorating bodies of those who were subject to constant disrespect. But who will believe such a claim coming from me? So, let me mention the medical evidence. Do you know the work of Dr. Arline T. Geronimus—a professor at the University of Michigan School of Public

Health? She provides empirical support for the conclusion that stress from ongoing discrimination can lead to premature death.

Is she the researcher who introduced the term "weathering"?

Yes. The term is a metaphor for what she documented was happening to the bodies of Black People, especially Black Women because they face discrimination for both their race and gender. Latinos/Latinas in the United States have also experienced something comparable. *Weathering* refers to the erosion of health caused by repeated acts of prejudice, disparagement, and hate. Dr. Roberto Montenegro, a psychiatrist at Seattle Children's Hospital, sums up the research on the effect of being a victim of frequent acts of bigotry: "Cumulatively," he tells us, "these acts of discrimination work like sort of low-grade micro-traumas."

The stress of repeatedly experiencing denigration can, over time, wear you down physically. It is of course normal for a perceived threat to produce certain physiological responses—higher levels of stress hormones, a faster heart rate—responses that usually subside once the threat disappears. But studies by Geronimus and Montenegro tell us that negative things happen to the body when it has to gear up for threats over and over again: the rise in the level of stress hormones as an ongoing process takes its toll on the body. To be consistently washed in stress hormones is a toxic thing that weakens the body's immune system: it can lead to hypertension and heart disease.

More specifically, Geronimus found that the toxic stress experienced by African American Women repeatedly exposed to a climate of discrimination and insults led to a premature deterioration of their health. When stress due to discrimination and disrespect occurs frequently over a long period of time, with constantly elevated stress hormones, this leads to wear and tear on the cardiovascular, metabolic, and immune systems, causing the bodies of these women to be vulnerable to illness and even premature death. It also explains why Black Mothers and their infants in the United States die at more than double the rate of White Mothers and their babies—namely because Black Mothers' dangerously high levels of blood pressure during pregnancy cause them to give birth to abnormally low-weight babies with low survival rates. Tragically, I saw all of this from above.

So, you're claiming—appealing to the research of Geronimus and others—that racial prejudice can be fatal to its targets, even if bigots do nothing directly to physically harm the people they belittle.

Precisely. But I don't want to deny the danger of physical threats to those detested because of their race. I, when I was God, knew of course the distress of human beings who were violently attacked by hate-filled racists, but of course I was never an actual target of murder-oriented bigotry. What I experienced earlier today changed that. In my life as God, I continuously witnessed hateful behavior but never, prior to becoming a human being, had the frightening experience of having my life threatened because of how I looked.

Now I have to deal with hate up close and personal. I was truly terrified when the pickup truck came close to ending my life. I now wonder if I have the courage of my convictions, the courage to confront racists and homophobes and misogynists, not to mention those who treat amputees with contempt. I hope I can stand up to all forms of hatred. But I'm now as fragile and vulnerable as every other sentient being. I'm now a mere mortal. I'm also now morally flawed. To be honest, I now feel so much fear that I'm not sure I have the courage to do what I know is right. At this moment, to be honest, I feel like withdrawing from this world I so recently entered, escaping all that is toxic in it.

It looks like you have a rather complicated story to tell me. Can I get you something to drink or eat? It's on me.

That's generous of you, but not just yet. I want to thank you for agreeing to meet. I didn't know whether you'd be willing to listen to someone claiming what I am claiming. All the others I invited turned me down, including a very liberal Christian who is an interfaith leader in Houston, someone with a reputation for promoting respect for religious difference and diverse views of all kinds. I'm sure you know her, but I won't mention the names of any of those who declined my invitation. Some I invited no doubt thought I was playing a trick on them they didn't want to be part of. Many may have believed, with good reason, that I was a head case, not in my right mind. Perhaps some of those who declined my invitation were a bit uneasy about being in conversation with someone so strange. Unhinged?

For all I know, I *am* self-deceived. You see, when it comes to absolute certainty, I confess doubt that I really was who I say I was. On the other hand, I do feel mentally healthy and am telling you what I genuinely believe to be true and what I truly remember. I was very much aware that the invitation to listen to my story about why I abandoned my life as God wasn't going to be well-received by most, if not all, of my invitees. I thought it might relieve some anxiety if I invited people to meet me in a public place. Until your positive response, that didn't seem to make any difference.

I wonder why you said yes. Maybe you were willing to meet because you're the director an interfaith organization. I know you get invitations from a lot of religious crazies. I remember you as a very receptive person, open to listening to almost anyone who had a spiritual, or even secular, story to tell. I would also guess that your own unorthodox theology played a role in your willingness to meet. You see, I don't know what's going on in your head at this moment, or how you now feel about meeting with me. In giving up divinity, I lost the ability to know what human beings are thinking and feeling, to literally read everyone's mind: a profound relief, to be honest—that is, to no longer know what every person on the planet is thinking and feeling, all the time!

This place is crowded and loud. I hope you can hear all I have to say. Let me apologize for that: when I've been here before on Sundays, it has been very quiet. I see you're recording our conversation as you warned me in advance. That's good: you can always listen to the recording to make sure you heard me correctly. And please forgive me if I adopt your vocabulary and speak like you. I often unconsciously speak the language, even use speech patterns, of the person with whom I am in conversation. That's not based on reading minds, but rather on divine memories I retain of individuals and their language habits.

Can you share with me some of my verbal habits, ones you remember from your former life when you allegedly knew me better than I know myself?

By the way—and you often say "by the way"—these are unconscious verbal habits: so, generally, if I had not informed you of this, you would not know that I'm doing it. I'll just mention a few. You often say: "the truth is" or "the fact is." And often utter "etcetera." Frequently you use the word "still" to begin a sentence. You seem to like the term "interlocutor." Also, when explaining something, your speech is peppered with "to wit," "namely," and "that is." You use the word "indeed" all the time. You have a particular vocabulary, a habitual way of talking, that is uniquely yours—a relatively large vocabulary, but not enormous, with a minimum of technical words, for an academic. As I said, my practice of adopting the speech patterns of my conversation partner—you may find this surprising—is itself automatic, really unconscious for me. It's something I do without thinking. Seeing someone triggers memories of their speech habits. If I catch myself, I can correct it. Generally, however, I find that if I use the vocabulary, and speak in the voice, of my interlocutor (there I go), there is less danger of a misunderstanding.

There is, as you may know, precedence for this in Judaism. We are told in the Babylonian Talmud (Berachot 45a for those interested) that "when God spoke to Moses, He spoke in Moses's own voice." Perhaps the God of the Torah did this to make sure Moses would more clearly understand the divine voice. When you say you will be speaking in my voice, clearly you don't mean this literally. I assume you will not be imitating my voice, but rather you will be adopting my manner of speaking, my speech patterns.

Correct. I am, however, also a talented mimic, as you will hear when I quote from others, but I will not be mimicking the sound of your voice, at least not intentionally. Back to your way of speaking: for someone raised in Texas, you speak American English without a Southern accent, indeed with a relatively neutral voice, but there is a subtle Texas twang one can hear in some of your language. Most listeners, unless they are linguists, wouldn't be able to tell what part of the county you're from. Your way of speaking is difficult to trace regionally because you worked hard at an early age to eliminate your Texas drawl, something that is still distinct in other members of your family—and your wife, also from Houston. You decided in the ninth grade that you didn't want to sound like a Texan because your career plan was to become either a CBS news anchor, like Walter Cronkite, or, failing that, a CBS correspondent.

You assumed that you would need to have a regionally neutral voice—with no trace of a Southern accent—in order to be hired as one of the voices of CBS News. So, you recorded your voice, listened to it carefully, and practiced losing the drawl. You used a recording of Walter Cronkite's voice as your model. Younger readers will have no idea who I'm talking about. You were successful. You still sound a bit like Cronkite. Only later would you discover that accent neutrality wasn't a requirement to work for CBS News. A young Dan Rather, working for KHOU, the CBS Houston affiliate, did such a professional and polished job of covering Hurricane Carla in 1961 (terrible hurricanes have plagued Houston for very long time, long before you were born, indeed from it's founding, August 30, 1837, by the Allen brothers, real estate swindlers from New York) that he was hired by CBS as a national correspondent. Rather had a Southern—specifically Texas—accent and was able to retain it while moving up the ladder at CBS, eventually becoming the anchor of the CBS evening news for twenty-four years, before being forced out because he (unknowingly) used bogus documents in a critical story on George W. Bush's National Guard service. Of course after junior high you discovered and fell in love with philosophy, making that your new career path.

That's an impressive bit of information about me. I probably told that story somewhere and someone wrote it down. Recordings of my voice are available on our interfaith organization's website.

Your speaking and writing are not always elegant or eloquent, but your language is usually lucid, a rare quality in an academic and a philosopher. I'm being up-front with you about my habit of adopting speech patterns and language of those with whom I converse—so, when I mimic your speech habits, you won't think I'm mocking you.

Thank you for the warning, and I'm glad it includes at least some praise for how I speak.

Maybe you'll interpret this extraordinary linguistic ability—which includes knowledge of the verbal habits and language of every person with whom I'm conversing—as a sign of my former divinity. Even I marvel at it.

This ability—because it is based on eroding divine memory—will eventually fade, but, for the time being, it is one of my assets. I was talking in German to a tourist from Berlin the other day and he asked me where I was from in Germany. I lied and told him Frankfurt. That's one liberty I allow myself, namely the freedom to lie.

To get by in daily life and not cause others to feel uncomfortable or want to avoid me like the plague, I don't tell people I was once God. I've contrived a story about my past. With you, I'm not pretending to be anyone I'm not. Even though I know you don't believe me, the truth is I haven't lied to you about my place of origin—or, if you wish me to qualify that epistemologically—where I sincerely, even if mistakenly, believe I'm from. For the sake of humility, I'll never deny I could be mistaken, but the fact is I don't think I am.

I appreciate your epistemological modesty, your willingness to admit that you may be an ordinary mortal who is self-deceived.

Let me repeat this question: Could my ability to converse in the language of the other, whether a native or foreign tongue, be evidence that I was Who I say I was? Could Jesus do this? Could he adopt the manner of speech and vocabulary of those with whom he conversed? You will not see any reference to this in the Gospels. And, although Jesus knew some Hebrew which he used in prayer, and had a little knowledge of Greek, which he occasionally spoke, he mainly conversed in his native Aramaic, in a Galilean dialect different from the Judean dialect spoken in Jerusalem. His cry of abandonment on the cross was in Aramaic. He was not the master of all languages.

Supposedly he established his credentials as God in the flesh by performing miracles, such as healing the sick, giving sight to the blind, raising the dead, turning water into wine, and walking on water. Did he really raise Lazarus of Bethany from the dead? If so, why does only the Gospel of John recount this story? What about the miracle of his resurrection, for those who believe that occurred? Did Jesus, identified by traditional Christians as the Son of God, raise himself from the dead, or was that the work of God the Father, or was it a miracle performed by the Holy Spirit? One can find in the New Testament a text to support each of these claims. Maybe all three at once raised Jesus from the dead? This gets us into the tricky territory of the Trinity about which I'll have something to say before we're done.

I'll eventually give you my take on Jesus. After all, he's the figure most Christians, and even most Jews and Muslims, associate with the claim that God became a human being. People in the West—present company excluded—are usually ignorant of the story of Krishna, believed by many ordinary Hindus to have been God in the flesh, God descended to earth to bring the world back to goodness, one of the ten avatars (incarnations) of the Hindu God Vishnu. Christianity is not the only religion to assert the idea of divine incarnation. Of course in the land where Jesus lived even some Roman emperors were thought to be gods: this was known as the imperial divine cult. For example, before the birth of Jesus, Julius Caesar was, shortly after he died, officially recognized by the Roman state as a god, becoming the divine Julius.

This brings me to the reason I invited you to meet me: to share with you my own story of incarnation, if that is the right word for my transition. It's not the right word if incarnation means that I profess to be both fully divine and fully human. Still, it's the best term I've found to describe what I did when I exited the transcendent realm, indeed my final act as God. I'm going to tell you a tale you probably will not believe. Ever since I arrived—that is, became a human being—I've wanted to have a conversation with someone who would really listen to me and be sympathetic to my strange narrative. It has been lonely not being able to share my story, lonely being the former Creator of the cosmos. Very isolating.

I thought you might appreciate my account of leaving heaven, even if you believe it's fiction. I'm of course hoping, against all odds, you will believe me—and, even if you don't, that you will share my tale with others. Although I know that you're a person who is deeply skeptical of all religious claims, I also know you remain open to theological exploration. You're a retired professor of philosophy who gives talks on the idea of a Self-limiting God. Your vision is of a Creator who, out of love and respect for freedom and creativity, chose to allow the world, within certain lawful constraints, to go its own way, allowing genuine chance and randomness to operate within an evolving universe that is still lawful enough for science to understand its operations and its development over time. That is also basically my story of Creation. During those moments you can bring yourself to believe—what you call "faith moments"—you affirm the existence of a perfectly compassionate God Who suffers with the world but Who, having surrendered omnipotence, now lacks the power to prevent suffering. That in fact was my situation as God. Given that, I thought you would find my story a plausible account of the life and death of God, even if you do not literally believe everything I am about to tell you.

When you give talks about God at area Unitarian Universalist churches, your own synagogue and others, Christian places of worship, philosophy departments, and seminaries, you always describe your view as a personal take on God, an unorthodox idea of the Creator for people who struggle, as you have all your life, to believe in God in a world so full of pain and evil. You usually tell your audience that you're a religious skeptic, but one who has always been open to the possibility of what the philosopher John Hick calls the fifth dimension, an invisible spiritual realm. A popular term for this is heaven. I've always valued skeptics, but even more skeptics who are willing to consider the possibility that the physical universe isn't all that is the case. Again, I'm hoping you will share my story with others. You could be my Moses. It is something you hinted at earlier.

You mean the Moses who supposedly recorded what God told him. You will probably not be surprised if I tell you that I am as hesitant as Moses was to be the conduit of a divine voice, even one that sounds like my own. Yet, here I am.

My voice is no longer divine. That's part of my story. I know my tale will sound incredible to anyone who hears or reads it, and may even strike them as madness. Again, if you think that I'm mentally ill or that I'm putting you on, I understand. The heart of the matter is that I exited my divine life for reasons I think you'll understand and appreciate.

If am to play along provisionally and entertain your odd tale, I need answers to some questions. Why did you decide to incarnate as a human being? Where were you born? Did you have a virgin birth? Who raised you?

A lot of questions to answer. The truth is that I entered the world already an adult about three years ago. No infant existence for me: no manger or crib. No childhood or adolescence. No time for those, even if it shortened my life. I am only twenty-three and healthy, despite the loss of a leg. I didn't go to college, but I am wise beyond my years for what that's worth.

After creating the world out of nothing—more precisely, after creating the point of infinite density that would trigger the Big Bang—I, as already mentioned, in order to make the cosmos a truly independent reality, with the power to develop on its own, gave up omnipotence. Thus, when I finally decided to exit my life as God and become a human being, I lacked the power to create for myself a human body out of nothing or even to resurrect a dead person. I did, however, have the power, really the only power I had left, to become a human being if I took occupancy in a living human body.

Taking up residence in a person's body meant taking over that individual's life. Would that be murder, I asked myself? I knew that God's mind would, if you can believe it, replace the chosen person's mind, literally replacing her consciousness with my formerly divine mind. But I didn't want to take the life of any human being who wanted to live. So, when I decided to exit my life as God, I considered only human beings on the verge of suicide.

Let me be more precise: I decided to take up residence in the body of a person who was about to commit suicide and would have successfully done so if I had not taken possession of her mind and body. That is, the circumstances had to be such that no person or event could prevent this individual's act of self-destruction. At any moment in time, there are, sadly, thousands upon thousands of individuals throughout the world who are suicidal and on the verge of ending their lives. Think of the numberless tragic suicides, often the result of mental illness or self-hatred, in the history of humankind, that God could not prevent—or, if one believes in an all-powerful Deity, chose not to prevent. The truth is that when I was God I was powerless to interfere in the free decision of any human being, including the free decision to take one's own life. I had to stand by helplessly, unable to stop any of the countless acts of self-destruction that occurred after human beings evolved an understanding of their power to destroy themselves.

Once I decided to leave my divine life behind, it was only a matter of which suicidal person. And remember: I had decided to dwell in the body of an Ebony Same-Gender-Loving Woman, a choice that you might think seriously limited my options. Unfortunately, or fortunately for me, many Black Same-Gender-Loving Women are suicidal. Because they internalize how their society or their religion views them—namely as having perverted, sinful, and abominable desires, desires that they cannot stop feeling—these individuals frequently come to hate themselves to the point of wishing they were dead.

As it turned out, I chose to take up residence in the body of a suicidal twenty-year-old woman who lived in Freetown, Sierra Leone. She became the Chosen One, deliberately chosen from the continent where human beings first evolved. As Shakira tells us in her song "Waka Waka (This Time for Africa)," "we are all Africans." Having granted human beings the power of choice and made myself powerless to intervene in human affairs, I couldn't prevent this young woman from killing herself, but I could take possession of her body and mind the very second she was about to end her life. You could say that I saved her life, but it would be more accurate to say that I *took over* her life, appropriated it. I will call her Esther. Esther, as you must know, derives from Hebrew verb "to hide." I will not reveal her actual name—a name I will not soon forget. I owe my life on earth to her. Esther was on the verge of destroying herself because her parents had disowned her.

Esther's father, who had come home from work early that day—her mother was outside talking to a neighbor—caught her passionately kissing another young woman in Esther's bedroom. Screaming at her, "Wetin yu de du" (Krio: What are you doing?!), he suddenly walked away in shock. Then, quickly returning to her bedroom from which the other woman had fled, her father told Esther how disgusted he was with her perverse behavior and how she was now dead to him. Her mother, when informed, was equally livid and agreed that Esther had to leave immediately. Esther's father gave her five minutes to collect her things and get out, time enough for her to stealthily grab a butcher knife from the kitchen and return to her tiny bedroom to end her life. As already explained, God couldn't wait for Esther to become a corpse, but had to enter her body as she was about to cut her throat.

You could say that I, or rather God, was a body snatcher. I would argue that Esther's act of starting to slice her throat amounted to virtual suicide: I can assure you that Esther would not have survived what she was about to do. And let me repeat the important point that most theists will find hard to believe—namely that God could not prevent her from killing herself. In becoming a human being by incarnating in Esther's body, I took the life she chose to give up. In doing so, I also completely emptied myself of divinity: that is, I gave up all my remaining divine attributes, including eternality. Christian theologians would call this an act of *absolute kenosis. Kenosis* means that God divests the divine Self of some or all of the divine attributes. In the case of Jesus, some Christians believe that the Son of God, when He became a human being, temporarily gave up the attributes of omnipotence, omniscience, and omnipresence—but retained other divine attributes, including perfect goodness and eternality. As God, when I became a human being, I in fact irreversibly emptied myself of every divine attribute. I'll say more about this later.

I want to return to the subject of Esther's hidden Same-Gender-Loving existence in Freetown. This is something that profoundly troubled me as God: namely human beings who must conceal who they are to avoid society's harsh judgment and who also feel rejected by God. Although males in Sierra Leone caught in Same-Sex couplings can be condemned to life imprisonment, this law is rarely enforced—and Lesbian Sex is not illegal. The fact is, however, that those in Sierra Leone believed to be Queer face harassment, ridicule, eviction, loss of employment, difficulty accessing medical care, and violence at the hands of very conservative religious people—both Christians and Muslims—who consider Same-Gender-Loving behavior a great sin, indeed an abomination. Those perceived to be Queer are often turned away from shops because shopkeepers fear that their money, simply due to the fact it was handled by people who engage in what they perceive as abominable acts, will bring bad luck.

Many in this country, including Esther's parents, believe that the outbreak of Ebola in 2014 was a plague sent by God as punishment for Same-Sex relationships. Her parents are very conservative Baptists—in a population that is 40 percent Christian and 55 percent Muslim. The two most widely read books in the country are, naturally, the Bible and the Quran. People perceived to be sexually perverted are sometimes beaten up while the police, if they do not themselves participate in the attack, look the other way.

There have been, over the years, planned sexual attacks, sometimes called "corrective rapes," arranged by family members, of women in Sierra Leone who are believed to be Same-Gender-Loving, targeted rapes motivated by the irrational idea that this will restore the women to so-called normal sexuality, cause them to change their sexual orientation. In October of 2004, the courageous Same-Gender-Loving activist and leader of the Sierra Leone Lesbian and Gay Association, Fannyann Eddy, was brutally raped by several men and then murdered. Esther may have feared that if others discovered her secret sexual life, she would also be targeted. But ultimately it was her parents' act of rejection, saying she was dead to them, that convinced her that life was no longer worth living. Because Esther had been very close to both her mother and her father, the idea of being permanently alienated from them was devastating: she reasoned that if she was dead to them, then she was also dead to herself.

Esther, struggling to reconcile her sexual desires with her conservative Christian upbringing, had internalized the hatred expressed by the largely homophobic community of Freetown: she loathed herself for having taboo sexual desires and for so frequently acting on those desires. Though intellectually she doubted that Queer sexuality was wrong or perverted, emotionally she could not escape deep feelings of shame and self-hatred. Because of this, she had been deeply depressed and suicidal for years. She could have easily said what the Same-Gender-Loving African American writer, Darnell L. Moore, stated in his coming of age story, *No Ashes in the Fire*: "It was a consistent voice in my head telling me to kill myself and that I was better off dead anyway."

As I have already said but need to repeat: at the very moment Esther was about to cut her throat I took immediate residence in her mind and body. The knife dropped from her hand when I did so. God suddenly, in a flash, transplanted the divine mind to a human brain. God's mind displaced Esther's—God's mind shrunk to a human level, depending on a human brain. As I have made clear, I no longer possess the all-seeing awareness I had as God, although I can draw on fading divine memory. Was this, according to Christianity, the Son of God's condition when he became a man? To what extent was the mind of the Son of God, the second Person in the Trinity, limited by being lodged in a human brain? Did the Jesus of Christian faith imperfectly remember his life as pure Logos, and did he lack the omniscience he possessed in heaven? Of course the Christian incarnation story is only a myth. And my tale is not a myth? Hear me out: I'm not making up my tale, even though I know it is as odd a story as the Christian narrative.

But no stranger than the Christian tale. According to one version of the Christian narrative, the Son of God became flesh as the child of Mary through impregnation by the Holy Spirit—and Joseph became Jesus' stepfather. The whole virgin birth thing is dubious, often justified on the basis of a Christian mistranslation of verse 7:14 in Isaiah, rendering the Hebrew almah *as "virgin"—a virgin who, we are told, "will conceive and give birth to a son to be called Immanuel." The correct translation of* almah *is "young woman." For Jews reading Isaiah in Hebrew, it would never occur to them to translate* almah *as "virgin" because it would have made no sense to say that a virgin—if by that one means a woman who had never had intercourse with a man— would conceive and give birth to a son. Only the Gospels of Matthew and Luke mention a virgin birth: there is no reference to this in the rest of the New Testament.*

The truth is that Joseph was Jesus' father. The genealogy in Matthew leading back to King David is that of Joseph—which makes no sense if Joseph was not Jesus' biological father. As the story is usually told, after he is crucified, Jesus is resurrected from the dead, bodily ascends to heaven to sit at the right hand of God the Father Almighty, and will one day return to earth. What about my story of incarnation? After I die, I will not be resurrected and return to heaven. God perished when God took on the flesh of Esther.

If we can, let's return to your story of incarnation in Esther's body. What happened after you took over her body?

After recovering from the shock of embodiment—the wrenching transformation from God to human being, when I suddenly became a flesh and blood creature limited to one place, no longer possessing divine awareness of what was happening everywhere in the universe, not to mention all over the earth—I left Esther's home in a kind of daze, with only the clothes on my back. Although possessing only a human brain, I was still able to recall, drawing on remaining divine memory, where I could find refuge in Freetown. I remembered that there was a hidden home owned by a young Trans Woman (whose name I cannot reveal for obvious reasons), a place of refuge for the members of the Sierra Leone Queer community, a home that came to be called "The House of Kings and Queens." Taking my first somewhat unsteady steps on earth, it took a while to walk to this location from Esther's home.

Quite the trek, it was well worth it. Although this house has no electricity or running water, with only an outhouse for elimination, this woman's welcome is so warm and inviting and reassuring that guests quickly forget about the lack of amenities. In this home, still operating as far as I know, those considered deviant no longer have to hide their forbidden lives.

Individuals judged perverse by the larger community can finally reside in a place where they don't have to worry about condemnation and the threat of violence. This is truly a safe house—a sanctuary of love and affection whose inhabitants can be who they really are.

Once embodied in and limited by human flesh, now dwelling on earth, I initially felt very vulnerable, fragile, and threatened. But when this generous and gutsy Trans Woman—some called her "the Queen of Queens"—took me in, I began to feel secure and safe, living there for about six months. Surrounded by other local Same-Gender-Loving women and now implanted in Esther's body, I began to feel the sensations of same-sex attraction, but I never acted on my urges. In taking over Esther's flesh I inherited her desires: what I felt sexually was clearly not a choice, only a fact about my recently acquired body. So, I didn't become a human being in some generic sense. As I've already told you, I very deliberately chose to become a Same-Gender-Loving Black Woman—initially, as it turned out, finding myself in a place where acting on my sexual desires could be dangerous, if not fatal. Thank God—well not really—Freetown had The House of Kings and Queens, a welcoming sanctuary in an otherwise largely homophobic and transphobic place, the port city and the capital of Sierra Leone.

Freetown is a West African city widely known for its breezy beaches but not for its maltreatment of members of the community I was now part of. Obviously, it's not a free town for those who are perceived to be sexual and gender freaks: abnormal creatures whose lives were thought to violate the order of nature and the will of God. I of course beg to differ about God's will in this matter—indeed, I wish to protest vigorously this ancient misrepresentation of God's will.

If, by the way, your readers think I'm making up The House of Kings and Queens, they should google "Freetown's LGBT Community Photos." The photos taken by Lee Price, were exhibited at the Humber Street Gallery in 2017, July through September, in the city of Hull, England. Your readers can go online to see a unique photo-story of what it means to be *different* in Freetown. Price, a Same-Gender-Loving Man who is an international photographer, took photos—obviously never showing faces—of a number of the then residents of The House of Kings and Queens. The exhibit in the city of Hull was designed to bring home to those who attended that despite progress in winning equal rights for Queer people in some countries, there are many places in the world where it's dangerous to be who you really are. There are still seventy-seven countries that make engaging in same-sex acts illegal. Photographs in the 2017 exhibit marked the fiftieth anniversary of the British Sexual Offenses Act of 1967, the law that decriminalized "homosexual behavior" in private between men. The law that was overturned like that which still exists in Sierra Leone, ironically a sister city of Hull, only applied to "male homosexual acts."

It should not go unremarked that the Sierra Leone region has the distinction of being the place from which some of the first slaves were brought to the United States in 1652. As the distinguished Black historian and authority on slavery Henry Louis Gates, Jr., observed: 90 percent of Black Human Beings shipped to the New World were enslaved by Africans and then sold to European traders. My choice to incarnate as you see me does not mean that I romanticize one group of people.

Anymore than the biblical God's choice of Israel as a Covenant partner meant God idealized the Jews. I'm actually moving away, theologically, from the notion of Jewish chosenness.

My decision to embody myself this way really means that I affirm a people who—although imperfect like any other people but no different in kind—still lack full equality and dignity in what's supposed to be the greatest democracy on earth. Returning to the subject of the slave trade in what is now Sierra Leone (founded in 1787): the truth is that the export of slaves captured in war was a major business in this West African country—from the late fifteenth to the mid-nineteenth century. Domestic slavery was only abolished there in 1928. There are even some inhabitants of Sierra Leone who are willing to admit that they are descendants of Black Slave Owners who became wealthy selling people of their own race. Enslaved Africans, captured in tribal wars, were held on a tiny strip of land, Bunce Island, in the Sierra Leone River, about twenty miles from Freetown: it served as the major post for the transatlantic slave trade during the eighteenth century.

On the other hand, I know that—drawing on divine memory—Esther was a member of the Creole (or Krio) people, an ethnic group in Sierra Leone who were descendants of freed slaves from the West Indies, Britain, and the United States. While slaves were still being transported for sale from Bunce Island, a small colony of liberated slaves, about four hundred men and women, was established by British Abolitionists in 1787 in the western part of Sierra Leone. It became a home for freed Africans—thus the name Freetown. So, Esther carried in her body the degrading heritage of slavery: she was a descendent of oppressed Africans who were treated like chattel and sold to the highest bidder. Esther, although not a slave, was never truly free. She was a victim of another kind of oppression and degradation, that issuing from hatred of Women who love Women. I now occupy Esther's body, carrying within me her past, the heritage of slavery as well as the personal sense of the oppression she felt as a Same-Gender-Loving Woman in Sierra Leone. I was glad I could find a way to leave that oppressive country to start a new life in Houston.

3

Shekhinah Travels to Houston and Becomes a Secular Buddhist

Houston is a cruel, crazy town on a filthy river in east Texas with no zon-
ing laws and a culture of sex, money, and violence. It's a shabby, sprawling
metropolis run by brazen women, crooked cops and super-rich pan-sexual
cowboys who live by the code of the west—which can mean just about
anything you need it to mean, in a pinch.

—HUNTER S. THOMPSON

How did you get to Houston?

Let me resume my story. Sierra Leone was only a way station to the
States and Houston. To expedite my exit plan from Sierra Leone, I knew I
would have to find a benefactor, and I knew, before I took up residence in
Esther's body, that there was a Same-Gender-Loving Man—an expatriate
of Sierra Leone whose home is now Paris—a man who, despite being open
about his sexuality, for many years frequently returned to Sierra Leone. His
name, Ibrahim Conteh, and how he helped me, can be revealed because he
no longer returns there. He has now become *persona non grata* in Sierra
Leone. I met him when he was visiting The House of Kings and Queens
during my stay there.

He had briefly resided in this Queer safe house—before he won
a fellowship in economics to attend the Sorbonne where he received his
PhD from the Faculty of Economics, one of the most respected economics

departments in France and in the world. Ibrahim Conteh eventually became a citizen of France and a professor of economics at the University of Paris. He is an internationally respected academic who is also a member of the group "Gay Muslims of France." He prays at one of Europe's first inclusive mosques, a place of worship in Paris that warmly welcomes Same-Gender-Loving, Trans, Feminist, and Progressive Muslims. He and his male partner were married—in a civil service—in Paris a few years ago. I knew of course, when I was God, not only that he returned to Freetown from time to time, but the time of year he returned. In the past when he traveled to Freetown, mainly to see his mother, he always made sure he was not followed when he visited The House of Kings and Queens. Professor Conteh had, over the years, visited this refuge to show support—often bringing groceries, large containers of water, and other necessities, including toilet paper for the out-house, everything packed to the top of a rented van. He even promised that someday he would provide the place with electricity and running water. I don't know if he ever did that. Professor Conteh told me, during his last trip, thinking I was Esther, that he would probably never return to Freetown because his mother had died: his father had rejected him when he came out. His international reputation protected him in the past, but that was changing.

The professor was warned by the Freetown police during his last visit that if he did return he might be arrested. They intimated that he could be charged with violating the anti-sodomy law, and he feared that he could be a victim of trumped-up charges. Freetown authorities had discovered that, on one of his visits, he met secretly with a group of Fourah Bay College students who these city officials believed were Queer. Professor Conteh was also well aware that the police had a history of harassing, detaining, and beating up those who they believe to be guilty of, to use their words, "acts of sexual abomination."

The professor seemed impressed with me—or rather Esther—especially her language skills: he thought Esther spoke perfect French, his newly adopted language. The real Esther had taken a class from Professor Conteh a few years earlier. He took an interest in Esther's/my plans, and offered to pay for a flight out of Sierra Leone. I told him that I wanted to live in a country where my sexual orientation would not be an issue and where I could pursue a doctorate in economics—the latter being a white lie, but I knew that was the real Esther's plan. And I knew that Esther had been accepted to begin studies in the PhD program in economics at Stanford University, an academic community she knew would be SGL friendly—indeed it topped the list of what the Princeton Review called "LGBT-friendly campuses." Still, I had no intention of moving there. Houston remained my final destination.

In earlier stays in Freetown, Professor Conteh hand been a guest lecturer at Fourah Bay College, teaching a class on macroeconomics that Esther attended. He found Esther's research papers brilliant and recognized early on that she was a gifted student. She graduated with honors early, at twenty, in economics. Believing I was she when he saw me at The House of Kings and Queens—and believing I would be starting graduate studies at Stanford, he invited me to attend an academic conference with him in Houston, a month before classes would start at Stanford. He also offered to pay for Esther's flight to San Francisco and even cover a cab from the airport to Stanford. Esther had graduated the year before and was living with her parents, working at odd jobs while she applied to various graduate schools. When he visited The House of Kings and Queens, Professor Conteh could see that Esther (I) was restless. I informed him that I'd become alienated from my parents because they caught me with another woman. In fact, I knew of course, prior to giving up my life as God, that the professor, who had just finished the last of his lecture series at Fourah Bay College, would, after what would be his last visit to Freetown, travel from Freetown to Houston.

Eventually, after helping Esther/me get a passport and an F Student Visa for graduate study in the United States, he booked us an early Sunday morning flight on Royal Air Maroc to Mohamed V International Airport, about twenty miles outside of Casablanca, then to Houston on Canada Airlines by way of Montreal, taking about thirty hours to get to our destination. He purchased first-class tickets for us. The professor and I were seatmates on the trip: so we had ample time to get to know each other. I told him about my/Esther's unhappy life in a religiously stifling home and, as he well knew, the sexually oppressive atmosphere of Freetown.

We flew to Houston with the official purpose of attending a global conference on "The Economics of Climate Change" at the Houston Ramada Inn Intercontinental, near the airport, where Professor Conteh reserved two rooms. To the authorities in both countries, this appeared to be a legitimate trip for Esther: she was a brilliant student, planning to pursue graduate studies and traveling with a recognized scholar to a professional conference sponsored by the American Economic Association. Arriving on a Sunday, Professor Conteth would be reading the following evening his paper titled "The Macroeconomics of Climate Change: Beyond General Equilibrium Modeling." The following Sunday Professor Conteh was scheduled to return to Paris and Esther was supposed to travel to Stanford to begin her graduate work, as stated on the application for her student visa.

That was August three years ago. My actual plan, which I conceived before I abandoned heaven, was to create a new identity once I arrived in

Houston. I didn't inform my new French friend of this: instead, I told him that I/Esther was going to apply for asylum status. He thought a Christian heritage might work in my favor, but given the Trump administration's hostility toward people coming from majority Muslim nations—and toward "aliens" in general—he thought that would probably be difficult to bring off. He wished me luck and said I could use him as a reference if I sought asylum. I stayed in the hotel until the end of the conference, actually attending Professor Conteh's presentation, thanked my benefactor when the conference ended, and told him goodbye. He wrote a check to pay for my travel to Stanford and gave me some cash to get me through a few days. I was unable to cash the check, and the money he gave me soon ran out.

I thus became, for a time, an undocumented person wandering the streets of Houston. If authorities ever discover I'm here illegally, will they extradite me to Sierra Leone? If I had kept Esther's actual name and her credentials, could I have successfully made a case for asylum in the United States? To technically qualify as an asylum seeker, you have to show you are being persecuted on account of religion, race, nationality, political opinion, or membership in a particular social group. Persecution for Same-Sex behavior does seem to count. Since, however, I could not prove that I was being persecuted for one of the officially recognized reasons (and I'm not sure under the Trump administration that really matters anymore)—I decided to create a new identity.

I thought the best strategy was to create a Texas as well as U.S. identity, making it appear I was a native of Houston. Just as I can speak Krio (the most widely spoken language in Sierra Leone, apart from English), French, German, or any language you name, I can speak English with a Texas accent if I wish. But you're living proof I need not do that to pass as a native. As you can hear, I've adopted a geographically neutral accent—like yours. But, as you can also tell, I don't sound like Walter Cronkite.

The truth is that I'm an extraordinary immigrant. You could say I freely chose to immigrate to the earth from what is now a God-forsaken place: what you call the fifth dimension. So, maybe I'm an illegal immigrant, one of the many the Trump Administration would like to deport. If so, I'm one of over six hundred thousand now living in Houston. I know Trump's underlings, through their use of the Immigration and Custom Enforcement Agency, are searching for us all the time, but we can be difficult to find. Will Trump deport me along with the two hundred thousand immigrants from El Salvador—who have lived in this country for a decade—that he decreed last January must leave? And the fate of the Dreamers—those eight hundred thousand undocumented immigrants who arrived in this country as children—is precarious at this time. Obama had allowed them to stay, but

Trump decided to terminate the Deferred Action for Childhood Arrivals program. Federal judges have ruled that his administration used a flawed process to end the program. but the administration is appealing.

The Trump administration has deleted the phrase "a nation of immigrants" from the United States Citizenship and Immigration Service's mission statement. Isn't that un-American? Separating children from their parents at the border with Mexico—to enforce his zero tolerance policy on illegal immigration—may have been Trump's ultimate act of cruelty, one that, due to overwhelming public disapproval, he had to reverse, but the damage was already done and it is probable that some children and parents will never be reunited.

I hate to say it but a Jew, a very conservative one, Stephen Miller, is the architect of Trump's anti-immigration policies. Apparently, Miller did not take seriously commandments in the Torah that require Jews to welcome the stranger, the foreigner: let us recall that there are thirty-six texts commanding equal treatment of resident aliens. Miller's childhood rabbi said he tried to teach him Jewish values but evidently failed.

I see myself as one of the over half-million illegal immigrants now living in the city. If by "immigrant" one means someone who moves from her homeland to another country to become a citizen, I'm an immigrant. Unlike other immigrants, my actual place of origin is unknown and unknowable. Whatever my status, I'm obviously a woman without a country: an alien in more than one sense, a being from another dimension. I'm the ultimate extraterrestrial. The important thing is that I, like other immigrants, arrived in Houston with plans for a new life.

After I left the airport hotel and spent the last of the money Professor Conteh gave me on another few nights in a cheap motel near the airport, I managed to hitch a ride to downtown Houston where I found myself suddenly living on the street. I was one of over five thousand (probably more now because of Hurricane Harvey) people experiencing homelessness in Houston, of which two thousand (usually undercounted by authorities) live unsheltered. I chose at first to live on the street. People operate with stereotypes of homeless individuals: they are often viewed as good-for-nothing bums, drunks, drug addicts, the mentally ill, and ex-convicts. What about ex-deities? I'm proof that even God can end up homeless. Did Jesus set a precedent? In truth homeless persons are human beings with problems anyone might have: an unlucky roll of the genetic dice that disposes you to a life of addiction or mental illness, a catastrophic accident that disables you, a natural disaster that destroys your home, a sudden loss of employment that makes it impossible for you to pay the mortgage or rent.

For a while, I spent the night in out of the way places, sleeping covered only in cardboard while lying on a strip of cardboard: a homelessness cliché, I know, but also a harsh reality. One day a very compassionate Catholic student—who attended the University of St. Thomas in Houston, someone who had walked past me several days in a row, and with whom I had a number of conversations about how I ended up on the streets—gave me a well-worn sleeping bag he had purchased from a thrift shop just for me. I can assure you that it was much more comfortable than my cardboard bed. And I eventually moved up from that to having a canvas roof over my head. One day a Black woman, maybe in her seventies, who saw me crawl out of my sleeping bag in an alley, motioned for me to get in her banged-up, ancient Volkswagen Beetle. She asked me if I wanted a ride to a homeless encampment below an overpass—a tent city, as I discovered, under Highway 59, stretching from Caroline Street to Almeda Road. I happily accepted her offer.

I spent many nights in a patched-up tent with three other women who generously invited me to join them, all of us Black. We often ate cold beans from a can, along with canned pineapple. This homeless village beneath Interstate 59 included 101 other tents of various sizes. It was hard to sleep because of the traffic above me, and harder when the storm hit. During Hurricane Harvey, our tent city, fortunately, was under a section of the interstate that was on high ground (much of the freeway became submerged), with tons of concrete above to keep us dry, as long as we stayed in our weighted-down-with-concrete-blocks tents when the driving rain and powerful wind arrived.

After the waters receded, I got used to sleeping with the sound of traffic overhead, sometimes very loud. It's amazing what you can sleep through when exhausted. But, after a while—with many people smoking crack or meth or injecting heroin, a couple of homicides and a stabbing in this increasingly littered, filthy encampment where people freely urinated and defecated on the concrete—I felt unsafe. Also it looked like hepatitis C was beginning to spread rapidly through our tent city. So, I exited this dirty and increasingly dangerous village of the homeless.

If I thought I had escaped danger, my violent welcome to Houston in fact happened shortly after I left the tent community. The evening I decided to leave, sometime after midnight, maybe around 2:30 in the morning, I hitched a ride with an elderly Black driver, someone who had been living in his car, to what I thought was the Montrose area of Houston, a place that has a rich Queer history and is still known for its Gay bars, a place I wanted to visit ever since I arrived in Houston. I thought it was very generous of this man to drive out of his way to do this. Unfortunately for me, this octogenarian got confused and dropped me off about 3:00 a.m. at Montrose Boulevard and West Gray Street, nowhere near the Montrose residential neighborhood. He ignored my protests informing him that he was in the wrong place. He dumped me out and said, "No, young lady, you in the wrong place." He then drove off in a huff.

Before I knew it, as I was walking in a very dark area, a couple of drunken White teenagers grabbed me off the street, forced me into a car and, after pulling into a remote parking lot, began to try to rape me. Imagine God being raped. Well no longer God, but still God's incarnation. They failed because of extreme inebriation and my ability to fight back. They probably weren't used to the physical power of a Black Amazon like yours truly. At that time I had both legs and was very strong.

I ran a long distance to get away from my attackers—and then, drawing from divine memory, recalled that the Bayou City Women's Center was only a few miles away. It is a safe place for women and children fleeing abuse. It offers shelter, counseling, advocacy, career development, and onsite early childhood education. After a long walk, I rang the bell and was asked by someone inside to talk into the outside microphone. I explained my situation. The person on the other end could see me because there was also a camera at the entrance: she could clearly observe my beaten up and bloody face, with my left eye already partially closed.

As luck would have it, one of the 120 beds at the Center was unoccupied, and I was allowed to sleep there, finally to experience the pleasure of a bed again. A friendly attendant on overnight duty quickly assessed my condition and clearly saw the need to shelter me, at least for the night. She took me to a small, very clean single room where four things were waiting on the bed for the next occupant: a bright blue quilt crafted and contributed by a local church, a fresh pillow with WELCOME printed in blue on the white pillow case, a stack of clean towels and wash cloths, and a care kit: a gallon ziplock plastic bag containing essentials such as deodorant, toothbrush, toothpaste, shampoo, comb, maxi pads, small water bottle, chapstick, granola bar, and peanut butter crackers. These items were designed to send a loving message: "You matter. You're worthwhile." Those who planned this welcome for newcomers knew it is likely that any abused woman who seeks refuge at the Center might not only be damaged physically, but probably be so beaten down psychologically that she would actually think her abusive partner might be right: she doesn't really matter.

Not having to sleep on the street wrapped in cardboard, or even in a sleeping bag in a tent, felt like a luxury. And I had the further luxury of a bathroom with private shower stalls down the hall, and being provided with a bathrobe and pajamas I could wear when I was done. It was good to wash the filth off my body and to be sheltered from the cold. In the winter, even Houston can at times be a difficult place to survive if you are living on the street or even in a tent. This past January, after the coldest night of the year, two dead bodies were found—clearly homeless men—one a short walk from Minute Maid Park (the home of the 2017 World Series–winning Houston Astros) and the other discovered near the recently closed iconic Midtown Sears Store on Main Street. I always found such deaths heartbreaking. There are over two hundred million homeless human beings in the world, with another near two billion people lacking adequate housing, many living in crumbling shacks. One of my dreams, as a human being, is to reduce the number of homeless people on the streets everywhere. It never occurred to me when I triggered the Big Bang, and after celebrating the emergence of human life on earth, that I would one day, out of frustration at my impotence, choose to cease being God and in fact become just another one of the many homeless human beings on the planet.

I think the staff at the Women's Center thought I made up the story about the teenagers and was really escaping from a violent partner. Since they figured out my sexual orientation, they probably suspected that I was fleeing from an unsafe relationship with a female lover. They knew that partner abuse in such relationships occurs at the same rate as heterosexual partner abuse and also that the abuse experience is similar.

As it turned out, the Center was looking for volunteers, and, after a stint as a volunteer helping them with a little of everything, I eventually got a position that paid, one I convinced them I was qualified for. The staff saw that I worked well with the children, knew just how to emotionally support them and make them feel secure. It didn't hurt that I could speak fluently any language an incoming child spoke. So I became a multilingual children's counselor. This ended my life as a homeless person and provided me with what the Buddha called "right livelihood": a way of making a living that does not increase suffering and, ideally, reduces it and even promotes the well-being of others.

To continue working, I had to purchase documents that would establish my new identity. Of course I knew, again from divine memory, where to find people in Houston who would provide this service for a reasonable price. I managed to pay for these credentials with the proceeds of my first paycheck. I lied to the HR people at the Center and told them that my Texas photo ID, etc. had been stolen by the guys who beat me up (after I convinced them it really was attempted rape) and that a head injury, probably a concussion from the attack, was affecting my memory, making it impossible for me to recall my Social Security number. That bought me time to create my new self.

My fences provided a phony academic transcript with my new name, listing, as I requested, a doctorate in counseling psychology from the University of Houston, a Social Security number, with the card stolen from a recently deceased twenty-year-old Black resident of Houston (who had no family and was not known to be deceased), and a certified copy of her birth certificate (good fit: born in Houston, Texas, September 27, 1997, 8 pounds, one ounce, 24 inches in length). Using these primary documents, I was able to get a Texas photo ID. I also eventually got two credit cards. In no time at all, I could afford a smart phone, allowing me to be just another human being staring at her phone much too frequently.

Thus, I became, in addition to being a body thief, an identity thief, stealing a dead woman's name, birth certificate, and government ID. She provided me with the credentials I required to pass as a United States citizen and Texas resident. I knew whose ID I was stealing. I remembered that this young Black woman had been abandoned when she was about a year old by her unmarried addicted mother, passed from group home to group home, finally escaping at sixteen to start life as a prostitute. In reality she was forced into this life by a sex trafficker who paid her very little, making a good profit from charging men who wanted to rape her.

He kept her under his control by beating her and getting her addicted to heroin. To get money for a fix, she was required by her owner "to do at least four tricks a night," performed in a seedy motel in a seedy part of Houston. This area, a historically Black community located off of Texas Highway 288, south of downtown Houston, is, ironically, named Sunnyside: in fact it's the sixth most dangerous place in the United States, a place where you have a one in eleven chance of being a victim of a crime. It is also drug-infested. This young woman's life was ruined by being made a nightly victim of multiple rapes arranged by her White male owner (really a modern-day "slaver") who eventually threw her away when her beat-up face, including knocked out front teeth, made her an unattractive sex commodity. Having lost her steady source of income, she struggled to find a way to pay for a fix, often stealing whenever she could, even breaking into houses of people who were at work.

This woman, whose identity I appropriated, an identity of course I cannot reveal, was close to becoming one of the sixty-four thousand who die of a drug overdose each year in this country, about as many people as the number killed in the Vietnam, Iraq, and Afghanistan (so far) wars combined. Even those who were once upstanding citizens have become junkies after getting hooked on a prescribed opioid. Pharmaceutical companies have aggressively and knowingly marketed a variety of addictive pain-killers and thus helped cause this crisis. As you are aware, the opioid crisis is the worst addiction epidemic in U.S. history. There is no way I can communicate the depth of suffering these addictions and subsequent deaths cause families: the suffering, including paralyzing fear and then the deep despair of each family, was something I well knew as God. Their suffering deeply pained God.

The woman whose identity I appropriated died, however, in a way that was more brutal than a drug overdose. When she could no longer pay her heroin suppliers and was deep in debt to them, they tortured and beat her to death and dumped her barbell-weighted-down-body in the Buffalo Bayou—a slow-moving dirty river full of alligators: running through Houston, it overflowed during the heavy rains of Harvey. The violence of the beating they gave her was one of the countless I witnessed over human history, something I never got used to. They took her Social Security card (something one might be surprised that she had), cheap cell phone, and the $11.53 in her pocket. Then they sold her personal information to those who sold it to me. Not a pretty picture of an ex-deity: the way I, after stealing Esther's life, created a new identity based on fraud. I'm benefiting from the untimely deaths of two women, one by virtual suicide, the other by actual murder. But I'm now only a flesh and blood person, flawed like everyone else. My life is based on a number of lies, but lying can be a relatively minor sin in the grand scheme of things.

Let's pretend you are telling me the truth, or what you believe to be true. I'm not sure I'm ready to call you a liar; it depends on whether I judge you to be sane. Maybe you, the victim of some pathology, are telling me what you sincerely believe is the truth. The question is: Why would God need to become a human being? Christianity has an answer to this question, but, from what you have told me, I assume that your answer is very different.

The short answer, already hinted at, is that I had wanted to vacate heaven, if I may again use that term, for a long time because I could no longer abide witnessing all of the suffering on earth. I . . . Excuse me.

(Shekhinah suddenly rose from our table, and, using her crutches skillfully, quickly moved toward the counter where a man and a woman were talking in Vietnamese. I don't know many words in this language, but I know how it sounds. The Vietnamese man seemed to be asking a barista something in very difficult, if not impossible, to understand English. Shekhinah started speaking to the couple in what was obviously very clear Vietnamese because they shook their heads in a way that indicated complete understanding. Indeed they began to smile as Shekhinah was explaining something and pointing in a particular direction. They appeared to thank her in Vietnamese, and also in very broken English, bowing graciously as they backed toward the door. They then, with large smiles on their faces, exited Starbucks. Was this further evidence that Shekhinah could do what she claimed: speak the language of any

conversation partner, perhaps in this case, for all I knew, a special dialect of Vietnamese? She returned to the table, smiling broadly, obviously pleased with what she had done.

As we resumed our conversation, I could not help but notice, as I looked around, most customers were staring at Shekhinah. Some looked puzzled, others amused, some amazed. One customer looked angry. It must have seemed incredibly strange to those who caught even some of what Shekhinah was saying to me that here, in their midst, was a young, very tall Black Woman, with a leg missing—obviously possessing superior language skills—who, for those few able to hear her, was talking to me about having been God. I have to admit I felt some embarrassment at being the one who was passively listening to her. Shekhinah seemed very focused on what she was saying to me, apparently not at all cognizant of others' reactions.

As Shekhinah might explain it, this was an advantage of no longer having divine awareness, namely knowledge of what is going on in the minds of others around her and throughout the world. Even though, if one believed her, she still retained fading divine memories, she was no longer omniscient. Of course she obviously possessed amazing linguistic skills and knowledge of many [all?] languages. Those who watched how Shekhinah handled the Vietnamese couple seemed to marvel at how she had just conversed in what must have been very good Vietnamese, before graciously sending these visitors on their way with a smile on their faces. After a while, most of these customers seemed to lose interest in Shekhinah and became absorbed in their own conversations, or, in many cases, what they were staring at on their phones.)

Please pardon me for interrupting our conversation. They are visitors from Saigon. They're touring the United States, visiting different Vietnamese Buddhist temples, of which this country now has many. Houston has the third largest Vietnamese population in the United States. The Buddhist temple in Sugar Land they want to visit is called in English "Vietnamese Buddhist Center." It has a very tall statue of *Quan Am*, the Vietnamese name for a figure better known in Chinese as *Guanshiyin or Kuan-Shi-Yin* (*meaning: who hears cries of the world*), a bodhisattva (enlightened being) revered almost like a deity: an exemplar of infinite compassion in Mahayana Buddhism. You could say that she was the first Transgender Buddhist, transitioning from male to female. That's a joke of course, but, as you know, *Guanshiyin* did start out as male figure in India and became a female in places like China, Japan, and Vietnam.

I'll be talking about her later when I discuss the important Mahayana Buddhist idea of the bodhisattva: a person who puts off entering nirvana in order to free others from suffering. I frequently visit the Sugar Land temple because of my affection for *Quan Am* and because I find it a very peaceful place at which to meditate. By the way, the Vietnamese Buddhist Center serves delicious vegetarian meals. Some weekend you might want to tour the temple and have lunch there. I would be happy to accompany you.

With pleasure. So, you now are attracted to Buddhism. Do you have a Buddhist practice? Some would of course find it odd that an ex-deity practices a nontheistic religion, or maybe that makes sense because, according to you, God is dead.

I've become a secular Buddhist, in the spirit of Stephen Batchelor, if you know his work. He is the author *After Buddhism: Rethinking the Dharma for a Secular Age* and *Secular Buddhism: Imagining the Dharma in an Uncertain World*. Secular Buddhism drops belief in the literal truth of metaphysical doctrines such as rebirth, samsara, karma, and nirvana in order to concentrate on what is judged to be the heart of Buddhism: namely the practice of meditation, the aspiration to be fully awake every day, and compassionate action devoted to the liberation of all sentient beings from suffering.

Black Buddhists are still a rarity in this country, Black Same-Gender-Loving Buddhists even more so, unless we are talking about cities like New York and San Francisco.

As I'm sure you know, a high proportion of the native born leadership of Buddhist sanghas in the United States are Jews by birth—individuals who converted to Buddhism because they found it preferable to Judaism. After the Holocaust, belief in God became impossible for many Jews. This, for a lot of Jews, was and is the attraction of Buddhism: namely that there is no Creator to blame for all the evil in the world. I had my Buddhist phase.

Yes, I know. This is sometimes called the JewBu phenomenon. And of course these Jews, along with many other leaders of American Buddhist sanghas, were and are overwhelmingly White. Buddhism in America as practiced by natural born Americans has been a White older, often male-led, heterosexual, and bourgeois enterprise—sometimes called White-Western-Convert-Buddhism (or simply WWCB)—making meditation and personal equanimity the heart of Buddhism, keeping Buddhism removed from radical social action for the sake of transforming society. It has often focused on expensive retreats in beautiful locations, something that those at the margins of society cannot afford. Indeed, I don't have the money for these retreats. And, frankly, I have no interest in them.

I want to inform our readers that many of the Jews who became Buddhist leaders retained their Jewish commitment to compassionate action, on behalf of the poor.

Yes, but many WWC Buddhist leaders still place too much emphasis on meditation and attaining a peaceful state of mind. Individuals who convert to Buddhism usually do so by pledging to take refuge in the Buddha (the awakened one), the Dharma (the Buddha's teachings), and the Sangha (the Buddhist community). Ultimately, according to traditional Buddhism, we will find our true home, our true refuge, within ourselves. The spiritual teachings of traditional Buddhism, like "home is within the heart," can be, according to the African American Buddhist Zenju Earthlyn Manuel—located, not surprisingly, in the San Francisco Bay Area—"off-putting" to those alienated from society when, as she remarks, "loss and disconnection are not also acknowledged." She maintains that, in addition to helping people find a path to a true spiritual home, Buddhism must also offer those who are "different" refuge from acts of prejudice and hatred, including racism, homophobia, and transphobia—and also from actual homelessness.

For Black Americans, many of whom experience racism daily, it can be difficult to feel at home anywhere—and finding refuge within themselves can be difficult. Some, internalizing racial hatred, come to loathe themselves, their very Blackness. How can Black Americans find a true home anywhere in this country when they suffer from continued discrimination wherever they live? It must not be forgotten that Blacks were forcibly extracted from their original African homeland, the loss of which, according to Zenju Earthlyn Manuel, remains in their bones. And since slaves weren't considered human, they were often given the name of their owners. So, Zenju can trace her lineage only back to the owner of her ancestors. Her last name, Manuel, is Portuguese. King Manuel of Portugal, the largest slave trader in the sixteenth century, brought Africans to the Caribbean, in particular Haiti. She laments that she carries the name of a man who was blind to her ancestors' humanity.

Far too many Buddhist practitioners in this country—especially those who are middle-class and White (really a minority of Buddhists here, the majority being Asian)—sit quietly and quietistically, understanding liberation to be a completely interior phenomenon, as essentially mental liberation. This focus on spiritual homecoming leads many WWC Buddhists to ignore the pressing need to provide actual houses for those who are physically homeless. These essentially contemplative Buddhists seem to have a difficult time connecting with the pain and misery outside their privileged world.

I've found that essentially contemplative Buddhists are not usually interested in discussing Sexism, Racism, Homophobia, Transphobia, Anti-Semitism (even if they are Jews), Islamophobia, or the degradation of other marginalized populations. Thanissara—a former nun in the Burmese school of Vipassana meditation and author of the important book *Time to Stand Up: An Engaged Buddhist Manifesto for Our Earth*—warns that "when dharma practice focuses primarily on individual efforts, leaving out the impact of systemic inequity, it reinforces internalized oppression." The privileged White Western Convert Buddhist community, an elitist sangha, needs to do more than sit quietly: they need, perhaps after quietly sitting, to create opportunities for dialogue between those in attendance, seeking to find out how people are doing and where they are in their lives, truly listening to those who feel "Othered."

If a Person of Color or a Trans Person or a Same- or Bi-Gender-Loving Person is present, White male, heterosexual, and privileged members of the sangha may need to hear what it's like to live in these too often disdained, even hated bodies—and what their experiences are in the larger community. As poet/activist/organizer Lama Rod Owens, an African American convert to Tibetan Buddhism, has argued, we should form sanghas that are supportive communities for people who are often mistreated because of their race, sexual orientation, gender identity, disability, age, or some other disrespected condition—and provide safe space for them to express themselves and tell their stories of suffering and alienation.

Although over the past decade more predominantly White sanghas in this country have begun to recognize the need to diversify, still a White Ethos tends to be central to their practice. Taking time to hear the voices of victims of discrimination and abuse may make members of an established previously middle-class, all-White Buddhist meditation group uncomfortable—because it will disturb what was, until then, controlled, peaceful space.

I've actually experienced prejudice at some overwhelmingly White meditation centers in Houston and haven't felt free to talk about my experience as a Black Same-Gender-Loving Buddhist Woman. I nearly lost it one evening when a middle-aged White woman asked to feel my hair, as if I were a strange creature she wanted to pet. Others have made remarks they thought I didn't hear about how Black I am. Maybe I'm being overly sensitive, simply imagining prejudice because I can no longer read minds. Prejudice is something I of course knew on high as God, but it's not the same as actually experiencing it in a Very Black Same-Gender-Loving Imperfect Female Body. The truth is that I was feeling increasingly isolated as a Black Same-Gender-Loving Buddhist until I discovered and made contact with Rev. angel Kyodo williams (she prefers a lowercase spelling of her given or birth names, inspired by the example of bell hooks), a convert to Zen Buddhism and a Zen teacher (Kyodo means "way of teaching") who has been described as "the most intriguing African American Buddhist in America." I attended, on scholarship, a workshop last December she organized in San Francisco called "How to Create Real Change." Had long talks with her. Openly Feminist and Same-Gender-Loving, she has shown me what is possible, against the odds.

Williams is a socially engaged Buddhist, someone who, like Thanissara, calls for Buddhists to get beyond a meditation-centered, insulated, quietistic, and largely silent practice in order to work with others to use love and Buddhist practice as a solution to problems of social injustice. Love for her begins with the healing of self, repair of the soul, something necessary before we can begin to heal society, but she also tells us we should never forget the need to heal the world. Famously, she has said, "Love and justice are not two. Without inner change, there can be no outer change; without collective change, no change matters." Inner change might involve, if one is White, Male, Cisgender, and Straight, recognizing one's privilege and, one's possibly unconscious, superior attitude toward Women, Same-Gender-Loving People, Trans Persons, and Blacks.

Or it might mean, if you are one of those whom society devalues, finding a way to overcome the self-loathing the dominant culture has caused you to feel—based on your skin color, sexual desires, sense of gender identity, disability, girth, or age. Kyodo williams is founder of the Center for Transformative Change, an organization dedicated, and I quote her, "to bridging the inner and outer lives of social change agents, activists, and allies to create social justice for all." She calls her work *Radical Dharma*, also the name of a book she co-wrote with Lama Owens.

I know her interfaith work. Williams is a member of the Auburn Senior Fellows program, connected to Auburn Seminary, a group of prominent leaders from different faiths committed to advancing multi-faith movements for social justice. It seeks to organize a Religious Left to counterbalance the long-established Religious Right by supporting liberal and progressive causes in the name of religion.

Yes, she's a Buddhist committed to interfaith work, but not if it's only about talk, mere conversation; on her view, the objective of interfaith dialogue should be collective action for the purpose of transforming society so that it's more humane and just.

Does socially engaged Buddhism completely dispense with religious ideas, such as rebirth, karma, samsara, and nirvana? I know the answer, but readers might not.

There are socially engaged Buddhists who do believe in another world, who believe in the literal truth of rebirth and nirvana. As a secular Buddhist, as I said earlier, I don't believe in the spiritual doctrines of traditional Buddhism. I could call myself an atheist Buddhist, but maybe that's redundant since there is no concept of a Creator in Buddhism. Some traditional Buddhists do, however, believe in gods, but the gods' heavenly life of contentment is not something Buddhists are supposed to aspire to. It's best to be a human being who knows suffering—because this can motivate you to feel compassion not only for yourself but for all who suffer—and to act to reduce suffering in the world.

Although I don't affirm any of the metaphysical beliefs of religious Buddhism, I'm able to interpret the language of Buddhism in a metaphorical way. I see rebirth as something that's possible each moment of life: that is, as free beings, we can always start anew, break out of samsara, understood as the vicious circle of negative habits such as a tendency to reactivity. Karma, as I use the term, is about understanding the consequences of actions in this life: we should seek to avoid acts that increase suffering and cultivate ones that decrease it. Nirvana is not for me a metaphysical state but rather a state of mind that is free from hatred, greed, and denial (of impermanence), the three poisons Buddhism warns us against. Nirvana means transforming these poisons into their opposites: hatred into love (even toward enemies), greed into generosity (a readiness to give everything away), and denial into acceptance (of impermanence, including death). I should add that Buddhism also helps me stay awake to what is going on around me—not only to my social and political environment, but also to my immediate physical surroundings.

After stepping in front of a car and losing a limb, mindfulness became for me an urgent practice, one I needed for survival, because, after arriving on earth, I was often lost in thought, not paying attention to what was right in front of me. After the accident that cost me my leg, I learned to look both ways, and I trained my ears to be more alert to ambient sounds, especially cars. This may be why I was able to quickly move out of the way to avoid being hit when the pickup suddenly approached me from behind this morning.

4

The Problem of Unbearable Sorrow and Impotent Compassion

She remembers . . . all the names of the children She has lost through war and famine, earthquake and accident, disease and suicide. And God remembers the many times She sat by a bedside weeping that She could not halt the process She Herself set in motion.

—MARGARET MOERS WENIG, "GOD IS A WOMAN"

I want to bring our conversation back to my original question, namely: Why did you want to abandon your life as God? If I understood your answer, it was because you could no longer endure witnessing suffering on earth. So, the problem of suffering became a problem for you as well as us?

Yes. Keep in mind that as God I was continuously aware of pervasive and massive suffering on this planet. I also perfectly loved all those who suffered, perfectly cared about them. Knowing and caring about the suffering of every creature, human and non-human, had become unbearable to me. The idea that God is perfectly happy, or serenely peaceful, in a world full of unspeakable cruelty, pain, and injustice makes no sense, especially if one conceives of God as truly compassionate and loving. For some theistic philosophers and some theologians, impassivity—the view that God has no changing emotions or feelings—is part of God's perfection. Unaffected by what happens in the world, God, on this view of divine perfection, is always in a state of perfect bliss, no matter how much suffering occurs on earth.

That is, God is always perfectly serene and is unmoved and unchanged by what goes on in the world. Nothing could be further from the truth.

This, as you know, is my theological and philosophical territory. You will get no argument from me. The traditional view is that to be perfect is to be changeless, which of course you well know—so I now say this for the benefit of readers who may not know (the philosopher-teacher in me must speak)—is grounded in an ancient Greek idea, developed by Plato, that conceives of perfection as inseparable from changelessness. So Plato's God, at least in The Republic, *is changeless. According to Plato, if a perfect being changes, that could only mean becoming less perfect. Plato also says this about objective, eternal value standards. For example, perfect beauty, what Plato calls the Form of Beauty, a transcendent eternal essence, is for him a changeless reality. It is the same with the form of Justice and all qualities of true goodness. Love, on the other hand, was for the Plato of the* Republic *something imperfect, something flawed, because it is a changing, unstable emotion. So, love, on this view, is by definition a lack, characterized by incompletion: it is a desire for something one does not have, either the beloved or some object in the world one strives to possess.*

A loving God would, according to this Platonic view, be an imperfect God because He would be affected by what happens to the beloved, would be changed by the suffering of the beloved, and made sad by the loss of the beloved. But this is precisely what those of us who affirm a process view of God want to assert: namely that God is a loving being Who changes in loving response to changes in the world. God is not a static or fixed reality, but a caring Creator Who is moved by suffering in the world. From a process perspective, God is a perfectly loving Subject of change whose moral perfection is found precisely in being deeply affected by those who suffer. Many Jewish, Christian, and Muslim philosophers and theologians, in opposition to Plato, assert that God is both perfectly loving and absolutely changeless. I think that this is a contradiction at the heart of the traditional Abrahamic view of God.

Yes, as I'm here to testify, a God who truly cares about creatures will suffer with them and be moved by their suffering. There are many defenders of traditional theism who think that a perfectly loving God's well-being is of another order and thus is unaffected by the misery occurring on earth. God, on their view, is, to borrow Aristotle's language, the Unmoved Mover. God is thought to be the Uncaused Changeless Cause of everything. The Eternal One never alters and so is never moved, emotionally speaking.

We should not leave out the dimensions of absolute power and perfect knowledge that are part of the traditional concept of God embraced by many Jews, Christians, and Muslims. God, on this view, is the perfect, changeless, omnipotent, and omniscient Creator of the cosmos. This vision of God is also often called classical theism. This God is a hands-on Creator, directing what

happens in the world guiding everything toward a good end, and thus fulfil-
ing the promise of what is called eschatology. (Note to readers: this is a part of
theology that deals with the final destiny of all souls and the final judgment:
the end of days). It is important to recognize that God so conceived perfectly
knows the future, knows absolutely in advance what will happen throughout
the universe, a capacity called divine foreknowledge. Of course, one serious
problem with this view is that it leaves all the evil in the world—both moral
and natural evil—unexplained. As you obviously know, one of my preoccupa-
tions has been theodicy, trying to solve the problem of evil. In the face of a
world full of loss and pain, I affirm a God who sympathetically suffers with
creatures, but does not have the power to rid the world of the forces, human
and natural, that cause pointless, malignant suffering—and did not know in
advance how things would turn out.

What troubles me about the classical idea of divine perfection is that
this God's well-being cannot be altered, diminished, or increased by what happens on earth—that God remains serene and unmoved, regardless of what
happens in the world. Apparently, this God is untouched by what I call malignant suffering. Indeed, any claim that our suffering is pointless or malignant
shows that our understanding of suffering is human-all-too-human: finite and
imperfect. Supposedly, our suffering makes sense from God's infinite vantage
point. In any event, according to this view, God is beyond sorrow because sorrow is a state that belongs to humans in all their limitations, not to God in
God's transcendence of all limitations.

This idea of God as the serene transcendent Other Who is beyond sorrow can also lead to the idea that God's justice transcends any human idea
of justice. Just as, on this view, no human emotions apply to God, neither
do human standards of justice. If one believes that God can remain serene
and unmoved while Nazi genocide occurs, one can also easily conclude that
God's justice is radically different from a human understanding of justice—
one that would demand intervention to prevent mass murder.

There are traditional theists—such as internationally know preacher and
best-selling author Francis Chan (Crazy Love: Overwhelmed by a Relentless
God) *who assert that God's moral way, God's sense of justice, is so far above*
human standards that we will never fully understand it.

Nonsense. Such thinking can lead to the justification of the worst horrors—whether inflicted by human beings or natural forces—in the name of
the inscrutable will of God. Abraham in Genesis 18 would not have been able,
in the name of justice, to challenge God, on behalf of potentially innocent
human beings, when God was about to destroy Sodom and Gomorrah, if God
had a different standard of justice, one that could justify the slaughter of the
innocent. Later, I will say more about the Abraham of this story, distinguishing

him from the Abraham who, in another story (what Jews call the *Akedah*: binding of Isaac), is ready to murder his own son because he believes God commands this. This Abraham story has been used to justify suspension of ordinary ethical thinking, attributing to God a standard of goodness incomprehensible to human beings. I think the view that God's moral standards are incomprehensible to human beings is a dangerous road leading to places such as Moriah where a father is ready to murder his son in God's name.

I think you're right. But many Jews and Christians, citing Isaiah (55:8–9), want to make the case that God's ways are not our ways, whether one is talking about God being unaffected by all the suffering on earth or about God operating with a standard of justice alien to our own.

In reality, for God, divine justice and divine suffering were intimately connected. It is because I as God suffered with creatures who suffered unjustly that I wanted to end this kind of suffering, not only to relieve divine suffering, but because such suffering is wrong.

The idea of a compassionate and just God who suffers when human beings suffer is as old as the Hebrew Bible. In another text in Isaiah (63:9) we are told that God is afflicted by Israel's suffering. God perfectly feels human pain—it is also God's pain—and seeks to relieve it. Maybe God's ways are not our ways in the sense that God is perfectly compassionate and we are not. On the view I defend, God's well-being is dependent on that of creatures. A God who wants creatures to feel joy—and takes joy in our joy—is necessarily a God Who shares also in our grief and misery, and wants us to be free from pointless pain and suffering. How could a truly compassionate God really know the sorrow of creatures, whether human or animal, and not also suffer?

A sympathetic God, if She really feels the suffering of creatures, will experience sorrow. An understanding of God's capacity for sorrow is well expressed in a poem by William Blake that my mentor, Charles Hartshorne, was fond of quoting, from "Songs of Innocence." In this poem, Blake rhetorically asks whether a father can see his child weep and not feel sorrow. And Blake also asks, recognizing God's compassion for non-human animals, how God could know a wren's sorrow without also feeling it. Blake imagines a God who sits with all suffering creatures and moans until their grief disappears. God, Blake tells us, will ultimately bring them divine joy.

Some philosophers of religion and theologians find it unacceptably anthropomorphic to attribute such feelings to God. They deny that God feels and is moved by the feelings of sentient creatures, that God shares their sorrow and loss. They deny that when creatures suffer God experiences sorrow because this makes God too much like us. Charles Hartshorne took issue with this. He liked to ask: "What does it mean to know what sorrow is, but never to have sorrowed, never to have felt the quality of suffering?"

The Jesus of the Gospel of Matthew tells us that God is aware of the fall of every sparrow. Hartshorne, as you know, would, in the spirit of Blake, add: God knows the joy and also suffering of every sparrow, its fear and pain. I agree: if there is a truly compassionate God, God's knowledge of the lives of all sentient beings necessarily includes feeling their feelings as vividly as they do. Otherwise, as Hartshorne also points out, God's knowledge would be abstract and incomplete. Complete knowledge involves not only knowing intellectually or cognitively that creatures have feelings and that they suffer, but also affectively or emotionally knowing this by sorrowing in their sorrow.

Yes, but it's not just a matter of feeling the sorrow that creatures feel. Let me repeat: I was deeply moved and indeed disturbed by all the suffering that occurred on earth not only because I perfectly knew and felt the feelings of all those who suffered but also because I was a God of justice. There's the rub. The book of Leviticus in the Torah contains a powerful ethical imperative that I would like to claim as my own, even though it was a product of ancient Jewish ethical wisdom, thus a human ethical discovery. The Israelites are told by Moses, supposedly channeling God, that they should not stand idly by while their neighbor's life is threatened or while their neighbor bleeds (*Leviticus 19:16*). Clearly this is a moral principle every human being should try to follow. Should God do less than is morally expected of human beings?

Despite their insight into God's intimate knowledge of the life of all sentient beings, God's capacity to feel the feelings of all sentient beings, what both Blake and Hartshorne—and I think you also, Jim—fail to appreciate is divine frustration: God's inability to intervene. Blake correctly asserts that God will moan until the grief of all creatures disappears. But when will all grief be gone? What more does God do, other than moan: sorrow in the sorrow of creatures? The grief of humans and animals was my grief, but the reality was that I had to stand idly by while humans and animals bled because I lacked the power to intervene. That was the source of my deepest sorrow.

Since I never slept, I could never turn away from the pain of the world. I could never close my eyes because I had no eyelids. Indeed I saw without eyes. My sight, to speak metaphorically, penetrated the very organs of creatures: I could see cancer eating away bodies, arthritic bones, deteriorating hearts, the wasting away of the bodies of starving children. I could also see all the mental pain hidden within the skulls of all those who suffer psychologically. I saw all too clearly the pain of mental illness, the unbearable darkness experienced by those with depression and the alien, disturbing voices heard by those with schizophrenia. I could see perfectly all the suffering of every creature that experienced any kind of pain, physical and psychological.

One could say I saw in a way more penetrating than the most extraordinary vision of any earthly creature. I had x-ray vision, if you will. I envied human beings who could deliberately choose not to look at the misery around them, not read or watch the news: to, if they wished, close their eyes to all the suffering in the world. I envied their freedom to shut their eyes to the pain that fills the world or turn their eyes away from unpleasant sights to pleasant ones. That was not a possibility for me. Or to use another metaphor, you could say that I could hear all those who cried out in agony, perfectly hearing the cries of physical and mental pain. There was no escape from the heart-rending voices of agony, both human and animal. Not one quiet moment, even a fraction of a second of silence. For the first time, when I became a human being, I could experience the peace of silence, of being able to go to a quiet place, one where I could not hear the cries of the world. In my life as God I heard everything all the time.

Admittedly, I could of course also hear all the laughter in the world— but the cries of pain somehow seemed louder than the sounds of joy. Let me make this clear: I don't deny that there was and still is joy on earth, including joyful sounds. There was and is, for example, the joy created by music and song—and these I celebrated. Friedrich Nietzsche said in his characteristically hyperbolic way: "Without music life would be a mistake." That goes too far, but . . .

Joyful music! Yes. Don't forget the way in which music enhances life and makes life meaningful in the face of loss, often inspiring to those who are struggling to persevere.

I must say that I came to view human music—don't forget there is music and even musical creativity in the animal world, among song birds and humpback whales for example—as an extraordinary invention, something again that I only vaguely anticipated. One of my divine pleasures was being surprised by the incredible range of human musical creativity. Not knowing what the future will bring, even the Creator could be genuinely surprised by human musical innovation and the great beauty and joy this brings into the world. A new and aesthetically wonderful sound suddenly appears in the world that was not there the day before!

Let me repeat: I was astounded by the breathtaking diversity of human musical creativity, and there is no end in sight to this, including innovation by both composers and performers. Jazz clearly illustrates both: think of the musical genius Charlie Parker (who died at thirty-five) on saxophone doing different takes on George Gershwin's "Summertime"—never doing it the same way twice. Of course music is only one domain of artistic creativity; I also marveled at the depth and range of creativity in the worlds of poetry, fiction, theater, dance, painting, sculpture, architecture, photography, and cinema.

5

Saying Hallelujah to Life

The Wisdom of Leonard Cohen

Music will help dissolve perplexities and purify your character and sensibilities, and in time of care and sorrow, will keep a fountain of joy alive.

—DIETRICH BONHOEFFER

(I read to Shekhinah the above quotation from Bonhoeffer, a Christian arrested by the Nazis for conspiring to rescue Jews. We will discuss his theology later.) Let's keep our focus on music. Don't you agree with Bonhoeffer? You said music brought joy to you as well as human beings, maybe a joy that redeems suffering?

No, music doesn't ultimately redeem suffering. Excuse me, Jim, but to say that it does reminds me of the Pet Shop Boys' song "It's Alright." After enumerating horrible events of a world in crisis—with lyrics describing the rapid destruction of forests, with deserts taking their place—they blithely and unconvincingly, ironically to be fair, tell us that everything is going to be alright because music will last forever. No offense, Jim, but music cannot redeem a world on the brink of ecological collapse. (*She must have known I liked the music of the Pet Shop Boys and was using this song to try to show the implausibility of making music salvific*).

And, yes, I did take joy in music and joy in the joy of human beings who create music and joy in the joy of those who experience pleasure in listening to music. I'll readily admit that music can sometimes turn sorrow into joy, at least momentarily. I don't want to deny this even as I tell my tale of unbearable divine sorrow in the face of massive suffering among sentient creatures and the massive destruction of life on this fragile planet.

Let me try to make the case for the redemptive power of music. And I grant you "redemptive" may be too strong a word. Still, the power of music to transform emotions is a wonder. Think of how Beethoven's "Ode to Joy" can raise human spirits. Even in the midst of slavery, consider how enslaved Blacks in the United States emotionally transcended their condition by making up songs called spirituals. Although they are often called "sorrow songs," African American spirituals served a powerful and positive double-function. First, the literal meaning of the words of these songs points to life in another world, the promised land understood as heaven, where those singing will be perfectly free and happy, thus bringing those who were enslaved consolation and hope in the midst of suffering and humiliation. And, when allowed to sing as they worked the fields, the act of joining their voices together in songs about crossing over to the promised land could lift their otherwise bleak mood. Let me quote the words of a freed slave, the brilliant and eloquent abolitionist, Frederick Douglass. About these songs, he said (reading from my phone): "We were at times remarkably buoyant, singing hymns and making joyous exclamations about as triumphant in tone as if we had reached the land of freedom and safety." That's strong testimony about the redemptive power of spirituals, coming from a former slave. Indeed, another name for spirituals is "redemption songs."

Second, many of these songs also contained hidden messages of physical liberation about which slave-owners were, in most instances, oblivious. For example, the lyrics of "Swing Low Sweet Chariot" could be used to signal the nearness of abolitionists who were ready to guide those enslaved to a network of secret routes and safe houses on the way to free states or Canada. This song could serve as a coded announcement that the "sweet chariot" (the network that was called the "Underground Railroad") would "swing low" (come South) to "carry me home" (North to freedom), a "band of angels coming after me" (abolitionists such as Harriet Tubman). A slave who suddenly starts singing has received and is spreading the word that help is on the way and that his or her fellow slaves need to be ready to leave: probably that night. The lyrics thus promised actual redemption from oppression, offering a real path out of slavery. The hidden meaning of words of spirituals literally pointed the way to liberation.

Another genre of original Black music, the Blues, music that is essentially secular and contains themes that are ostensibly the opposite of joy, has, since its creation, brought Blacks great pleasure. This unique African American inven-tion—which may have begun as the musical cry of so-called "free Blacks" who continued to be devalued and mistreated even after they lost their chains—can, paradoxically, lift the mood of both singer and audience. Ironically, the Blues can bring a smile to listeners who find the virtuosity of the performers uplifting: think of the music of Robert Johnson and Bessie Smith.

Again, Black solidarity in suffering—the realization that in listening to words of disappointment and melancholia you are not alone in your hard-ship—could and can be strangely therapeutic and actually reassuring. And Blacks could and can take pride in an original art form they created in re-sponse to a world where their dreams had been denied. That's why I believe music has redemptive power. Indeed, I think that both sacred music, such as African American Spirituals, and secular music, such as the Blues, have the potential to enable those who suffer to affirm life as they listen to songs that can touch their heart.

As God, I appreciated both secular and sacred music, at least some of it.

What about a piece of music that creatively combines the spiritual and the profane? I want to propose an example of a popular song that does this while providing those who are suffering, indeed those who have in fact experi-enced brokenness, with a message of redemption, a way to say yes to life.

You have in mind Leonard Cohen's "Hallelujah."

I thought you could no longer read minds. Or am I that transparent?

I remember your taste in music. You have picked a song that has been performed by over three hundred major artists and continues to be per-formed at both weddings and funerals. You could call it an enduring piece of pop music, but it is much more than that. Of course the name of the song literally means "praise God." But Cohen's take on the word "Hallelujah" goes beyond praising the Creator, something, to be honest, I never felt comfort-able hearing. In fact, when I was God, I despised religious praise music. The lyrics seem to ignore the dark side of creation.

This could be said about some Jewish prayers, including Psalms, we sing in synagogue: songs full of exaggerated praise for the Creator.

Clearly, Cohen's "Hallelujah" is not a hyperbolic praise song directed at God, but rather a complex composition that involves saying yes to something very mundane: failed erotic love and the human brokenness it can bring.

Yes, and that's why it's surprising to encounter the song in popular en-tertainment. You can of course find it on the soundtrack of the blockbuster animated film, Shrek, as well as other films and on many television programs. Over the years it was performed so often that Nick Murray in a September 19, 2016, article in the New York Times called for a moratorium on it, and that was not the first time a news outlet made such a demand. Good luck with that,

Nick. I rather think, as a Cohenphile, maybe there should be a moratorium on moratoria.

Adam Cohen, Leonard's son, has said that the family would like a moratorium on the song. Even if possible, that would deny new generations the pleasure and wisdom of this remarkable song. It continues to be performed by new generations of musicians and to win fans who fall in love with some version of it. I want to linger on "Hallelujah" because I know it's one of your favorites, because many of your readers will be familiar with it, because it brings together the sacred and the sensual in a very creative way, and because it lucidly illustrates what I, as God, felt wonder about, namely the way a single piece of music can show the creativity of the composer—in this case both the lyrics and the melody—while also lending itself to an amazing range of creative interpretations by performers.

Reflecting on the richness and depth of this one song will allow us to explore not only the nature of musical creativity but also what it means to say "Hallelujah" in midst of failed love and human brokenness—indeed what it means to sing "Hallelujah" even if there is no God! I think this song by Leonard Cohen shows how human beings can say yes to the messiness of love and life, even if God cannot. Both the song's form and its content deserve attention.

I've long enjoyed listening to it in its many versions. And I agree that it has something important to say on the subject of sexual love. About this song, the R&B singer John Legend said, "It is as perfect as you can get"; and Bono stated that "it might be the most perfect song in the world." This praise may seem inflated, but the high praise for "Hallelujah" tells us something important about this piece of music.

As you probably know, "Hallelujah" was written at a low point in Leonard Cohen's career in 1984: he was turning fifty and his last three albums, stretching over the preceding decade, had not done well. Cohen, after a career as a novelist and poet, didn't start writing songs and singing music professionally until the late 1960s when he was in his early thirties. He wrote over eighty verses of "Hallelujah" from which he selected four to create the original 1984 version, a rendition that because of its biblical references has been dubbed the religious version. A 1988 rendition, found on *Cohen Live*, is sometimes called the secular—or more specifically erotic—version because it drops the biblical verse and deals with a sexual relationship. In truth even the so-called religious version contains a sexual theme.

I think one needs to hear all the verses he ultimately released to get a full picture of what Cohen was after. In the end, not even God could do justice to the words of this song because it, like the best sacred texts, is rich in meanings and is open even to conflicting interpretations. Some unimaginative critics wonder why Cohen didn't make his meaning clearer.

I think Herb Bowie, rock critic, gets it just right when he says, "If there was another, simpler way for Cohen to communicate what he wanted to say, then he wouldn't have to spend years creating the song." I don't think Cohen had one meaning in mind. I believe that Cohen, who, as a Jew, celebrated endless creative and even conflicting interpretations of texts in the Torah, deliberately gave the song layers of possible meanings and was personally open to interpretations that might surprise even him.

So, any interpretation you or I provide will be just that, one interpretation among countless possible ones. What complicates things is that over the years Cohen added verses to the original released in 1984 and changed some words in different verses. We can identify seven verses that ultimately made their way into different performances of "Hallelujah." Your readers can find all of them online. After the additional verses were made public, those who performed the song always had to decide which verses to use.

Cohen spent close to five years attempting to draft multiple verses of the song (he lied when he told Boy Dylan it took only two years) and then, in the end, reduced it to only a few. I remember—admittedly, a fading divine memory—that during one frustrating night in a hotel room, Cohen, clothed only in his underwear, literally banged his head on the floor, saying, "I can't finish this song. I can't finish this song!" "Hallelujah" in its original version was not immediately recognized as a great song. In fact Columbia Records executives turned it down, questioning Cohen's talent, with the president, Walter Yetnikoff, rejecting the whole album on which it ultimately appeared (*Various Positions*), saying about "Hallelujah," "What is this? This isn't pop music. We're not releasing it. This is a disaster." Cohen's second version, the secular one, released in 1988, didn't do much better when it first appeared.

The 1984 religious rendition of "Hallelujah" on Various Positions *was a little cheesy with its choir, and I can see why those hearing it might be puzzled, given the biblical references and the chorus repeating a term that seemed to belong in a synagogue or a church. Someone even described it as "a funeral synth-laden dirge." This edition of the song was probably confusing to commercially minded executives who may have been reluctant to take a chance on what struck them as a solemn religious hymn when what they wanted was a promising pop song that would make them some money.*

The Columbia Records executives were right. The song released in 1984, on an independent label, wasn't a winner commercially when it hit the market. It took Jeff Buckley—American singer, songwriter, and guitarist, who died too young, at thirty, of drowning—to get "Hallelujah" the attention it deserved and to create a huge cult around the song. Even that took a while. Buckley was working with a version put together in 1990 by John Cale, co-founder of the Velvet Underground and a producer, composer, and performer in his own right. Cale had asked Cohen to fax him verses of the song. Then, while Cale was away from his apartment one evening, a long roll of fax paper poured off his machine, covering his floor with fifteen verses of "Hallelujah." Choosing the verses he thought "were cheeky and mischievous," Cale combined the religious and secular versions to create a song in five verses, with some minor editing of words. In 1990 he recorded his version of the song, alone, seated at a Steinway piano. It can be heard on the tribute album to Cohen: *I'm Your Fan.*

As chance would have it—and I can assure you it was chance alone, not fate or divine intervention—Jeff Buckley discovered the tribute album while he was cat-sitting in an apartment of a friend. When I was God, I saw Buckley fall in love with Cale's version. Buckley's album, on which the song appeared, was at first a flop, although some leading musicians were high on Buckley's take on "Hallelujah." It was, however, Buckley's rendition that eventually struck a chord with a wide audience, with most listeners assuming that Buckley wrote the song. The version Cale chose, which Buckley simply appropriated, is what many consider the canonical edition. Jeff Buckley's "Hallelujah" can be found on his only studio album, *Grace*: his version of the song made the music world and music lovers sit up and take notice and finally say *Hallelujah* to "Hallelujah."

I like both Cale's and Buckley's "Hallelujah," and also Rufus Wainwright's—but k. d. lang's take on it, especially the way she sang it at the opening ceremonies of the 2010 Vancouver Olympics, is one of my favorites. Each of these performances of the song has its distinctive appeal.

And I assume that you like some of Cohen's versions. This makes my point about the creativity of the performer. We have the songwriter's interpretation, and even that sounds different in different versions. Then we have qualitatively different interpretations by John Cale, Jeff Buckley, Rufus Wainwright (on *Shrek*), and k. d. lang—just to name a few. Your readers should go online to hear all of these versions as well as the 1984 and 1988 renderings by Cohen—so you, Jim, don't have to pay the expensive permission to quote Cohen songs.

Thanks, I'll second that, to keep permissions costs under control, since my publisher requires me to get permissions and pay for them. Besides, it is not enough to read the lyrics: one needs to hear this song sung by different artists.

By listening to many different versions of this popular song, people can appreciate the art of musical interpretation. As I've already said, I was amazed, not only by human musical creativity, by the range of musical compositions, but also by the creativity one hears in different takes on the same work. This applies to most forms of music.

(*I felt Shekhinah was obviously making musical, cultural, religious, and philosophical references—such as to Cohen and the history surrounding his most famous song, not to mention all of her references to Jewish practices and even to the* New York Times—*she knew I would understand and appreciate, part of her uncanny ability to speak the language of her interlocutor. If I had been a young Black man, the musical and other cultural references, I am sure, would have been very different. For example, she does not immediately mention hip-hop in discussing music—something she would later instruct me about—because she had not seen any indication that I liked this genre of music. So just as she had adopted my speech patterns, she was speaking my language in more ways than one.*)

As you know, but many readers may not, "Hallelujah"—which really should be spelled Hallelu-yah—means "praise Yah." "Yah" is a Jewish term for God derived from the first letter of the Hebrew name for God: YHVH. In one verse of the song, a woman is being addressed, maybe a lover, who has evidently accused Cohen of taking God's name in vain. This may refer to the charge that he is using the word "Hallelujah" profanely, to which Cohen responds that he doesn't even know the Name, reflecting the view that Jews use terms such "Yah" or "Adonai" or "Lord" because they don't know how to pronounce God's personal name in Hebrew. Out of reverence, Jews never try to do so.

This extraordinary song, when we consider all the verses that Cohen ultimately released to the public, mixes the sacred and profane in a very interesting way. It's both an unorthodox hymn and an unorthodox love song. I want to say yes to Cohen's union of the sacred and the sensual. In an interview shortly after Cohen's death, k. d. lang insightfully said that she thought the song was about "the struggle between having human sexual desire and searching for spiritual wisdom." This song is not only about an "unbroken Hallelujah," namely praising God understood as the Lord of Song, or a Hallelujah praising successful human love, but also a Hallelujah praising tormented sexual love, failed love, the "broken Hallelujah." We need to remember that for Cohen there can be at least two kinds of Hallelujah: a celebration and a lament, an expression of joy and a cry of pain. In the Psalms God is sometimes praised in the midst of pain, even in human brokenness. (See Psalm 42 for example.) Cohen thought (he says as much) that perfect and broken Hallelujahs have equal value. This song reflects, he tells us, his desire to affirm life, with enthusiasm and emotion, not in some religious way but in a way that that works even for those who live a purely secular life.

We must remember that, religiously speaking, Cohen was complicated: a Jew by birth who kept the Sabbath, he immersed himself in Buddhist practice—he in fact spent years in a Rinzai Zen monastery—dabbled in Scientology, and included many Christian themes in his music.

Let me jump in. He left Scientology behind and never became a Christian—even temporarily like Bob Dylan during his brief born-again period. The fact is that Cohen, whatever his interest in other faiths, always identified as a Jew. Yes, Cohen did have, for a number of years, a serious Zen practice, but this in no way contradicted his identification as a Jew. When asked once if there was not a conflict between Zen and Judaism, he answered that he did not think they are mutually exclusive, depending of course on your take on Zen.

The kind of Zen Cohen practiced involved no prayerful worship and did not require him to give up belief in God. About Judaism, in an interview with Arthur Kurzweil, he said: "I've inherited an extremely good religion. I have no need to change it." He told Kurzweil, unambiguously: "I am a Jew." Cohen wanted to promote both a deeply spiritual and also a very tolerant Judaism, while trying to recover the prophetic voice of the Jewish tradition. He was a practicing Jew until his death.

(*The following response to my remarks again surprised me. Did she have an encyclopedic mind, a mind that could internally google anything?*) I don't want to dispute that he remained a Jew. In fact, the Buddhist monk he worked with at the Mount Baldy Zen monastery, Joshu Sasaki, in the San Gabriel Mountains of the Angeles National Forest—where, starting in 1994, he lived for six years, even being ordained as a monk in 1996—said to him once: "Leonard, I've known you for twenty-five years, and I've never tried to give you my religion. I've just poured you Sake." Cohen then lifted his glass and said, "Rabbi, you are indeed the light of your generation." Cohen called him rabbi—which, some of your readers may not know, means in Hebrew "my teacher"—because he felt that the Zen wisdom he learned from this monk opened him up to a new appreciation of Judaism. As he colorfully remarked about the monk's contribution to the rediscovery of his birth religion: "He provided a space for me to kind of dance with the Lord." Unfortunately, this monk's career was tainted later by a tide of charges of sexual abuse, something Cohen knew nothing about.

Yes, I know—but let me, for the moment, stick with Cohen's faith. In the interview with Kurzweil, Cohen said that he was never really interested in a new religion. He states that, although he had always been a Jew, it was only after studying with his old Zen teacher for many years, when he broke his knees, tripping in the dark outside the monastery, that he really began to practice Judaism again in earnest. Because he could no longer sit in the required Zen meditation position, he began to stand in Jewish prayer, at first propped up by crutches, and then on his own. Indeed he began to recite prayers from the Amidah (Hebrew for "standing"), nineteen Jewish standing benedictions that Cohen said lifted his soul and brought him a deeper appreciation of Jewish spirituality. As he concluded a performance attended by fifty thousand at Ramat Gan Stadium in Tel Aviv in September 2009, Cohen recited—in Hebrew—the Birkat Kohanim (priestly blessing) from the Torah, Numbers 6:22–27 (here is my translation): "May God bless and keep you, let God's face shine upon you. May God be gracious to you. May God look kindly on you and bring you peace." As he said the last word of the prayer, "Shalom" Cohen raised his hands and formed with his fingers the Hebrew letter Shin, representing another term for God: Shaddai.

I was never sure what people expected of me when people recited the priestly blessing, a benediction found in Christianity as well as Judaism. The truth is I could not be gracious, and although I could look kindly on all creatures, I was not able to bring peace to anyone who was troubled. Wish that I could have, but I could not. *Shaddai* is sometimes mistranslated as "All-Powerful," which of course God was not. The name actually derives from the Hebrew word for breasts, suggesting that God is the One Who nurses or nourishes all who are needy, which God did not do.

Let's return to Cohen's take on Judaism. After his time in the monastery, Cohen reclaimed Judaism with a new resolve, finding new meaning in its prayers and rituals. He was never, I want our readers to know, a Jew who thought that Judaism was the only way. He never thought that Jews were holier than any other people. What Cohen found unacceptable in any religion was exclusivity. With some ultra-Orthodox Jews, there is an arrogant emphasis on chosenness and contempt for those pejoratively referred to as "goyim": non-Jews. Cohen by contrast wanted to recover the kind of openness that existed when Jews used to study with Sufi masters. Cohen asserted that confident Jews are never closed off to other faiths. He was very open to interfaith dialogue and cooperation. He said in the interview with Kurzweil: "A great religion affirms other religions. A great culture affirms other cultures. A great nation affirms other nations. A great individual affirms other individuals, validates the being-ness of others and their vitality." Although Cohen was a very serious Jew, he was also truly tolerant of other faiths—indeed he valued religious diversity.

That's something I as God also celebrated, namely human beings who are open to learning from those who are religiously different and from those who are not religious at all—something you, Jim, are in the business of promoting. Openness to listening sympathetically to the other, to truly hearing what is central to the religious or spiritual or the secular life of another person, was for me a truly holy thing.

I want to return to the song "Hallelujah." We should try to hear what Cohen is telling us about his inner life, or the life of the singer who at that time wrote this. The song is, on the face of it, about praising God. It also, as I mentioned already, about saying "Hallelujah" to life even in the face of failed love, affirming life even when love hurts. Cohen perceptively brought the world of frustrated human-to-human love into the category of Hallelujah—into a place that enabled him to praise love, despite its frequent failures and defeats. Love, he tells us in this song, is not a form of combat, even if failed love sometimes—especially if one partner falls in love with another person—feels like a contest that one lover loses and the other wins.

(She quietly sings the opening lines of "Hallelujah." Shekhinah amazingly captures, through a modulation of her voice, Cohen's voice at fifty, different from his voice at thirty-three when he launched his musical career.) The first words of the song refer to a secret chord that King David played on his harp that pleased God, and then the singer suddenly accuses his lover of not caring for his, Cohen's, music. The singer of this song is clearly unhappy with his lover—there is an antagonistic tone between them—because he feels that she doesn't appreciate his work. And Cohen identifies with "a baffled King David" who is given credit for writing the songs of praise we find in the Psalms. Remember: scripture tells us that this is a king who has a sexual relationship with a married woman, Bathsheba, and arranges to have her husband killed on the battlefield. Is David described as "baffled" because he suddenly realizes that his passionate love for Bathsheba has turned him into an adulterer and a murderer? But "baffled" could also refer to his ability to create lyrics of praise, despite heartbreak.

Yes. Alan Light in the must read The Holy or the Broken *explicates the reference to a bewildered King David this way: "It is a comment on the unknowable nature of artistic creation, or romantic love, or both."*

I would have to agree. Even from my perspective as God, neither the creation of a song nor erotic love was completely comprehensible: at the dawn of creation, I didn't know the songs that would be created or who would fall in love. Getting back to "Hallelujah," I must add (*again Shekhinah's encyclopedic knowledge surprised me*) something that Alan Light, as you know, wants to remind us to think about: namely that for all the ink devoted to the lyrics of the song, we wouldn't still be talking about "Hallelujah" if it did not have a simple yet unforgettable melody; to use Light's words, "it sways, gentle but propulsive, a barely perceptible waltz rhythm adding to a singsongy lilt." Daniel J. Levitin, professor of psychology at McGill University and the author of *The World in Six Songs: How the Musical Brain Created Human Nature*, says this about "Hallelujah": "The music is timeless and modern at the same time." "It has," he insightfully tells us, "elements of

17th-century harmony—big, classical themes—but also an almost 50s retro ballad arpeggio, combined with modern harmonic moves." I would add that the song endures because its melody strikes a deep pre-verbal chord within listeners.

Still, the lyrics are also important. We should recognize, as Light also observes, that the words of "Hallelujah" hold our attention with their sharp juxtapositions, taking, as you pointed out, the form of both celebration and lament. Cohen sings about how King David saw Bathsheba bathing on the roof, was overcome by her beauty in the moonlight, and was brought down by his sexual relationship with her. Like David, the Cohen of this song seems both pulled toward and baffled by the perplexing power of intimate love.

Cohen was, more than once, seduced both by sexual love and his lover only to have it all fall apart and bring him down. Cohen likened himself to David, a holy sinner. Cohen found the sacred in the sensual. Indeed, erotic love became for Cohen something holy. In sexual love, lovers worship each other through their bodies. "Hallelujah" for Cohen is a natural response to the ecstatic embrace of lovers, even when the relationship is, from a traditional religious point of view, broken or illicit in some way, for example, outside of marriage.

Cohen had two children but was never married. Clearly, when it came to Cohen's sexual relationships, he lived outside requirements of Jewish law. But then so did the lovers who are depicted in one of the most erotic books of the Hebrew Bible, the Song of Songs. Indeed, "Hallelujah," with its spiritualization of sexual relations, was inspired by this biblical poem. The Song of Songs makes no reference to God and its unwed young lovers describe in great detail what they find attractive in each other's bodies and the passion they feel for each other. Later, I will say more about this wonderful sacred book of erotic poetry.

In describing what Cohen is doing in "Hallelujah," Maureen Kendler of the London School of Jewish Studies puts it this way: "The carnal is seen through the spiritual." In A Broken Hallelujah: Rock and Roll, Redemption, and the Life of Leonard Cohen, *Liel Leibovitz tells us that Cohen's maternal grandfather, Rabbi Solomon Klinitsky-Klein, a Talmudic scholar, gave his grandson something that was for Cohen a far more stirring vision of Jewish life than the dispassionate Maimonidean rationalist approach of the Montreal synagogue of his youth, Congregation Shaar Hashomayim (Gate of Heaven), the place of worship the Cohen family attended, co-founded by his other grandfather, Rabbi Lyon Cohen.*

Rabbi Klinitsky-Klein's more sensual approach to Judaism was grounded not only in the Song of Songs, but also in Hebrew prophets. The prophets can be understood as passionate poets, men who understood that—to borrow

Leibovitz's words—"humankind's spiritual and sexual yearnings were inter-
twined." For instance, in the book of Isaiah Jews who stray from God are com-
pared to a woman who uncovers herself to another lover in an act of infidelity
(57:8). In the book of Hosea God even commands the prophet Hosea to take
a whore as his wife so Hosea can understand how infidelity, unfaithfulness,
feels, how God suffers in the face of "children of harlotry." Israel, according to
scripture, was often unfaithful to her Eternal Covenant Partner, worshiping
other gods (Hosea 1:2). She is often described metaphorically in the Bible as
God's unfaithful spouse.

(*What follows again surprised me, in both its insight and, from what*
I knew, its historical accuracy.) You're right. Cohen's maternal grandfather,
Rabbi Klinitsky-Klein, showed Cohen that the prophets brought the sexual
into the realm of the religious. This spoke to the adolescent Cohen who
was just discovering both yearnings—the spiritual and the erotic—within
himself. One of the most damaging things that religions such as Christianity and Buddhism, in their most anti-sexual and ascetic forms, have done
is to separate sex and holiness, creating in some cases a view that sexual
desire is dirty or impure in itself, implanting in their adherents the idea that
the highest spiritual life can only be experienced by those who remain (or
become) celibate, abstaining from entering into any sexual relationship, as
Jesus of the Gospels was his whole life and the Buddha was after enlightenment. Like the passionate verses of the Song of Songs, "Hallelujah" challenges this kind of thinking about spirituality. In one famous eye-raising
verse, Cohen reminds his lover that, before their love failed, there was a
perfect sexual moment, a moment that he frames in deeply spiritual terms,
recalling this moment of erotic pleasure as evoking from them a perfect
"Hallelujah." Cohen tells us, in effect, that each lover's breath, in the ecstasy
of coitus, is a form of divine praise, every breath a "Hallelujah," hallowing
the act of sexual intercourse.

This reminds me of words of David's original prayer, also called "Hal-
lelujah," that we chant in our religious services. Cohen in his youth must have
voiced this prayer countless times in the Montreal synagogue he attended
with his family. The prayer ends with these words: "Kol han'shamah t'haleil
Yah, hal'lu Yah!" Here is one translation, mine: "Let every breath praise God,
Hallelu-Yah."

This prayer, with words taken from Psalm 150, recounts the many ways
we can praise God, such as "with lute and harp, drum and dance." Why not—
and this, albeit within the framework of marriage, is consistent with traditional
Judaism—praise God with the passion of sexual intercourse? Although a kind
of outlaw Jew, Cohen was only doing what Jewish tradition urges—namely,
whenever possible, making holy what is usually considered profane. The song

tells us that every breath Cohen and his lover drew in their ecstatic moment of sexual pleasure was an act of praising God, and also an act of celebrating the holiness of their momentary, perfect sexual union. This is not too far off from lovers, even atheists, calling out in the midst of erotic ecstasy: "Oh God, Oh God!" Such intense sexual pleasure elicits, even from nonbelievers, spontaneous "Hallelujahs."

(Smiling) Very good, Jim! And Cohen means something even deeper. Despite ultimate disappointment in love, he can still say: "Hallelujah." Cohen can say this even to the experience of flawed, failed love. He confesses in one line of "Hallelujah" that he has been hurt in love and maybe all he has learned from love was how to hurt in return the one who hurt him first. But he ultimately transcends this petty feeling. Indeed, we are to imagine he never stopped loving this unnamed lover, despite the fact that she hurt him. In an earlier song, *Ain't No Cure for Love* (1968), Cohen tells us that love is still love even if everything goes wrong.

Let me reiterate: "Hallelujah" is a song written to praise even failed human love, even love in which you feel the beloved has betrayed you! Despite this failure, you can still see love as something to be thankful for, as something worthy of a "Hallelujah." This brings to mind Lord Tennyson's famous last line—now a cliché, but still insightful—in his poem "In Memoriam" that tells us it is better to have loved and lost than never to have loved at all. Cohen is able to sing "Hallelujah" and thus affirm life despite the collapse of a love relationship—despite, after a broken relationship, feeling cold and alone. Most people tend to idealize romantic love and think that only perfect or successful love is worthwhile or worthy of praise. Cohen possessed a deeper wisdom about intimate love: despite the fact that it failed miserably, we should appreciate what we had. Keep in mind that we are talking about not just sexual pleasure, but a loving relationship. That is something I wanted to risk when I chose to become a human being. I now want the experience of intimate love, a love that I well know can always go wrong and bring deep hurt and disappointment, indeed a feeling of brokenness.

Brokenness is, I think for Cohen, unavoidable in this life: what we offer to the God of Song in singing about love is often a gift of a flawed love, a love that may end in heartbreak. As Cohen tells us in the song "Anthem" (1992), we should give up the idea of bringing to God a perfect offering. Cohen, as a Jew and thus a God wrestler, is metaphorically challenging God's command in the Torah to ancient Israel, when the Temple existed, that it offer only perfect animals as sacrifices to God, and that the offering must be performed only by a Kohayn/Cohen—how interesting that this is the Hebrew term for priest—who himself is without any blemish. On Cohen's contrarian view, everything is broken—cracks appear everywhere—and, paradoxically, Cohen seems to believe, this is necessary in order for light to shine through. (I pulled up on my iphone an article I remembered from The Daily Beast.*) Jay Michaelson, an insightful Gay Jewish writer, says, affirming Cohen's theme, that "precisely in the broken, frail frame that is the human condition—precisely in vulnerability, failure, and loss—is where the light gets in."*

Cohen tells us it is only with the peaceful acceptance of cracks in everything—because this allows light to break through—that we can avoid irretrievable gloom. He said this once in an interview: "The light is the capacity to accept that sorrow as well as joy may be part of every day that dawns. It is this understanding that allows you to live life and embrace disasters and sorrows and joys that are our common lot."

Cohen knew the Psalms well (wrote his own version called Book of Mercy*): he knew their soaring words of ecstatic joy and also their despairing words of deep sorrow. Cohen thought that the light breaks through in every word of his song about broken love. Maybe the light shines through especially in the broken "Hallelujahs," because he believed, as we are told in Psalm 34, that "God is close to the brokenhearted." And we all know that what inevitably breaks many hearts is love gone wrong, unsuccessful love, or unrequited love. "Hallelu-Yah" in the Psalms can be both a word of praise in the midst of joy and a word of praise in the throes of despair. I think Leonard's "Hallelujah" is a twentieth-century psalm that offers a path to healing in a world that is irreparably broken, where love often fails.*

Psalm 34 is right about the nearness of God to the brokenhearted. Speaking from painful experience, I can assure you that God was always near those whose hearts were broken, as close to them as their own breathing. Indeed, that was the source of my great agony: to be so close and yet so far away.

For the author of the song "Hallelujah," we live in a world of absolutely irreconcilable conflicts and differences, even between those who supposedly love each other. For Cohen this is a world in which we can only live peacefully when we embrace its failures and conflicts and cease looking for a final resolution.

In other words, for Cohen only when we can say yes to the brokenness of life, only in that moment do we live here fully as human beings.

I agree. Yet, despite the theme of irreconcilable conflict, the song was for him an affirmation of life, an act of uttering yes to life, not only to all its joys and pleasures but also to all its losses and pain: holy or broken, we can still sing "Hallelu-Yah." Cohen once said: "There are moments when we can embrace the whole mess, and that's what I mean by Hallelujah. That regardless of the impossibility of the situation, there is a moment when you open your mouth in song and you throw open your arms and you embrace life, and just say Hallelujah." Let me repeat. Cohen's song is a way of saying yes to this life, despite all its misery and imperfection. This is music with a life-affirming, redemptive theme.

Jim, this was something that I, as God, could not do: namely say yes to all of life. I can actually come closer to life-affirmation as a human being, probably because I no longer know and immediately feel the totality of suffering in the world, and probably because I can now do something to lessen suffering, no matter how limited this may be.

And it may be, given the tentative theism in this song—in one verse Cohen expresses doubts about God's existence—the "God of Song" is only a metaphor for what inspires Cohen to write songs like "Hallelujah." To be more precise, we might conclude that, in the end, the song isn't really about God at all, Who, from the perspective of the Cohen of this song, may or may not exist, but rather is essentially about human love, both unbroken and broken. That's why the song resonates even with secular people and atheists. He once said: "I wanted to push the word 'Hallelujah' deep into the secular world, into the ordinary world. I wanted to indicate that 'Hallelujah' can come out of things that have nothing to do with religion." We might want to say, with the Right Reverend Nick Barnes, Bishop of Cryodon, speaking in a BBC documentary about the song: "He's rescued the word 'Hallelujah' from being just a religious word."

What did Cohen, at the end of his life, believe about God? Many Jews struggle with belief in God. Did Cohen accept a traditional understanding of the Creator, as all-powerful? One might even ask: Did he begin to doubt the existence of God—or, if he did believe, did he come to doubt the goodness of God? His final album is full of lyrics that seem to offer a very dark view of both God and human nature.

Toward the end of his life, Cohen seemed to believe in an all-powerful God and saw much of the darkness of the world as coming from the Creator precisely because he retained this belief. Cohen never hesitated to name what was dark in religion and the world, and he never lost the Jewish habit challenging and arguing with God.

As I said, this seems to be especially the case with the last songs he wrote.

Yes. Cohen's last album, which he composed as he was dying of cancer, *You Want It Darker*—released 2016, October 21st, nineteen days before his death at the age of eighty-two—contained one of his most religious and also, paradoxically, his most irreverent songs, the one for which the album is named. Cohen sings defiantly, in the title song, that God wants the world to be darker, which I understand to mean "more evil."

You can hear in the recording of this song, if you are listening for the sacred, the voice of Cantor Gideon Zelermyer, tenor leader of the Montreal synagogue that generations of the Cohen family attended. The song makes reference to the Kaddish, the Jewish prayer for the dead (with its words, "magnified, sanctified be thy Holy Name"). We can also hear the synagogue choir in the opening and closing of this song. Most important, at the end of the song, Cantor Zelermyer can be heard chanting the Hebrew word "*Hineni*": "Here I am." I was bothered by this because during the song—and here is another profane element—Cohen sings about God giving us permission to kill and to wound each other. Was Cohen willing to affirm—say "*Hineini*"—to a God of murder?

Maybe Cohen is thinking of all the texts in the Torah that sanction atrocities, such as Deuteronomy 20:16–17 where the Israelites are commanded, when conquering a city in the promised land, to kill everything that breathes. I could never believe in this God.

Did Cohen really believe that God gave permission for some human beings to slaughter other human beings? It saddens me to think so. Some traditional Jews and Christians see every word of scripture as God's word and every act of God described in the Bible as the literal truth—and some fanatical true believers seem ready to act out the worst in these texts. I thought Cohen was beyond this kind of literalism. Why did Cohen think that God wants it darker? I entered the world before he wrote this music. Thus, I didn't know his mind at that time he penned the words of *You Want It Darker*.

He does say in this song, in seeming explanation of his words, that this is written in the scriptures, namely that God wants it darker. Maybe he had in mind Isaiah 45 where God is quoted as saying "I form light and I create darkness, I make peace and I create evil." This of course would explain the claim that God wants it darker in the world.

On this view, not only did I allow evil: I chose it; it was my will. Despite his accusation that God wants it darker, Cohen seems ready to surrender to God when he too sings the word "*Hineini*." Suddenly we have an unexpected submissive tone at odds with the God-challenging words of much of the song. I didn't welcome this shift.

The language sounds too much like Abraham in Genesis 22 when the patriarch says "*Hineini*" to what he misperceives as a divine command to murder his own son, to make a burnt offering of Isaac. A God who would command this does indeed want it darker because He commands Abraham to do what is unquestionably evil. This is a tale of cruel temptation because this God, after mentally torturing Abraham by asking him to cut Isaac's throat, has, at the last minute, an angel tell Abraham to drop the knife. It is as if this God is saying: "Never mind: I really didn't mean it; just a test and you passed." This is religion at its most perverse. No, I didn't deliberately create darkness: I did not will evil. I did not want it darker. But it became darker and darker, to my profound disappointment and surprise. And maybe Cohen, believing in an omnipotent God, can only conclude that a world full of cruelty and murder is what God wills—or at least permits, standing idly by while blood is being spilled.

As you know, but our readers may not, a Jewish blessing we chant before reciting the central prayer of Judaism, called the Sh'ma *("Hear O Israel, the Eternal is Our God, the Eternal Alone."), edits and corrects Isaiah to say. "I make peace, and I create everything." The ancient rabbis who wrote this prayer changed the words of Isaiah because they could not bring themselves to write a blessing that says God creates evil.*

And this is closer to the truth. I did, in a sense, create everything. As I have said already, when I was an all-powerful being, I created out of nothing the infinitely dense and infinitely hot point that expanded into the cosmos humans now know, a cosmos that includes evil as well as good. I intended good but could not prevent evil. I keep saying "I" but the truth is I'm no longer God, any more than you, Jim, are still a professor. Both of us are emeriti. The readers of this will by now know that when I say "I" in referring to God, this is a reference to my past life as God.

6

Poetry, Music, and Darkness

Songs are as sad as the listener.

— Jonathan Safran Foer,
Extremely Loud and Incredibly Close

Let me return to the power of poetry. The world of poetry, like the world of music—whether mocking, skeptical, spiritual, or completely secular—provides the poet with endless opportunities for creativity and her audience with an immense variety of aesthetic pleasures. In this urgent time, however, maybe poetry needs to do more than play with words or even engage in clever God-wrestling. When the planet is in crisis, maybe we can no longer afford the luxury of poetry for its own sake. The award-winning poet Christian Wiman asks: "What is poetry's role while the world is burning?" One answer is that poetry can communicate a revolutionary message: it can be pedagogy for the oppressed. That is, poetry can be a creative tool for liberation, for introducing new ways of experiencing the world and radical ways of changing the world. It can be a medium for social transformation.

I want to revisit Audre Lorde, my inspiration. She describes herself as a Black Lesbian Feminist Mother Warrior Poet. Lorde cultivates an identity based on a relationship to many divergent perspectives and movements that at one time were perceived to be incompatible. You will find a collection of her essays and speeches in *Sister Outsider* where in the late seventies and early eighties she dared, as the young African American playwright Antoinette Nwandu states, "to critique a mostly white, academic community of second-wave feminists for overlooking blacks, gays, lesbians, the elderly, and the disabled in their theories." Nwandu, writing in 2017, recommends that we take another look at *Sister Outsider* as we reflect on White Nationalist rallies such as the one in Charlottesville, Virginia, in August of that year—as a way of learning the importance of building a justice movement across differences, creating a coalition of progressives—and I would add even libertarian social activists—in the fight against bigotry.

Lorde describes herself as "intersectional" (now a buzz word), meaning that she is a person who seeks to unite members of disparate oppressed communities while never asking individuals to give up their particular identities. Although in what I'm about to quote she is speaking to Women, Lorde could also be speaking to other oppressed groups—Black Men as well as Black Women, SGL Men as well as SGL Women. In a famous essay—published first in 1977 in *Chrysalis: A Magazine of Female Culture*—she gives an explanation of why poetry is a serious enterprise. Lorde says *(and now she begins to speak softly in a different voice and accent, presumably mimicking Lorde)*:

> For women . . . poetry is not a luxury. It is a vital necessity of our existence. It forms the quality of the light within which we predicate our hopes and dreams toward survival and change, first made into language, then into idea, then into more tangible action. Poetry is the way we help give name to the nameless so it can be thought. The farthest external horizons of our hopes and fears are cobbled in our poems, carved from the rock experiences of our daily lives. . . . It is our dreams that point the way to freedom. They are made realizable through our poems that give us strength and courage to see, to feel, to speak, and to dare.

Lorde thinks poetry has the power not only to express beautifully our otherwise hidden feelings but also to help transform an oppressive world into a free one. That at least is Lorde's dream: to wit, a world without any form of oppression, a dream I share. I now consider her my mentor, model, and the mother I never had. I will say much more about this complex and courageous woman before I'm finished.

I appreciate your admiration for Lorde—and I love poetry—but the fact is that, contrary to what Lorde wanted, poetry has become a luxury, a medium of enjoyment and enlightenment for an ever-shrinking minority, a literary elite. The percentage of individuals in this country who have read at least one poem in the past year has, according to a New York Times *article I recently read, declined to about 6% of the U.S. population. If I may, I want to briefly return to Leonard Cohen. Beginning at the age of thirty-two, he made a decision to leave his modestly successful career as a fiction writer and poet to become a song writer—or, maybe it would be more accurate to say: to give most of his attention to song.*

Inspired by Bob Dylan, Cohen decided to record himself singing his poems. He had a number of things in common with Dylan: both of their grandfathers were rabbis, both Dylan and Cohen attended Zionist summer camps, and both were taken with Jewish folk songs. Cohen saw how Dylan's song "I and I" brought together the sensual and the spiritual: it begins with Dylan singing about having a strange woman in his bed and moves to a line from Exodus (33:20) that warns us that no person can see God's face and live. Dylan exemplified for Cohen what was possible, and Cohen ran with it. The important point is that Cohen suddenly understood that for his words to have a real impact he needed the medium of music. You should know that! But of course what I'm saying is for the benefit of those who may read a transcript of this conversation.

Cohen began to imagine his poems, in retrospect, as one big diary, set to guitar music. More important, he saw music as a medium that could reach a larger audience. Also, compared to poetry only in words, he thought poetry put to music could more effectively, emotionally and spiritually, communicate what was in his heart and mind. He remembered of course how the Psalms chanted in the synagogue had moved him. More than this, he saw music as a vehicle for prophetic communication, as a herald of the future. Dylan told us through music that the times are changing. Plato in The Republic *saw the revolutionary potential of music and warned that musical innovation is a threat to the state and can even bring about fundamental changes in the law. In this country protest movements often inspired and were inspired by protest songs.*

Politically charged lyrics put to music can serve the function of warning people about what is coming if a society stays on the same path. Cohen's dark, dystopian song "The Future" is an example: he tells us bluntly that he has seen the future and it is murder. One of The Beatles suggested that the power of music rivals, indeed exceeds, the power of religion. John Lennon may have seemed arrogant when he said that The Beatles were more popular than Jesus, but he was on to something. Hearing is one of our most powerful senses, and music can reach the soul and, compared to poetry only in words, reach a significantly greater number of people not only nationally but also internationally. Cohen's unique, sometimes sensual-spiritual themed music ultimately reached a global audience. He had a talent for translating his unique vision into words and chords. If he had stuck with poetry only in the medium of words, his audience would have remained very small, minuscule compared to the enormous impact of his words put to music. So, looking back I would argue that Cohen was more insightful than Lorde.

You're probably right, as much as I don't want to admit it: Lorde's concept of the power of poetry now seems too optimistic. Indeed, I think if she were living today, she would agree with what you are saying about the power of music, especially words put to music, compared to poetry only in the form of words. I think she would still call this poetry. If you want poetry expressed in music that reaches an incredibly large audience, you might want to check out hip-hop, another largely African American invention, with West Indian and Latin influences. Originating in the mid-1970s in a place with a dizzying diversity of musical traditions—the Bronx—hip-hop brought together multiple art forms, including not only the rhymes over beats of rap but also deejaying, graffiti art, and break-dancing. It immediately appealed to those who felt disenfranchised and marginalized. Ultimately it created a revolution in music. From the Bronx it became a national and then an international phenomenon.

I know little about hip-hop. My point is that Cohen saw music as having the power to redeem human life. I appreciate—and I think you must too—what Liel Leibovitz in A Broken Hallelujah *said about Cohen's approach: namely that Cohen is telling us what worldly inclined rabbis had been, for thousands of years, telling Jews, who were waiting for a messiah, to solve their problems themselves. Cohen's message, according to Leibovitz, is this: although the world is a place of suffering, there are things here on this planet—art, love, friendship, kindness, music, sex—that have the power to redeem us. I think Cohen would have said "Hallelujah" to that as a summation of what he hoped his music conveyed, whether or not it actually did.*

But it is not just music with words that has the power to penetrate deep into our psyches, raise us up, give meaning to our lives, and bring us aesthetic pleasure. Music without words can do the same, depending on the piece of music and depending on the listener. In fact some music without words can do the same more powerfully. Consider Mahler's Sixth Symphony: I find all four movements deeply inspiring. We can rejoice in the fact God created a world in which music like this has, over time, brought joy into billions of lives, and that—and here I agree with Nietzsche—life would be profoundly impoverished without it. Indeed, despite what you say, I still believe music has redemptive power.

Classical music itself has unfortunately a rapidly shrinking audience, showing a decline comparable to interest in poetry. Mahler may inspire you, but many younger people, if they were to actually listen to his music, would be bored to tears. Although Mahler's Sixth Symphony may lift your mood, conductor Wilhelm Furtwangler calls it "the first nihilist work in the history of music," and it often carries the subtitle "Tragic." I of course know that other commentators, such as music critic Tom Service at *The Guardian*, assert that it has a cathartic and even life-affirming power. This is a lesson in the ambiguity of the meaning of great instrumental music. In any event, I'm glad music, in all its variety, with or without words, has produced joy and provided, over the centuries, meaning for countless human beings.

There are, however, two problems with your praise of music and confidence in its redemptive power. First, despite your love and knowledge of Cohen's music, you don't seem to recognize how dark much of his work is, thus reinforcing a mood of negativity. And, since you admit that you don't listen to a lot of current popular music, especially hip-hop/rap, you are not in touch with music that reaches an extraordinarily large audience because of streaming on services such as Spotify. Thus you may be unaware of how pessimistic is the message many younger people are internalizing. Popular music has become, more recently, a voice of depression and hopelessness for many.

If we consider the year 2017, we can get a clear picture of how negative music can be for millions of human beings. This is documented in an article (written at the end of 2017) by popular music critic John Pareles in your favorite newspaper, the *New York Times*. His article captures the mood of the year in its title: "Pop Music 2017: Glum and Glummer." The 2017 article begins with an excerpt from Lil Uzi Vert (the professional name for Symere Woods), then one of the top hip-hop artists; he sings about being pushed to the edge and tells us all his friends are dead, maybe from overdoses. The lyrics are from "XO Llif3" in an album happily called *Luv is Rage 1.5*. He sings about wanting to leave a bad relationship, his girlfriend's threat to commit suicide, his use of Xanax to dull the pain, only to fall into an addiction to "xanny." And that's not all of the bad news the song has to deliver.

By the time the article appeared, the song had streamed half a billion times on Spotify alone. In Pareles's words: "the tone of that song—mournful, dazed, sullen, traumatized, self-absorbed, defensive, remote, morbid—was pervasive in the pop of 2017." He states that the somber tone of rap music is not surprising given the reality young people face: increasing income inequality, social media that gives its consumer the idea that everybody else has a better life, a staggering debt burden for those who choose college with the hope of avoiding a dead-end job, the shredding of safety nets, and Trump's dismantling of environmental regulations as climate change looks unstoppable—to mention a few things that feed hopelessness. Maybe this dark turn in pop music will pass, but I wouldn't count on it anytime soon. Those who read this a decade from now will be able to judge that. The point is that music can be life-denying and soul-draining as well as life-affirming and soul-lifting. So while you may listen to inspiring music, millions upon millions, indeed billions, listen to music that reinforces a mood of depression and despair.

I don't want to say that all of rap is negative and pessimistic. There is positive and politically conscious rap music. Consider Mehak Ashraf of Kashmir, who goes by the stage name Menime, American rapper Eminem's name spelled backward. This seventeen-year-old girl is a voice against oppression in Kashmir, indeed Kashmir's first female rapper. She says rap is her way of expressing resistance—resistance against what she perceives as the occupation of her country by India. She has shown enormous courage because she could be targeted like other rappers in her country who had to go underground. The fast, indeed dizzying, tempo of her rap first drew attention from local radio producers—then from the world. She now has a global voice.

By the time this is published, she may be silenced or simply be a musical blip, but the point is that rap can also serve as a pedagogical tool for the oppressed, something Lorde wished for poetry. And, again, I contend that rap is poetry set to music. Politically conscious rap music, emphasizing a theme of liberation and hope, may be the exception right now, but it has potential to replace, or at least compete with, more self-indulgent dark rap. For more positive and/or politically conscious rap in the United States, you should check out Common, Chamillionaire (from Houston), Lupe Fiasco, Lil' Mama, Invincible, and early Queen Latifah, names that may be soon forgotten. Positive rap, oriented toward affirmation of life and themes of social liberation, has an uphill climb.

You might also want to listen to Janelle Monáe, a singer who raps but more recently has sung across musical genres. Her most recent album, *Dirty Computer*, is, as musical journalist Jenna Wortham puts it, "a celebratory ode of femininity and queer people." The singer told Wortham she wanted the album to be especially relevant to Black and Same-Gender-Loving Women. In *The Guardian*, Kitty Empire explains the title song this way: "We are the dirty computers, with our corrupted drives." Empire says that Monáe brings a liberating message on behalf of those who don't fit what Empire calls "the Trump-era matrix" they are, as she puts it, "the marginalized, the highly melanated, the non-straight, and the poor." This talented woman is not just a singer: she is also a talented actor. In the movie *Hidden Figures* she portrayed one of the Three Black Women whose mathematical genius contributed to NASA's early success, although one would not have know this from history books, not until recently.

I discovered this only when I saw the movie.

Returning to music: you need to listen to Kendrick Lamar's album *DAMN* that recently won the Pulitzer Prize for music, first time for a rap album. It's not uplifting. On the contrary, it's profoundly disturbing—politically, socially, racially, religiously, sexually, and personally. It appears to be a rebuttal to any call for radical social action. You of course should be interested in Lamar's statement: "Don't call me Black no more. I'm an Israelite." Lamar even titles one song "Yah." A theme of the album is what it means to be DAMNED, to live under a curse.

After the album won the Pulitzer, I did try to listen to it. It seems to be, in large part, very angry music, endorsing along the way a strange theology, using language that makes me personally uncomfortable: for example, references to "bitches" and "motherfuckers." It made me want to listen to Nat King Cole's song "Smile" as a way of washing myself clean of the album's lyrics. DAMN felt toxic to me. But I'm an old guy.

Yes, toxic is a good word for some of the music on *DAMN,* but not all of the pieces. There is nothing toxic about the song "Love," but then again there are those who say it's out of place on the album. Despite the album's virtuosity—and its unanimous endorsement by the Pulitzer jurors speaks to that—it clearly belongs under the heading "bleak." Here we have deeply pessimistic music that received one of the highest honors that can be bestowed on music in the United States. This is music that may influence many Black Americans who love Lamar's work. Clearly Lamar has been theologically influenced by his cousin, Carl Duckworth: indeed, "Duckworth" is the title of one song. Cousin Duckworth, who also goes by the Hebrew name Karni Ben Israel, is a member of a Black Israelite organization called Israel United in Christ.

People of Color, not Jews, were, according to Duckworth, the biblical Israelites. Christ, who is viewed as having come to fulfill the Torah, is depicted as Black. IUIC theologians interpret the Torah as explaining the troubles of Blacks in the United States and elsewhere—in effect providing a theodicy that purportedly explains all the suffering Blacks have endured in this country: slavery, Jim Crow laws, poverty, racism, violent attacks, mass imprisonment, diabetes, addiction, continuing discrimination, and all their other afflictions. The explanation: all of this is punishment for disobedience to God's laws. Lamar was especially taken with Duckworth's focus on Deuteronomy 28:68: this text describes cursed Israelites being taken back to Egypt on ships. This is imaginatively interpreted by Black Israelites as prophetic, as predicting that enslaved Blacks, because of their sins, will one day be transported from Africa on ships to various "Egypts" in the world, including the United States.

Many theologies are of course created on the basis of selective biblical quotations, ignoring the full text from which the words are taken. This is no exception. What's missing in this quotation from Deuteronomy 28 are the final words. Here is my translation: "And the Eternal One will bring you back to Egypt again. You will offer yourselves as slaves for purchase by your enemies, but they will refuse to buy you." I've puzzled over this text for years. The most plausible interpretation is that Israelites will be so accursed that no one will employ them, even as slaves: they will be shunned by everyone when they are returned to Egypt—and Egypt means Egypt. To say that they will be brought to places like the United States as slaves is not true to the text. And notice that the biblical text actually says that they will not be accepted as slaves: they will be so shunned that no one will buy them, or even take them for nothing. Thus they will not become slaves. Of course Jews themselves have, over the centuries, played fast and loose with scripture—and many liberal Jews also have been guilty of this—but we need to be especially critical of any interpretation of a biblical text that is used to morally justify slavery, to hold that it was actually God's will for some people to be enslaved. In this case, we are told that Blacks were enslaved as punishment for disobedience to God's law.

I agree and will say more about the religious justification of slavery later. The dubious theology Lamar seems to be espousing in *DAMN* tells us that the original Israelites were—to repeat the wild claim—People of Color, not Jews: on the Israel United in Christ website, it says that "Blacks and Hispanics were the original 12 tribes of the nation of Israel." As this version of the story goes, after the destruction of the Israelite Temple by the Romans in 70 CE, the Israelites were scattered into western Africa and then, after being enslaved, were scattered from there to the four corners of the earth. This peculiar theology, which has no basis in fact, understands the slavery of Blacks—and indeed every form of suffering experienced by descendants of the original Israelites—as a deserved curse for their ancestors' disobedience to God. All have been damned.

I'm not really bothered by the claim, even though it is obviously false, that Blacks and other People of Color, not Jews, are the true Israelites. Again, what I find most disturbing is the contention that enslavement of Blacks was God's will. Isn't this a form of blaming slaves for their enslavement?

Of course it is. I'm concerned that, in the age of Trump, the message of political quietism in *DAMN* may appeal to an increasing number of Black Americans, communicating to them a dangerous message: to wit, that political activism is useless and so there is no point in voting. Those on the right who have tried to suppress the Black vote will of course welcome this. We are supposedly, according to Israel United in Christ theology, living in end-times, and hardships will continue to plague People of Color until they return to their Israelite heritage—until they follow the laws of the Bible: laws, by the way, that can be interpreted as condemning Same-Gender-Loving and Trans Persons. The lyrics of *DAMN* in some of Kendrick's songs suggest that an ancient curse may be in his DNA and that, whether due to wickedness or weakness, he and people like him may be lost.

To return to my original challenge to you: Lamar's music, like much of rap, is not uplifting but, on the contrary, discouraging and depressing. It reinforces a bleak view of the world and is politically reactionary. Although I do think there is much to celebrate in the musical world, there is also reason to doubt that music can redeem the world in the way you suggest, a world that I as God feared was close to the point of being beyond redemption—thus a world I could no longer abide observing as a helpless witness. The state of popular music, so full of themes of despair and hopelessness, provides a further challenge to your confidence in the saving power of music.

The second problem with your hyper-praise of music, your exalted view of the importance of music—and I don't doubt that the kind of music you like, including the Hebrew words chanted in your synagogue, can work wonders for *your* spiritual life—is that you run the risk that Nietzsche did: of hyperbole, of misleading and dangerous exaggeration, of making music something more than it can be or should be. Even if, ignoring what I just said about the bleakness of current rap music—you still want to make a case that music can redeem life and that life would be profoundly impoverished, indeed "a mistake," without music, to use Nietzsche's words—what do you say to the deaf population? Are their lives necessarily impoverished because they cannot hear the sound of music? Are people who cannot hear beyond redemption? If Nietzsche is to be believed, their lives are a mistake! My work in the disability rights movement motivates me to warn you and others who get carried away celebrating a particular medium, or a particular ability, that you are creating a standard for meaningful life that devalues the lives of those who cannot participate in a life so described, whether it is a life of hearing, seeing, walking on two legs, or what have you.

I stand corrected. Still, I think we should give God credit for bringing forth a cosmos in which there has emerged amazing aesthetic creativity—including music and poetry, the play and the novel, painting and sculpture, photography and cinema—arts that can bring cathartic release for both creator and audience, communicate a deep emotion shared by artist and audience, create a new way of seeing the world that radically alters the perception of its audience, and even move those who experience socially conscious artistic works to transformative social action.

The problem is that I as God could not, after human life evolved, avoid knowing, once sufficient time elapsed, the often degrading suffering and pain of countless human beings who never experienced the joy of music, sculpture, painting, literature, or any art form—really anything positive in their lives for that matter. I had direct intimate knowledge, over the course of human history, of billions of lives where pain was definitive and over-whelming. I came to know a planet on which too many human beings de-rive pleasure from killing and torturing others, and a world in which too many animals survive by tearing other animals apart and also gain pleasure from doing so.

In the case of both human beings and animals, I think you err on the side of pessimism. We know, for example, that people, during and after natural disasters, surprise us in the extraordinary ways they are willing to help vic-tims. Rebecca Solnit, focusing on five major disasters—the 1906 San Francisco earthquake, the huge explosion in Halifax, Nova Scotia, the devastating 1985 Mexico City earthquake, lower Manhattan after the 9/11 terrorist attack, and the deluge of Hurricane Katrina in 2005—demonstrates this in her book Para-dise Built in Hell *by bringing our attention to the altruism, courage, and com-passionate action of people in these crisis situations. I saw this recently when great numbers from different faith communities and many secular individuals showed up to rescue Hurricane Harvey victims and to help people rebuild af-ter the disaster. And you also seem to underestimate the capacity of animals to care about other creatures. Nature red in tooth and claw is not the whole story. Your fellow Buddhist, Matthieu Ricard, as you must know, documented empathy as a widespread phenomenon among animals as well as humans in his comprehensive empirical study:* Altruism: The Power of Compassion to Change Yourself and the World. *For example, altruism—intervening to save other species, including human beings—has been documented among hump-back whales. Shouldn't this have consoled God somewhat: namely, the reality of empathic behavior throughout the animal and human world?*

Despite the existence of empathy across some species, and the al-truistic behavior of different creatures, the amount of human and animal suffering that is unrelieved is enormous. Again, I don't deny that there is much good in the world—including the creation and enjoyment of beauty, recognizing that some level of aesthetic enjoyment occurs in humans and other species in the animal world—and that many acts of compassion occur, including those acts that flow from both human and animal empathy. The problem is that as God I was aware of a greater number of creatures that never practiced or benefited from altruistic behavior.

To be aware of every sentient being that pointlessly suffers in the ani-mal and human world and not be able do anything about it is agony for a Creator who feels perfect compassion for every creature. I did not choose to give myself the capacity for such compassion. It was as much part of my divine nature as my desire for perfect justice. I could not help wanting a world in which meaningless suffering and gross injustice were absent. Some suffering may be conducive to certain kinds of growth, but much of it is useless and degrading to the sufferer. I saw this kind of suffering as pro-foundly unjust.

My unrealizable desire for perfect justice and the end to pointless suffering made my existence as God unbearable, intolerable. The mistake of many who believe in a Creator is to think that God has the power to intervene to relieve suffering and correct injustice. And of course there are those who believe that, even if injustice is now pervasive, God will bring about perfect justice at the end of time: the dangerous myth of eschatology, the idea of a divinely guaranteed good end to world history. I had no such power. Let me repeat: what motivated me to give up my life as God was my powerlessness to help those who pointlessly suffer.

7

God's Suicide

Nietzsche's Insight

Even God has a hell: it is God's love for humanity. God is dead. God died of compassion for humanity.

—FRIEDRICH NIETZSCHE, *THUS SPOKE ZARATHUSTRA*

So, you are telling me that is why you left your post as God—because you were unable to intervene to prevent suffering?

Yes: because of the breadth and depth of the suffering that occurred in the world, suffering I could do nothing about. Leaving my post may not be the best description of what I did in dissolving the fifth dimension because it suggests the possibility that I might return to my life as God. There is no post to which I can return. The truth is that I, after centuries of being a powerless witness, and after contemplating suicide, finally decided, irreversibly, to give up my life as God.

The philosopher Nietzsche wrote that God died because He could no longer endure the suffering of human beings but never meant by this that God literally died. Nietzsche, an atheist, was of course using language metaphorically when he wrote about the death of God. At a very young age he had, with good reason, reached the conclusion that God does not exist. So, for him it was the idea of God that died. Still, Nietzsche showed great insight in grasping that if there existed a Creator who truly loved human beings, the Creator would ultimately prefer death to witnessing the enormous amount of meaningless human suffering that occurs on this planet. Implicit in Nietzsche's viewpoint is the realization that if there is a loving God Who lacks the power to end human suffering, this would be hell for the Creator, thus motivating divine suicide.

Divine suicide strikes me as a contradiction in terms, a logical and metaphysical impossibility. Can an uncreated eternal Creator really cease to be?

My answer is clear: yes. I embody this truth.

I want to better understand your claim that this extraordinary suicide occurred, something that I have never considered a possible divine choice, but I first want to understand the nature of divine despair. Was your problem the amount of pointless suffering, or the fact that there was any pointless suffering at all?

In a sense, one case is too many for a God Who deeply loves every creature that suffers. Just imagine one instance of unjust human suffering: your child being raped, tortured, and murdered by a pedophile. Keep in mind that as God I knew in a personal way everything this child experienced: her horror, terror, fear, pain, desperation, and confusion were as much mine as the child's. Sadly, I was a witness to countless cruel and deadly attacks on children that I could do nothing to stop—but also could never turn away from.

Let me return to the case I just mentioned. One of the abnormalities that occurs in some human beings, an aberration of evolution, is that some individuals develop a powerful urge to act out murderous pedophilic sexual desires, a sexual lust that finds pleasure in the torture, rape, and murder of children, one after the other. An aberration I, quite frankly, never anticipated when I gave up omnipotence and let the cosmos develop on its own and life to evolve freely. Thus, we have a phenomenon no truly loving, all-knowing, and all-powerful God would allow: namely, individuals who feel a compulsion to rape and murder children. These human monsters—who did not create their own monstrous nature and in some cases hate themselves—not only cause terror and pain to the children they sexually attack, torture, and murder, but also inflict unbearable pain on the parents who suffer the loss of their child in this horrible way. The parents' grief was unbearable, and so was mine, as if these murdered children were literally my own children. Of course they were, in an ultimate sense, my children. If I had possessed the power, I would have intervened. How could a truly loving God with the power to intervene to prevent the torture and murder of children not do so?

Tragically, there have been and are too many instances in which the parents are the ones who inflict enormous suffering on their own children.

Recently there was a story in the news about a California couple who had imprisoned their thirteen children, ages two to twenty-nine, in a dirty and foul smelling home, many of the children shackled to beds and furniture with chains and padlocks. By the way, these parents won permission to homeschool their children, requiring them to memorize long sections from the Bible. These starving children were allowed only a few bites of food a day. In effect, the house became a torture chamber. This was discovered only because a seventeen-year-old daughter of the couple managed to grab a cell phone, slip out of the house, and call 911. When the police arrived they thought the caller was only ten years old because she was so thin and small. All the children were stunted in growth and skeletal in appearance.

This is not what I had in mind when I created a cosmos with the possibility of creatures like human beings falling in love and raising families. Even if only one child is tortured by her parents, that in itself is a great injustice which raises questions about the goodness of God if God is conceived as having the power to intervene. Fyodor Dostoevsky, the great Russian Orthodox Christian, a genius of fiction, well understood that the torture of even one child is a serious moral problem for traditional theism. In his brilliant novel *The Brothers Karamazov*, one of his famous characters, the atheist Ivan Karamazov, remarks that children up to the age of seven are innocent, even like a different species of human beings. The chapter where Ivan says this and brilliantly lays out the problem of the suffering of children is aptly titled "Rebellion" because it makes a case for rebelling against God. Ivan tells Alyosha, his deeply religious brother, the story (based on an actual case Dostoyevsky saw in a Russian newspaper) of a five-year-old girl who was treated hatefully by her parents. They kicked and beat her until she was bruised all over. One evening, in an act of great cruelty, they locked her in a freezing outhouse; before doing this, the mother smeared her face and filled her mouth with excrement. The frightened, shivering child screamed in horror through the night, to no avail.

According to Ivan, this young girl, imprisoned in this frigid and dark privy, breathing in and tasting shit, cried out and beat her tiny chest, weeping and pleading for "dear kind God" to protect her. Ivan asks his pious brother: "Why is such infamy permitted by God?" Speaking to his brother, this is Ivan's complaint, one that I really could not argue with: Don't tell me, Alyosha, that this evil—a child's pain and degradation—is justified by the great good of human free choice, a freedom to choose between good and evil that necessarily brings with it the power to choose cruelty as well as kindness. Ivan is in effect asking his deeply religious brother this question: Why should human beings be free to choose between good and evil when the costs are so high? Ivan concludes that the whole world of moral choice does not justify the pointless and cruel suffering of even one child. Even if, contrary to the facts, only one child on earth suffered, the good of human freedom would not, according to Ivan, be worth the pain of this child.

Let me press you on this, perhaps playing the devil's advocate. What if, contrary to the facts and consistent with Ivan's thought experiment, there had been only one instance of an innocent human being, a child, suffering in this universe? Would that have been enough to drive God to self-destruction? Would that really be an unjust universe? Couldn't an otherwise good world compensate for the unjust suffering of a single child?

Probably not, but hypotheticals like Ivan's are really beside the point when the earth itself, over time, became a place occupied by billions of creatures who suffer for no good reason. The truth is that countless human beings have suffered unjustly and will continue to do so. And, again, remember this: It was not just human suffering that disturbed me; it was the suffering of all sentient beings. An animal—for example, a fox—caught in a steel-jaw trap is an instance of unjust suffering. Your readers can find graphic descriptions, like the one I'm about to give you, of the cruelty of these traps, in PETA literature. (*A reference to People for the Ethical Treatment of Animals.*)

When a fox steps on a steel-jaw trap, the trap's jaws slam shut, clamping down on the animal's leg or paw. As the fox struggles in excruciating pain to get free, the steel vise cuts more deeply into the flesh—often down to the bone—mutilating the leg or paw. Some foxes, especially mothers desperate to return to their young, will attempt to chew or twist off their trapped limb. Foxes caught in a trap often struggle for hours, sometimes days, before they finally die from exhaustion, exposure, frostbite, or shock. I suffered with all the animals caught in such a trap—felt their desperation, their terror, their agony—every moment of terror, from the time the jaw of the trap was triggered until they finally died or chewed off the trapped leg.

The suffering of animals on this planet has been and is enormous. In some cases, the causes of animal pain are natural: attacks by predators, drought, floods, and fires started by lightning can all cause painful animal deaths. Imagine the horror and pain a deer experiences burning to death in a forest fire caused by a lightning strike. In other cases, animal suffering is caused by human beings, as in the case of the steel-jaw trap. Factory farming, a very profitable human enterprise, has, since its inception, caused extreme suffering to livestock, including chickens, cows, and pigs. Many veal calves and gestating sows are so tightly confined—by "producers" who want to make them a more tasty product—as to suffer painful joint and bone problems. Chickens on many factory farms—some farms now allow chickens to roam freely part of the day—are locked up twenty-four hours a day in cages in which it is impossible to turn around. Faulty or improperly used stun guns have caused and continue to cause the painful death of thousands of cows and pigs each year. Billions of animals, each with complex sensations and emotions, die on production lines all over the world. It is not clear that one form of animal suffering and death is better than the other. Is it better to be devoured by a lion than caught in a trap set by a human being? With respect to a painful death, are crocodile teeth preferable to steel blades?

The suffering that producers inflict on farm animals is not only physical: it's also emotional. Yes, animals have emotions. Have you ever heard milk cows when their calves are taken away? There is very loud moaning day and night. Those who don't believe the sounds the cows are making are cries of sorrow, the act grieving the loss of their newborns, lack empathy and emotional intelligence. It was once argued by White slave owners that slave parents do not emotionally suffer when their children are sold off because Blacks are nothing more than "beasts." Yet even "beasts," non-human animals, experience grief. The cows are as distressed as human mothers would be if their newborns were suddenly ripped away from them. For milking cows, the whole process will be repeated over and over until the cows' bodies are spent. And what about the calves taken away from their mothers? Does anyone really believe they lack a capacity for grief, for feeling the loss of their mothers, and how much suffering this causes them?

Of course many who read this will say we are anthropomorphizing when we say animals grieve, that we are projecting our own emotional life onto them without scientific justification.

Don't take my word for it. This is another area where Darwin was ahead of his time. In his study *The Expression of Emotions in Man and Animals* (1872), Darwin states that many animals, like human beings, feel not only pleasure and pain, but also joy and sorrow. He observed that the grief of female adult monkeys for the loss of their young can be so intense as to cause their death. As with Darwin's views on the place of beauty in evolution—how, for example, the female bird's sense of beauty can shape the evolution of the male's appearance and the sounds it makes (what he called sexual selection)—so most of his contemporaries also dismissed his attribution of emotions to animals.

Of course some scientists, dismissing Darwin, still accept Descartes's view that animals are robotic beings without feelings. In the late twentieth century and into this century, however, many biologists have changed their views, based on careful observations of animal behavior. Consider the reported behavior of orca mothers: orcas are large-toothed whales with distinctive black and white markings and a prominent dorsal fin. Recently, for example, a twenty-year-old female orca, given the name Tahlequah (a

Cherokee word meaning "just two"), also known as J35—a southern resident of the the critically endangered population based near Puget Sound—on July twenty-fourth of this year gave birth to a female calf who lived just thirty minutes. The calf, emaciated and lacking enough blubber to stay afloat, was kept afloat for two weeks by Tahlequah, who balanced the dead baby on her head—on what some orca researchers called a "tour of grief." Other orcas have exhibited similar behaviors after their calves died.

For those who doubt the orca mother was grieving, keep in mind that the orca brain, bigger than the human brain, has a paralimbic lobe that is highly developed, and, like the human brain, contains von Economo neurons: rare, specialized cells that relate to empathy, communication, intuition, and social intelligence. Researchers have in fact reported grieving behavior in a variety of cetaceans (whales, dolphins, and porpoises). Italian biologist Melissa Reggente documented fourteen such observations involving seven species of marine animals in a 2016 article in the *Journal of Mammalogy*. I observed such grief behavior—and literally felt the grief—in animals with much less developed brains than those mentioned.

So, a growing number of scientists are challenging the claim—which seems to contradict the continuity of evolution—that humans have a monopoly on grief. Mourning-like and depression-like behaviors have been observed not just in cetaceans but also in dogs, elephants, giraffes, chimpanzees, gorillas, and birds. For example, chimps and gorillas are known to carry their dead offspring for days or even months, and female elephants stand vigil over their dead offspring. What has been observed in many cases are mothers who stop eating for days after the death of a newborn, or the death of a young animal to which they have given birth. Recognizing the fact that *our* emotions are largely driven by hormones, and that hormones are likely to have evolved similarly in other animals, why should it be a surprise that non-human animals experience similar emotions, including grief and depression? I could say that I know this to be true from divine memory, but I will let the reader investigate the growing scientific literature that supports my claim.

Notice what this means. Not only do animals experience physical pain: they also suffer emotionally. The amount of emotional suffering in the animal world has been and remains enormous. Most philosophers and theologians who struggle to reconcile belief in God's omnipotence and goodness with pointless human suffering have ignored the suffering of animals. Would a truly loving God be concerned with human suffering alone and be indifferent to the pain of animals? Wouldn't a truly compassionate Creator have compassion for all sentient creatures?

One of the Jewish prayers—P'sukei D'zimra (Verses of Praise)—that I say daily states precisely this: "Blessed is the One Who is compassionate toward all creatures."

Human suffering by itself is great beyond measure. Add animal suffering to this and you have a planet on which the level of misery is beyond the comprehension of human beings. Imagine affectively knowing and sympathetically feeling, which I did as God, the suffering—physical and emotional—of all humans and animals on earth from the beginning of complex sentient life, and never being able to act to relieve any of it. That was my life as God, my existence as a perfectly loving and perfectly just Creator.

What is the value of the divine attributes of love and justice if they cannot be actualized in the world? I was like a painter who has in mind the most beautiful painting imaginable but has no hands or even feet to paint with, and not even a mouth to hold the paint brush, indeed no way to ever realize her artistic vision. This was my life as God: a perfectly loving and perfectly just Creator who could not actually practice love and justice by intervening in the world to show love or bring about justice. And, despite the widespread belief that God can do these things, there is no compelling evidence for this: quite the contrary. Those who believe in an intervening God need to ask themselves: Where is the evidence that divine love and justice are at work in the human and animal world? There is no such evidence.

8

A Tragic Divine Choice

Creation of an Independent World

Freedom contains the mystery of the world. God wanted freedom, and from this came the tragedy of the world.

—NICHOLAS BERDYAEV

How do you answer a predictable question, and of course you knew this question was coming: Couldn't you have created a universe that did not contain pointless suffering? After all, you were once omniscient and omnipotent. You told me a few minutes ago that you created the cosmos out of nothing. It would appear, as you yourself suggested, that a Creator with such power and knowledge would be able to create a better world or arrange to intervene in the world to prevent terrible things from happening to innocent creatures.

When I created the initial conditions for the universe to develop on its own, to evolve into a cosmos, I irreversibly divested myself of absolute power. It was my free decision to create a world that would be independent of my control. I gave up the option of intervention the moment I created a world that was genuinely other than me. Using my infinite power, I created a singularity of infinite density—the infinite point out of which the cosmos evolved, out of which mass and space-time emerged. Once I allowed it to become a free universe, a universe free to develop in its own way, governed only by the fundamental physical constants necessary for the emergence of life, including life capable of awareness and free choice (thus made in my image), it was out of my hands. I could not intervene. I did fine-tune the world for intelligent life, but I also gave it autonomy. Without the fine-tuning, there would have been no intelligent life. If I had retained omnipotence and omniscience, there would have been no genuine freedom and chance.

The fundamental constants I established include of course the well-known four physical forces: electromagnetic, strong and weak nuclear forces, and gravity. Consider the attractive force—really the force field—we call gravity. If this force—using this word metaphorically since matter really moves in certain ways in response to the curvature of space-time—that holds people on planets and holds planets, stars, and galaxies together had been even slightly weaker, then stars and planets could not have formed and the matter needed to form them would have been dispersed. If gravity had been slightly stronger, then stars would have burned up too quickly to make the components necessary for life: for example, the sun would have burned faster and exhausted its energy before even the first steps in organic evolution could begin. Even a slight difference in strength would have made it impossible for life to develop.

Or consider the strong force that binds together the fundamental particles of matter to form larger particles. It acts between subatomic particles of matter, binding quarks together to form more familiar subatomic particles such as protons and neutrons. It also binds together the atomic nucleus and underlies interactions between all particles containing quarks. If this strong force were slightly stronger or weaker (by just 1 percent in either direction) there would be no carbon or any heavier elements anywhere in the universe, and thus no carbon-based life forms like human beings to ask why things are just so.

Even scientists who are atheists admit the universe looks fine-tuned for life. The now deceased atheist and mathematical genius Stephen Hawking said this: "The remarkable fact is that the values of these numbers [the constants of physics] seem to have been finely adjusted to make possible the development of life." But Hawking concludes in his book *The Grand Design* that the universe created itself, out of nothing! Christian columnist Tim Morris well states our choice between divine creation and Hawking's view: "One sees God creating everything. The other sees a self-creating universe. Which is harder to believe?"

Another brilliant atheistic scientist, the cosmologist Martin Rees, acknowledges that if these numbers (the physical constants) had been even slightly different, life, including life conscious of itself, would never have emerged. Rees recognizes the improbability of life and acknowledges the universe looks designed for life. His explanation: we got lucky because we are in one of the few universes containing intelligent life. Rees hypothesizes a Multiverse: countless universes. This looks like an ad hoc explanation of why this universe appears designed for the existence of intelligent beings. Christian philosopher Richard Swinburne sums up the problem with the Multiverse hypothesis when compared to the God hypothesis: "To postulate a trillion trillion other universes, rather than one God in order to explain life in our universe, seems the height of irrationality."

Some Christian thinkers make the fine-tuning argument part of Christian apologetics, as evidence for the truth of Christianity. A number of Christian philosophers of religion, such as William Lane Craig, have er-roneously concluded that this is evidence for the existence of the personal God of traditional Christianity, a Creator who remains, after the creation of the world, all-powerful and therefore able to intervene in evolution and human history, purposefully directing things while also allowing human freedom. Not so. Even if one accepts the fine-tuning argument as providing good grounds for believing there is a Designer, it does not follow that this Creator is the God of any of the Abrahamic faiths.

The acceptance of the idea that the universe was fine-tuned for the emergence of intelligent life does not establish the existence of the God of traditional theism in general or the God of any particular Abrahamic reli-gion. The emergence of life conscious of itself—for example, human life—required of course a complex set of conditions that appear to be the result of divine fine-tuning, but this doesn't require one to conclude that the cosmos was created by a providential God Who oversees and purposely directs the whole process, from the beginning to the end.

What traditional Christian theists can never show empirically, even if we grant that the appearance of fine-tuning is prima facie evidence that there is a cosmic Designer, is that the Designer is the Christian God, or that this Designer is perfectly good, all-powerful, and omniscient. A successful design argument based on the appearance of fine-tuning clearly is not the same as a successful argument for the God of Christian theism or any other Abrahamic faith: for example, Judaism, Islam, or the Baha'i Faith. As I've already said, there is no compelling evidence that this world is *overseen* by a Creator who loves all creatures and justly orders the world. Therefore, there is no good empirical reason to conclude that, even if you grant that there is a transcendent Designer, this is an omniscient, omnipotent, just, and loving God Who reveals in scripture a divine plan for the world, intervenes from time to time, and directs human history toward a good end.

If there were an all-powerful and all-knowing God who retained abso-lute control over the evolution of the cosmos each step of the way, with the primary aim of bringing forth human beings, creatures made in the divine image who are commanded to love, obey, and worship "Him," why did it take billions of years to bring us into existence? This extraordinarily long process suggests either a limitation of power and knowledge or that the Creator allowed the cosmos to develop on its own. For an all-powerful and all-knowing God, who remains always in control of the process of cosmic evolution, this is an astoundingly long time to achieve the goal of creating intelligent life: billions of years with no life at all, not to mention human life. Why would an omnipotent and omniscient God of love who seeks, above all, a reciprocal loving relationship with human beings—a God Who always has mastery over how things proceed—need such a cumbersome and protracted process?

If the Creator's ultimate aim was the creation of human beings with whom He could have a loving relationship, why did God need to start the process fourteen billion years ago? And why would an omnipotent and omniscient Creator allow a long, messy evolutionary process during which many species emerge and then become extinct? To be more precise, based on the fossil record, paleontologists tell us there were five periods of mass extinction during which most of the species existing in each extinction period disappeared. I can assure you that there were in fact many more extinction events, as a result of which 90 percent of all organisms that have ever lived on earth became extinct. Does this look like the work of a perfectly intelligent Designer, a Creator Who is in control of evolution? Was this process of hit and miss evolution, including the loss of so many species, really necessary to produce human beings who the New Testament says were crowned with glory and created a little lower than the angels (Hebrews 2:7)?

The young-earth creationists—who claim the earth is six thousand years old—have a point: an all-knowing and all-powerful Creator who remained omniscient and omnipotent could achieve His aims more directly in much less time, with no "mistakes" along the way. The problem is that young-earth creationists—biblical fundamentalists—need to deny what science tells us in order to make their case. So, if we accept the age of the universe and the time period for evolution science gives us, the question remains: if God wanted to bring human life into existence in order to have a being with whom God could have a reciprocal relationship, a being who could freely obey divine commandments, why do this through such an inefficient, long drawn-out process? If, as Genesis says, God speaks the world into existence, then God must be a very sluggish talker. Maybe, like Moses, this God was slow of speech, since it took God billions of years to speak human life into existence. Instead of this lengthy process, wouldn't we expect that as soon as an omnipotent Being spoke the words "let it be," the *it* would immediately materialize?

Jonathan Sacks—the great British Orthodox rabbi and philosopher— recognizes this. He claims that when it comes to God, there is no gap between intention and execution. God spoke and the world came into being, according to Rabbi Sacks. But the rabbi is an old earth creationist who accepts the claim that the formation process took billions of years. So, he needs to explain the huge temporal gap between intention and execution.

Wouldn't we expect the time period to be no more than the six days described in Genesis where each day God speaks new creatures into existence? Or did God lack the power and the know-how to create human life within that short, biblical time period, or, more to the point, instantaneously?

Despite this, many Christian philosophers who are old-earth creationists—Big Bangers—have tried to use the fine-tuning argument to serve their cause. Let me repeat my point and make it more specific: one cannot logically move from acceptance of the fine-tuning argument for a Creator to the conclusion that this Creator is the perfect Triune God of Christianity, the second person of which, the Son, born of a virgin two thousand years ago, incarnated as a Jew, preached the gospel, was crucified, and then raised from the dead on the third day. None of the components of Christian doctrine follow from acceptance of a fine-tuning case for a cosmic Designer. The truth is that the fine-tuning argument for a Designer is, given what we know about the evolution of life on earth, more consistent with an indifferent, uncaring, and/or imperfect Designer.

What should we conclude from looking at what is supposed to be the creature God made a little lower than angels? Just consider the design flaws in the human being: the blind spot in the eye, resulting in less than optimal sight; the shared passage for breathing and swallowing that allows food to sometimes fall into and block the windpipe, creating a threat of choking to death (thus the need for the Heimlich maneuver); in women the narrowness of the birth canal in relationship to the large-headed human fetus, thus causing labor pains; the useless organ called the appendix that is vulnerable to infection (appendicitis); a brain whose chemistry can seriously malfunction, resulting in mental illnesses such as schizophrenia and clinical depression, contributing to suicidal impulses—to name a few problems in the design of a creature who is supposedly the crown of God's creation. And there are human beings who are born with what they experience as the wrong gender, others with sexual desires oriented toward the same sex (leading to sexual behavior that many religiously conservative defenders of intelligent design condemn), still others with painful disorders that raise questions about either the intelligence or the justice of the Designer. The idea that the Designer is the God of traditional theism—conceived as an omnipotent, omniscient, perfectly loving, and absolutely just Creator who oversees the world each moment—requires a very large leap, having nothing to do with what science tells us.

Although I'm claiming that I as God did possess the attributes of perfect love and perfect justice—because they, unlike omnipotence and omniscience, were the essence of God's holiness—I don't see how anyone who is aware of all the terrible things that happen on this planet could reasonably conclude that the Designer has these moral attributes. On the contrary, let me repeat: from all appearances, this is a world untouched by divine love or divine justice, a planet where there are countless cases of bad things happening to innocent creatures and where, if things keep moving in their present tragic direction, human beings may bring about not only the continued destruction of other species and the earth but also their own demise. I did of course know, in the words of another great Russian Orthodox Christian thinker, Nicholas Berdyaev, that if I wanted freedom, "from this would come the tragedy of the world." I allowed for tragedy, but I didn't anticipate its breadth and depth.

Here is my message to the world, a divine revelation if you will: if human beings want to survive, they must take matters into their own hands, change their ways, and abandon the idea that an omnipotent God will deliver them.

As you know, I agree. We need to give up belief in an omnipotent God. If one is going to believe in a God worthy of reverence, some adjustments must be made. Rabbi Harold Kushner in his best-selling When Bad Things Happen to Good People *was one of the first popular religious writers to defend the idea of a God limited in power. Alfred North Whitehead and Charles Hartshorne of course had made the case for such a God decades earlier for a philosophical audience.*

Rabbi Kushner's motivation for writing this book was a theological crisis, his personal encounter with inexplicable evil. His son was diagnosed with progeria, the rapid aging disease, and died from it at a young age. Victims of progeria tend to die as teenagers of ailments that usually strike only the very old. His son's hair began thinning at twelve months; he never grew taller than an average three-year-old. By the time he was ten he was physiologically in his sixties. Near the end his bodily systems were so weakened that in order to breathe he had to stand leaning against the wall all night. When he died in his mother's arms two days after his fourteenth birthday, he weighed twenty-five pounds. This was for Kushner truly heartbreaking and faith-shattering.

With this, Rabbi Kushner's belief in a God who was both omnipotent and perfectly good could not be sustained. To continue to believe in the goodness of God he would have to cease believing in God's omnipotence. Kushner con-cluded that God does not have the power to intervene to save people from disease, natural disasters, or human atrocities. He stated once in an interview: "I would rather believe in a God of limited power and unlimited love and justice rather than the other way around."

To hold on to the goodness of the Designer, I am convinced—unless one wishes to make God's failure to intervene to correct unjust suffering a great mystery beyond human understanding—one needs to give up belief in God's omnipotence. I spent many years arguing this in papers I published, talks at philosophy conferences, and guest lectures at seminaries, synagogues, and churches. By now the case against omnipotence has been repeated ad nauseam in the literature of philosophy and theology: it is the argument that thought-ful theists must choose between goodness and omnipotence; they cannot have both. Although many attempts have been made by clever philosophers of religion and theologians to reconcile goodness and omnipotence, I remain unconvinced. As you know, I personally concluded long ago that belief in the goodness of God requires positing a God limited in power. So, we are on the same page, theologically speaking.

Not necessarily. I am adding a dimension to this that neither you nor any other apologist for a limited God ever considered: divine suicide. It was Nietzsche, as I have repeatedly said, who clearly saw why the life of such a Creator would be an unendurable hell. Let me return again to my account of why I, when I was God, wanted to die, something you and others have invariably missed in proposing the possibility of a God limited in power, namely how unsatisfactory the existence of such a Creator would be. Some who propose the idea of a limited God conceive of God as inherently lim-ited; others understand God as a self-limiting being. I am telling you that the truth is the latter. I chose irrevocably to relinquish omnipotence, to give up power over creation, once and for all time. Wish that I had not, but I did.

After irreversibly giving up control of the cosmos, I eventually found myself impotent in the face of horrible human behavior, some of it commit-ted in God's name. Let me reiterate what the fictional character Ivan Karam-azov so forcefully and eloquently asserts: even the suffering of one child tortured by her parents is too high a price to pay for the good that freedom brings. Did Dostoyevsky, the Christian creator of this fictional character, really think otherwise?

Of course that is one explanation that theologians and philosophers still give to explain evil: namely that we cannot have freedom without unjust suf-fering. This is the so-called free will theodicy we have been discussing. You, obviously, don't find this theodicy convincing. I want to revisit this question: is human freedom really not worth its costs? No defender of the free will theodicy

denies that freedom has brought with it great tragedy. Yet freedom is an ex-
traordinary good: maybe it is worth the costs. Freedom necessarily brings the
suffering of the innocent. And you have confessed that you knew this when you
created a world within which free beings would emerge.

Obviously, when I created the conditions necessary for the evolution
of intelligent self-determining beings, I did think the good of freedom
would be worth the costs. That was my wager and my hope. Because I gave
up omniscience, I could not know how things would turn out. Although I
originally thought the good of freedom would be worth the risks, over time
the immense suffering of innocent creatures caused by the misuse of freedom led me ultimately to doubt whether freedom was worth all the misery
it brings. But even if I could have been persuaded that a positive moral cal-
culation can be successfully made—to wit, that the good of human freedom
outweighs the suffering it causes—a free will account of evil does nothing
to explain or justify all the suffering caused by natural phenomena: earthquakes, tsunamis, hurricanes, tornadoes, and disease. A free will theodicy
doesn't solve what philosophers call the problem of natural evil. Natural
events alone have brought, since the emergence of sentient life, destruction
and misery to billions of human beings and animals. Obviously, the terrible
suffering caused by natural processes cannot be explained by human misuse
of free will.

The suffering caused by natural events alone is massive in and of itself.
This is not something human beings can prevent. Nature is not self-destruc-
tive, but nature, even independent of humanly produced changes within it,
can cause widespread suffering and tragic loss. One should not romanticize
nature—as some pantheists do—even as one sees nature's preservation and
protection from destructive human behavior as a sacred duty. I was always
bothered by the dishonesty of hymns that praised God for the beauty of
nature, hymns that ignored its ugliness: its potential to bring catastrophic
death, destruction, and emotional pain.

Think about the enormous misery a single tsunami can cause. On
December 26, 2004, a tsunami—with its epicenter off the west coast of
Sumatra, Indonesia—killed close to 300,000 human beings (the official
count of 228,00 was incorrect). Think of the panic, terror, and loss of life
by drowning—and, on top of that, all the suffering felt by the survivors who
in most cases never found the bodies of their loved ones. I could add to
this the terror, death, and suffering earthquakes, hurricanes, and tornadoes
have inflicted on their victims in the history of the earth. In Houston the
memory of Hurricane Harvey should bring home to its residents the terrible, indiscriminate destruction that even one natural disaster can cause.
And of course human beings are not entirely innocent when it comes to the

destructives forces of nature, with humanly caused climate change making storms more frequent and more severe. But, again, even apart from problems caused by humans, nature, on her own, can be a terrifying source of profound physical and emotional pain.

The enormous suffering of both humans and animals, whether caused by human agency or natural forces—suffering that I could do nothing about—was so disturbing to me that my continued impotent existence as God became unacceptable, and so I decided to give up my eternal existence. One false assumption of all forms of theism, including limited theism, well articulated by the eleventh-century theologian-philosopher St. Anselm, is that God's mode of being, unlike that of creatures, is *necessary*. Anselm distinguishes God's necessary existence from the contingent existence of all created beings. Contingent beings come to be and pass away; a necessary being's nonexistence is impossible. On this view, God must exist: God's nonexistence is thought to be as inconceivable as a square circle.

Yes. Agreeing with Anselm, Charles Hartshorne maintains that the idea of a God Who could cease to exist is a contradiction in terms. For Hartshorne, as for Anselm, God necessarily exists. For Anselm and Hartshorne, it is impossible for there not to be a God. The implication is that God does not have the power to destroy God: to commit suicide.

Couldn't this assumption be mistaken? Isn't it possible that philosophers who assert the necessity of God's existence and the necessary eternality of it, are in error? Are you absolutely certain, Jim, that the Creator cannot commit suicide? To reframe the question more philosophically: Do you really know with certainty that God cannot exist? Do you rule out divine suicide a priori? Do you really know that the death of God is impossible?

I will be calling you a liar if I say yes, but the truth is I have ruled out divine suicide, maybe dogmatically. And I know you know that I don't believe your story. Still, I will admit that it is a reasonable philosophical question, one, I agree, that has not been sufficiently explored by traditional theists or even unorthodox theists like James Friedman. I have to confess that I never considered this a real possibility and don't know any philosophical theists who have. An important function of philosophy is, I also have to acknowledge, to challenge what is taken for granted, what is thought to go without saying, what is considered self-evident or necessarily true. Of course meeting you personalizes the philosophical question of whether God can cease to be, of whether God can commit suicide—even if I don't believe the story you are telling me.

You might want to ask yourself, Jim, whether eternal existence is as much a fixed attribute of God as compassion and justice. You have often argued that a God lacking omnipotence is conceivable and no less worthy of reverence if that God is understood to be perfectly loving and just. What about eternality? Could that be like omnipotence? If God can give up omnipotence, maybe God can also give up eternality.

Although I once believed that God gave up omnipotence, I no longer believe God was ever all-powerful. So, that's where we also differ. But let's keep the focus on God conceived as an eternal being. There is a strange asymmetry in the concept of a God Who has always existed but can one day cease to exist. Do you agree that God has no beginning, was uncaused, without an origin?

Yes.

My question remains: If God has no beginning, how can God have an end?

Strangely enough, the answer is this: only by incarnating, and thus becoming a finite being in the fullest sense. This is my autobiography I first moved from being Infinite in power before Creation, to, after Creation, becoming a God Who was finite and powerless—while retaining the moral attributes of perfect compassion and justice. And then a few years ago, I made the decision to become completely finite: mortal. This is my first—and last—incarnation. Heaven is forever empty: no angels or souls reside there. Indeed, there is no longer a transcendent, spiritual world. This world is now all there is.

God in fact was the only spiritual reality, the only transcendent being. I was the All-in-All. Before I created the cosmos, I was alone and self-sufficient, the fullness of being. When I started to create the physical cosmos I was the Absolute, the Infinite One. There was no court of angels in my midst to advise me, with some arguing against creating human beings because they knew they would be liars and never cease quarrelling, as one Jewish midrash asserts. God alone existed. The Infinite was everything: that's what the word means. When I was omniscient, I didn't need angels to advise me about anything.

And if I had remained omnipotent, angels would have been superfluous. I wouldn't have needed them to do my bidding. So I never, contrary to what some religions mistakenly assert, assigned guardian angels to protect favored persons. An all-powerful being does not require special agents. But once I decided to let the world go its own way, to give up omnipotence, I was unable to create angels or any other special spiritual beings—or even create new physical beings for that matter. Indeed, as I have so often said, I could not, after I created the seeds of what would become this cosmos, intervene in the created world.

Alone and self-sufficient, why then did you suddenly decide to create? Why did you decide to create after being by yourself for eons? If I may be so bold, what were you doing all that time before Creation?

You probably know what St. Augustine jokingly tells us is God's response to this question, namely, "I was preparing a place in hell for those who ask this question." This is Augustine's idea of theological humor. This of course was not his actual answer. Unlike Augustine's God, I created neither heaven nor hell. I intended for intelligent, free beings to live moral lives without these external incentives. As John Lennon tells us in his surprisingly popular song "Imagine," there is neither heaven nor hell, just this world.

Lennon is telling us, quite correctly, that there is no place—neither heaven nor hell—that immortal souls go to after death because there are no immortal souls. If, contrary to fact, there had been a hell for the unsaved to descend and a heaven for saved souls to ascend, heaven would not have been a place of peace and perfect happiness. How could any compassionate inhabitant of heaven really be happy and peaceful knowing that others, including even some of their loved ones, are writhing in pain forever? Even apart from hell, the knowledge of pervasive suffering on earth would make perfect happiness in heaven impossible for its occupants if they were truly caring. Or do those who believe that the saved are perfectly happy in heaven imagine that the residents of paradise are ignorant of what happens on earth or in hell? If so, then it would be a false, deceptive, blinkered, dishonest, and amoral happiness. Despite this, I know that there are many Jews, Christians, and Muslims who hold out the hope of finding peace in the next life.

An ancient Jewish prayer already mentioned, the Jewish prayer for the dead, the Kaddish, in its final line, makes this request: "May the One who creates harmony in heaven bring peace to us below."

Did I really create harmony in heaven? Was I even at peace with myself? The answer should by now be clear. I have explained why, if heaven existed, its inhabitants would not be perfectly happy, but let me strengthen the argument by addressing those who also believe in the story of fallen angels: for example, many traditional Christians. They have to concede, on the basis of their own worldview, that, after God created the world, a rebellious angel, Satan, and his followers, a third of all angels on one count, disrupted the peace of heaven. Supposedly, these rebellious angels had everything that those who believe in heaven hope for—and yet they were not satisfied.

When Christians who believe that angels once rebelled in heaven say the Lord's Prayer they utter the words "Thy will be done on earth as it is in heaven." They cannot mean "as Thy will was always done in heaven"—and cannot know that, should they go to heaven, there will never be another angelic rebellion. The story of the revolt of angels is a story of a disruption of the peace of heaven by Satan and company who refused to obey the will of God. Why did they rebel? On one account, Satan and other disobedient angels were full of false pride and wanted to take God's place. As the story goes, God threw them out of paradise to maintain the peace. How can those who believe this tale be certain that there will not be another revolt, maybe after they've arrived in heaven? Based on their own understanding of the history of heaven, these believers must admit that for all they know, if past is prologue, conflict may break out once more in paradise. Indeed, they cannot be certain that the peace of heaven will not be shattered again and again.

Isn't it possible that angels who have hitherto remained passive and submissive while God failed to intervene to correct injustice on earth—failing, for example, to intervene to prevent genocide, slavery, abuse of children, etc.—may one day conclude that God has not done a good job of overseeing the world? Indeed, if God really could have intervened to prevent massive injustice but chose not to, it could be argued that angels would be justified in challenging God's rule.

There is a Jewish midrash, Lamentations Rabbah, in which angels do precisely this. As the story goes, after the destruction of the Temple, lamenting this tragedy, angels, arranging themselves in rows, like mourners, speak to God, accusing the Creator of breaking the covenant. We must remember that a covenant is a two-way agreement: there are expectations of God as well as human beings. The charge here is that God did not keep the divine end of the agreement, failing to prevent the destruction of the holiest place in the world. So, although very different from Christian accounts, Judaism also has literature about the rebellion of angels.

The point, let me reiterate, is that those who believe that angels rebelled in the past cannot rule out another revolt in the future. The eternal peacefulness of heaven cannot be a sure thing if you believe stories of angels revolting against God. The truth is, however, that heaven, hell, angels, and souls don't exist—and never existed. I understand why heaven and hell were invented. Belief in a future world where the good are rewarded and the evil punished enables many believers to accept injustice on earth and to have faith that one day all human beings will get what they deserve. But how, I must ask again—forgetting for the moment the possibility of a recurrence of rebellious angels—how can there ever be joy in heaven while there is still unjust suffering on earth and, for those who believe in it, eternal suffering (of unsaved people) in hell? And I must also repeat this: belief in hell, eternal torture, pain without end, is incompatible with belief in a perfectly loving and just Creator.

The rabbis of the Talmud, for the most part, never affirmed an eternal hell. A year at most, according to some sages in the Oral Torah, the Talmud! Probably most Jews don't believe in hell at all, and many don't believe in heaven.

As imagined by traditional Christians and Muslims, hell will be popu-lated by those who fail to profess the true faith—and of course Christianity and Islam make conflicting claims about what constitutes correct belief. On either view, ethical individuals who strive to do good on earth and try to make amends when they do harm will also suffer forever if they die as un-believers. And of course many people cannot honestly believe in the truth of either Christianity or Islam. Will disbelievers be punished eternally because they cannot truthfully believe what a particular religious worldview asserts? Is that justice? I was troubled by this kind of religiosity, one that increases suffering on earth through its intolerance of people who are, in all honesty, skeptics, atheists, or agnostics—and in its attempt to terrorize people into believing what they may find incredible.

(Suddenly a well-dressed man, maybe in his forties, was standing over us. He seemed very angry and agitated.)

Young woman, I have listened long enough to you trash Christianity and make the outrageous claim that you were God all the while denying that Jesus is God. You're a willing instrument of the Devil. Whether you believe it or not, the truth is that your perverted lies will send you straight to hell. You show no respect for Jesus, our Lord. I cannot believe you are quoting the hippie John Lennon as if he was an authority on heaven and hell. You know what happened to him on earth. He paid the price with his life. After his death you can be sure he paid even a higher price for his atheist views.

(To me, with his voice getting louder and many customers staring):

Old man, why are you listening to this theological garbage? I figure you're a left-wing professor. I can spot you professor types a mile away. If you had any decency, you would've walked away long ago. You are as guilty as she is. Your own views will also send you to hell. I should pray for your students.

(His voice was becoming even louder. Even more customers were star-ing.) You should both fall on your knees and ask Jesus for forgiveness. Not that God needs me to defend Him, but I would dishonor Jesus Christ, the Father, and the Holy Spirit if I said nothing. You both need to profess your sins and accept Jesus Christ as your Lord and Savior. Jesus rules. Yes, God's all-powerful, has been, and always will be, as you both will one day find out. And let me tell you another thing . . .

(A young male barista came over, interrupting the sermon of the angry man.) Sir, you need to leave these customers alone. They're not bothering you. I'm going to have to ask you to either sit down or leave.

Don't worry, I'm leaving! *(He walked over to his table, very close to ours, grabbed what appeared to be a well-worn Bible and walked out quickly.)*

(Not wanting to provoke the irate customer, we had quietly signaled to each other not to respond. We did, however, give him our full attention as he spoke. As if nothing had happened, after the irate man left, Shekhinah continued talking. Her focus was not broken by the rude interruption. The other customers at least pretended to get back to their own conversations or their smart phones or iPads. No doubt some of them were whispering to each other about what they had just witnessed and perhaps feeling even more curiosity about the Young Black Woman.)

9

Why God Created the World

From the creation . . . God's self-humiliation and self-emptying deepen and unfold. Why? Because the creation proceeds from God's love, and this love respects the particular existence of all things, and the freedom of human beings who have been created.

—Jurgen Moltmann, "God's Kenosis in the Creation and Consummation of the World"

Let me return to my question about the moment of creation, about what God was doing before Creation.

St. Augustine's serious response to this question is that God created time: that is, time did not exist before God created the cosmos. This response is correct. Time becomes a reality only with the Big Bang. It emerged with the expansion of the primeval point into the massive temporal universe we now observe. So, the words "before creation" really have no meaning because *before* is a temporal term. I, when I was the Infinite One, dwelled outside of time: thus there really was no *moment* of creation. Since human beings necessarily think in temporal terms, what I am saying will probably be unintelligible to most of those who read this.

Enough said about that. Although you may have hinted at an answer earlier, the question I really want you to answer is this: Why did God create the cosmos?

Why did God create at all? The simple answer: out of loving generosity. The greatest gift God could give, an act of infinite generosity, was independent existence: the creation of beings that were truly other than the divine Self. The decision to create the world, to make real something other than God with an existence of its own, independent of divine will, was a profoundly risky act. It was, to use a spatial metaphor, the act of shrinking the divine Self, a transcendent act not only of infinite generosity but also of infinite humility. It was, to borrow Christian language, creation as kenosis. This refers to God's act of emptying divine reality of some of its attributes—attributes that, as I have said more than once, traditional theism mistakenly assumed to be fixed and unalterable, such as omnipotence and omniscience. God gave up Fullness of Being—the state of being the Only Reality—in order to make room for genuine otherness. It was, as it turns out, God's first move toward finitude, the beginning of the end of God as the Absolute One: the Infinite.

Your description of creation as the act of shrinking the divine Self, of God giving up Her existence as the Only Reality, the Absolute, is very similar to the view of Jewish mystics who describe the creation of the world as an act of tzimtzum, *a Hebrew word that means "contraction." It refers to the contraction of the Infinite to allow "breathing" space for another reality: namely a cosmos with a capacity to develop on its own and give rise to free individuals: self-determining beings capable of moral agency.*

Yes. When God gave up omnipotence, omniscience, and Her existence as the Absolute—the Only Reality—She radically diminished Herself. That is what makes the creation of the world an act of divine humility, generosity, and love. The loss of absolute power occurred about 14 (to be exact, 13.8) billion years ago when God created the infinitely dense, ultra-hot point that contained the seeds of the large-scale structure of the cosmos, including the potential mass and space-time that constitute the universe as humans know it. What came to be called the Big Bang was first discovered by Georges Lamaitre—a Belgian Catholic priest, astronomer, and physicist—who in 1927 discovered that all the galaxies we observe in the universe are speeding away from us. He then reasoned backwards to a beginning, postulating what he called the "Primeval Atom Hypothesis" which stated that the universe expanded from a single point. Our galaxy is not the home of that single point, but rather only another galaxy moving away from it like the others. This Catholic priest was the first theist to recognize God as the initiator of what was later derisively named the Big Bang. It was Lamaitre who first discovered the cosmos was expanding from a primeval point—and not, as often claimed, Edwin Hubble, who of course had a telescope named after him.

The Big Bang was not, as it is sometimes described, an explosion in space—space did not yet exist—but rather an expansion from an infinitely dense point out of which the fabric of space-time emerged. The truth is that space, like time, never existed independent of the universe; the cosmos didn't expand in space but rather space itself, a product of the Big Bang, has been stretching and carrying matter with it. When the cosmos was a fraction of a second old—more precisely, a hundredth of a billionth of a trillionth of a trillionth of a second in age—there was a burst of expansion known as inflation in which space itself expanded faster than the speed of light. After inflation, the universe continued to expand but at a slower rate. About ten billion years after the Big Bang, the universe began gradually to expand more quickly and is still doing so today. At the outset, as space continued to expand, the universe cooled enough to allow the formation of matter: first subatomic particles, and, after that, simple atoms. Huge clouds of these primordial elements later coalesced through gravity, eventually forming the stars, planets, and galaxies.

I have to warn you that here is where you may trip yourself up, namely by adopting the cosmological theory that is now dominant but is subject to revision and even challenge: I have in mind of course Big Bang cosmology. As you must know, there are competing theories on the rise that, if research comes to support one of them, will be enough to refute your story of creation. It is risky to make your story of creation dependent on the currently dominant cosmological theory, because scientific knowledge, being empirical, open, and subject to change, may one day become your enemy. We should not forget the misplaced confidence of the defenders of the once reigning Steady State theory of the universe.

The name "Big Bang" was coined as a term of derision by Fred Hoyle, a proponent of the once dominant view that the universe has always been as we now observe it: this was the Steady State theory. For those who follow research in cosmology, much in the news lately has been the Big Bounce theory. In some versions of this, the cosmos is said to expand and contract eternally, having no absolute beginning. Unlike defenders of the Steady State theory, defenders of this cosmology grant that the current iteration of the cosmos did begin about fourteen billion years ago and that expansion has been going on since then—but they argue that this universe will eventually collapse on itself, only to expand again in an endless cycle of expansion and contraction. On this view, there was no absolute beginning of the universe because there has always been a cyclical cosmos. In other words, there has always been a universe of some kind, and the current universe did not just pop into existence fourteen billion years ago, nor was it created by God from nothing. From this perspective, it could even be argued that the universe needs no Creator.

So, the Big Bounce hypothesis gives us a cyclical model, with a new universe created after an old one collapses, each, according to some advocates of this view, having different physical laws. Given infinite successive universes, we thus get by chance a universe that looks like it was fine-tuned for life, but that is really an illusion. There is of course also the Multiverse proposal that some cosmologists, such as Martin Rees—someone you mentioned earlier—propose that holds that there are different, maybe an infinite number of, universes that coexist with each other like bubbles lying side by side, each independent of the other, each with different physical laws, and maybe only a few, as chance would have it, governed by what you call the fundamental constants necessary for life. You have dismissed this idea, but be careful what you dismiss: remember the Big Bang theory itself was once ridiculed.

In your tale of creation you assert an absolute beginning to the cosmos, an act of creation from nothing. My view, consistent with that of Charles Hartshorne's, is that God is always related to some coexisting material, even if it is only primordial chaos. The idea of a cyclical cosmos with no beginning is a view that those of us who affirm a process concept of God can live with. Indeed, it is a better fit than creation from nothing: the idea that the universe had an absolute beginning, with nothing before that. Actually, I welcome both ideas: Big Bounce and the Multiverse. Growing evidence for one of them may be the undoing of your tale of how the world began, not to mention your story of God's death. Even a different version of Big Bang cosmology, one that does not fit your description, would undercut your story of creation. Because you are making empirical claims—to wit, one version of Big Bang cosmology—your creation story may one day be refuted. And I think your account of Big Bang cosmology may contain errors. But I have to admit that your claim that the Big Bang was a result of divine humility and generous love has a certain appeal to me. Whatever the truth, you spin a very strange tale, by anyone's measure.

Yes, a queer tale by a Queer storyteller. I could respond that since my human memory of my life as God is less than perfect, I may be misremembering. It is, after all, human memory of divine memory and therefore fallible. In fact, I'm not worried about the Big Bounce or Multiverse hypotheses. You're correct: it will depend, over time, on what the empirical evidence shows—or on which of the theories best fits observations of the known universe and yields confirmable predictions. In this respect, the Big Bang theory has done well: many predictions of those who first proposed it early in the twentieth century have been confirmed. For me this will be a test to determine whether my memory of Creation is accurate, and maybe whether my memory of being God is correct.

I have admitted my own uncertainty, but I have also been telling you what I seem to remember and what I believe about the formation of the cosmos. If you have not already done so, you might want to look at the letter the late Stephen Hawking and thirty-two of his fellow scientists sent to *Scientific American,* a magazine that featured a version of the Big Bounce theory in an August 2016 article. They angrily expressed their "categorical disagreement" with the Big Bounce proposal and strongly asserted that traditional Big Bang cosmology, including its claims about singularity and inflation, remains the most defensible account of the origin of the universe.

You raise questions about empirical support for an alternative view of the universe. Let's not forget that when Einstein proposed views that challenged Newtonian physics, there was no empirical evidence for what he claimed. That came later—so may evidence for the Big Bounce or Multiverse proposals.

If I may return to my account of why God created the world, I want to make clear to you—and your readers—what God intended, as I now remember it, when God created an independently evolving cosmos. Above all, God wanted to create a world that was truly other—a universe that would be independent of divine will, a cosmos with its own mode of being. This, as I have said repeatedly, meant generously and lovingly giving up absolute power and absolute knowledge: the absolute power to control all creatures, or even to intervene from time to time, while also giving up perfect knowledge of the future of the cosmos. God could have created a cosmos completely under divine control whose future She could perfectly know—but God, out of infinite generosity and infinite humility, chose otherwise. Creation was a self-emptying act of love, a divine love that—to borrow Christian theologian Jurgen Moltmann's language—"respects the particular existence of all things and the real freedom of human beings."

To have complete control over everything and perfect knowledge of all future events in the cosmos would have meant creating a universe that lacked genuine independence. I would have been like a playwright who creates characters whose every word and action are only those the writer has consciously plotted out in advance, instead of a playwright who creates characters that suddenly take on a life of their own, even surprising the author in what they say and do. The latter is closer to what God did. God created a lawful universe, but one still containing significant randomness, freedom, and unpredictability. From God's perspective, this meant the possibility of surprise, for good or ill. Again, sadly, I mistakenly thought the good would substantially outweigh any evil.

What were there the good things that you hoped would emerge in the universe over cosmic time?

Creativity, beauty, diversity of life forms, and ultimately creatures with moral agency and a passion for knowledge. I envisioned a self-organizing and self-evolving universe that would give rise to multiple forms of life, including forms of life capable of creating and experiencing varieties of beauty, always beauty perceived from a subjective point of view. The evolution of beauty in the animal world was, as already mentioned (I refer you and your readers to *The Evolution of Beauty* by Richard O. Prum, Professor of Ornithology at Yale University who expands Darwin's view), often shaped by the eyes of the female of a particular species.

Think of the eyes of a female peacock focused on and attracted to the tail of male peacocks, a female who will sexually select only the male she perceives as having the most beautiful tail. Or consider the ears of the female wood thrush as she selects as her sexual partner a male wood thrush whose songs are more beautiful and pleasing to her than those of his competitors. As it turned out, what members of one species find beautiful may also strike members of other species as beautiful. For example, human beings also tend to perceive the male peacock's tail as beautiful (its image was used by NBC in 1956 to announce its color programs), and the male wood thrush's songs are perceived by many human beings as among the most beautiful bird songs they have ever heard. This appreciation of beauty across species is something I anticipated. And for me what happened over billions of years of cosmic evolution, even before life emerged, was itself a beautiful thing to behold: a great cosmic fireworks display in an ever-expanding universe, with new stars, planets, and galaxies forming all the time.

I made possible and anticipated, by the initial conditions I established and the precise values I gave physical constants, the emergence of highly intelligent beings capable of self-consciousness—beings that I anticipated would one day be capable of forethought, scientific investigation, moral agency, endless forms of play, expansive imagination, and aesthetic creativity. It came to be. Think of how extraordinary human beings are: despite the general continuity of evolution, they constitute a break, a radically new mode of being through which the universe becomes conscious of itself and knows its own evolution and laws.

Moral agency, an amazing offshoot of human evolution, requires conscious choice and unpredictability: self-determining beings who can go their own way, possessing what philosopher Daniel C. Dennett calls "elbow room." Creating a world in which free moral agents can emerge means taking a great risk. As I have said, God could have exercised absolute power over creation and could have known all future events in the cosmos, with every creature conforming to the divine will. God could have created a world in which all sentient beings would be perfectly happy and, in the case of human beings, perfectly good. God could have chosen to create a world in which nothing could go wrong and everything would go right: a utopia, heaven on earth. That was a possibility, and maybe, foolishly, I, or rather God, rejected it. Yes, I am thinking this was foolish.

God valued freely given love and so, out of love and respect for freedom, God created a world in which beings capable of loving behavior could freely choose to live in a loving way, or not. God recognized this meant that such beings would also be free to choose a life of indifference or even hatred. Again, God could have created a world where human beings automatically relate to each other in a loving way, a world that would have only positive human relations built into it, with no possibility of hate or war. Maybe that would have been the wiser course, but it was not God's choice. As I said before, God deliberately chose a riskier course, one that would allow the evolving cosmos room for freedom, chance, and novelty—a universe that could genuinely surprise God. That surprise would include the behavior of the most intelligent beings, beings whose acts would be under their conscious control: again, for good or ill.

This reminds me of a statement made by Karl Popper, one of the twentieth century's greatest philosophers of science. Popper takes issue with Einstein's famous theological claim—namely, "God does not play dice with the universe"—and affirms an opposing viewpoint. I have memorized these wonderful lines:

> *If God had wanted to put everything into the world from the beginning, God would have created a universe without change, without organisms and evolution, and without human beings and the human experience of change. But God seems to have thought that a live universe with events unexpected even by God, would have been more interesting than a dead one.*

Well-said by Popper. I cannot repeat this often enough: allowing conscious beings the choice to behave compassionately or not was profoundly risky. Why did God create? Not out of need or necessity, but, as I have insisted, out of a free, generous love, with humility and respect for the freedom of creatures like us. The love God felt for human beings did not carry with it an expectation of a return. Let me make this clear: God never commanded human beings to love God. The idea of a God who commands or demands love from those whom God loves is incompatible with the notion that divine love is unconditionally generous and unselfish. Indeed, because God let the world go its own way, independent of God, the Creator had no way of communicating divine love and/or the divine will.

Although I, when I was God, loved all the creatures that emerged in evolution, I had a special fondness for human beings, maybe because they were most like me, evolving in my image, to use traditional theological language. Deeply concerned with the well-being of human beings while also respecting their freedom, I did not seek to control them but did want the best for them. Allowing freedom meant living with uncertainty. To use Popper's language, I welcomed a "live universe with events unexpected even by God," a world that could surprise me. This meant, however, not only that I couldn't know the future but also that I had no control over what happened in the present. A lack of control also brings a sense of helplessness in the face of those who unjustly suffer and die.

So, you gave up sovereignty over the cosmos, surrendering something traditional Jews, Christians, and Muslims believe makes God God. Many Jewish blessings begin with these words: "Praised are You, the Eternal our God, Sovereign of the universe. . . ." For those who doubt God's omnipotence—the view that God is Sovereign—Jewish mysticism offers an alternative by telling us that the Hebrew word translated as "universe"—olam—can also mean "hiddenness." So we could translate the beginning of a blessing this way: "Praised are You, Sovereign of Hiddenness." A recurring theme of Jewish scripture is anxiety about a God who hides or is absent (hester panim). In the Psalms, we often see the complaint: "God, why do you hide Yourself?" On your view, if I understand it, in line with the Jewish mystical idea of tzimtzum, God chose to withdraw—disappear, hide God's existence—at the moment of creation, in an act of supreme self-renunciation, love, and generosity. Is that correct?

Yes. You could say that God became the Master of Concealment. The existence of God was hidden at the foundation of the world. This necessarily follows from God's choice not to exercise power over Creation. And not just power. Let me repeat: God also gave up omniscience—understanding that to include foreknowledge—allowing for God to be disappointed and disturbed by the way things turned out. If I as God had retained the capacity to know the future, that would have meant that no creatures could act in a manner other than I knew they would. Omniscience brings with it determinism. Omniscience would have been the death of freedom. That is why God gave up foreknowledge.

My act of bringing into existence an unpredictable world, a world containing events that could surprise me, made foreknowledge impossible: it meant that I could not have precise knowledge of how things would go. More specifically, it meant I could not know fourteen billion years ago the decisions human beings would make over the course of human history. If the intelligent creatures I brought into existence were to be truly free and independent individuals, truly other than God, and not puppets, I had to give up both absolute power and perfect knowledge of the future.

I wagered that if a creature with self-consciousness, a capacity to reason, and a potential to care about others emerged out of a long evolutionary process—having both a head and a heart (to use two more metaphors)—this creature would, more often than not, see the advantage of love over hate, empathy over antipathy, compassion over cruelty, justice over injustice. I was surprised by how often human beings chose hateful acts, even on a mass scale. Human history may not end well.

Eschatology, as I have already said, is a fiction in a world where individuals are free to go their own way. No good end can be ordained for the history of humankind or individual human lives. As a result, in a free universe where both human actions and natural events are unpredictable, there is no way to guarantee that every human life will be meaningful and worth living. Despite this, there are religious individuals who say God is good and make the sweeping claim, against all evidence to the contrary, that life is unequivocally good. Is life really good? Whose lives are they talking about? Certainly not the countless lives where tragedy is definitive. Does tragedy strike every life? No. It is, however, an overwhelming reality in too many lives, lives in which there is relentless pain or lives that end much too early.

Of course there are individual human beings—and animals—whose lives, after they have ended, could be described as on balance more enjoyable than miserable. But there have been and are billions of lives where pain is debilitating and crushing. There have been and are whole societies where the misery is so profound, where starvation, murder, and cruelty are so widespread, that pockets of happiness never compensate for overall pain and loss. Some individuals may feel content and even joyous in their protective palace (to borrow a Buddhist metaphor), and foolishly conclude, in the spirit of Voltaire's character Candide, that life as such is good and that this is the best of all possible worlds. When individuals declare that life is good, they are usually generalizing from a moment in their own lives. And there may well come a time when those who make such a naïve, egoistic declaration, in the ecstasy of the moment, say the opposite: like Job, who went from a state of blessedness to a time when he cursed the day he was born.

Individuals who declare the goodness of life (again really their lives at a particular time) never actually see, as I did when I was God, the totality of suffering on the planet, including the long history of human and animal pain and misery. So a person who says cheerfully that life is good is, to repeat an important point, really telling us only that *his* life is good at the time he is speaking. Is life as a whole really good? Sadly I did not see it as such, and, remember, I saw everything. Again, I am not denying that some human lives are indisputably good: morally good, characterized by thoughtful acts of caring behavior; aesthetically good, marked by a rich enjoyment of artistic creativity; relationally good, wealthy in love and friendship; and vocationally good, defined by meaningful and fulfilling work. Do you know how rare this has been on earth?

What deeply disturbed me, during my life as God, was how much unhappiness on earth is humanly caused. Human beings, to my great amazement, were extraordinarily creative in their infliction of death and suffering on fellow human beings, often in the name of a religion or a political ideology. And I could not stop this. The *Shoah* is an especially disturbing example. One insightful thinker, Hans Jonas, who reflected deeply on the nature of God and Creation in light of the Holocaust and other evils—not surprisingly a Jew—constructed a vision of God's intentions that is close to the story of Creation I've been telling you. This brilliant twentieth-century, German-born American philosopher, calling his account a myth, puts it eloquently. Jonas says:

> In the beginning the Divine chose to give itself over to chance and risk and endless variety of becoming. And wholly so: entering the adventure of space and time, the deity held back nothing of itself; no uncommitted or unimpaired part remained to direct, correct, and ultimately guarantee the devious working out of its destiny in creation. . . . In order that the world might be, and be for itself, God renounced his being, divesting himself of his deity—to receive it back from the Odyssey of time weighted with the chance harvest of unforeseeable temporal experience: transfigured or even disfigured by it. In such a self-forfeiture of divine integrity for the sake of unprejudiced becoming, no other foreknowledge can be admitted than that of possibilities which cosmic being offers in its own terms: to these, God committed his cause in effacing himself for the world.

I know Jonas's work. I often assigned the essay from which you are quoting, "The Idea of God after Auschwitz," when I taught my course on the Holocaust. (Did Shekhinah do research on my classes?)

What Jonas's myth of creation—the story of a God divesting Godself of power over creation and control of events, allowing for the uncertainty freedom brings, including an unknowable and uncontrollable future—means is that God is, in the face of evil and loss, powerless: unable to intervene in the world to stop awful things from happening, including genocide. For Jonas, when God allowed the cosmos to develop uncontrolled and undirected by the divine will, God ceased to be God. I of course take issue with that, but I understand why Jonas reached this conclusion. Clearly, Jonas's Creator after creation does not fit the traditional view of God, but that does not mean this Creator Who divested the divine Self of power ceased to be God: rather this Creator became a different God. My point is this: what Jonas calls his creation myth is very close to reality. What is missing in his myth is that the creation of the world was an act of generous humility and selfless love, showing absolute respect for an independently evolving cosmos and human freedom. My choice to be powerless was intended as a loving gift to the world: the gift of liberty. So, God's creation of the world began with good intentions, but, clearly, good intentions are not enough.

In the face of Nazi genocide, there was at least one Christian thinker who shared Jonas's viewpoint: Dietrich Bonhoeffer, whom I quoted earlier. A great Lutheran theologian, Bonhoeffer describes a similar idea of God as he awaits execution in a Nazi prison for his involvement in Operation 7, a scheme to help Jewish men and women escape Germany, but also for his involvement in the resistance.

This, you need to realize, is the same Bonhoeffer who said to a colleague that Jews were cursed to a long history of suffering because they, in his words, "nailed the Redeemer of the world to the cross."

Even if he did say this, as a Jew, more important to me than Bonhoeffer's theological beliefs are his self-sacrificing actions. He risked his life to save Jews: he dared to resist a murderous Nazi regime. Most important, Bonhoeffer came to realize that we live in a world where we cannot rule out the possibility of victory by ruthless leaders like Hitler. As he began to rethink his theology in prison, he must have asked himself: Where is God? He, like Jonas, ultimately concluded that the Creator had divested Himself of power. As Bonhoeffer moved toward this new radical theological conclusion—which can be found in his Letters and Papers from Prison—*he did not understand God's powerlessness as a bad thing. It was something he came to see as necessary for human autonomy, and, indeed, something that you have been saying: as God's loving gift. Bonhoeffer of course interprets divine powerlessness in Christian terms: indeed, as the central message of the crucifixion of Jesus. (I googled and brought up on my phone a text to read: an excerpt from* Letters *and* Papers from Prison.)

Bonhoeffer tells us, referring to the Gospel of Mark, that "the same God who is with us forsakes us" (a reference to Mark 15:34); And I quote again: "The same God who makes us live in the world without the working hypothesis of God is the God before whom we stand continually. Before God, and with God, we live without God. God consents to being pushed out of the world and onto the cross; God is weak and powerless in the world. . . . The Bible directs people toward this powerless and suffering God. Only the suffering of God can help."

So says Bonhoeffer. Long before Bonhoeffer and Jonas, some ancient rabbis reached a similar conclusion about God. You must know that, after the destruction of the Temple in Jerusalem, there were midrashim, such as Lamentations Rabbah, where Jewish sages concluded (and this was and is shocking to other Jews) that God was helpless to prevent the destruction of the Temple and that God, conceived as Shekhinah—understood as God's presence in the world—went into exile with the Jews. Thus, from the point of view of these

ancient rabbis, God was banished to wander with the Jews and appears to be
as powerless as the Jews themselves

Yes, Shekhinah now dwells in the world with Jews and all human beings, but I'm no longer powerless. The paradoxical message Bonhoeffer was
trying to teach fellow Christians—and all theists—shortly before he was
executed, was that we must learn to live in a godless world—that humans
must learn to make it on their own, without divine intervention, and that
this was as God intended. He is right about this.

*Yes. He tells us that we are entering a period he describes as "a coming
of age." By this he means an age of human adulthood, one beyond dependence
on God. His message is that human beings must learn to live without a God of
intervention, the deus ex machina, the God who solves all human problems.
We have to learn to live in the world etsi deus non daretur ("as if there were
no God"). God, he says, "helps us, not by his omnipotence, but by virtue of his
weakness and suffering."*

But how does Bonhoeffer's powerless, suffering God actually help
those human beings who suffer atrocities, human beings who, in the words
of great twentieth-century Jewish philosopher Emmanuel Levinas, "experience pain in its undiluted malignity, suffering for nothing"? Levinas was
thinking of Nazi death camps.

*Maybe human beings must help God in God's suffering. I am reminded
of the words of Etty Hillesum, the Dutch Jew who died in Auschwitz in 1943 at
the age of twenty-nine. (I searched the Kindle on my phone to find An Interrupted Life.) In her diary she writes something I find surprising: "And if God
does not help me to go on, then I shall have to help God." She also writes: "I
shall merely try to help God as best I can, and if I succeed in doing that, then I
shall be of use to others as well." She actually tries to reassure God—Who she
recognizes does not have the power to help her—with these words addressed to
the Creator that amazed me: "Believe me," she says, "I shall always labor for
You and remain faithful to You, and I shall never drive You from my presence."
The idea of consoling God in God's grief is remarkable.*

Hillesum and others like her did somewhat console me when I was
God, with their extraordinary spirit, demonstrating transcendent concern
for others who suffer, including God, while remaining celebrants of life in
the midst of death. I have to admit that there is something ethically impressive about those who, like Hillesum, accept divine powerlessness and actually show compassion for, and seek to comfort, the Creator. Compassion
for a suffering God is something I found generous and loving in a way that
deeply moved me.

*As you know, there is a prayer for the dead, already mentioned, that
Jews say at the graveside following burial and in the synagogue to remember*

the dead: the Mourner's Kaddish. The twentieth-century Hebrew writer S. Y. Agnon speculates that this prayer, in its extraordinary praise of God—"may God's great name be magnified, sanctified, blessed, acclaimed, glorified, revered, raised, beautified, honored, and praised"—was first recited to comfort God Who was said to grieve over the death of every human being.

I did appreciate those Jewish mourners who said this prayer to comfort God: it shows real insight into the plight of God. For God, the death of any human being was a permanent loss to the universe because she or he is gone forever. Human lives are unique and unrepeatable. Remember, I deny that anyone has an immortal soul, or that in the future the dead will be resurrected. I know that belief in an afterlife can be comforting to mourners—but the fact is that death is annihilation, pure and simple. Human beings, like other animals, are mortal and perish forever when they die.

Contrary to Agnon's view, the Mourner's Kaddish was in fact originally recited to prompt mourners to praise God when in reality they felt anger at God, or felt disappointment in God—especially if the death was premature, for example, a child. Again, the traditional Jewish view—which, as you know, became part of Jewish High Holy Days liturgy—is that God decides who will live and who will die—meaning that God determines when an individual's life will end.

I have never believed this. On my theology, this is out of God's hands.

Every time the Kaddish was said I had a difficult time abiding this prayer's unjustifiable profuse praise of God. I appreciated those who said the Kaddish to comfort me, but I completely understood those who reluctantly repeated words of praise when they were furious at me. I preferred honest curses to dishonest praise.

Why praise God when what we are looking for is within ourselves? Isn't that your message? I want to return to Dietrich Bonhoeffer for a minute. For the imprisoned and doomed Bonhoeffer, the heart of Christianity was not belief in a God who intervenes to save us from agents of evil, such as the Nazis, or a God Who offers us heaven as compensation for suffering on earth. Rather his mature Christianity calls us, above all, to lead a Christlike life. This is a life in imitation of Jesus, the person Bonhoeffer aptly describes as "the man for others." If, however, I understand you correctly, human beings do not need Christ or any religious exemplar to show them how they should live. And human beings do not need the Torah, New Testament, or Quran to provide them with ethical direction; human beings do not need any scripture to provide them with moral guidance. According to my take on what you have said, human beings do not need any religious exemplar or divine revelation in order to discover how they should live because they can find this by examining their own hearts and minds, by exercising their inborn rational and empathic capacities. Is that correct?

Yes. And the Bonhoeffer awaiting execution would, by his own logic, have to agree. Although he lauds Jesus as a man who demonstrates what it means to live for others, Bonhoeffer, at the end of his life, seems to be moving toward the view that ethics can be found within, if we make use of our full powers of sympathy and our inborn sense of justice. The affirmation of human moral autonomy in a world come of age is what he embraced as he sat in prison with only a short time to live. It follows from this that human beings no longer need to look to God for moral guidance. Remember Bonhoeffer tells us that we must live—to recall your quotation from him—as if God does not exist. Bonhoeffer's conviction, a religiously shocking one, is that God wants us to edge God out of the world. If that is the case, then humans don't need an image of Jesus to know how they should live. If we take seriously Bonhoeffer's idea of a world come of age, one that accepts human autonomy, self-determination, then we can come to recognize that human beings, without God, are able to discover on their own what is right and wrong. This doesn't mean that for Bonhoeffer there is no place for revering and praising God—for example, for God's willingness to grant us autonomy, but Christian liturgy should no longer include words affirming an intervening God.

My hope, once human beings emerged in the evolutionary process, was that most would aspire to a morally good life, something they can discover through self-reflection. The values of such a life include compassion, generosity, kindness, justice, and peace; embodying these values is what it means to live a truly holy life. This is precisely where the divine can be found, namely in acts of goodness. Bonhoeffer was trying to tell us that one way to experience God in this world is to live for others. Bonhoeffer's language in the prison letters implies that human beings do not need the life of Jesus to know what a good life looks like. This is because human beings have an inborn sense of what is good that enables them to recognize the goodness Jesus exemplified, namely a life in service to others. Indeed, we could never recognize that Jesus' loving behavior is a paradigm of goodness if we did not already know that loving others as yourself is good.

Without any scripture to guide them, almost all human beings have the capacity put themselves in the place of others and ask themselves how they would want to be treated if places were reversed. In God's mind, holiness and ethical goodness were always intertwined. For God, holiness was never about private piety, faith despite doubt, fear of God, submission to divine commands, or hyperbolic praise of God. It was and is about treating others in the same loving way you want to be treated. Even without God,

God knows, human beings can discover what is good and be good. Knowledge of the good doesn't depend on divine revelation. Indeed, God can be judged truly good only if God instantiates goodness. In truth, when I was God I could not actualize goodness because I had no power to act.

Ethical thinking, at its best, is progressive and increasingly inclusive. The scope of ethical concern has in fact widened since Jesus' time as human beings made progress in expanding the domain of their ethical responsibility. Jesus' ethical worldview, though insightful in many ways, was anthropocentric. Ethically progressive individuals have come to see that a truly ethical life involves not only compassion for human beings, but also compassion for nonhuman sentient life. We have seen that animals also suffer—physically and emotionally—and so we must enlarge our ethical universe to include them. This concern is missing in the teachings of Jesus.

And plants should never be ignored as we think about what is ethically required of us. The plant world is a diverse kingdom with its own way of being, its own kind of intelligence and way of communicating that humans are only beginning to understand as we, at the same time, annihilate more and more plant species. Some Native American practices are attuned to this world. There are of course hundreds of Native worldviews, with significantly different spiritual practices, but if we inform ourselves about some Native teachings that are truly wise about nature, including plant life, we can learn from them. I urge your readers to read *Braiding Sweetgrass: Indigenous Wisdom, Scientific Knowledge and the Teaching of Plants* by Robin Wall Kimmerer, Professor of Environmental and Forest Biology—and also a member of the Potawatomi Nation.

Just as it took a long time to come to see the need to value every human life, so we have come very late, maybe too late, to the understanding that it is an ethical imperative to show respect for nonhuman sentient life, for the earth itself, and the ecosystems we depend on for our very existence. My hope is that more human beings will come to share this larger vision of what deserves ethical consideration. Unfortunately too many politically powerful people in this, the most advanced society on the face of the planet, remain married to a reactionary ideology that denies humanly caused climate collapse, embracing a short-sighted ideology that focuses exclusively on profit-making at the expense of a healthy planet. My hope is that more individuals and more societies will eventually wake up to the need to, in addition to treating all human beings with dignity, honor non-human life and the earth.

The imperative to show reverence for the earth cannot be ignored much longer. Surprisingly earth is the only planet on which complex life has emerged so far in this vast universe. Human beings need to "care for their common home," as Pope Francis so eloquently puts it in his 2015 encyclical on climate change. As the pope clearly recognizes, care for the earth and care for the poor are intimately related. He argues that we need to recognize our social debt to the poor and the need for global ecological conversion. In *Laudato si'* ("Praise be to You"), Pope Frances says: "The deterioration of the environment and of society affects the most vulnerable." He recognizes that the poor suffer disproportionately when the climate warms, the sea rises, and storms become increasingly severe. Thus, to work to diminish the effects of climate collapse is also to work on behalf of the marginalized and impoverished. Our urgent task—time is short—is to work for climate justice.

I'm not sure religion has been very helpful in this struggle. Genesis calls for humans to have dominion over and to subdue the earth (1:26). If we read the text carefully, it tells us that *man* is to rule over *her*, the earth—*aretz*, the word translated as "earth," is feminine in Hebrew, as you know—and, endorsing a chauvinist view of marriage, it tells us later in Genesis (3:16) that *the husband is to rule over his wife*. The requirement should have been for men to respect women as their equals (since they were both created in the image of God), and for all human beings to respectfully care for the natural world, to view the earth as our sacred home. If truly the word of God, this would have been as much a part of Jewish and Christian scriptures as the explicit prohibition of slavery. Neither was. Not only is scripture unneeded to discover how we should live: it sometimes gets in the way of creating a truly comprehensive morality that summons humans to equally respect each other and to respect the earth.

10

What about the View that Scripture Is God's Word?

There is no sense in God writing a book for me and then making me in such a way that I cannot believe his book.

—Robert Green Ingersoll, *Why I Am an Agnostic*

Are you saying that God didn't communicate the divine will in any of the scriptures of the world's great religions?

There are many scriptures purporting to be God's will, God's words, God's commandments. All of these so-called revelations are human creations. But some texts coincidentally express God's actual intentions for humankind, such as the call to love others as you should love yourself, welcome the stranger, free those unjustly held captive, feed the hungry, protect the vulnerable, impartially apply the law, etc. There is, however, much that is wrong in the scriptures of many religions, including texts purporting to be divine that actually reveal what contradicts God's will for humankind.

It is even reasonable to ask whether on balance the major world religions have brought the world more darkness than light. When I saw in Torah, Leviticus chapter 19, the command to love neighbor and the stranger as self, I wanted to shout: "Yes that's a beautiful moral law for all to live by." But I also saw in the Torah, in the same book, Leviticus (chapter 25), my Jewish friend, something that was mistakenly accepted as divine law: namely that Israelites are permitted to own non-Israelites permanently and pass them on to their children, and that Israelites may treat these non-Israelite slaves as ruthlessly as Israelites were treated in Egypt. I wanted to shout: "No, not so!" Slavery was never God's will. There are scriptural apologists who say God was only giving these human beings what they could handle at that historical time. I don't buy that. If those who originally received the Torah had seen in it an explicit divine condemnation of all slavery, do you think they would have ignored this, especially if the God of this text had threatened them with awful consequences for disobedience as He so often did? And even if these recently liberated slaves defied God's prohibition of all slavery—paradoxically wanting others to suffer as they did in Egypt—God would at least be on record condemning all slavery as an unholy practice. After all, the biblical God is on record condemning the enslavement of Israelites and calling for their liberation. Why in the Torah is permanent slavery wrong for Jews but not for all other communities?

You will get no argument from me. This is a question I ask out loud every Passover.

The failure of both the Bible and the Quran to absolutely condemn slavery led to the legitimation of an institution that brought enormous pain and degradation to those who were literally owned as one owns a piece of property. If the Bible (both Jewish and Christian versions) and the Quran had really been authored by God, they would have contained an unambiguous prohibition of slavery. Of course, many Jews, Christians, and Muslims have argued that the condemnation of slavery is implicit in their scriptures. The truth, to repeat, is this: the absolute condemnation of slavery in Jewish, Christian, and Muslim scriptures would have prevented untold misery and death—but in fact there is no unequivocal prohibition. The condemnation needed to be loud and clear, and it was not.

In his memoir *Narrative of the Life of Frederick Douglass*, the famous former slave, already mentioned, who became an eloquent leader of the abolitionist movement, graphically describes the indignities of a market where human beings could be purchased, where members of families could be sold to separate buyers, as if Blacks, young and old, were no different from the livestock being bought and sold in the same place. His words:

> We were all ranked together at the valuation. Men and women, old and young, married and single, were ranked with cattle and horses, sheep and swine. There were horses and men, cattle and women, pigs and children, all holding the same rank in the scale of being. At this brutalizing moment, I saw more clearly than ever the brutalizing effects of slavery upon both slave and slaveholder. A single word from the white men was enough—against all our wishes, prayers, and entreaties—to sunder the dearest friends, dearest kindred, and the strongest ties known to human beings.

Douglass tells us that one of his owners, recently converted to Methodist Christianity, found religious sanction and support in scripture for his slave-holding cruelty. Indeed, any owner of slaves could quote the Gospel of Luke (12:47) where Jesus says that the slave who knows his master's will and does not do what his master wants shall be beaten with many blows. In *12 Years a Slave*, this is the very verse that the narrator, Solomon Northup, a former slave, says one of his masters, Peter Tanner, quotes to justify whipping his slaves. Indeed, in conformity with scripture, Tanner tells them, he has a God-given right to inflict "many—forty, a hundred, a hundred and fifty—lashes."

This biblical text is of course part of a parable Jesus is telling about his future return to earth, and so the language is allegorical—a servant (symbol for believer) is impatient for his master (symbol for Jesus) to return—rather than literal, but the point is that Jesus is never quoted as saying that it would be wrong for a master to inflict many blows, or that slavery is wrong. What if Jesus had been quoted in even one Gospel as saying: "Slavery is a terrible sin; no human being should own another human being. It is an abomination." If Jesus had truly been God, wouldn't he have condemned slavery? Supposedly, Jesus had no fear of those in power and wasn't shy about expressing his mind. If Jesus had absolutely condemned slavery and the whipping of slaves, Christians in the South who owned slaves would not have been able to defend slavery so religiously and to feel that they had a divine right not only to own slaves but to beat them, and even beat to death disobedient Black Human Beings.

Many Southern slave owners (many in the North said the same thing when slavery was legal there) felt it was their biblically sanctioned right to enslave those with a dark pigment, because they believed that Blacks were divinely ordained to be slaves. One source of this belief is found in Genesis when Noah, apparently with God's permission, condemned Ham's children, Canaanites, to slavery (*Genesis 9:25–26*) for an unknown shameful act committed by Ham against his father, Noah. The Genesis narrative refers to a curse on Canaanites, justifying enslaving them, but says nothing about Blackness. Despite this, there were slave-owning Jews, Christians, and Muslims who interpreted the text as saying that all of Ham's descendants were cursed with Blackness—and this became both an explanation of Black skin and a justification for enslaving dark-skinned human beings. The very name Ham was associated with blackness.

In his book The Curse of Ham: Race and Slavery in Early Judaism, Christianity, and Islam, *David M. Goldenberg, a historian who spent thirteen years investigating every reference to Blacks in Jewish literature up to the seventh century, found that a misreading of Hebrew and other Semitic languages led to the mistaken belief that the word "Ham" meant "dark" or "black." Inaccurate translation can prove tragic.*

The point is that, no matter how linguistically shaky it is to equate the name Ham with blackness, the enslavement of Blacks was, for many slave-owing followers of Abrahamic faiths, a deserved punishment for the sin of Ham, an adoption of the paradoxical, indeed irrational, view that children can be held culpable for the sins of the father. This accords with the same irrationality that characterizes the Christian doctrine of original sin developed by Augustine. My liberal Christian friends repudiate this doctrine.

To be honest, there are texts in the Torah that say that children will be punished for the sins of their fathers: for example, Exodus 20:5–6. Other texts reject this. But of course you're right: what is most disturbing are texts in the Torah that sanctify and sanction slavery.

The long degradation and humiliation of enslaved persons in the United States may be difficult for Americans, including Blacks living now, to fully understand. Many people mistakenly think that house slaves were well treated. Evidence of how horrible slavery was, even for slaves who lived in the home of the master, is disturbingly illustrated by the famous case of Margaret Garner. The case was the inspiration for the 1858 poem "Slave Mother, A Tale of Ohio" by the Black abolitionist and suffragette Francis Harper; the 1867 painting called *Modern Medea* by Thomas Satterwhite Noble; Toni Morrison's novel *Beloved*; and the opera *Margaret Garner* composed by Richard Danielpour, with an English-language libretto by Toni Morrison.

Born in Kentucky in 1834, Margaret, called Peggy—the child of a rape by her enslaved mother's owner—was also an enslaved woman married to an enslaved man, Robert Garner. In 1849, John Pollard Gaines, the owner of the plantation where Margaret and her husband lived, sold his plantation and all the human beings he owned to his brother, Archibald Gaines. In 1856, after Archibald Gaines had repeatedly raped Margaret, she and Robert decided to flee, taking with them their four children. On a frigid winter night in 1856, they crossed an iced-over Ohio River to free Cincinnati to stay in the cabin of Elijah Kite, Margaret's uncle—who, although once enslaved, was now living as a free man. Margaret and Robert were tracked down by Gaines and U.S. Marshals, who surrounded the cabin and then stormed it with warrants for the arrest of the Garners.

While Robert was trying to defend his family with a pistol, even wounding one of the Marshalls, Margaret, horrified by the prospect that she and her children would be returned to a life of slavery and sexual abuse, slit the throat of her two-year-old daughter with a butcher knife, stabbed her other children, and then herself. Her infant daughter died immediately, but

Margaret and her other children survived. She obviously believed it would be better to die than live enslaved. Given the humiliation, pain, and violence that characterized their daily lives, this was not an uncommon feeling for enslaved human beings. That Margaret thought she and her children would be better off dead is no surprise. Of course it was also a degrading life for her husband. Sometimes Robert Garner was ordered to whip Margaret if she resisted Gaines's sexual advances: this was not an unusual demand of owners who wanted their way with an enslaved woman. It was of course also a way to emasculate a female slave's male partner.

How can anyone believe that a perfectly just, compassionate, and omnipotent God would not only fail to prohibit slavery but, furthermore, would not intervene to prevent the cruelty of slavery? It is now clear that you and I both want apologists for the God of the Bible to answer another question: Why would the Creator, Who, according to the Torah, liberated the Israelites from slavery, stand by while the worst forms of humiliation and degradation were inflicted on other enslaved human beings?

Yes, yes, and yes! If God really liberated the Israelites from oppression in Egypt, why would God, if truly omnipotent and just, not have freed enslaved Blacks in the United States and elsewhere who suffered as much if not more than the so-called Chosen People? If God had the power to liberate Blacks from the degradations of slavery, but refused to do so, He would, I agree with you, be guilty of idly standing by while blood was being shed—while enslaved people were being beaten, tortured, raped, and murdered. I of course share your view that God in fact lacked the power to intervene. And, again, you are right in saying that if, as so many Jews and Christians claim, God was truly the omniscient and just author of scripture, knowing what the future would bring if He remained silent, He could and should have made it clear that slavery is absolutely wrong—always a violation of God's will.

As God, I saw it all, completely helpless to do anything about countless sexual atrocities that occurred under slavery in the American South. To read disturbing first person female slave accounts of physical and sexual abuse, your readers might want to look at the memoirs of former slaves Mary Prince and Harriet Jacobs—also the various narratives dictated by the illiterate ex-slave Sojourner Truth who, despite her lack of education, became a persuasive voice for abolitionism and women's rights.

Let me return to the inadequacy of scripture in the Abrahamic religions. During the Civil War both sides quoted scripture and argued that God was on their side. Christian abolitionists argued that slavery was inconsistent with the Golden Rule, the belief that all human beings are created in the image of God, and the conviction we are all one in Christ. Christian Southerners who owned slaves believed, many sincerely, that the Bible supported slavery and could cite specific texts while also pointing out that neither the Old nor the New Testament explicitly condemns this practice. Jews were equally on both sides of the issue in their conflicting interpretations of the Hebrew Bible. And Muslims could not point to any verse in the Quran quoting God as absolutely forbidding slavery.

Couldn't you as God have done this: clearly revealed your intentions to us, provided us with absolutely correct guidance on this question and others?

I must remind you: when I gave up omnipotence and omniscience, when I hid myself at the foundation of the world, I gave up the possibility of directly communicating with human beings. That was part of what it meant for the world to develop on its own. As I tried to make clear a few minutes ago, in order for human beings to be truly autonomous, they must be morally self-directing. Bonhoeffer was right about this. Remember, I didn't think a divine revelation about the nature of good and evil was necessary. As I've so often stated, human beings have the capacity to understand the right way to live, apart from all scripture. Human beings, if they had used their capacity for sympathy and their inner sense of justice, should have been able to see that slavery was indefensible. Understanding what is right does not depend on divine revelation. That's why atheists can be good without God, despite what many theists claim. That's why Buddhists can also live truly ethical lives without belief in a Creator.

Human beings, using their capacity to reason and their capacity to put themselves in the place of others, can recognize that cruelty and treating others with disrespect is wrong. They can understand, without recourse to religion, that compassion and justice are good. This does not mean that there aren't hard cases where values may conflict—for example, when one must choose between justice and mercy in dealing with an offender in a criminal justice system. No one seriously disputes that justice and mercy are important values we should live by, but we sometimes struggle when we have to choose between them. The important point is this: the claim that people cannot know what is good—or be good—without God is a false idea that needs to be discarded. Some of the most immoral acts in human history have been committed by individuals who believed that they were doing God's will, guided by this scripture or that. There is in truth a long history of theists committing great evils (consider the Crusades and ISIS).

Indeed, although we can document atrocities justified by nontheistic religions such as Buddhism, theistic religions have sometimes provided the most powerful incentives to immoral behavior. What has led many self-described believers astray, even to the point of going against what their own conscience tells them, is the view that they should always obey God's will as they understand it, no matter what: the view that being religious means absolute obedience to divine commands. If, for example, someone truly believes that God's will trumps everything and sincerely believes that God commands us to enslave a certain group of human beings, then slavery is for that believer absolutely right. On this view, to be religious is to submit to God's will, even if that means doing what your conscience tells you is wrong.

This, however, is only one idea of what it means to be religious, namely to obey God, no matter what God commands. There is an alternative view. In the Torah, your holy scripture, Jim, the reader encounters two conflicting models of religiosity, two different ways of being religious, based upon two different understandings of the relationship of God to human beings. Let me speak to you as a religious Jew who claims Abraham was the first Jew, the spiritual father of Judaism, maybe a model Jew. The question is: Which Abraham do you emulate, the one who models moral autonomy or the one who exemplifies absolute submission? Of all the stories in the Torah, one that I most celebrated was Abraham's challenge to God when he hears that God is about to destroy the cities of Sodom and Gomorrah. This Abraham is an individual who aggressively asserts his moral independence, implicitly challenging the obedience model of religiosity. The Abraham of this story (Genesis 18) shows ethical *chutzpah* by questioning God, asking God whether God plans to kill the innocent along with the guilty. He boldly asks God: "Would the just judge of all the earth ever do what is unjust?" The question—Will You kill the innocent along with guilty?—is one that the God of this text does not see as irreverent because the God of this narrative clearly shares Abraham's sense of justice.

This Abraham does not uncritically submit to the will of God nor does he get his sense of justice from God. This story in Genesis precedes revelation at Sinai, the handing down of the divine law through Moses. As a thoughtful human being using both heart and mind, *this* Abraham knows, prior to revelation of ethical commandments at Sinai, that it is wrong to deliberately slaughter innocent human beings, wrong for God as well as for us. This Abraham holds God to a standard of justice valid for both God and humans—and the God of this tale never disputes the claim that there is a universal standard of justice according to which both human beings and God can be judged.

This is the Abraham I admire, in contrast to the Abraham who is willing to sacrifice his son, to literally make a burnt offering of Isaac, because he believes God commands this. This other Abraham, who (in Genesis 22) is ready to murder his own child, without questioning or challenging God's command to do so, provides a religious model of absolute obedience. There are Jews, Christians, and Muslims who, over the centuries, have praised this Abraham as an example of true religiosity, a model of the life of faith, where a truly religious life is understood as a life of uncritical submission to the divine will. The two Abraham stories really provide two conflicting examples of what it means to be religious. One makes everything turn on God's will to which humans are expected to be absolutely obedient, no matter what God commands. The other is based on an idea of universal values valid for both God and human beings, a model of religiosity that affirms the moral autonomy of human beings, their capacity to think for themselves and discover standards that should govern not only all human life but also the behavior of the Creator. And the God of this story seems to expect Abraham to challenge Him.

My own view is that a long Jewish tradition favors the Abraham who challenges God. After all, another name for the Jewish people is Israel, meaning "God-wrestlers." The Abraham of this narrative exemplifies God-wrestling. Jacob, following in his footsteps, also challenges God and gets his new name, Israel, because of his willingness to make moral demands of God. Moses, considered our greatest prophet, not only argues with God to save his fellow Jews, but wins this argument, several times, when God is bent on killing all Israelites. Jeremiah dares to ask God why the wicked prosper and the good suffer. And Job, though not a Jew, does something very Jewish when, as someone suffering unjustly, he utters these defiant words: "Though God may slay me, I will argue my case. I have prepared my case: I know I am right. Why do You hide Your face?" So, arguing with God, on the basis of our conscience and a clear sense of what objective justice requires, is very much in the spirit of Judaism—Judaism at its best, in my opinion. I have never been drawn to the Abraham who is ready to cut his son's throat simply because God so commands.

Elie Wiesel, who suffered through the horror of Auschwitz as a teenager, wrote a novel, Night, *about his experience in this death camp: this is really a story about God's abandonment of his people. Wiesel also wrote a play,* The Trial of God, *in which God is put on trial by Jews in a Ukrainian village in 1649, after a pogrom, a brutal anti-Semitic Cossack attack on the Jewish population in that village. Jewish survivors stage a mock trial, indicting God for failure to intervene in the face of evil. The play was based on an event Wiesel witnessed at Auschwitz: three rabbis—brilliant and pious Jews—decided one day to indict God for allowing Jews to be massacred by the Nazis. God was convicted of allowing the massacre of Jewish people. Reflecting on youthful years spent at Auschwitz, Elie Wiesel published a letter to the editor in the* New York Times, *October 2, 1997. It was addressed to Master of the Universe. Wiesel's powerful words, challenging and questioning God, are for me unforgettable. I remember clearly what he said in that letter, namely:*

Why did you allow if not enable the killer day after day, night after night to torment, kill, and annihilate tens of thousands of Jewish children? Why were they abandoned by your Creation? These thoughts were in no way destined to diminish the guilt of the guilty. Their established culpability is irrelevant to my "problem" with you, Master of the Universe. In my childhood, I did not expect much from human beings. But I expected everything from you.

(Shekhinah's response to this again surprised me. How could she be knowledgeable about so much, including the conclusion of this obscure letter by Wiesel?)

You have neglected to quote the final words of the letter: "Let us make up." Wiesel seeks to reconcile with God. This I never understood because Wiesel believed God was omnipotent and could have intervened. Are Jews to believe that an omnipotent God stood idly by while six million human beings were slaughtered, including over one million Jewish children? Remember, Wiesel addresses God as Master of the Universe, and takes it for granted that God had the power to prevent these atrocities but failed to do so.

On my view, Wiesel was too forgiving. If the Creator after creation really remained Master of the Universe—retaining the power to intervene—then this God should have asked Wiesel and other survivors of genocide for forgiveness. A truly loving God Who possesses absolute power should and would intervene to save the innocent and would be culpable if He did not. Again, I have never understood how anyone could believe that divine love is at work in this world, that an omnipotent and just being has the power to intervene but allows gross injustice, such as the Holocaust, one of many genocides.

If omnipotent, I must repeat: God is profoundly guilty of violating the moral law attributed to him in Leviticus, one to which we have both alluded, namely: "One should never stand idly by while another bleeds." This applies to all cases of unjust suffering. Would an omnipotent God Who is also perfectly loving and just really remain idle while countless enslaved human beings are degraded and tortured by their owners, while genocide decimates whole ethnic communities, while cancers ravage countless bodies, too often bringing with them excruciating pain and then death, while natural disasters destroy lives indiscriminately and make life intolerable for survivors? The list of inexplicable evils goes on and on. Where is God's perfect justice, or perfect compassion, in any of this?

I could, when I was God, completely understand why skeptics reject belief in God altogether as they daily observe a world so full of evil and unjust suffering. They see how questionable it is for anyone to believe in a God Who, although having the power to act, allows so much misery and pain, never offering any clear explanation. A God of resounding silence! Thus, I always had a warm place in my heart for atheists and agnostics. I felt just the opposite toward those who uncritically believe in and worship a God who either wills or permits the mass suffering of the innocent. I found too uncritical and submissive those who passively accept all the evils of the world as part of an inscrutable divine plan!

Leaving my transcendent, potentially eternal life beyond this world for a mortal life on earth actually brought me a sense of relief and liberation. As I've said, there could be no peace in heaven because there was no peace on earth. Again, I must ask you: How could heaven be a peaceful place, how could God be at peace, as long there was so much suffering on earth?

Did you find some peace when you became a human being?

Once I became a mortal creature—my ultimate and final act of self-limitation—I could actually shut out the lack of peace on earth. I could escape the explosive, awful noise of warfare—where children are often bloodied and even blown apart, as, most recently, in Syria—and the agony of minds so tortured by mental illness that suicide seems the only recourse. I could finally look away. I could finally cease being a helpless witness to pointless suffering. When I became a human being, I could no longer directly feel the suffering of all sentient beings. I finally ceased to feel the pain of every creature—the breadth and depth of the sorrow and misery on this damaged planet. That again was Nietzsche's brilliant insight: to see how unbearable, how hellish, this would be for a truly loving God. Maybe it took an atheist to see this—namely that compassion for a suffering world would ultimately kill an impotent God.

Once I completely emptied myself of divinity and became a human being, I could literally close my eyes to the suffering of others. I could escape to a quiet place where no disturbing sounds could be heard. Having physical ears, I could even put my fingers in them to block out unpleasant noises. As I sit here and speak with you, I can hear about your troubles, if you wish to share them, and I know abstractly that there are others in this coffee shop who may be struggling with loss or experiencing physical pain. But I have no direct awareness of what is going on in their hearts, minds, or bodies. This is a protective ignorance, a freeing ignorance I never knew as God. Although I still retain a memory of all the suffering that occurred on earth, this memory lacks the vividness and the intensity of directly feeling this suffering that I possessed as God.

Although you sometimes play along, you don't believe a word I've said, do you? I should not have expected you to believe me, but somehow I hoped you would. If someone claims she became a disillusioned God Who abandoned heaven for earth, there is of course good reason to suspect madness or deception or dark humor. I of course welcome skepticism. As I've said, even as God I welcomed skepticism about my goodness, even my very existence. I think I would have been a religious skeptic if I had been born a human being with the ability to think and reason. Now I'm only a human being. I carry only weakening memories, slowly fading, of my previous life. I do appreciate your willingness to listen, even to play along.

In a sense, I am playing along—with, for all I know, your sincere, even if mistaken, belief that you were once God. Playing along, let me ask you this: What did you know when you were God? From what you have said, it appears that although you did not have perfect knowledge of the future, you had perfect knowledge of the past and the present.

Yes, that's correct. I was omniscient in the sense that I knew all there was to know. I had perfect knowledge not only of the feelings of all sentient beings and all events that occurred everywhere in the universe, but also perfect knowledge of mathematics, cosmology, physics, chemistry, biology, etc. I had perfect knowledge of everything that occurred from the moment I created the cosmos out of nothing—starting with the Big Bang. I had perfect recollection of what happened during the billions of years when the cosmos cooled downed, stars and planets formed, and life emerged on the earth in all its diversity: life that, to my surprise, survived despite multiple mass extinctions. I can recall my excitement and hope when human beings emerged from a hit and miss evolutionary process. Finally, there were creatures who had the potential for self-consciousness and the capacity for moral agency, aesthetic creativity, and scientific understanding. As I've already stated, as God I lacked what philosophers and theologians call divine foreknowledge: perfect knowledge of the future.

Although lacking perfect foreknowledge, I still had perfect awareness of everything that had occurred in the cosmos and everything currently happening. Since future events were not yet a reality, I could not know them. There was nothing to know because the future, marked by freedom and chance, had yet to unfold. I could not know when I created the cosmos what human beings would decide because their future was theirs freely to determine.

This, as you know, is what philosophers now call "open theism."

Yes, meaning the future is open, waiting to be freely decided and also subject to chance. Thus, the only reality I could perfectly know was the past and the present. Despite the laws I established that allow science to predict the behavior of a wide variety of phenomena, many things remained unpredictable because there is genuine chance, random variation, and, with the emergence of human beings, free choice. Clearly, it would be an understatement to say that many things in the cosmos did not turn out as I expected, as I desired. This applies to the emergence of intelligent life.

For example, I was surprised that—given the number of planets in a cosmos containing three trillion galaxies (the Royal Astronomical Society undercounted them, estimating two trillion), with many earth-like planets positioned just the right distance from sun-like stars, many conducive to diverse forms of life—intelligent life emerged on only one planet. There were and are primitive life-forms on many planets, but, as chance would have it, human-like species have not evolved on any other planet. When I made my exit from the fifth dimension, there were no planets with the potential for the development of intelligent self-conscious life. Of course this form of life may still emerge on some planet in the distant future, maybe with better results. This possibility did nothing to mitigate my suffering or the suffering on earth.

Although I made sure that the cosmos contained the conditions necessary for the emergence of complex life forms, it appears that, after the Big Bang, there was, after all, no necessity for intelligent life to appear anywhere! Human life may have been a lucky hit. Maybe I left things too random. Although one might think that in a universe so vast there must be intelligent life elsewhere, physicist Paul Davies, director of the Center for Fundamental Concepts in Science at Arizona State University, correctly points out in a *Scientific American* article that the vastness of the cosmos "may be dwarfed by the odds against forming even simple organic molecules by random chance alone." As it turns out, he is right. Despite the number of earth-like planets and sun-like stars at earth-like distances from them throughout the cosmos, no scientist has found any decisive evidence for extraterrestrial intelligent life because in fact, other than yours truly, there is no such life.

(Thinking I might stump her, but not betting on it, I brought up something she might not know; in case she did, I wanted her response.) So, we are left with Fermi's Paradox.

Yes. For those readers who don't know, the paradox was named after the great twentieth-century Italian physicist Enrico Fermi who in 1938 won the Nobel Prize in physics and has been called the architect of the atomic bomb. Not a great gift if you're Japanese. Fermi's Paradox refers to the contradiction between the high probability estimates for intelligent life on other planets (based, to repeat, on the number of galaxies and the probable number of earth-like planets in earth-like distances to stars like ours) and the lack of evidence for such life. Or as Fermi asked at Los Alamos during the summer of 1950, while at lunch chatting with two other brilliant physicists, Edward Teller and Herbert York: "Given the high probability of intelligent life like us elsewhere in the cosmos, where is everyone?" Do you know the song *Fermi Paradox* by the American heavy metal band Avenged Sevenfold? The lyrics, which describe the search for extraterrestrial life, include words that tell us there is no one home on other planets. And, despite claims to the contrary, the truth is that I'm the only intelligent extraterrestrial who has visited earth: indeed the only such being in the whole cosmos. All other ETI claims are bogus.

This makes our situation even more urgent: the fact that there are no human-like beings anywhere else in the universe. What struck me as unspeakably tragic was that life on this small planet had become so fragile because it was daily being threatened by the activities of its most intelligent inhabitants. The eco-destructive behavior of human beings has already led to the extinction of many forms of life and hourly threatens the future of others. It now threatens even human existence. There are scientists who believe we are in the period of the sixth mass extinction of life. A recent article in the *Proceedings of the National Academy of Sciences* reveals that billions of animals have been lost in recent decades. The lion is an emblematic case. Historically the lion was distributed over most of Africa, southern Europe, the Middle East, and all the way to northwestern India. Now the vast majority of the lion population is gone.

(After looking up a reference.) American biologist Edward O. Wilson in a 2018, March 18 article in the New York Times *maintains that the extinction of life by human activity is accelerating at such a pace that it may eliminate more than half of all species by the end of this century. He points out that the worldwide extinction of species is not reversible: once a species is gone, it is gone forever.*

(Surprising me again.) Yes, and Wilson also points out that scientists estimate that of all the known species that currently live on earth, 1.3 million, there are probably about 8 million species (actually the correct number is 12.4 million) that have not been identified. Most of these species will disappear without ever having been recorded. Wilson, giving us reason to hope, believes that we can solve the problem of disappearing species and prevent tragedy if we only have the will to apply the knowledge and resources we possess. But another disturbing reality is that the world is losing biodiversity at an alarming rate—biodiversity is of course the wonderful variation in species that occupy the planet. Since all species are interconnected in complicated food chains, whenever we wipe out one species that means the destruction of many others. This biodiversity—something that God did anticipate and came to highly value—evolved over millions of years, but it can be destroyed in no time at all. Much of the damage is already beyond repair. Action is urgent. Now I feel like I'm preaching, giving an ecological sermon about the coming biological apocalypse.

*Tracy Chapman, a very socially conscious African American song-
writer, sings about this assault on the earth in her pleading, moving song, "The
Rape of the World." Chapman mourns the way we have stood by while the
earth, the mother of us all, has been raped. She sings about this as one of the
greatest crimes of all time.*

I've always appreciated her music. The destructive behavior of human
beings and the immeasurable pain it inflicts on fellow human beings and
animals was too much for a perfectly compassionate God Who could do
nothing to stop it. I have repeatedly said that, but I want you to know that I
ultimately saw this as a call for me to stop moaning and do something. How
could I stand aside and watch the assault on the earth and the other injus-
tices occurring daily? I could not. Not to stand by idly meant for me only
one thing: becoming a human being who could actually act in the world
and join in the fight against what Chapman calls "the greatest violation of
all time."

But apart from what we have done to make natural disasters more destructive, nature on its own, through the very processes that made evolution
and the diversity of species possible, has also caused much misery. Consider
the suffering caused by naturally occurring DNA mutations (hereditary
mutations or an error made as DNA copies itself during cell division). Mutations, essential to evolution, the raw material of genetic variation, necessary for evolutionary change and development, can, for example, take a dark
turn when they produce cancers that end human lives and, in too many
cases, lead to painful deaths.

Mutations can also result in tragically premature death. Progeria, already discussed, is caused by a mutation in the LMNA gene: we have seen
how it turns a child's body into a body that should belong only to a very
elderly adult, bringing about, in many cases, a miserable end, often by heart
attack, during the teenage years. Genetic mutation contributed to the disease that killed Stephen Hawking: amyotrophic lateral sclerosis. Those who
develop this progressive neurodegenerative disease can lose the ability to
move, communicate, and even breathe. ALS is fatal and, before death, can
cause some victims to feel like they are suffocating or drowning, a very cruel
way of dying. Would an all-powerful and perfectly loving God really do
nothing and allow human beings to be tortured to death by such diseases?
The truth is that much human misery is the product of mutations. Although
I did not intend, and could not prevent, these painful diseases from occurring, I plead guilty to creating, then stepping back from, a universe that I
knew would be full of random events.

Fatal cancers that strike children are especially tragic. It can begin with
random changes in the DNA in normal bone marrow cells that cause them

to become leukemia cells. Think of the physical pain of a child and the emotional suffering of parents who watch helplessly as their child dies of acute myeloid leukemia. This child may experience severe bone pain before death occurs. The loss of this child was also my loss. At least a human parent can hold the child's hand and try to comfort her. Although some believers think so, there is no divine equivalent of holding a child's hand. I now can visit children in cancer centers and literally hold their hands and comfort them. I plan to use my remaining divine knowledge to help cure these diseases. So, that no time is wasted in medical school, I will have to acquire phony medical credentials that will allow me to join cancer research teams sometime in the near future.

As the Creator who became causally disengaged from creatures, I couldn't cure any child's cancer, despite all claims about God's miraculous power to heal disease. Why would God, if all-powerful and all-knowing, and in control of what happens in this world, from the beginning to the end, allow the existence of terminal, painful diseases, diseases in children that this God is often asked to cure? Do you know how many parents earnestly and desperately prayed to God to heal their child, with no result? Too many to count. Of course there are many religious parents who believe, in cases of unexpected recovery, that God, working a miracle, cured their child. But why would God, if all-powerful, just, and perfectly loving, choose to heal this child but not that one when both sets of parents prayed equally hard to God for a miracle? And why should God ignore a child whose parents did not pray at all, maybe who were, with good reason, hardened atheists? Should children suffer for the sins of their parents? Would God discriminate by saving only those children whose parents have faith, or the right faith, or pray to the right God?

Of course, when children die, many parents who are believers often console themselves by saying that God called their child to His heavenly home because God needed another angel. You can find such language in the obituaries of many of these children. Why would a God Who, according to these parents' own theology, already has countless angels need another one, especially when calling the child to heaven causes so much suffering to those living on earth? Or, in the words of a grieving mother who has just lost her son in David Lindsay-Abaire's play (also a movie), *Rabbit Hole*: "He's God, why didn't He just make one. I mean, He is God, after all. Why didn't He just make another angel?" Isn't this mother correct? Wouldn't an all-powerful God Who wants another angel simply create one instead of selfishly taking the child for Himself? And why would such a God, if He wanted another angel, allow, as happens in too many cases, for a child with cancer to die in great pain before calling her to heaven? Why would a truly all-powerful God Who is also perfectly merciful engage in divine kidnapping when it causes parents to experience a wrenching loss?

As Ivan Karamazov rightly contends, the suffering and death of very young children is a special problem because of their obvious innocence. Yet in an important sense most parents who lose a child are also innocent—or at least undeserving of this kind of loss. The horrible emotional pain of losing a child through terminal illness has repeated itself over and over in numberless lives. I created a cosmos in which, because I left things to chance, young lives are extinguished all the time, causing tragic loss for both these children and their parents. Remaining an impotent witness to tragic loss and suffering was something I could no longer endure. So God committed suicide.

11

Divine Suicide by Full Kenosis

Human Embodiment

In its most absolute and most consistent form the theory
of kenosis teaches what La Touche calls "incarnation by
divine suicide."
—Louis Berhkof, *The History of Christian Doctrines*

*But how did God destroy God? How were you able to end your divine life? I
still don't understand how it's possible for an eternal being to become temporal:
to lose eternal existence. That remains a profound philosophical and theological puzzle to me.*

I've already given you the short answer to this question: I ended my
existence as God through incarnation—by becoming a human being. Let
me give you the longer version of my answer, hinted at earlier. When I, as
the Infinite, contracted myself, metaphorically speaking, to make room for
genuine otherness in creating what would become an independently evolving universe, I knew that I could continue diminishing my divine Self if I
so willed. When I moved from being the Infinite, the only Reality, to becoming a limited God, when I made my first move toward finitude, toward
self-limitation, it was, I knew, a process of divine contraction that I could
continue until I gave up my divine existence altogether.

So when I relinquished my existence as the Absolute, surrendering omnipotence and omniscience, I was aware that I had the power to contract my being even more, indeed to become, if I wished, a finite being in the fullest sense by incarnating, taking on flesh and blood, and becoming a mere mortal. I knew that I could become a human being, but, if you remember what I said in the beginning, to do so I had to enter and take possession of the body of a living person. I also knew that, once embodied, I could never regain my eternal existence as God, just as I could never recover omnipotence once I gave that up. To be honest, when I surrendered the attributes of omnipotence and omniscience to make room for an independently evolving world, I did not know—could not know because the future was unknowable—that the end result would be so troubling that I would want to give up altogether my life as God. Fortunately, I retained the power to exit my divine life and become a human being.

Once I became a human being, I did not remain—as orthodox Christianity claims about the Son of God when He became fully human in Jesus—also fully divine. On the contrary, when I chose to become a human being, I knowingly gave up divinity. Some Christian theologians, viewed as heretical by other Christian theologians, affirm something I have only briefly touched on but which best describes what I did as God, namely the act of *kenosis*. This term, from the Greek verb "to empty," refers to God's act of emptying Godself of divine attributes. Applied by some Christians to the Son of God, it is the view that when He became Jesus, God incarnate, the Son of God renounced His divine nature—wholly or in part, temporarily or permanently.

For example, according to one theory of kenosis, the Son of God, when He became a man, temporarily gave up some divine powers while retaining others. On this view, when the Son of God walked on earth in the flesh of Jesus, He, for His time on earth, temporally lost the divine attributes of perfect foreknowledge and eternality. Those Christians who say Jesus lacked omniscience quote from Matthew (24:36) and Mark (13:32) where Jesus says that no one except the Father knows when Jesus will come again, not even the Son. And there are Christians who say that the Son of God lost, while He was a human being, eternality because the Gospels tell us that the Son of God literally died on the cross: that is why He had to be resurrected. More orthodox Christians say any claim about Jesus' limitations constitutes heresy. But those who affirm some form of kenosis insist, thinking they are being faithful to the Gospels, that the Son of God, when He became a man, was limited by time and place, diminished in significant ways, as he lovingly took on the role of humble servant to humankind.

Some more extreme expositors of the idea of kenosis interpreted the Son's self-emptying of divine attributes as absolute and permanent and thus viewed the incarnation as a form of divine suicide. For most Christologists—an ugly word meaning Christian theologians who develop theories about the nature of Christ—this is an unacceptable view because if the Son of God irreversibly gave up all of His divine attributes, He would of course cease to be God in the person of Jesus, clearly a heretical view. Even those who assert kenosis in some limited and temporary way have, as I pointed out, also been charged with heresy because this would mean that Jesus was not *fully* divine. After all, the official doctrine developed by the Catholic Church, and adopted by most Protestant denominations, is that the Son of God remained fully divine when he became Jesus.

Jesus himself never claimed to be both fully God and fully Man. This view of Jesus is a product of the theological imagination of self-described Christians who came after Jesus. The orthodox doctrine is of course that Jesus was "truly God and truly Man"—that although Jesus the Christ (*"Christ" being a Greek term meaning "messiah"*) possesses two natures, one divine and one human, they are, it is claimed, united in the one person: Jesus. The bishops of the Council of Chalcedon voted to accept this as orthodox (correct) doctrine in 451. Can theological truth really be a product of a vote? As a matter of fact, it wasn't the theological truth. As I've already said, Jesus never claimed to be God and never was God. Let me repeat: the idea that Jesus asserted that he was fully divine and fully human was an invention of Christian thinkers.

But the Gospel of John (10:30) quotes Jesus as saying: "I and the Father are one." Why should anyone doubt that Jesus claimed to be God? I ask this for the benefit of our readers. I have my own view.

More revealing than this sentence from the Gospel of John are the final words of Jesus according to the Gospels of Mark and Matthew: "My God, My God, why have you forsaken me?"—a cry of despair uttered by Jesus as he was hanging in agony on the cross. They are the words of a man who felt abandoned by God. This is what Jesus actually said. Think about it. What purpose would it serve the writers of these two Gospels to make up such despairing final words, words that attribute to Jesus a sense of feeling totally deserted by God? Obviously Jesus was not speaking to himself when he cried out to God: he was speaking to the God that he, a purely human Jesus, believed was his loving, heavenly Abba: Father. Jesus felt abandoned by God during his final agonizing hours on the cross, a period when he experienced hopelessness, excruciating pain, and the agony of suffocation—a degrading death.

Jesus—a good Jew who knew the Hebrew Bible, indeed the only Bible he knew—is here of course quoting the beginning of Psalm 22 where the Jewish author of this text, the one that begins "My God, my God, why have you forsaken me," like so many Jews before and after, is expressing a cry of the heart, a powerful feeling of anguish and desertion. No doubt many religious Jews in Nazi death camps uttered these same words. Cruelly treated by people who hated and despised them simply because they were Jews, they saw the Nazi world of death as God-forsaken and could not understand God's absence. The point is that the historical Jesus deeply felt God's absence as he died in misery, hanging on a cross. I would argue that Jesus—who studied Torah like a Jew, dressed like a Jew, argued like a Jew, and prayed like a Jew—would not, as a good Jew, ever claim to be God. And if Jesus claimed to be the Christ ("messiah"), he knew that the Jewish messiah would never claim to be God in the flesh. That would be both blasphemy and self-idolatry. Even as he was breathing his last breath, Jesus, like a good Jew (an Israel: "God wrestler"), challenged God and accused God, as more than a few Psalms do, of hiding His face.

I of course do claim I was God, a God Who took Her own life. The truth is that even before God died, this world was God-forsaken. Bonhoeffer was right about that. I took kenosis, the act of self-emptying, a step further than the mythical Christ of "relative" kenosis—the Son who temporarily emptied Himself of some divine attributes—when I permanently gave up all divine powers. Thus, what I did is closer to the view of those radically heretical Christians who assert that God, in taking on flesh, permanently emptied the divine Self of all divine attributes and thus committed suicide. Remember: I started this process of kenosis when I permanently gave up omnipotence and omniscience in creating an independently existing universe, or at least the seeds of what would become the self-evolving cosmos that we now know.

In becoming a human being, I finished the process of kenosis by surrendering my remaining divine attributes: eternal existence, direct divine awareness of everything that happens in the cosmos, and moral perfection. I am no longer perfectly compassionate or just; like all other human beings, I can fall into selfishness and lose my way ethically. I am as morally flawed as any other person. But, despite my moral limitations, I've resolved to live, even if imperfectly, a life of compassion and justice, to act in the world to reduce suffering and to work to correct injustice where possible: in other words, to do what I could never do as God when I possessed moral perfection, a perfection that could not be actualized in the world.

Now I walk on solid ground—in a mortal body, destined to age and die, maybe incognito. Will anyone believe I was God? It appears that even you, despite this direct encounter, will never believe what I've been telling you. And the readers of a transcription of my words will also greet them with disbelief. Thus, no one may ever know who I was. Unlike Gautama who became the Buddha, I have no visible traits that set me apart. Gautama was reputed, even before he became the Buddha, to have thirty-two marks that would show the world he was a Buddha-to-be (Awakened One), including, to name a few, hands that reached below the knees, a thousand-spoked wheel sign on his feet, toes and fingers that were finely webbed, thighs like a royal stag, a curl that emits light between his eyebrows, a fleshy protuberance on the crown of the head, and elongated ears. There is nothing about me that would lead one to say: "Yes, clearly she was once God." Unlike Gautama whose thirty-two marks allowed those in the know to identify him as a Buddha-to-be, I have no perceivable traits pointing to my former divinity, establishing my credentials as the woman-who-was-God.

Your memory for detail and knowledge of different disciplines would probably not be considered proof that your mind was once divine. At most it would be evidence of a photographic memory, an encyclopedic mind. Of course, as you mentioned earlier, you are able to adopt the language and speech patterns of any interlocutor, to speak in foreign tongues, maybe even speak in tongues of the Holy Spirit, for all I know. You could probably perform masterfully in an assembly of Pentecostals, joining with them in speaking charismatic glossolalia. But this would not establish you were once God.

You're correct. My ability to adopt the speech patterns and speak the language of any interlocutor cannot be taken as proof of my former divinity. Who in the world would be so impressed that they would conclude that Shekhinah must have been God because she can speak Russian with Russians, Chinese with Chinese, Urdu with Pakinstanis, Swahili with Tanzanians, Krio with Sierra Leoneans, etc., etc., while adopting the peculiar speech patterns and the regional dialect of her conversation partner? At most I would be viewed as a linguistic genius.

Unlike the Buddha I lack characteristics that set me apart, and my fate will be the opposite of that of the Buddha. Let's review the myth of the life of Gautama: while being sheltered as a prince in a palace where he was not allowed to see anyone who was diseased, elderly, or dead, the Buddha-to-be, when he was finally exposed to these harsh realities, suddenly recognized the central problem of life is suffering and went in search of a solution. His solution was liberation from all incarnations. The key for the Buddha, as the story is told by many Buddhists, was not a better rebirth, but complete liberation from samsara, the realm of death and rebirth—never to be reborn again, not even in the most favorable human life. Human beings, according to traditional Buddhism, must be liberated from all forms of incarnation because as long as we are embodied and draw a breath, we will experience dissatisfaction, unhappiness.

The Buddha promised what he thought was the only path to freedom from suffering and sorrow: nirvana, the end of all incarnations. This of course is another religious myth, unless by nirvana the Buddha really meant complete annihilation—which his followers explicitly tell us he did not mean, but neither, they also tell us, does nirvana mean immortality of the individual self or soul which, according to Buddhism, is itself impermanent rather than eternal. Whatever its meaning, nirvana, as it is usually understood by traditional Buddhism, is about escaping the slings and arrows of embodiment: it means never being reborn into this vale of tears; never being embodied again.

I, on the other hand, found existence beyond this life, beyond human embodiment, to be a life of unbearable suffering and preferred suffering in this world to the overrated glories of divine existence. As should be clear by now, my divine existence was not nirvana. As God, I tended to identify with another mythical Buddhist figure, one I mentioned at the beginning of our conversation, Guanshiyin, a figure from a later iteration of Buddhism. In Mahayana Buddhism, we encounter the idea of the bodhisattva, a being who practices perfect compassion. Guanshiyin—pictured, if you recall, as female in places like China, Japan, and Vietnam—is the clearest example of what it means to be a bodhisattva: a term that literally means an "enlightened being." Remember, the name Guanshiyin means "one who hears all the cries of the world." She is often depicted as holding a willow branch in one hand and a bottle of nectar in the other. The willow branch is a tool for healing the sick and the nectar is the dew of compassion that relieves suffering. Again, I recommend that you see the impressively tall white statue of this bodhisattva at the Vietnamese Buddhist Temple here in Sugar Land.

The idea of the bodhisattva is an inspiring myth in Mahayana Buddhism. Guanshiyin is one of the most famous bodhisattvas in all of Buddhism. More precisely, a bodhisattva is a being who has become enlightened and can enter nirvana—but chooses to stay in samsara, the world of pain and sorrow, until she has freed every sentient being from suffering: that is, until she has led all other sentient beings to nirvana. Only then will she enter nirvana. If this time of helping others is infinite, then the bodhisattva will never enter nirvana. Maybe a bodhisattva is morally superior to God, because I as God could not endure even a few more years of listening to all the cries of the world. And there was no path out of suffering, such as nirvana, to which I could lead sufferers.

The truth is that there was no end to my suffering as long as I was God—and there was nothing I could do about any creature's suffering as long as I was God. Although I could identify with Guanshiyin, I wondered how she could bear to hear all the cries of the world. Even believers in Guanshiyin agree that those cries will never stop as long as there is a world of sentient beings. If Guanshiyin really hears all the cries of those who suffer, she, like God, must feel, at least sometimes, overwhelmed by all those voices of pain.

Will there not come a time when Guanshiyin will want to exit her condition of listening to the sorrow-filled sounds of all sentient beings? Her aspiration is that one day she will actually lead the last suffering sentient being into nirvana, at which time she too will end her sorrow. But can this day ever come for this bodhisattva of infinite compassion since, on the Buddhist view, worlds come and go forever (an early version of Big Bounce cosmology)—thus, sentient life and suffering will never end? To be fair, those who pray to Guanshiyin may find some relief from their suffering to the extent they believe she can intervene to help them. On my view she is just another mythical figure whose help is only imaginary. No bodhisattva, any more than any deity, can help anyone because the promise of transcendent help is always illusory. But of course, as we have seen, illusions can be consoling.

If for traditional Buddhism all forms of human embodiment bring unacceptable suffering that can only be solved by liberation from all incarnations (rebirths), for God embodiment as a human being was, despite the suffering it involves, the only thing that could bring the Creator relief from eternal suffering. God would experience suffering as long as She remained God. Embodiment, although inevitably bringing with it both pain and death, was for me preferable to an eternal life of impotent compassion and endless misery. The cries of the world became unbearable precisely because I, unlike the mythical Guanshiyin, was unable to respond to those cries: I had no soothing nectar to offer those who suffered.

I think traditional followers of Buddhism, like many of those who believe in God, desperately want permanent freedom from suffering, want a place of rest beyond this world. This is not something that has very much interested me, and very few liberal Jews I know. For me as a progressive Jew, the important thing is repair of this world that badly needs healing, living a truly ethical life, and appreciating ordinary things, indeed making everyday experiences holy.

12

Shekhinah's Human Mission

Against eternal injustice, human beings must assert justice.
And to protest against the universe of grief, humans must
create happiness.

—Albert Camus

I can say "amen" to your Jewish ethical ideal, and also the call to appreciate
ordinary things.

*Before we touch on ethical matters, I'm curious: What ordinary things
do you appreciate?*

I've come to enjoy walking, or often hobbling, around on this amazing
planet. Walking is a remarkable capacity that most ambulatory persons take
for granted. I took walking for granted during my first few months on earth.
Losing a leg brought me a sudden appreciation of what I had now lost. Then,
I adapted to my one-legged existence, and now consider my mode of movement normal, whether using crutches, prosthesis, or wheelchair. I prefer being bipedal. Like seeing, hearing, smelling, tasting, and touching—walking
upright should be appreciated as an extraordinary achievement, a product
of a long evolutionary process.

People should savor and make full use of the powers they have. On
the other hand, we need to be careful about treating people who lack one
of these so-called normal powers—for example, seeing or hearing or walking—as somehow lesser human beings, creatures to be pitied. A person can

have a meaningful life without the ability to walk. Still, those who can walk should feel gratitude that they have this amazing power.

As you know, appreciation of the ordinary is built into Jewish daily prayer life. In the morning many religious Jews recite a list of Hebrew blessings called Nisim B'chol Yom: Daily Wonders. *The daily wonders include breathing, seeing, standing, walking, excreting, dressing, freedom of movement, and other everyday activities we tend to take for granted. This is prayer as an expression of gratitude. According to the great Jewish philosopher and civil rights activist Abraham Joshua Heschel, we should inculcate in ourselves an attitude of "radical amazement" about ordinary activities and abilities. I glory in these everyday things, especially in my old age. When I wake up in the morning, I try to follow the advice of Heschel: to take nothing for granted and see even the most ordinary things as phenomenal. My first words in the morning, even before I open my eyes, are the first words from the Jewish morning prayer script*—Modeh ani: *I am thankful. This blessing expresses thankfulness that one is alive another day.*

I try not to take for granted the privilege of being a human being. I daily celebrate that I now have the power to act, something I can use, joining with fellow human beings, to literally change the world—again, a capacity I lacked as God. Never take for granted any power you have to bring about change, no matter how limited. The powerlessness of God—something Bonhoeffer, awaiting execution, seemed to celebrate for humanity's sake— was in fact for me, when I was God, nothing to celebrate. On the contrary, it was a curse.

Why then didn't you abandon heaven earlier? Apparently you found your life as God unbearable for a long time.

Your question about why I waited so long is a good one, and sometimes I now wonder why I didn't make my exit sooner. At first, I thought that if I waited a bit longer, things would improve. Given the freedom of human beings and their ability to change themselves, I could not rule out, in an earlier period, the possibility of human self-transformation. People are capable of transcendent acts of altruism and self-sacrifice. That gave me false hope.

Human beings can, theoretically, change course, indeed reverse course, and engage in acts that lead to the Jewish project you just mentioned: *tikkun olam*, the healing of the world. I had, however, become concerned that human beings might not change course soon enough. The hope I held out was drying up. I was becoming a witness to the destruction of countless forms of life on earth and ultimately human self-destruction. The rate of climate collapse had become alarming. Either humans would destroy the natural eco-foundation of their very lives through their degradation of the planet or they would destroy themselves and much of life on earth with weapons of mass destruction. I saw the production of nuclear weapons proceeding apace and new biological and chemical arsenals being produced at an equally alarming rate, in secret compared to nuclear explosives.

So three years ago I recognized that there was still a possibility of preventing disaster, but I could do nothing to help as long as I was literally removed from the world. Only by becoming a flesh-and-blood person, only by entering the world, would I be able to make any difference. Being idealistic and perhaps naïve, I thought that if I became a human being, I could join a successful fight for global justice and the work needed to repair a damaged planet, alongside like-minded persons.

To answer your original question: Because of the cumulative effect of so much senseless human and animal suffering—and the daily destruction of the earth—I reached my breaking point. I could no longer endure being a helpless bystander. Why this didn't happen earlier I can't say. I know it was grandiose of me to think that by becoming a human being I could actually help save the world, but that's what I believed.

You seem to have, if you don't mind my saying so, a messianic complex. Clearly, you suffer from delusions of grandeur, in more ways than one.

Maybe I do have such a complex. In a sense I'm truly a God-sent messiah. To be more accurate, my message is that we must all become messiahs. Actually, after I entered the world, there was an early period during which I had to work on myself, to engage in what Jews call *tikkun ha-nefesh*: the act of healing the self. I have to admit that there was a time when I was tempted to destroy my newly acquired human life. That would have been a second suicide. I lost eternity, but, as I said, I thought I could actually make a significant difference in this world. Before I knew it, after arriving on earth, I found myself experiencing something very human: in the face of all the suffering in the world and the permanent damage humans inflicted on the earth that suddenly seemed to me beyond repair, I experienced hopelessness and a deepening depression. The brain I acquired had a disposition, like too many human brains, to clinical depression if the right triggers are there.

Remember, I took up residence in the brain of "Esther" of Sierra Leone: although the memories that occupy her brain are God's, not Esther's, indeed displacing hers, still my physical brain, with its particular chemistry, is Esther's, a person who had for years struggled with dark moods. I of course knew this when I appropriated her body, but I thought I could transcend this. Not so. My loss of a leg probably contributed to my fall into psychological darkness—as did the constant throbbing pain in my stump, and sometimes even pain in the missing parts of my leg, in my missing knee, ankle, and foot; this is called phantom pain. Fortunately, I had the good sense, before it was too late, to stop taking addictive painkillers. Or I might have been another death by fatal overdose.

The healing of the stump after the amputation was taking a long time. My mobility as a human being was suddenly impaired. I also suffered PTSD, with flashbacks, nightmares, and severe anxiety from the trauma of being hit by a car. And of course I felt stupid for stepping in front of traffic, felt like an idiot. In addition, I was feeling overwhelmed by the good I wanted to do in a limited amount of time. So, it looked like I would also probably fail as a human being.

I couldn't help feeling that I'd failed as the Creator, as God. I of course couldn't tell my psychiatrist this. She would've thought I was crazy! Fortunately, these days, when you suffer from clinical depression you don't have to talk to psychiatrists for any length of time about what you feel is making you miserable. They know that a person's fall into darkness is probably chemically triggered and therefore needs to be chemically corrected. It was only because of a health care plan provided by the Bayou Women's Center that I could afford professional help. Even an ex-deity needs health insurance. Without a psychiatrist, I, given my deep depression and constant suicidal ideation, would probably have taken my life. I wasn't sleeping and lost my appetite and became physically weaker and more defeated day by day. Wheelchair bound, my depression was not helped by an ill-fitting prosthesis and my failure to find one that I could use for over thirty minutes, after which the pain was too much to bear. It took a while for my psychiatrist to find the right combination of medications to bring me out of my suicidal condition. Finally, she hit upon antidepressants—two different ones—that worked.

So I got lucky and finally recovered from what my doctor called a "major depressive disorder." Although I felt suicidal most of the time during my struggle with depression, I could still dimly see that life would be preferable to death, and so convinced myself, despite my doubts, to take what turned out to be life-saving medications. Many people aren't so fortunate: they never recover and eventually kill themselves, something I witnessed all too frequently when I was God. It also helped that crutches provided the walking mobility I needed when, because of the pain, I was unable to use my artificial leg and didn't want to use a wheelchair. The crutches gave me another option for traveling upright: I'm sure you've noticed the ease and speed with which I move with them.

Yes, very impressive. I'm glad you didn't take your life.

Keep in mind that the being I originally wanted to kill was God, the Creator Who could no longer abide Her powerlessness. Divine suicide, the self-termination of my life as God, was my goal, not complete annihilation— because, after all, I did want to *live* as a human being. Having recovered my mental health, I no longer feel hopeless and impotent. In fact, I now feel more powerful than God, although that's not saying much. That I can now do something to reduce suffering in the world makes all the difference.

I of course had to face what most human beings face who are committed to changing the world: a choice of causes. And like most people, in order to eat I have to make a living. The job at the women's shelter provides me with a way to support myself while also giving me the opportunity to help women and children who have suffered trauma. As I've already said, such employment allows me to follow the Buddhist principle of right livelihood. And since I don't drive, I am lucky to have a fellow worker who lives in Sugar Land—which is why I reside here—to provide me a way to and from work. I pay half the fuel costs. So, as an ex-deity, I've had to learn how to deal with the practicalities of everyday life, including making enough money to pay for food, clothing, rent, and transportation. By the way, as you no doubt know, Sugar Land is considered part of the Greater Houston metropolitan area. I think of myself as a Houstonian.

I suppose Houston should be proud that an ex-deity chose to live here. What else do you plan to do? I don't mean to diminish the importance of your work at the women's shelter, but it seems you have a more ambitious agenda in mind. You have already mentioned your plans to enter field of medical research—once you are fraudulently credentialed.

I'm determined to do what I couldn't do as God. I have limited time. Since I cannot fight for all the causes I believe in, I've decided, in addition to, once credentialed, working on cures for multiple diseases, to spend my time on five other projects, all of which I consider God's work: the struggle against racism, work to promote equal respect for women, the fight for rights of the LGBPTTQQIA+2 community, work to halt the climate crisis, and the struggle to win justice for the disabled. So, I am a member of Black Lives Matter: Houston (its work is intersectional and inclusive); Pride Houston, Inc.; WatchHerWork (a Houston organization whose aim is to empower women in the workplace); the Houston branch of the Grassroots Global Justice Alliance (an organization committed to climate justice, gender justice, an end to war, and transition to a just economy); and the local chapter of Disability Rights Texas. I also recently joined the Houston chapter of Democratic Socialists of America as a way to fight locally for economic justice and more democracy in the workplace. So you should add that to my list.

Since I don't drive, I have to find transportation to meetings of these organizations, but I have made friends in each organization willing to go out of their way to give me a ride. Each night after I come home from work and grab some dinner, I'm usually off to a meeting of one of these groups, each of them action oriented. I may be spread thin, but it doesn't feel like it.

It feels good, after billions of years of idleness, to be able to actually work for justice: for example, by being part of Black Lives Matter. I wear this t-shirt to make a public statement.

Let me stop you so I can raise a question about a recent statement Black Lives Matter made about Israel and Palestinians in which it used such words as "genocide" and "apartheid" to describe Israel's actions against Palestinians. I am not uncritical of Israel, but I think the language is extreme. I am generally sympathetic to Black Lives Matter, but perhaps the organization should concentrate on fighting injustice against Blacks rather than venturing into international matters.

Without getting into a debate with you about the legitimate scope of the work of Black Lives Matter—and I agree genocide is too strong a word, even if Israel's abuse of Palestinians is a serious problem just as much as is Hamas's terrorist attacks on Israeli civilians—let me say something about the origin of and distinctive nature of this movement. What's impressive about Black Lives Matter is that it represents, to quote African American historian and social activist Barbara Ransby, "democracy in action." It embodies a twenty-first-century model of a racial justice movement. Its actions, according to Ransby, arise not from a top-down model in the style of a Martin Luther King, Jr. or a Malcolm X, charismatic, messiah-like figures, but instead solutions created by Blacks in their local communities.

Keep in mind that this movement was a response to police shootings of Black people; in many cases it was White policemen killing young Black men: think of Eric Garner, Sean Bell, Michael Brown, Alton Sterling, Philando Castile, and Stephon Clark. In 2013 three Black Female organizers—Alicia Garza, Patrisse Cullors, and Opal Tometi—created this Black-centered movement, originally a response to the acquittal of George Zimmerman, the murderer of Trayvon Martin. And we should add a young Black woman, Sandra Bland, who was arrested for assaulting an officer in Waller County, Texas, after a traffic stop, only to be found, three days after being arrested, hanged in her cell, suspiciously labeled a suicide. The killing of Blacks by the police is not something new, not a recent phenomenon.

Black families mourning the killing of a son by police has been going on for a long time, far too long. Audre Lorde published a poem in 1973 called "Power" that was a response to a White policeman's murder of a ten-year-old Black Boy. Lorde writes that after the policeman shot the boy, he said, "Die you little motherfucker." She points out that there are tapes to prove the policeman said this, and that he also said that he didn't notice the victim was a child, only that he was Black. The policeman was acquitted.

Lorde wrote the poem to express her rage, an emotion that was an appropriate response to this racist murder of a Black Child. She was often criticized for being an Angry Black Woman, but sometimes that is what is needed if one wants to be heard when speaking against repeated acts of lethal violence directed against Black Human Beings, namely to openly express one's rage against murderous racism. Here we are, close to half a century later, dealing with the same tragedy and abuse of police power. Whatever its flaws, Black Lives Matter is a movement that brings attention to, and fights against, racial injustice, activating people at a local community level. Whether police killing Blacks is a result of outright racism or implicit bias (*unconscious racism*) doesn't really matter. Black Lives Matter was and is a rational reaction to the repeated killing of unarmed Black Men by the police, with the police often acquitted. Anything I can do to contribute to the diminution of this injustice—which is really a manifestation of the devaluation of Black Lives—will make my life worth living.

Are police always in the wrong?

I'm acutely aware that police are sometimes unfairly charged with injustice and that police are feeling increasingly under unfair scrutiny by residents of Black communities—their every move recorded on the cameras of cell phones. And many who police our streets are also feeling physically threatened, in some places targeted for death by those, Whites as well as Blacks, who hate them. This attack on the police includes cops who are Persons of Color. I know that police these days, when they answer certain 911 calls, experience a lot of stress and anxiety. Police who are doing their jobs responsibly—that's most of them—deserve justice and respect. On some weekends, I, following the example of LA, teach meditation to receptive local Sugar Land police officers; there is evidence that, if practiced regularly, meditation can reduce both stress and aggressiveness. The number of police who attend these sessions has grown significantly.

Also, as part of a diversity training class I volunteered to teach, I, very gently, attempt to communicate to these mostly White officers what it is like to be Black in the United States. I also try to educate them about the racist history of Sugar Land, largely concealed until recently. I see this as my civic duty as a resident of this thriving city on the Brazos River. It clearly is not part of the narrative city officials wanted to tell over the years about this growing, prosperous Houston suburb of ninety thousand. What they want people to know is that Sugar Land is the single most ethnically diverse county in the nation, was voted one of the best places to live in America, and has been praised for its top-tier public education. I always remind a new group of officers that it's important to know how this city got its name. It was once the center of sugarcane plantations whose profits were made possible by the ruthless exploitation of the labor of enslaved Blacks who cut sugarcane stalks. At least 70 percent of the roughly twelve million

Blacks who were forcibly brought from Africa to the Americas on slave ships were destined for sugar colonies.

I also inform them that with Emancipation and the abolition of slavery, the sugar industry in Sugar Town, after briefly going under because it lost slave laborers, solved its crisis by leasing prisoners to harvest the cane. Sadly, the prisoners supplied by the Texas prison system were Blacks, including former slaves. Southern state legislatures, including Texas, after the abolition of slavery, quickly passed "Black Codes"—new laws that applied only to Black People. These laws subjected Black Males to criminal prosecution for minor offenses such as loitering, not carrying proof of employment, flirting with a White Woman, petty theft, walking alongside railroad tracks, or vagrancy. Upon conviction for one of these minor offences, African American Men were then given felony-level sentences. This virtual re-enslavement of Blacks was made possible because Texas penal authorities were able to exploit a loophole in the Thirteenth Amendment, ratified in 1865, that outlawed slavery. The loophole: the enslavement of felons is constitutionally permissible. These convict-laborers, newly enslaved Blacks, also worked on railways, in mines, and constructed the capitol building in Austin. Those who purchased prison labor paid minimal fees. This new penal-based form of slavery endured from 1878 to 1911.

The working conditions for Blacks who harvested sugarcane, under the brutal convict-leasing system that proliferated across the South in the late nineteenth and early twentieth centuries, were actually worse than they were under slavery. Many Blacks were literally worked to death, dying from dehydration and heat stroke in temperatures reaching over one hundred degrees, or dying from dangerous working conditions, conditions so terrible that prisoners called the Sugar Town plantation on which they labored, namely the Imperial State Prison Farm (the beginning of the Imperial Sugar Co.), the "Hellhole on the Brazos." And those who leased Black prisoners didn't have any incentive to keep their workers alive—unlike slave owners, who saw Blacks as an investment—because, when a prisoner died on a prison farm, the sugarcane producer could get a quick replacement from the prison system.

Sugar Land police officers became, I think, fascinated with me, and really didn't know what to make of me when I told them that there would be a sobering discovery on a construction site for a new vocational school in Sugar Land: namely that the remains of ninety-four bodies of Males and one body of a Female, all African Americans, would be discovered in the near future. I told them that the bones of these individuals would be found in unmarked decaying pine coffins, two to five feet beneath the soil. I even specified the general build of these leased convicts, with age and height ranges.

I made this prediction before construction crews during February of 2018 found human bones jutting out where they were about to build. The site was the land of the old Imperial State Prison Farm: the "Hellhole on the Brazos." The bodies were later confirmed to be prisoners leased for sugarcane work: skeletal remains of African American individuals, as young as fourteen and as old as seventy, most muscularly built, many with misshapen bones that suggested repetitive wear through hard labor, heights ranging from five feet two inches to six feet two inches, everything I had predicted. The depth at which the bodies were buried, which I had predicted, also proved true—of course.

When the gruesome discovery was finally made, the officers asked me how I could have possibly known this. Of course, before beginning construction on the school, there had been historians and bioarchaeologists who recommended careful fieldwork, prior to school construction, because they had good reason to believe this was a burial site for prison laborers. But no one predicted there would be exactly ninety-five unmarked pine coffins and the other details I provided. I told the officers that I was there when the bodies were buried, and left it at that. Some laughed nervously, others just seemed baffled. Some may have thought, because I identified as a Buddhist, that I was claiming to have seen this during an earlier incarnation. It was not the last time I would reveal something to them that no else knew, taking advantage of divine memory. These recollections can be a useful tool for winning respect and impressing people, making them pay attention and listen to you. Readers can verify for themselves the discovery of these graves in Sugar Land. Maybe you'll take this as further evidence of my claim about who I was.

I would have to know more. In any event, what happened to the remains?

I'm a member of a group of concerned citizens led by a wonderfully aggressive African American, Reginald Moore—former prison guard, prison reform advocate, and amateur prison historian who had long believed the land in question would prove to be a burial ground. We requested that the gravesite be memorialized on the spot where the bones were found. Many city officials want to move the remains to a nearby cemetery and not bring attention to this shameful period of Sugar Land history. Following Reginald's lead, some of us will continue to be silence breakers until we get our way.

Silence breakers about Sugar Land's history of ruthlessly exploiting Black labor? Since you claim that the Creator now occupies your body, Black history is now your personal history.

Yes. I'm a human being with very dark pigment who personally knows why we must keep saying that "Black Lives Matter." To reiterate: I see the world differently now that I am encased in Black Skin. I'm not sure I can any longer be completely impartial or objective. And of course, to repeat something else I've also conceded: "Black" is as much social construct as "Jew." Still, when you feel hostility directed at you because your skin is very dark, it doesn't matter whether race is a construct or a reality: bigots don't make this distinction. I'm now defined by multiple disrespected identities. My perspective is that of someone labeled a "crip dyke nigger," someone who finds herself targeted by individuals who hate one or more of her perceived identities. I could have died earlier today simply because of how I look.

I also know what it feels like to be devalued simply because I'm a Woman, not only by White Men but also by Black Men whose consciousness has absorbed rap lyrics that reduce Women to "hoes and bitches." I see evidence of misogyny everywhere every day. I am fortunate to be able to work at a women's shelter, to be able daily to provide support for women who have suffered verbal and physical abuse, and, in some cases, near-death experiences. Those who survive beatings and verbal abuse often are left with little or no sense of self-worth. Whatever I can do to help ease the pain of these women and help them to rebuild their lives and gain a new sense of self-respect I see as God's work. Some theologies see human beings as the hands of God—and rightly so.

Since God literally had no hands, human beings alone have always been the necessary means for realizing sacred values such as justice and compassion. Some people perceive me, hobbling on one leg, as partially disabled. The truth is that as God I was completely disabled, absolutely paralyzed. Human beings can at their best be hands of goodness—instruments of constructive social change. Work on behalf of those who are disenfranchised, marginalized, and abused—not only Women and People of Color, but also Individuals within the Queer Community, and Persons with Disabilities—is the practice of true holiness, as opposed to praying, worshiping, reading scripture, attending a religious service, or seeking to submissively do God's will, to do whatever one believes God commands. I know I've said this before, but it bears repeating.

Of course the cause of saving the planet should not be forgotten, another holy task. Of all the projects I'm working on, it appears to me that nothing else will matter if we don't stop the destruction of the earth. So I'm trying to figure out what contribution I can make to help repair the planet and what tasks I can individually perform to lessen the damage being done daily. This of course needs to be a mass movement informed by science. My own efforts in this area are works in progress. Given that I created the conditions necessary for the emergence of life in first place, I of course feel a special responsibility to save not only life on the planet but also, as already mentioned, to prevent further destruction of biodiversity, something beautiful that was a long time in the making. I sometimes have to fight hopelessness about this, but I know, on most days, that defeatism is a luxury we can't afford.

The Grassroots Global Justice Alliance connects the movement to stop climate change with the needs of those who are impoverished. My focus now, after Hurricane Harvey, a disaster made worse by climate change, is to help protect low-income Houston communities that are close to refineries, chemical storage facilities, and industrial zones because flooding can spread toxic chemicals to these vulnerable populations.

I'm also a volunteer at Texas Environmental Justice Advocacy Services, a member of GJA and the oldest environmental justice organization in Houston. Although not a lawyer, it helps that I perfectly know the law. I understand the applicable environmental laws and regulations and work with the lawyers in this organization to make sure they're enforced. When those with law degrees puzzle over my expertise in environmental law, I lie and say I specialized in this at the University of Texas Law School, leaving them with the impression I had to drop out for financial reasons. Given Trump's anti-environmental agenda, this kind of work has become much more challenging.

Aren't you exhausted most of the time? Don't you feel overwhelmed?

I've learned to cultivate moments of peace in quiet places where I can withdraw from the world, a luxury I never had as God. I practice meditation daily, drawing insights from Buddhism. When I meditate I have to use a chair or a raised seat because my missing leg makes any floor sitting position uncomfortable and often painful. Meditation can bring me at least momentary mental peace. I am able, temporarily, to block out the world by, during meditation, following the advice of tenth-century Indian master Tilopa:

> Let go of the past.
> Let go of the future.
> Let go of what is happening in the present.
> Don't try to figure anything out.
> Don't try to make something happen.
> Just rest, relax this moment, just rest.

The Vietnamese Buddhist Temple in Sugar Land I mentioned earlier is one of my places of retreat, especially when there isn't a crowd. Outside the temple there is a long white beautiful statue of the Buddha in a reclining position, the so-called death pose. On a weekend day, especially if the weather is nice, I meditate, sitting on a bench in front of this figure, relaxing while being reminded of my mortality. Because of prejudice I often encounter in WWBC groups, I have created an all-Black Female/Feminist Sangha in Sugar Land: after a twenty-minute period of meditation, we discuss how the problems of race and gender impact our daily lives. We find this very therapeutic. The group meets in my apartment one evening a week; otherwise I meditate nightly right before going to sleep. Throughout the day I also practice deep breathing exercises to reduce the stress of my job; working with abused women and their often equally traumatized children takes its toll.

So these are practices that bring you some calm and peace? Anything else?

Yes. You'll appreciate this. I also observe a Sabbath. My Sabbath, when I am able to fully observe it, is more than a day: it is forty-eight hours, Friday at sundown to Sunday at sundown. This is a time set aside for the cultivation of peace of mind, joy, pleasure, rest, recovery, being with friends, and withdrawal from the world of suffering. As God, I could never, once complex sentient life emerged, enjoy even one peaceful Sabbath because I could never turn away or escape from all the suffering on earth: never a moment when I was not a witness to all the pain in the world.

So, when I was God, I could not observe a Sabbath of complete peace. Now, as a human being, I can I turn off the news, not look at newspapers, not use my smart phone, TV, or laptop. Sometimes I seek out friends for conversation about peaceful topics at their place or mine—or simply hangout alone here at Starbucks, thinking only pleasant things while I just sip tea. The Sabbath was a brilliant Jewish invention. I wish I could take credit for it, but it was sages within the ancient Jewish community who came up with the idea and gave God all the credit. It was great gift to the world that too few human beings choose to enjoy.

Judaism was also wise in making the Sabbath a *mitzvah*, a commandment, a requirement. I am an ethical workaholic; so, I treat the Sabbath as a weekly necessity for my refreshment—a time when I don't allow myself even thoughts about work or what's wrong with the world. I strive during this period of time to ignore the troubles of the planet. I take a break from even thinking about the battered women I see during my workdays. Given all my commitments, I want to avoid burnout. I burned out as God: I don't want to burn out as a human being. I of course realize that there's little time to lose in a world of impermanence where life is fragile and short. But I also know that I, like most human beings, need time for rest, renewal, and recovery

So you give yourself a moral holiday as a way to experience some peace of mind?

Yes. And like other mortals, I also need sleep. Indeed, I achieve a measure of peace through sleep. Like most human beings, I need seven or eight hours to function efficiently. To repeat the truth of Psalm 121: as God, I never slumbered nor slept. I've come to appreciate this period of unconsciousness, a period of time that allows a nightly exit from the real world, often a wonderful way to escape all the seemingly endless bad news that can disturb us when we are fully awake. This is another advantage of being human: I can, during sleep, enjoy a period when I'm unaware of what's happening in the real world. I can take flight in a world of dreams, indeed a pleasant world of fantasy, where logic loses its hold on the mind—pleasant as long as I don't have nightmares. I do, however, sometimes have bad dreams, waking up in a cold sweat, from a nightmare during which I see all the horrors taking place on the planet, horrors that I can do nothing about. Then I rejoice as I wake up from the nightmare of being God! I wake up thankful I'm no longer the impotent Creator, the powerless Witness to suffering everywhere.

For recreation, I also do things with my body that are celebratory, things I could never do as God: joyful activities like dance that have nothing to do with acts of moral goodness. Yes, you might call these moral holiday activities. Nietzsche said that he could only believe in a God who danced. What an image! Maybe he was thinking of the Hindu deity Shiva who is sometimes pictured in a dancing pose. Shiva is described as *Nataraja*: the Lord of Dance. There is a well-known image of Shiva with one foot on the demon of ignorance and the other foot raised in a dynamic pose, his four arms outstretched, dancing within a ring of fire. This deity is sometimes depicted as the God of destruction, the destroyer of worlds.

Dance can of course represent something very different, namely a life-affirming act in which you try to defy gravity—if we can play with the double meaning of that term—by lifting your body into the air and by doing so also lifting your soul that may be weighed down by the troubles of the world. Sometimes, as Nicholas Kazantzakis's famous character Zorba the Greek puts it, reflecting on the death of his son, it is dancing and only dancing that can stop pain; he proclaims: "to dance is to live."

According to Hindu legend, another Hindu God, Krishna, the incarnation of the God Vishnu, described as the preserver of life, taught his followers how to dance for joy, even in the face of danger. According to Hindu legend, Krishna demonstrated this by dancing on one of the hundred and ten hoods of the giant poisonous snake Kaliya. When the people on the banks of the Yamuna River saw this, they too jumped on the hoods of Kaliya and danced ecstatically. Dance was once part of temple ritual in Hinduism just as it once was in the Temple in Jerusalem. The truth is that God could not dance. God lacked arms and legs—had no physical body. God couldn't move—was immobile.

I wonder, however, given your concern with a suffering planet, how you can justify dancing while so many creatures suffer on earth?

As a human being I have a different take on these things. As I've made clear, to stay sane, mentally healthy, it is best not to keep the suffering of the world on one's mind all the time. Remember what I said about my Sabbath and another reason I gave up my life as God: to be able to have moments of complete peace. But neither do I necessarily forget that there is suffering in the world, even in the midst of my happiest moments. Human beings are able to remember loss even when experiencing joy. You should know this. When Jews celebrate one of the most joyful events in a Jewish life, marriage, they don't deny there is heartbreak in the world. At the end the marriage ceremony, there is the ritual of breaking a glass.

One traditional interpretation of the groom's act of crushing a wine glass beneath his right foot is that this as a reminder of the destruction of the Temple in Jerusalem, an event that is a source of profound Jewish mourning. At our egalitarian temple, both the bride and groom break their own glasses.

The important point is that Jews recognize that at this most joyful time they need not be oblivious to suffering and loss. The happy union of the married couple can also symbolize the possibility of starting anew, of healing a broken world.

On another interpretation, the fragility of the glass reminds the couple and those gathered of the fragility of even the most intimate, loving relationships, something we saw that Leonard Cohen appreciated.

This ritual of taking a moment to remember loss does not, however, prevent a continuation of the marriage celebration. In fact, you can be sure that most Jews, after this brief pause to recognize the dark side of life, don't give it another thought for the rest of the wedding celebration! On the contrary, as you know, after breaking the glass, there is much joyful dancing at traditional Jewish weddings, joyful celebration uncontaminated by lingering memories of suffering. Even the most ethical of Jews take moral holidays, take moments to forget the sorrows of the world. At weddings, momentarily forgetting the worries of the world, Jews dance and enjoy the pleasure of wine and food in the company of friends and relatives.

You said that you dance.

Remember, despite Hindu mythology, a God cannot dance. It was, to be honest, a selfish reason that I wanted to enter the world bipedal. One of the first things I did when I could finally afford a place to live was to dance privately in my small one-bedroom apartment. So as not to disturb my neighbors, I put in earbuds as I move quietly on the carpet in my living room. I dance daily, moving to a variety of music. Last night it was SZA's "Drew Barrymore," Lady Gaga's "Just Dance," Beyonce's "Halo," Katy

Perry's "Power," Kendrick Lamar's "Love," Nicki Minaj's "The Night Is Still Young," Kaskade's "4 AM," Shakira's "Waka Waka," and Janelle Monae's "Americans"—to give you a sense of some of the music I dance to. I try to deeply feel the music and then create dance moves that reflect the mood of a particular song. Sometimes, when I want a demanding workout, I choose music with an especially fast tempo, with very high beats per minute, music that can lift my mood while working my lungs. After I lost my leg, a blow to my dreams, I was wondering whether I would be able to continue dancing.

Bipedal human beings should never take for granted their capacity to dance on two legs, no matter how unskilled they may be. When I'm ready to dance these days, I often put on my prosthetic leg. I can wear it for about thirty minutes before I feel discomfort and then, as I've said, if I continue, I experience unbearable pain in my stump. I do sometimes dance with crutches and at other times move my wheelchair to music, but the prosthesis enables me to have the advantage of two legs. As God I found dance another extraordinary human invention, something I vaguely anticipated but again was surprised that it could take so many amazingly different forms. As God on high I envied human dancers. That's why I looked forward to entering the world with two legs.

Don't you feel at least some guilt dancing while there are people you could spend time helping? And such a long Sabbath! After all, you left heaven so you could act in the world to relieve suffering. This time could be used to work for one of your causes, maybe even add another one.

You seem unwilling to let that go. (*She suddenly smiles and laughs.*) Jews historically have always been good at cultivating guilt and encouraging guilt feelings. There is even the story of a rabbi who believed that all the world's troubles were caused by his own sins. Of course, as God, I could easily identify with him. I can justify dance as aerobic exercise that I need to do to stay physically healthy, to keep my heart and lungs functioning as they should. The same with my long Sabbath: I have convinced myself that I need the renewal my Sabbath brings. I probably do indulge in rationalization, part of what it means to be human. Also, keep in mind that I'm no longer God: you need to hold me to a lower moral standard. I'm only human.

Moral holidays are permissible and helpful for human refreshment. As God, although unable to act, I could never take a moral holiday. I always felt guilty because I could do nothing to help those I created who were in dire straits. I felt responsible for every creature's pain and misery because I brought them into existence—or at least created the conditions necessary for their emergence. Now, I, more often than not, dance without guilt just as I observe my Sabbath without guilt. Remember: I left heaven not only to make a difference in the world, but, to be completely truthful, also to find periodic relief from suffering and maybe even to experience pure joy. Buddhist meditation, something that enables me to truly rest my mind on the Sabbath, has taught me how to stay focused on whatever I'm doing—for example, dancing, without distracting thoughts or feelings, without, for example, worrying about the fate of the world.

Did Jesus ever dance? If he did, would his followers have said that it was wrong to do so while so many were suffering around him, people he might heal, and while so many needed to hear the good news? According to the Gospel of John (2:1–12), there was a wedding at Cana attended by Jesus, his mother, and disciples where, when liquid fruit of the vine ran out, Jesus turned water into wine. Wine, as you know well but many readers may not, is a symbol of joy in Judaism and in Jesus' day was consumed heavily at weddings. We can imagine that Jesus consumed some of the wine he miraculously made available. After all, he had a reputation as drunkard—undeserved—but the truth is that he did enjoy drink. And food: he also had a reputation as a glutton, but wasn't.

The Gospels of Luke (7:34) and Matthew (11:19) do suggest that Jesus found pleasure in eating and drinking. Jesus, like most of his fellow Jews, enjoyed these sensual pleasures, but, I assure you, never ate and drank to excess. Did he also enjoy dancing? Did Jesus ever dance at weddings? No, and no Gospel reports that he did. At the Cana wedding, if we listen carefully to the tone of his voice in this text in the Gospel of John, he seems out of sorts and is a bit short and impatient with his mother. Despite the festive occasion, he seems to be in a sour mood. Maybe he envied the husband-to-be, wishing for himself a normal Jewish life, including marriage and a family. Because he was Jewish and only human, that was tempting to him. Later, I will say more about this when I discuss Nicholas Kazantzakis's insightful novel, *The Last Temptation of Christ*.

What I find inspiring about the Jesus of the Gospels are those moments he encourages his listeners to practice what Christians call *agape*: a love that is completely generous, expecting nothing in return, a love so generous it is even directed towards one's enemies, toward those who abuse and mistreat one, even toward those who crucify one. Jesus is quoted as saying from the cross: "Father forgive them, for they know not what they do." This is something I am trying to do after the two young White Nationalists attempted to kill me this morning with their truck—namely forgive them because they, at a deep level, truly lack knowledge of the harm they do. I should be able to forgive these young, confused men bent on my death: they lead ignorant and poisoned lives from which they need to recover. Maybe because it was so recent, I'm not there yet.

As a human being, I'm having a difficult time practicing this kind of love. Practicing *agape* means humanizing, and even having compassion for, those who hate and demonize you, those who you in return are tempted to demonize and hate. *Agape* is a form of love that is given regardless of circumstances, the behavior of the other, or whether it is reciprocated; it is a genuinely transcendent love. Jesus recognized the toxic nature of unforgiving hate and the healing power of forgiving love. So Jesus in fact revealed the meaning of truly divine love. It was this idea of love, inspired by the life of Jesus, that motivated the strategy of nonviolent, loving resistance practiced by Mahatma Gandhi and Martin Luther King, Jr.

Let me return for the moment to the idea of hell as eternal pain that so many fundamentalist Christians don't blink an eye at while also proclaiming that Jesus embodied perfect love. The preaching of forgiving, *agape* love is inconsistent with the threat of hell that some Gospel writers falsely put in Jesus' mouth. When Nietzsche tells us, mocking Dante, that over the gate leading to hell are the words "I too was created by eternal love," he is of course being sarcastic and ironic, suggesting an obvious contradiction in any form of Christianity that affirms both *agape* and eternal torture. *Agape love* is what I as God felt toward the world, and I could have never ever, even if I had possessed the power, sentenced any creature to endless pain. Neither did I create an otherworldly paradise.

What I profoundly wanted, to borrow the title of another Leonard Cohen song, was for everyone "to dance me to the end of love." Dance to the beauty of music and love in an all-too-brief life. As you probably know, Jim, this song was inspired by the Holocaust. Cohen discovered that at certain death camps there was, by a crematory, a string quartet made up of inmates who performed while their fellow inmates were being incinerated in ovens. And these performers too would of course eventually, after being gassed, be thrown into a furnace. This is what he means about dancing to beauty with a burning violin.

13

The End of Divine Loneliness

Cultivating Friendship and Seeking Erotic Love

Do you think I Who have been alone from all eternity am really happy?

—A PARAPHRASE OF THE VOICE OF GOD
IN JOHN MILTON'S *PARADISE LOST*

Can I buy you a cup of coffee? We probably shouldn't continue to occupy a table without purchasing something else. Maybe tea? I need to use the bathroom.

Thank you, herbal tea, any kind, nothing in it.

(At least I didn't wet my pants during our long conversation. Incontinence can be one of the embarrassing humiliations of old age. That's why I've started wearing Depend for Men: adult diapers. It took me a while to get over the embarrassment of having to buy them. In a few weeks I'll get an implant that will allow me to use an electric current to restore control of urination. As I slowly emptied an all-too-full bladder, I tried to process Shekhinah's tale. On the one hand, it made perfect sense to me, in terms of my own experimental theology. I have to admit, however, that when I thought about the idea of a God limited in power—not only a God who doesn't cause cancer but also a God who can't cure it—it never occurred to me to conclude that such a God would find the suffering of sentient creatures so overwhelming that She could and would commit suicide. Incarnation meant for Shekhinah both the death

of God and the beginning of her human life, a life that, if one believed her, included divine memories that would ultimately disappear.

I didn't know what to make of Shekhinah. Was she an amazing actress that someone put up to playing this bizarre role, maybe to toy with me, to have me confront a person who mouthed many of the things I had been writing and lecturing about for decades, while also giving this theology a surprising Nietzschean twist? But Shehkhinah knew too much to be just an actress, even an exceptional one who was also a quick study in philosophy and theology and music and literature and cosmology. She did not seem to be following a memorized script. On top of all this, she appeared to be truly a master of languages and speech patterns, including mine, having what one might be tempted to call a transcendent ability. Could I possibly be thinking she might be who she said she was?! I said to myself: of course not. I wasn't a fool. I was, at the time, feeling both puzzled and curious.

As I was returning to the table, I saw Shekhinah in a far corner having a lively conversation with what I assumed was a Black friend whose gender was unclear. I couldn't believe the number of expletives both she and this person were uttering. I guess she was speaking his/her language, just as she spoke mine when we conversed. I was never comfortable with such language, even though I know many of my contemporaries use it. Maybe that makes me a linguistic conservative. So be it. When Shekhinah saw me, she returned to our table. Our conversation took a different turn when I showed up with her tea and my coffee. Since Shekhinah referred to her friend as "they," I assumed the person identified as Non-binary.)

Tell me about your wife. (Wouldn't she, if really a former deity, already know the answer? Of course three years had passed since she, supposedly, had direct knowledge of my wife's condition.)

A leader in the Houston business community, she was a brilliant executive. Beth had been president of an eco-friendly construction company, Southern Green Builders. Although Houston has its share of climate deniers and environmentally indifferent people, it also, as you must know, has become an increasingly environmentally conscious city, moving progressively in a green direction. According to the New York Times—and I would imagine that when you were God, despite the disdain for the newspaper at Fox News and by Trump, you must have thought highly of it—well, according to the Times, the municipality of Houston relies more on renewable energy than any other big city in America and has more green space, relative to paved, than New York. In any event, Beth created SGB and made it financially successful. She retired in in 2010 and became a kind of ceremonial chairwoman of the board until Parkinson's did its job on her mind and body. We celebrated fifty years of marriage last year. Now, I spend a lot of time going over and over with her

*what day it is, telling her repeatedly it is Sunday or Monday or whenever, and
what is planned for the day, something that is on a calendar right in front of
her. I finally purchased a device that shows the hour, day, date, and year in big,
well-lit letters. I placed it by her bed. She often forgets to look at it.*

*Still, every Friday night we watch a movie together as we have done for
half a century. We no longer go the cinema: all films are viewed at home. She
is still able to enjoy and understand most movies; if, however, the plot is a bit
complicated, I may have to explain it—more than once. She can usually then
follow the story. Her challenge is a short-term memory deficit that makes it
difficult for her to remember what I just said. On the other hand, she can
retrieve from her memory the color of the wallpaper in our first house where
we lived forty years ago and the first words of our daughter and only child who
is now forty-one. What has disappeared from my memory remains in hers. So,
we have different memory abilities: you might call them complementary. Who
is to say one is better than the other? She helps me remember the distant past
and I help her recall something from a few minutes ago.*

As God, I envied loving couples: a shared life with another person
where there is mutual love and physical intimacy, a truly caring relationship. I know there are also times of disagreement, anger at the other, even,
at moments, feelings of hatred toward the one you supposedly love. Yet, if
it is a healthy relationship, there are also healing acts of forgiveness. There
is, above all, the give and take, positive and negative, of being together,
and good conversations, maybe even good arguments, with someone you
think you know well, but who may also still surprise you in what she says
and does. Also, there is someone to embrace physically, to touch and to be
touched by. As we saw in our discussion of Cohen's "Hallelujah," even failed
love relationships are worthy of our praise. For a perfectly loving God, being
alone is torture, especially if it is for eternity.

Are you saying God was lonely?

Yes. That turned out to be another price I had to pay for giving up my
existence as the Infinite, my status as the Absolute, the one and only Reality,
Being-Itself. As I mentioned already, once I gave up my life as the Infinite
One, I found myself dependent, for my own well-being, on what happened
in the world. And I could not have a person-to-person relationship with
any human being. This is something that most believers don't understand,
especially those who believe that God is a God of love Who seeks (and even
commands) reciprocation of divine love from human beings.

It never occurs to most believers that God can be lonely. Milton's *Paradise Lost,* taking its cue from *Genesis,* tells us that being alone is the first
thing God names as not good. Although Milton is too theologically cautious
to say so explicitly, he hints at the Creator's loneliness. More boldly, James

Weldon Johnson (1871–1938)—African American poet, song writer, and early NAACP activist—in his 1927 poem "The Creation" tells us that God made the world because He was lonely. So, on his view, God created the world because God could not stand to be alone. My claim is that God created the world not because God was lonely but as an act of loving generosity. The loneliness of God became a problem *after* creation.

One of the few to recognize this possibility, reflecting on it in a playful way, was a Pulitzer Prize–winning twentieth-century Black poet: Gwendolyn Brooks (1917–2000). In an early poem she shows an understanding of the problem, expressed in her poem "The Preacher Ruminates: Behind the Sermon," which begins with the line, "I think it must be lonely to be God." (*Shekhinah continues in a different voice which I can only assume mimics that of Brooks*):

> But who walks with Him?—dares to take His arm,
> To slap Him on the shoulder, tweak His ear,
> Buy Him a Coca-Cola or a beer,
> Poo-poo His politics. call Him a fool?
>
> Perhaps—who knows—He tires of looking down.
> Those eyes never lifted. Never straight.
> Perhaps sometimes He tires of being great.
> In solitude. Without a hand to hold.

Brooks is right in saying that God grew tired of being called great. In the words of the title of a book by an eloquent, brilliant, and acerbic atheist, Christopher Hitchens, may he rest in peace: *God Is Not Great*. Being called great made me feel even lonelier. In a prayer spoken by Moses, God is described as powerful and awesome. I wanted to shout at those who called on me to free them from poverty, oppression, war, and disease: "I cannot help you!" I found it refreshing that the Hebrew prophets Jeremiah and Daniel, who lived in times of terrible Jewish defeat and subjugation, would have none of this, omitting the words "powerful" and "awesome" from their prayers. You must know these texts in the Talmud, Yoma 69b.

Yes. Jeremiah, who prophesied during the destruction of the First Temple, wonders where the evidence is of God's awesomeness as invaders romp in and desecrate God's Temple. The prophet Daniel who lived during Israel's Babylonian Captivity—a second place of bondage for the Israelites after forced removal from their homeland that followed the First Temple's destruction, wonders: "Where is the proof of divine power as His children are being enslaved?"

Both had rightly concluded that, to borrow Rabbi David Hartman's language, "God hates lies," and so they refused, in all honesty, to affirm what seemed incredible to them: the awesomeness and omnipotence of God. To be called great is very isolating when You know You are not great in the sense that believers use that term: all-powerful and able to intervene to prevent death and destruction or correct injustice.

Brooks was right: the life of God was a lonely one. Maybe if I had had a divine partner, it would have been easier. That could be the origin of the doctrine of the Trinity, the attempt to see God as a community, having an eternal fulfilling love relationship before there were any creatures or any human beings. The Trinitarian God—the community of Father, Son, and Holy Spirit—is conceived as a perfectly loving threesome so in sync they are one. The three could be seen as united by their mutual love. We are to imagine three perfect co-eternal persons who forever dwell in perfect reciprocal love. Since the Trinity is conceived as an eternal relationship that preceded the world, on this view God was never lonely and never will be. The Trinitarian God never suffers from solitude.

In reality there was no partner: "Allah has no partner," as the Quran correctly says repeatedly to rebut the Trinitarian view of God. The Muslim God has no co-eternal partners and needs no other beings to feel complete. The Muslim Creator seems, however, a bit too content in His oneness. God in the Quran is depicted as the Compassionate Creator who never suffers loneliness. I beg to differ. Don't get me wrong: insofar as the God of Islam is described as a God Who is supremely merciful and calls upon believers to help those in need, I celebrate Islamic theology. To the extent that the God of Islam affirms human diversity, I have nothing but praise for Him. The Quran tells us that God could have made humankind one community—one race, one religion, and so forth—but decided to make us different in order that we might compete with each other in the performance of good deeds. This I liked.

Still, the Muslim God seems insecure about whether people will do His will, for example perform charitable acts, or even believe that He is the author of the Quran, if He does not threaten them with eternal fire. Throughout the Quran, if we take it literally, the Creator seems to want to put the fear of God in people to deter them from becoming disbelievers. My liberal Muslim friends interpret the eternal fire texts metaphorically. The same is true of my liberal Christian friends when they talk about how they construe references to hell in the New Testament. Of course my Jewish, Christian, and Muslim friends are all very liberal theologically since they all affirm me as Same-Gender-Loving Woman. I of course say nothing to them about my previous life and speak from the perspective of a secular Buddhist, which is what I truly am—now. So they are also okay with atheism and secularism as long these ideologies are genuinely ethical in orientation. Totalitarian Marxism would be an example of an unethical atheist ideology

But I digress. I simply wanted to point out that, contrary to popular theological thought, being God is—or rather was—a painfully lonely business.

Abraham Joshua Heschel—whom I have already mentioned, a great Jewish theologian as well as social activist—did recognize this. In fact, he wrote a book with the title God in Search of Man. *Heschel asserts that God suffers with us and needs human beings, needs our cooperation to save the world, and argues that there can be no redemption of the world without human action. By the way, as I'm sure you know, Heschel's term for the dimension of God in search of human beings is "Shekhinah," the name, as we have seen, Jewish mystics give for the dimension of God that dwells on earth.*

(*Again, Shekhinah shocks me with her knowledge of Jewish thinkers.*) But I'm not God dwelling on earth: I'm a mere mortal. Heschel does assert that God and human beings need each other, and God's presence is said to be the solution to human loneliness, thus the title of another of his books: *Man Is Not Alone.* Although he argues that God's presence is the cure for *human* loneliness, Heschel does not say that God is lonely: he writes that "it is as if God were unwilling to be alone"—the "as if" language suggests that he is not willing to literally assert that loneliness is a divine state. But he does correctly assert that God needs human beings to complete the work of redemption. On his view, God needs us to do the work of healing a broken world. Heschel doesn't, however, fully recognize divine loneliness as a source of divine suffering, not to mention God's growing inclination to become a human being in order to solve this problem. Maybe this is because Heschel believed that God and human beings could have a mutual loving relationship: that God could share divine suffering with others just as they could share their suffering with God.

As God, I couldn't share my suffering with anyone. I had no one to walk with, no one who could take my arm. As Brooks puts it: God lives "in solitude without a hand to hold." She provides an accurate image of a God who grows tired of looking down, eyes never lifted, who sees all who suffer and can never look away, dwelling in total solitude. I couldn't have a genuine intimate relationship with any human being, if one thinks of such a relationship as something open to mutuality, real dialogue, actual two-way communication, and the possibility of physical embrace.

There are of course those who thought I had a relationship with them, who thought I even talked to them, maybe even walked with them, and who thought I answered their prayers. Traditional Christians of course believe that God in the flesh literally walked and talked with human beings.

But those who think God in the person of Jesus once physically interacted with human beings are mistaken. Those who think God is somehow now in a loving relationship with them are self-deceived. I'm happy people have drawn strength from this illusion, felt my love in times of loss and suffering. As I've stated, there's something to be said for the power of religious illusions. I don't expect religious illusions to disappear, and maybe that's for the best. Many people need them.

My point is this: despite the widespread belief in the possibility of an I-Thou (interpersonal) relationship with God—to borrow Martin Buber's language—there was never such a relationship. I was completely alone, and divine solitude would have been eternal if I hadn't ended it. In exiting heaven, I escaped divine loneliness and now can be in a genuine relationship with others. I can now enjoy having someone actually take my arm, slap me on the shoulder, buy me a beer, and poo-poo my politics. As God, I longed for the possibility of a passionate loving relationship on earth, of living literally face-to-face with another person, sharing her bed. I was willing, in the spirit of Leonard Cohen, to say "Hallelujah"—using the term metaphorically of course—to even a failed love relationship. I too concluded with Tennyson that it would be better to have loved and lost than never to have loved at all—that is, never to have experienced a relationship of mutual love. I'm speaking of course of an intimate, affectionate, physical relationship. This was and is the appeal to me of Nicholas Kazantzakis's remarkable novel *The Last Temptation of Christ*.

Those who have read the novel know that, on Kazantzakis's imaginative account, Jesus' final temptation was to escape from the passion of the cross (suffering) in order to experience the passion of marriage (sexual love). While hanging on the cross, Jesus fantasizes, tempted by Satan, a different life: he dreams that he is married, with children. According to Kazantzakis's tale of Jesus' fantasy on the cross, after the death of Mary Magdalene, whom he loved, he comes to know Martha and Mary of Bethany, beautiful sisters who opened their home to Jesus. Mary's attraction to Jesus is more than spiritual, and Jesus begins to feel something more than spiritual love for her. Both experience a desire for a sexual, loving relationship. On the cross Jesus dreams that Mary and Martha persuade him that the way to truly please God is to have a home, marriage, and children. He dreams that he weds Mary, and then out of a sense of responsibility (more compassion than passion) also weds her sister. Jesus dreams that they have many children together, living out a normal human life.

A very Jewish dream.

Yes. But many conservative Christians were outraged by this novel—and Martin Scorsese's bad movie based on it. I am using the term "bad" cinematically, not morally. Was the depiction of Jesus as married to women with whom he had sex the source of the outrage? Maybe this is a scandal to traditional Christians who cannot believe that Jesus—who they contend was fully human—actually experienced something very human: sexual desire and a desire to experience marital love. If Jesus was truly human, then he felt not only hunger and thirst, but also sexual arousal. And his marriage to two women was not scandalous from an ancient Jewish perspective. Remember, in the Torah, the only version of divine law that Jesus knew, polygamy is not prohibited. In fact some of the most revered Jewish figures—Abraham, Jacob, David, and Solomon, for examples—had more than one wife. Most women during that time lived in a state of economic dependence on men, and polygamy could be practiced humanely and lovingly.

You're right. There is no prohibition of polygamy in the Torah. However, as far as the Talmud is concerned, of all the rabbis named in this multivolume work, not one is mentioned as living in a polygamous marriage and the general sentiment is against it. Over time monogamy became the norm for Jews. Marriage between one man and one woman came to be considered a holy, sacred framework for sexual relations. In Judaism, as already mentioned, the idea that there is something especially holy about a celibate life never got a foothold. Is marriage something you seek?

I hope some day to have an intimate, loving relationship, whether it's within the framework of marriage doesn't matter. A Same-Gender-Loving-relationship is something I aspire to have—without apology. To avoid loneliness, there is, however, much to be said for friendship and even conversations with strangers—face-to-face relationships—something I never experienced as God. As you know, the great French Jewish philosopher Emmanuel Levinas, already mentioned, viewed face-to-face encounters as the foundation of ethics.

Levinas is a philosopher I feel close to and not only because he was Jewish. I am attracted to his emphasis on intersubjective—or as you put it, face-to-face—experience, the encounter of two persons with each other, individuals who can look into each other's eyes. Yes, for Levinas the ethical arises from such human relationships. The gaze of the other generates an ethical imperative. Levinas dramatically asserts that the other's face implicitly communicates the command "Do not kill me!"

On my interpretation of Levinas, persons don't need literally to see each other (so we don't exclude those who are blind), but rather they must in some way be in each other's presence and able to communicate—and this experience of another's presence is what grounds the imperative not to kill the other. Perhaps we should call these person-to-person relationships. Levinas' "do not kill me" imperative can be taken figuratively to mean: Do not annihilate or negate my personhood, treat me as less than human, with contempt, or communicate the wish that I not exist—as, for example, some White Supremacists do when they are in the presence of a Black or a Jew.

This clearly is what the two young men wished when they saw me: they wished for my annihilation. They violated the imperative of a person-to-person encounter because they never truly saw me as a person like themselves. Intimate person-to-person relationships can embody very different forms of love. In addition to *apape* and *eros*, we should add, picking up on what I said a few minutes ago, that special form of love the ancient Greeks called *philia*, love between friends. I hope we can continue our relationship and achieve that. I've come to value friendship as my ultimate protection against loneliness, as the kind of relationship that provides me with ongoing, nourishing companionship, even if I fail at sexual love. I hope we can become friends.

It would be my great pleasure, in spite of my inability to believe your story. Friends in the deepest sense, on my understanding, are those who enjoy each other's company, want to be together frequently, share things in common, and develop over time great affection for each other. I agree: that is as high a form of love as any other.

I don't take for granted the experience I'm now having, one of being in conversation—even though I know it's sometimes closer to a monologue—with another human being whose mind I cannot read, who can surprise me with his words, who may even conceal from me what he is thinking and feeling. To be in a dialogical relationship with another person (something Martin Buber correctly saw as truly holy), to be in the presence of a human being who truly listens to you, and to whom you truly listen, is an extraordinary thing. This is not something most human beings think about or fully appreciate. As God, my loneliness was cosmic and the feeling of being separated from those I loved extremely painful. In most cases, when I make friends—of course again present company excluded—I have to hide who I was. But telling friends the whole truth is not always the wisest thing to do.

And, as I've said, I welcome the possibility of one day having an erotic, loving relationship. To experience sexual love would be a marvel for me. Many conservative Christians were outraged by *The Last Temptation of Christ* with its story of Jesus having, even if only in a dream, sex within a polygamous marriage: that was somehow a bridge too far. Although the idea of God in the flesh involved in a loving sexual relationship may strike many Christians as unholy, many Hindus, on the other hand, enjoy and celebrate a story of the passionate love that Krishna—who, as I have already mentioned, was asserted to be the God Vishnu in the flesh—and Radha, a milkmaid, felt for each other.

So uncharacteristic of a Jewish man, Jesus never enjoys one of the great pleasures Jews who are married are commanded to enjoy, especially on the Sabbath: sexual intercourse.

Some pious Christian types, maybe people who see sexual abstention as necessary for spiritual purity, may find the coupling of the name "Jesus" with the term "sexual desire" irreverent, maybe even obscene. Nicholas Kazantzakis well understood that Jesus the human being, the historical Jesus, actually felt sexual desire, experienced the need for sexual intimacy, and desired to have a family. Thus, despite its status as fiction, Kazantzakis's *The Last Temptation,* more accurately than the Gospels, describes the very erotic dreams of a fully human Jesus. Jesus, who was a hetero Jewish male, did in fact dream of having a loving, sexual relationship within marriage.

As you have already mentioned, there is a book in the Bible that poetically celebrates the sacred nature of the human longing for sexual love and sexual union: namely the Song of Songs.

Yes. Let's talk about this. The author of the Song of Songs, a woman (not, as tradition has it, Solomon!), understood the holy power of sensual love. The female who composed this sacred poem, Hannah, imagines the male lover saying:

> Your lips are like crimson thread,
> Your mouth is lovely
> Your breasts are like two fawns,
> Twins of a gazelle,
> Browsing among the lilies.
> You have captured my heart,
> My own, my bride,
> How sweet is your love,
> My own, my bride
> You have captured my heart.
> How sweet is your love,
> My own, my bride!
> How much more delightful your love than wine.

And the female lover reciprocates with equally erotic imagery:

> He is majestic as Lebanon,
> Stately as the cedars,
> His mouth is delicious
> And all of him is delightful
> Such is my beloved
> Such is my darling.

A female author actually makes sense. Some religious commentators have called the Song of Song the Holy of Holies—but only if they can interpret this erotic poem allegorically: according to Jewish tradition, the lovers are God and Israel; in Christianity, Christ and the Church. In fact, this, the most erotic book in the Bible, says nothing about God and, uncharacteristic of books of the Bible, a woman's voice predominates.

Yes. Song of Songs scholar Benjamin Segal, who has created a wonderfully annotated translation of this sacred poem—so your readers should consult it—points out that nearly two-thirds of the verses are in the voice of a woman, and even some of the words of the male lover seem to be spoken by her.

Also, this woman, the central character of the poem, says, "I am black and lovely." Female Black readers can read this with pride, even though this woman was not an African. The point is that she defiantly celebrates her dark skin in a society where this was a sign of being of a lower class, of a woman who works in the sun.

And this dark young female lover in the Song of Songs will not be deterred, either by threats or ridicule, in asserting her passion for the young man, a shepherd. The Song of Songs is sacred poetry that depicts the deep longing of two lovers who, despite the use of the word "bride," are not married. Maybe a marriage is in the offing, but the two lovers in this biblical poem are not marriage partners. The sexual relationship is clearly reciprocal and egalitarian: they are pursuing each other, yearning for each other, and seeking fulfillment in each other's embrace. The poem celebrates the human body in a tale of extraordinary—or maybe not so extraordinary—sexual love. I, like the woman of the Song of Songs, and the Jesus of *The Last Temptation of Christ*, long for a loving sensual relationship. What could be more human—and holy?

That, to be completely honest, is another reason I made my exit from heaven: not only to make a moral difference in the world by becoming a human being, and not only to be able to withdraw, from time to time, from hearing all the cries of the world, but also to experience the delightful intimacy of a loving relationship, something that was impossible for God. I wanted to end the loneliness I experienced in a transcendent realm where I had no partner, where there was no possibility of physically touching others or being touched by others. Even if Jesus never had sexual relations, we are told that he was physically touched by people and he touched others (in some cases, to heal them)—something apparently God the Father and God the Holy Spirit never experience.

I was willing to take on mortal flesh, to embrace a life that I knew would end in death, indeed annihilation, in order to experience all forms of intimate love—including *eros* and *philia*—that most people take for granted. I needed to lose my life as God, to give up eternity, in order to escape the solitude of divinity and live in close relationship with people on earth, a world I can now sensually enjoy and possibly help change. But even here on this planet, so crowded with people, there are countless lonely individuals who cry out silently, suffering profound solitude, people who resonate with the words of a song written and made famous by soul singer Sam Cooke. The title is "Mean Old World" because that's how it feels when you try to live all by yourself and have no one who truly loves you. Still, lonely human beings, unlike God, have the potential to end their loneliness, maybe by connecting to someone on social media, or simply by initiating a conversation with the next person they meet at the grocery store.

14

The Chosen One

Black, Female, and Same-Gender-Loving in Houston

Yes, this is Texas, but Houston bucks many rules and gay-hating trends seen in other Southern cities. As an openly bi writer and young woman in search of finding out more about myself and sexuality, I couldn't have hoped for a better city.

—DREA, "QUEER GIRL CITY GUIDE: HOUSTON"

(Suddenly there was a young man, maybe in his late twenties, standing at our table.)

May I interrupt? I overheard much of your conversation. My name is Dan Walker.

(Although he seemed friendly, I didn't know what to expect.)

Nice to meet you Dan. I'm James and this is Shekhinah. (We both shook his hand.)

I'm a reporter for the *Houston Chronicle*—the religion beat, actually the editor for a section of the paper that appears on Sundays called "Houston Belief & Religious News." I would like to have your permission to do something. I'm here to cover an international conference of Catholic philosophers and theologians that is being held at the Town Square Marriott in

Sugar Land. It starts tomorrow. The conference attendees include a long list of respected Catholic thinkers who will be talking about The Relevance of God in the Twenty-First Century. Ironic, huh? I'll be interviewing a professor of Catholic theology who is a keynote speaker at the conference. He would probably also be interested in your conversation. I came in here to grab some coffee and look over the program before the interview. I have a PhD in Religious Studies from the University of California at Santa Barbara, so I'll be able follow most of what is said at the conference. There were no tenure track teaching positions in my specialty when I received my doctorate. I needed to earn a living, and the *Chronicle* was looking for someone with a broad knowledge of religion. My areas of study were comparative religion and Christian theology.

Maybe that's why this place is so crowded. Perhaps it's packed with conference speakers and attendees. What kind of permission are you seeking?

I would like to report, in some fashion, on what I overheard. I'm asking permission to write a story about your exchange, with, if permissible, excerpts from your dialogue. I won't reveal your names or even provide a physical description of either of you, apart from gender, age, and race, if that's ok. Also, I will not disclose the location of your conversation, or include any information that could make it easy to track you down.

You can imagine how fascinating this would be to our readers, regardless of beliefs. The story will no doubt anger some, but that's what the letters to the editor page is for. So we will provide an opportunity there for at least some of those who want to vent—and readers are also free to express their views through the online *Chronicle*. Confession time: I took notes on your conversation. I use a version of Gregg Shorthand that's very accurate. (*He shows me a long yellow legal pad covered in what appears to me to be another language. I quickly look through his notes and cannot decipher much except for an occasional word or word fragment here and there, like "eschat" and "eros."*) The piece would have to be a very abbreviated, edited down version of your exchange. If you say no, I'll turn my notes over to you, James, to destroy. If you say yes, I will, if you wish, upon completion of a draft of the article with excerpts from your dialogue, let you read it for accuracy. Since I can see that you, James, are recording the conversation, you'll be able to send corrections, if needed. This is something I rarely, really almost never, do: let those I am reporting on read a draft of my article—for the purpose of making corrections before publication. I'm making an exception in this case.

(*Shekhinah smiled at the reporter.*) I have no reason to hide from the public what I've been saying. On the contrary, I'm happy to share this. I cannot, however, reveal who I am for fear of being targeted by haters who may

be able to discover where I live. Unfortunately, these days people who hate
your ideas or what you stand for often threaten to kill you, informing you
they know your address. Terrifying really. Are you ok with this article Jim?
    (I nodded yes and also smiled.)
    May I pull up a chair and sit down for a few minutes to clarify some
things. Then I'll leave you alone. (*We signaled approval. He pulled over the
chair from his nearby table.*) There is just a question or two I need answered
that was not covered in the Q and A I heard. It's possible of course I missed
something because I arrived a bit after you started your conversation or
couldn't hear what you said because of all the noise. Houstonians will want
to know, Shekhinah, why, of all places, you chose to "immigrate" here, if I
may borrow your language. And is there anything you want to say about
God's choice to incarnate as a Black Woman? I intend nothing racist or sexist by this question, but you can be sure that this will be a question on the
minds of our more conservative readers, those who in fact tend to think of
God as, no matter how absurd it may seem, a White Heterosexual Male, an
image that has not yet disappeared. It goes without saying, you must know,
that no reader will believe the story you have to tell, Shekhinah.
    (*Shekhinah smiled again at the reporter, conveying clearly that she was
a person with nothing to hide as long as it didn't threaten life or limb. She
would remain incognito while allowing her story to reach a large audience
since articles in the* Chronicle *are accessible all over the world. Maybe she was
not sure I would really share her story, put it on our website and later publish
it in book form. In any event, she seemed very open to any questions Dan
had and to the publication of her answers. So, before this book was published,*
Houston Chronicle *readers had an opportunity to see very abridged version,
really a preview.*)
    Not just Female and Black, but also Same-Gender-Loving. You must
have missed what I said earlier. I want to make that clear before I talk about
the choice of Houston. To the question about God's choice of gender, race,
sexual orientation, and place, one could just as reasonably ask Christians:
Why did the Son, the second member of the Trinity, decide—maybe in
consultation with the other two persons in the Trinitarian Tribunal—to incarnate in the body of a (heterosexual?) Jewish male in Judea, specifically in
the form of an infant born in an obscure town, Bethlehem, of all places—if
your readers believe the Gospels of Matthew and Luke? Why not some town
in India or China or Ethiopia? Why not a Chinese or an Ethiopian God-
Man or God-Woman? Of course the Christian answer is this: because it was
prophesied in the Hebrew Bible/Old Testament. For example, in the book
of Micah (5:1–2) we are told that in Bethlehem a new David will come, one
who will rule Israel.

Christians can only say that the messiah must be a male who comes from the House of David, from a Jewish line, and be born in Bethlehem, because the Bible tells them so. Why Bethlehem? (Impartial biblical scholars of course dispute the claim that this was Jesus' place of birth.) Some Christians answer that precisely because the town was small and insignificant it magnified the glory and greatness of God. Why male? Why from Jewish lineage? Why did God choose the Jews as the community from which the messiah must come, and why were they God's Chosen People? Please forgive me, Jim, if I quote the twentieth-century British journalist William Norman Ewer who dared to remark: "How odd of God to choose the Jews." Some have labeled that statement anti-Semitic, but I think Ewer makes a good point.

Let me jump in. Excuse me Dan. You may not want to include what I'm about to say in your article. My comments may offend Jews as well as Christians. I want to support Ewer in expressing puzzlement over God's choice of the Jews. Even Jews who believe they were divinely chosen sometimes think it odd that they are supposed to be God's Treasured People and see this as anything but a blessing. Given what has happened to Jews throughout history, Jews would be hard-pressed to make the case they are God's favorites. Think about our history: from four hundred years of enslavement in Egypt (if one believes the Torah) to the charge that we are Christ killers, an accusation that led to the massacre of Jews during the Crusades, centuries of pogroms, the burning of Jews at the stake during the Spanish Inquisition, and the continuing history of Christian anti-Semitism and anti-Judaism, all setting the stage for the Holocaust.

Many Christians in Germany, after years of hearing vile things said about Jews in their churches, including the charge of deicide, became so contemptuous of Jews that they were ready to look the other way as Nazi soldiers, serving a pagan regime, took Jews away from their homes to a fate supposedly unknown to good German Christians. Well, the truth is that anti-Semitic German Christians didn't really care where the Nazis took these killers of Christ, as long as they were out of their sight. And anti-Semitism is again on the rise. One can understand why many Jews might say that if this is what chosenness means, they wish God had chosen another people. This is precisely the message of Yiddish poet Kadya Molodowsky (1894–1975) in her poem "Merciful God." She asks God to choose another people because Jews are tired of being murdered simply because they are Jews, chosen to be candidates for death everywhere they live.

What is the biblical origin of chosenness? Taking the Torah as their authority, many religious Jews—many Jews are not religious and some are even anti-religious—believe that God chose Abraham, the first Jew, to be the person with whom the Creator wanted to establish a special covenant, an agreement sealed by the blood of Abraham's self-circumcision at the age of ninety-nine (ouch!), a covenant which, if the Jews lived up to the new law-filled version of it revealed at Mount Sinai, would allow them to enter a land flowing with milk and honey, a land where their troubles would be over. As the story goes, God would, if Jews kept the covenant, ensure their success by partnering with them in the annihilation of those who occupy the promised land when they enter it.

The story of the Jews as a people really begins in the Torah when God, after slumbering for four centuries while the Israelites were severely oppressed by the Egyptians, is suddenly awakened by the loud cries of Jewish slaves. Apparently God finally decided, after their four hundred years of hard slave labor, that the time was ripe to liberate the Chosen Ones. The process of liberation was rather ugly. To win the freedom of the Israelites, the God of the book of Exodus inflicted on Egypt ten plagues, including turning water into blood, spreading frogs everywhere, infesting Egyptians with lice, inflicting them with boils, infecting livestock with a deadly disease, and other very unpleasant things.

The tenth plague, the final blow to the Pharaoh—whose heart, we are told, was hardened by God so that God could demonstrate His power and glory—was the killing of the firstborn males of the Egyptians, including the Pharaoh's son, the firstborn males of non-Jewish slaves, and the firstborn males of livestock. The killing of the firstborn was, by any rational moral measure, cruel and undeserved punishment, something I protest every Passover, not allowing my fellow Jews at the table to gloss over—or should I say pass over— how really terrible this story is. If this God had been truly omnipotent and compassionate—and the plagues seemed to be God's way of showing off his power by ruthlessly inflicting on Egypt ten dark miracles designed to make not only the Pharaoh, but also ordinary Egyptians, quake in their sandals—could He not have simply softened the Pharaoh's heart so he would release the Israelites the very moment Moses asked the Egyptian king to let his people go? That would have been a more humane form of liberation.

I personally could never worship such a God, a God of indiscriminate slaughter. That's why I am not a biblical literalist: there are too many atrocities committed by the God of the Hebrew Bible for me to believe God really did what is depicted. As for God's choice of the Jews as his special people, let me be the first to say that, if you know your Torah, God clearly did not choose the Jews for their inherent goodness or their moral superiority. Jews were of course supposed to be a light to other nations—to liberate others who are oppressed, welcome the stranger, feed the hungry, and house the homeless. But the Jews who were liberated from Egypt were, according to the Torah, ungrateful and anything but a light to other peoples.

No sooner had God set the Israelites free and prepared a set of tablets inscribed with the Decalogue than these stiff-necked people were caught worshiping a calf idol made from molten gold. In fact this God had to kill off almost the entire generation liberated from Egypt. They had to die so a new generation could take their place. Why? Because those who left Egypt were such an ungrateful, kvetching, and disobedient people that they lost the right to enter the promised land. It is not clear that the next generation was much better. In Isaiah 41 God says this about His so-called "Treasured People": "Who is so blind as the Chosen?" Is God saying this only about the Israelites He freed from Egyptian slavery because they proved to be morally blind and unappreciative of all that God had done for them? Or does God have in mind all of those who make up the Chosen People, generation after generation? A case can be made that God is referring to all of the chosen: that we are all blind.

Picking up on this, the view of many Protestant Christians is that God chose the Jews despite their moral weakness, or better, precisely because God knew they would fail to keep divine law. Indeed—if we believe the account of many Christians who adopt a very Lutheran reading of the apostle Paul— Christianity preaches a very un-Jewish message: beliefs, rather than ethical deeds, redeem us. That message, say many conservative evangelical Christians, a message they want all Jews to hear, is this: no human being can be saved by good works, but by faith alone in the saving power of Jesus the Christ: Jesus understood as the divine messiah, the God-Man. We Jews, however, as long as we truly are Jews, will never buy stock in this saved-by-faith-alone business. We contend that behavior is more important than belief: a famous midrash even quotes God as saying that He does not care whether Jews believe in Him as long as they obey His laws.

Let me return to the puzzle of chosenness. Couldn't we say that God would have done just as well, maybe even better, if He had chosen Ethiopians, maybe even making all Blacks his chosen people, from which the messiah could have emerged? A Black messiah would have been an excellent choice. That would have made it difficult for White Jewish and Christian slave owners in the South to justify the enslavement of Africans, to declare them less than fully human simply because they were Black. On the other hand, that might not have made any difference. After all, if God really chose the Jews, that clearly did not prevent the abuse and degradation of Jews, even by those who believed the messiah was a Jew.

Why did God choose the Jews instead of the Ethiopians? There's no good answer. It could have been the Ethiopians if we believe the prophet Amos who quotes God as telling the Israelites that they are just like the Ethiopians (9:7). Let's not forget that the book of Numbers (12:1) tells us that Moses was married to a Cushite (thought by many scholars to mean Ethiopian) woman: in other words, Moses had a Black Wife. Black Africans, who, as biblical scholar Robert Alter observes, might seem like an ultimate other to Israelites, were apparently scattered among those who left Egypt—and there is no suggestion of racial prejudice. Indeed, Moses's marriage to a Cushite could be taken as his and God's affirmation of Black Human Beings. There is a remarkable 1650 painting by the Flemish artist Jacob Jordaens of Moses standing beside his Black Wife. It is striking in this painting how dark she is and how beautifully she is dressed, even wearing a stunning African sun hat.

So—despite claims of some slave-owning Jews and Christians in the South—the God of the Hebrew Bible does not look down upon people with Black skin and did not curse them: again, God tells us that they are just like the Israelites. Black Africans could have been the chosen people. The choice of Jews looks like an inscrutable divine decision. God's choice was, ultimately, arbitrary, puzzling, and without rational justification: what many Christians like to call the grace of God. Still, it does seem odd of God to choose the Jews. And I speak as a faithful Jew. Remember the Jewish people are also called Israel—God wrestlers—for a good reason. We argue with God and even with the idea that we are God's chosen people. One Jewish movement—Reconstructionist Judaism—has in fact explicitly rejected the claim of chosenness. Maybe I'm really a Reconstructionist Jew. I've now finished my defiant speech, my irreverent sermon, on the arbitrariness, oddity, and unkindness of God if God really did choose the Jews as His Treasured People. So, rather than seeing it as anti-Semitic, I applaud the brilliance of Ewer's statement: how odd of God to choose the Jews.

Thanks for your support, Jim. Let me return again to your question, Dan, about the rationale for the form of embodiment I am claiming that God actually chose—the form you see in front of you—and why Houston. My answer may not be very satisfactory, but it's the truth. You might also ask: Why the United States? Does God especially bless America, as some super-patriotic Americans believe? Not any more than God blesses other countries, whatever it means for God to bless a nation-state. God's final act as God was to choose embodiment as Black, Female, and Same-Gender-Loving. Nothing compelled God to choose this form of incarnation. Yet I *can* give you reasons. I gave them before, but let me briefly repeat them since you evidently missed my earlier remarks. Indeed, these reasons need to be repeated, like a refrain in a song.

As God, my choice of how to embody myself was an act of saying yes to the dignity and worth of forms of human life that for too long have been disparaged as less than fully human. Being Black in White majority societies can still be a curse, triggering belittlement, suspicion, and even physical attacks. Being openly Same-Sex-Loving, unfortunately, can often evoke feelings of hatred and hateful acts in too many places in the world and this country, including Houston. And I chose to be a Woman, knowing full well that the subordination of women, their treatment as inferior, and their abuse is far from over here as elsewhere: indeed the fight for the rights of women all over the world is a difficult, often discouraging, uphill struggle.

That is why I welcome the new life given to the #MeToo movement, revived when women stepped forward to accuse Harvey Weinstein of being a chronic sexual abuser. I see the results of the degradation of women daily when I report for work at a shelter for battered women. God's choice to incarnate in the body you see in front of you was a divine affirmation of these different ways of being human. It really should be no more objectionable than the Christian God's decision to incarnate as a Jewish Male, presumably heterosexual in orientation, although in the Gospels we have no texts dealing with Jesus' sexual behavior or sexual desire.

I'm claiming that God chose what many perceive as stigmatizing forms of embodiment. And now, as an amputee, I find myself being stigmatized in four ways: for not being White, Male, Heterosexual, and Able-bodied. I have joined the struggle of the disability community for respect, a struggle to be treated with dignity, and not to have obstacles put in our way when we try to enter this public place or that. My membership in this last category of too frequently disrespected human beings was not a divine choice, but truly an accident, one that, however, has been morally instructive.

Why Houston? After all, as God I was free to choose any place on the planet. I could have chosen any city in any country, any city in the world. And, if you heard the earlier part of our conversation when I explained where I first incarnated, you know that I claim to have arrived in Houston by way of Freetown, Sierra Leone. I could say that I chose Houston because it is racially, ethnically, and religiously diverse, something important to me as God. I wanted to live in a city that had made progress on issues of race and the rights of the LGBPTTQQIA+2 community, but still needed to be pushed to move in a more egalitarian direction, to promote genuine respect for difference.

This city has one of the largest Queer communities in the state, and one of the largest in the South. Houston fit the bill, but of course so do many other cities. Houston has a rich Prideful history, but I think we can make it richer and more welcoming. That's not what many of Houston's more conservative Jews, Christians, Muslims, Baha'is, Hindus, etc. will want to read. Indeed they will probably be outraged by anyone saying that this is one reason God chose this city as *Her* preferred dwelling place.

I have other reasons for my choice of Houston. The great historian Douglas Brinkley, who teaches at what has been called the Harvard of the

Southwest, Rice University, here in Houston, said this: "Today Houston's tradition of 'transition' consists of arriving immigrants from places like Mexico, Vietnam, and Nigeria, all striving for a fresh start, forced to negotiate new identities, believing that all whimsical fantasies are within grasp." I see myself, like these dreamers, as a new immigrant from a foreign land, trying, like other aliens, to negotiate a new identity, bringing with me the perhaps whimsical fantasy that I can change the world, starting of course with Houston. Brinkley imagines Danny Deck—a character in the novel *Some Can Whistle* by the talented Texas novelist Larry McMurtry—as Deck approaches Houston again, after being gone for years, feeling the excitement of being back, thinking: "Anything is possible in Houston." As Brinkley also points out, this is the place that pioneered the moonshot, built some of the world's finest heart and cancer hospitals, nurtured musical talents like Lightnin' Hopkins and Beyoncé, and established temples for the artists Mark Rothko and James Turrell.

Despite these observations, it must be said that nothing compelled me to choose Houston. I can give reasons, but none of them, in the end, ultimately explains or justifies God's choice to reside here. In that sense, I cannot make my choice any more explicable than that of the New Testament God Who decides to incarnate as a Jew in a small town in Judea. Thus, we are back to the freedom of the divine will. I made a free decision, a choice I was not compelled to make. It was, however, God's last choice, one that annihilated God. You might say that God died on the way to Houston.

To be honest, after living in Houston, there are times I wonder why I chose it rather than, say, Portland, Oregon. Of course, I'm still free to move there. In a sense, I welcome the challenge I knew I would face here. As God, I also knew that, given the way I chose to embody myself, if I placed myself in some parts of the world I might be imprisoned for my sexual behavior or killed if caught in the act. What I didn't count on is the possibility I might be killed here in Houston for being Black, Female, and Same-Gender-Loving.

Today I was the target of two young men who saw me as an abomination, someone best eliminated by a quick hit and run. Why? Simply because they perceived me as, to use their language, something, Dan, your paper may not be able to print: a "*nigger bitch filthy dyke cripple.*" To them I'm a ghastly creature that it would be good to erase from Houston's landscape. For these two young men so full of hate, my body was a target-rich environment. If they had thought I was also a Jew or a Muslim, I would have been even a more valued target for destruction. Still, as I have said, I try not to hate them. I would truly like to understand them and, if I felt safe, have a conversation with them about their views. Again, blessed be the name of Emmanuel Levinas, it's possible that a face-to-face encounter with me, in a coffee shop like this, in a long conversation about race, sexual desire, and gender, might lead them to hate me less and make it more difficult for them to kill me. Just possibly: one never knows.

Of course many religious people will find me hateworthy when they read my tale about the death of God. If, Dan, you got the drift of what I was saying to Jim, then you know I'm proclaiming something most believers, including my new acquaintance, Jim, don't want to hear. Like Nietzsche I am announcing the death of God, but, unlike Nietzsche, I don't mean this announcement to be interpreted metaphorically, because I'm asserting that God once existed and that God literally died. Many will not receive this as good news; indeed they will see it as blasphemous and nihilistic. And of course they will declare it fake news.

I know that you, Dan, have read Frederick Nietzsche's only work of fiction: *Thus Spoke Zarathustra*. (*Dan showed surprise and seemed somewhat mesmerized by what he was hearing.*) Like Nietzsche's Zarathustra—a name you also know as a serious student of religion, the name of the founder of Zoroastrianism but who Nietzsche uses to voice his own views—I am aware that any announcement of the death of God will fall on unreceptive ears. In Nietzsche's "Parable of the Madman" in *Thus Spoke*, the madman's proclamation of God's death—insisting that human beings have killed God (really the idea of God)—is greeted with mocking disdain and disbelief. The madman concludes that he has come too soon, that people were not yet ready for the message of God's demise. On my view, it will always be too soon to declare the death of God. Whatever the wishes of atheists, belief in God will be with us for the indefinite future.

In my case, if I announce openly that God died three years ago, and that I *was* God, people will say that I too am mad, speaking nonsense, and probably need to be institutionalized. Or they might say that I'm sneering at religion, putting on an act in order to ridicule belief in God. If I could precisely proclaim my message, I would simply quote Nietzsche, taking literally words he meant figuratively, to wit: "God is dead. God had his hell. It was his love for humanity. God died out of compassion for human beings." Actually, I would amend the final statement to read "compassion for all sentient beings" because, as I said earlier, there is massive suffering, physical and emotional, among non-human animals, whether caused by human beings, other animals, disease, or natural disasters. The God who truly suffered with all sentient beings on this planet—and could do nothing to help the creatures that She perfectly loved—preferred death to impotent love. This Nietzschean message has been one of my other recurring themes today. I know of course that people in significant numbers will continue to believe heaven is occupied by God and even, despite evidence to the contrary, that

God lovingly intervenes in the world. As you know by now, Dan, it is my claim that when God entered this body you see before you, God perished.

Just so I'm clear about this: You are claiming that God committed suicide?

Yes. The moment God became flesh, was incarnated in the body of a Sierra Leone woman I'm calling Esther, God died. As I said before, the term "incarnation" may not be the best word because I don't claim to be God in the flesh. God ceased to exist the moment God took on Esther's flesh. I have no divine attributes, except maybe lingering divine memories that are weakening.

Thank you. Thank you both for giving me permission to write about this fascinating conversation. Shekhinah, you have now made clear what you have been telling Jim. So, I'll be reporting on what I will have to call— please forgive the word, Shekhinah—a "bizarre" conversation between— and here is the language I will use, again with your permission—"a retired philosophy professor and a young black lesbian who claims she was God." It may be the strangest story that I have ever published in the religion section, assuming those in charge allow it to see the light of day. I cannot guarantee that they will permit publication, but I think I can persuade them. It will depend on how I pitch it. As I said, it will no doubt outrage many readers.

Jim, if you give me your email, I'll send you a draft of the article when it's done. (*I handed him my card. He stared at it with interest.*) That adds a fascinating twist. So you're the head of an interfaith organization. I won't disclose this. You must have conversations with a lot of people with unusual beliefs, but, I'm sure, nothing like this. It was a pleasure to meet both of you. Your cooperation is greatly appreciated.

(*Dan returned to his table.*)

Let me quickly text my sitter to tell her that I will not be home until much later. (I sent a text informing my friend that I might be in Starbucks until closing time.) I need to eat something to keep going. Can I get you anything?

Nothing for me. Thanks for staying longer. I have to make a quick trip to the bathroom.

(*I came back with a cheese and fruit plate. While Shekhinah was in the bathroom, I quickly consumed the Brie, Cheddar, and Gouda cheese, grapes, and multigrain crackers. A delicious snack, it gave me a shot of energy.*)

15

The Fight for Equal Rights

Being an American is about having the right to be who you are.
Sometimes that doesn't happen.

—HERB RITTS

*Tell me about your work for the Pride Community of Houston. Again, you
realize that the idea of a Lesbian God will be over the top for many religious
people who read this. Also, I would be interested to hear about your work for
Women's Rights.*

  I didn't say God was a Lesbian. God had no gender or sexual desires. It
is, however, telling that people who don't bat an eye at male terms for God
are bent out of shape by any reference to God that uses female language,
and of course it is out of the question for countless believers that the words
"God" and "Lesbian" could be connected in any positive way. You and I both
know, and Dan said this, that there are still people in the world, numbering
in the millions, maybe the billions, who still think that God is a Heterosexual White Male. So, I'm not saying God was a Lesbian, but I am saying that
God chose to become embodied as a Same-Gender-Loving Person—again,
one of a number human identities God chose before taking on flesh.

  *I stand corrected, but—as I think you've admitted—this will be equally
blasphemous to many conservative Jews, Christians, Muslims, Baha'is, and
other believers who read what you have to say. Putting aside for the moment
the sexual orientation and gender God chose, let's talk about something practical, such as changing the law. Getting religious conservatives in Houston on*

board to support the rights of the LGBTQ community, not to mention get-
ting them past the idea that same-sex relationships are sinful, is an ongoing
challenge. A liberal Christian friend of mine is a Methodist minister in the
Montrose area. Her congregation is 80 percent Gay, with many Transgender
members. She has to be careful because the denomination she serves, the
United Methodist Church, although progressive in some ways, still officially
condemns homosexuality. So she cannot perform same-sex marriages. The
UMC will take up the issue of human sexuality in February 2019; let's hope
they come down on right side. (They in fact came down on the wrong side.)

One of my projects is to join the Houston campaign for equal rights,
to revive the Houston Equal Rights Ordinance for a vote—when the time
is right. We face, in many cities, a challenge that the Supreme Court ruling
on marriage didn't solve: continuing discrimination against Same-Gender-
Loving and Trans Persons in housing, employment, and business services.
A city that can elect a Same-Gender-Loving mayor to two terms can surely
one day pass this.

You're going to face opposition from a lot of people here who believe that
a Transgender life and same-sex relationships are sinful and unnatural—
against the way God created human beings.

A question I have for all opponents of Same-Sex relations who are also
traditional theists is this: Why would an omnipotent and omniscient God,
the God they believe in, intentionally design a world in which there are human beings who have powerful sexual desires that God forbids them to act
on? Where did those desires come from if not from a God Who, according
to these believers, was completely in charge of creation and still controls the
world? Forbidding SGL consenting adults from acting on their desires seems
like cruel and unusual punishment to those of us who are naturally attracted
to members of the same sex. If the Creator is conceived as an all-knowing
and all-powerful Designer Who oversaw every moment of the evolution
of species—for those who believe in divinely directed evolution, or, if one
adopts the fundamentalist view that God created all species by speaking
them into existence in six days, then they must believe that God could have
created a world in which *no* human beings and *no* animals (since same sex
behavior is well-documented in the animal world) would have such desires.

Are Same-Sex desires supposed to be a temptation to the human beings who feel them, a test of some kind? Are those who feel attraction to the
same gender supposed to, out of love (or fear) of God, sacrifice their sexual
life, remain celibate, always having to deny in practice who they really are
sexually, thus never finding the fulfillment they seek in a Same-Gender-
Loving relationship? To reiterate: when I talk about Same-Sex relationships
I am of course only talking about consenting mentally competent adults,

not those disposed to pedophilia. Of course it also remains a puzzle why an all-knowing and all-powerful God would deliberately design a world in which there are adults who lust after children. Couldn't God, if a hands-on Creator, overseeing every detail of Creation, have designed the world otherwise? Traditional, God-is-in-control theism has to say yes.

And why would God create a world in which there are human beings who are born with a powerful sense of belonging to a gender different from the one they were 'assigned' at birth? Since they didn't choose to feel this way, why should they be condemned for seeking to create or construct for themselves the gender they most identify with? Clearly, an all-powerful and all-knowing God, directing every stage of creation or evolution, could have made a world in which there are no Trans Persons. But the Creator obviously did not. So, if God was omnipotent and omniscient at the moment of Creation, and remains so, it's God's fault if anyone is a Trans Person.

I did want to say a few more things—for the record, as they say—about my life as an LGBPTTQQIA+2 activist in Houston. Let me return to the subject of the Montrose neighborhood. I see myself as doing God's work, or the work that God did not do but wished She could have done. That includes fighting for equal rights for all those who are perceived as "Queer." In creating actual space for an alternative way of loving and gendering in Houston, Montrose, one might say, was the birthplace of freedom in Texas: freedom to be who you are. Sometimes I wish I lived in Montrose just to be in the location where, for the first time, people in Houston, in significant numbers, did not have to hide their true selves.

I'm surprised you don't live in the Montrose area.

Are you really? I knew of course when I arrived here that Montrose had a history of being friendly to difference. Actually it didn't get this reputation until the 1980s when for the first time it had a significant Queer population and was becoming the center of alternative culture in Houston. The 1990s were really the beginning of the heyday for Montrose. And by 2008 there were some forty active locations, mainly bars, in Montrose catering to SGL clientele. And although other parts of Houston have become welcoming and Montrose is no longer the special place it was, Montrose remains a center of strong support for the movement toward equal LGBPTTQQIA+2 rights.

And women's rights, also one of your causes?

One of the things that has recently inspired and given hope to those of us working for women's rights is the number of women who stepped forward in in great numbers in 2017, and continue to do so, to report sexual harassment and sexual assault. This was organized as a revival of an earlier #MeToo movement. It seemed to be the start of a cultural shift that was recognized even by Rich Lowry, the editor of the thoughtful conservative magazine *National Review.* The title of his November 24, 2017 article is "After Weinstein: A Cultural Revolution, Ending a Model of Abuse." Giving me hope about the power of news—real news, not fake news, the term Trump uses for news not to his liking, a president who himself bragged about sexual assault—this cultural revolution appears to be a result of an article in the *New York Times* that was published October 5, 2017.

My readers are going to think our conversation is a running ad for the Times. *So be it.*

The article by Jodi Kantor and Megan Twohey provided credible support for the claim that Harvey Weinstein had a long and dreadful history of sexual misconduct and intimidation, and how for decades he bought the silence of his accusers while also intimidating them. Almost in the blink of an eye, we saw the beginning of a movement in which women boldly went public, bringing down very powerful men everywhere, marking the end of the silence of women.

Suddenly, women naming their abusers meant for powerful men a career death penalty—rather than what it had been in the past, the end of the careers of the women charging abuse. Witness the quick collapse of Charlie Rose's rising star at CBS and PBS, and the end of Matt Lauer's morning reign at NBC, as more and more women voiced similar descriptions of inappropriate, indeed gross, behavior on the part of these two men. Some have called this sudden change Hurricane Harvey (Weinstein), comparing it to the storm we are all too familiar with around here. May this storm gather force and continue to bring down powerful, abusive males in all areas of American life: business, politics, entertainment, religion, education, and the arts.

And sports. Let us not forget the downfall of a man who was untouchable for decades because he was very clever—disguising his abuse of young girls and women in gymnastics as medical treatment. Larry Nassar finally faced justice after sexually abusing untold numbers of women, close to 300, since the 1990s and was forced, at the end of his trial, to face 156 women who told him about the pain he inflicted on them. The judge sentenced him to 175 years in prison, writing what she called his death warrant. I think the #MeToo movement helped inspire the great number of those who came forward. One of the first women to call Nassar out—Rachael Denhollander—told the world that she personally paid a heavy price after filing a police complaint in 2016 for abuse that occurred in 2004 when she was fifteen. Dismissed by some people as "just looking for a payday," she was at first not believed, losing her church, many of her friends, and every shred of privacy. Still, she must have felt vindicated by Nassar's fate.

And the spirit of the #MeToo movement appears to be happening elsewhere: for example, thousands of French women came forward after the Weinstein event. I wish I could describe it as a world tsunami. Unfortunately, this is not the case. In France the central place of seductiveness in French culture slows the progress of this movement. In places like Indonesia sexual harassment can best be described as an epidemic. Indeed mistreatment of and violence against women worldwide might be best described as a "global pandemic," to borrow a term used by Tarana Burke, the social activist who started the #MeToo movement.

It's no small thing that *Time* magazine named the Silence Breakers of the #MeToo movement the Person of the Year for 2017. The movement was originally created by Burke, an African American, in 2007 to help survivors of sexual violence. Audre Lorde would like that phrase—"Silence Breakers"—and be proud that a Black Woman started the movement. #MeToo was originally part of a grassroots campaign to promote "empowerment through empathy" among Women of Color who experienced sexual abuse. Burke said she was inspired to use the phrase after being unable to immediately respond to a thirteen-year-old girl who confided to her that she had been sexually assaulted. Burke remembers that she didn't have a way to help her at that time. Burke wishes she would have responded to the girl's story of sexual abuse by simply saying the words "me too."

I have some concern that although the American #MeToo movement was founded by a Black Woman, so far it has been predominantly an upper class White Women's movement, this despite the fact that Women of Color—for example, Black, Asian, and Hispanic—face sexual harassment and assault at higher rates than White Women. It should be noted that Burke was not in the picture on the *Time* cover. We must not forget that Burke's original campaign aimed to provide support to survivors of sexual violence who were marginalized, poor, underrepresented, and without a network of community support.

This meant that it originally focused on Low-Income Women and Girls of Color who lacked support and resources. The fact is that many Poor Women of Color working the night shift all across the country have frequently been victims of sexual violence; only recently have they received the attention they deserve. The #MeToo movement must never forget women at the margins in every society. So it cannot be only a movement of Silence Breakers who are White and Privileged: it must also work on behalf of Girls and Women of Color who often suffer in silence. We have to keep in mind the countless women who are too afraid to speak out, to break their silence because, according to Burke, they "fear denial, shame, punishment, blame, further violence and retaliation against them and their families." To reach out to these women #MeToo in the United States has joined forces with Unicef USA to say: #HerToo. Unicef's work—work we must all undertake—is to end discrimination and violence against Girls and Women worldwide through education, protection, and policy reform. Here is another cause I've taken up and to which I hope to make a contribution in doing work that God wanted to do but could not.

Maybe the Women's March the day after Trump's inauguration set the stage for defiance of what was for too long the expected behavior of women, namely to stay quiet about abuse by powerful men who can ruin your career if you dare to speak out. Over two million people across the planet took part in this march, a massive protest uniting people of all ages, races, and religions, calling for respect for human rights, with a special emphasis on women's rights, immigration reform, reproductive rights, racial equality, LGBPTTQQIA+2 rights, and workers' rights: in other words, fundamental progressive causes. The second march occurred a year later with the theme "Look Back, March Forward." It was also about a wide range of progressive issues, but the empowerment of women took on new urgency when the #MeToo movement revealed there was still much work to be done. The problem is that marches like this don't have a lasting effect.

We do need to ask: Is #MeToo a movement that will endure or just a passing moment of feminist activism? I'm working with various women's coalitions in Houston to keep the movement alive here. Even as God I could not have predicted the future of #MeToo because it depends on what women and men do to sustain this cause. There needs to be a movement from the personal to the political, really to the legal. There is a need to move from the "me" to the "we," to move from stories to legal actions that penalize and legally correct abuse. Toward this end Time's Up has been created. Administered by the National Women's Law Center's Legal Network for Gender Equity, Time's Up connects victims of sexual harassment, assault, and abuse to local lawyers who will take their case, sometimes pro bono. In all this, care must be taken to make sure those charged with sexual abuse receive due process. Justice requires that, but so does the integrity of what I hope is a sustained revolutionary movement.

Maybe this is an area where we also need to go beyond retributive justice—although that has its place—and supplement it with restorative justice. In some cases—where women have suffered psychological damage and the offender, despite compelling evidence of criminal behavior, never admits wrongdoing, and so never apologizes to his victims—time in prison is what justice requires. But not all sexual misconduct reaches a criminal level. Someone fired for making sexually inappropriate remarks may suffer a great financial loss, but will his behavior change when he finds employment again?

Katie J. M. Baker, an investigative reporter for *BuzzFeed*, asks an important question: "What should happen to these men?" Do we want those who do not go to jail to just go away, to somehow disappear? Although she acknowledges that it will not be appropriate in every case, she asks us to explore whether restorative justice is not sometimes the best way to go. In restorative justice, concerned citizens (including the victim if she wishes) and the wrongdoer meet together to discuss the offense committed and what can be done to make amends and to change offensive behavior. Offenders must of course be willing to admit wrongdoing, and there must be an emphasis on repairing, if possible, the harm done. Most important, people must work with the offender to prevent a repetition of the offensive behavior. Baker's point is that most offenders are going to return to society, and so we need to have a conversation about whether their redemption is, at least in some instances, a possibility.

Unfortunately the message of the #MeToo project has not penetrated some important areas of our culture. One domain of entertainment unchanged by this movement, a form of entertainment that, as I pointed out earlier, reaches a massive audience, is rap. In this musical world, misogyny and depictions of physical attacks on women don't bring the disgrace they deserve. A *New York Times* headline reads: "In Rap, Little Reckoning for Misconduct." Some leading rap artists who have either been charged with or convicted of sexual misconduct remain very much on the scene. Their audiences have not deserted them and they have suffered no serious public consequences. Some of these artists seem to thrive on and even commercialize their outlaw status. If they are Black, they can, according to *New York Times* music critic Jon Caramanica, exploit skepticism about the fairness of law enforcement in the United States and cleverly play the role of antiauthoritarian folk heroes.

It is not only the behavior of popular rappers that concerns me. What about rap lyrics? I have been put off by the language, the way it refers to Women as bitches, and to its general vulgarity. Maybe this reflects my age and my cultural conservatism. Maybe I simply don't get it.

No. On the contrary, you get it. There is a serious problem with the language of hip-hop when the lyrics become misogynistic and its consumers are silent about this. Silence Breakers are also needed in the rap community and among the countless people who support this industry with their dollars. Right now there are rappers who are getting a free pass for misogynistic lyrics. As Shanita Hubbard points out in a recent article in the *Huffington Post*: although Black Women like Sylvia Robinson, Queen Latifah, Missy Elliott, and many others helped mold hip-hop into the musical powerhouse it is today, hip-hop lyrics too frequently fail to show respect for women. Record producer and rapper Chief Keef, for example, in his song "You" sings that if a certain woman says no to his sexual advances and refuses to suck his penis, he will kill her. Here we have lyrics that literally threaten a woman with death if she does not perform oral sex.

Hubbard wants us to think about the following fact: This line made it past each level of production—writing, recording, mixing, distribution—seemingly without a single person saying that maybe we shouldn't normalize lyrics that involve a man's threat to kill women who refuse to have oral sex with him. The problem is that such lyrics are not unique to this rapper. And Black Women in this industry have in some cases conspired with men to make misogynistic music. Women in the hip-hop world need to step forward to become Silence Breakers. I think we should take seriously Hubbard's important question, to wit: "What are we going to do about the silence around violence in hip-hop?"

Before we leave this subject, I have a question. Are Women the only ones who suffer abuse? Are heterosexual men the only abusers?

Of course there are cases where Women sexually harass and abuse men, but in far smaller numbers. Sadly and ironically, it was recently revealed that one of the first women to accuse Harvey Weinstein paid off an ex-child actor who accused her of sexual misconduct. And obviously sexual abuse doesn't occur only in the Straight community. Same-Sex Oriented individuals in positions of power have also exploited their power to impose their will on individuals of the same gender. Victims who say, in the face of such abuse, "me too" in order to bring down an abuser have performed an important service to others.

Notice how accusations of sexual assault quickly finished the career of a truly gifted actor: Kevin Spacey. Of course acts of sexual assault and harassment have been and are daily committed by Same-Sex-Oriented people, and we know that those in powerful positions have misused their power for sexual ends. Obviously there is the long history of pedophilic Catholic priests sexually abusing children. What we are talking about in many cases is an adult male raping a child. I don't think Pope Francis has done enough about this, despite all his talk. (*The next month, after this conversation, the pope announced a conference on this issue, scheduled for February 2019.*)

And we should not ignore sexual abuse by Catholic men in high office of their adult male subordinates. Consider the case of Cardinal Theodore McCarrick, former Archbishop of Washington D.C., called "Uncle Ted," who was accused of coercing seminarians to sleep with him. In June 2018, the Vatican removed McCarrick from public ministry for "credible sexual abuse allegations." We have discovered that this was another case, like Weinstein, where "everyone knew" but for a long time no one would go on record against this powerful man. We also know in some Chabad communities there have been cover-ups of sexual abuse of male students by rabbis, teachers, and staff. It cuts across denominations and religions.

While I don't want to deny abuse committed by Same-Sex-Oriented individuals—whether adult on adult or adult on child—I also don't want people to lose sight of the distance this society needs to go in recognizing the worth of Consenting-Adult-Same-Sex relationships. People need to treat such relationships, especially if they are loving and mutually respectful, the same way society views Consensual-Caring-Heterosexual relationships. Many Houstonians are not there yet. Same-Gender love needs to be recognized as having the same potential for depth and meaning equal to the best Heterosexual relationships.

Houston, as you suggest, still remains in some ways a very conservative city, and is not unequivocally Gay friendly. Are you sure you want to stay here?

The recent defeat of the Equal Rights Ordinance is discouraging. Despite this, I still believe radical change is possible here. One reason I entered the world is because I knew that even one individual has the power to act to correct injustice. That's what struck me and led me to abandon my divine life: namely the power of a single human being, compared to the powerlessness of God. Although I think the key to radical social change is the creation of a coalition of diverse allies willing to work together (such as civil rights activists, environmentalists, disability rights activists, feminists, libertarians, members of the LGBPTTQQIA+2 community and their allies), I believe it's always possible for even one person—for example, even a single Houstonian—to move things in a radically different direction.

In 1950 Heman Marion Sweatt, a Black Baha'i Houstonian—Baha'is have been great proponents of racial equality and opponents of many forms of prejudice, even though their official position on Same-Gender-Loving Persons is wrong—took his battle against the "separate but equal doctrine" in education to the United States Supreme Court. Sweatt was denied admission to the University of Texas Law School in Austin. When he applied in 1946, the president of the law school, Theophilius Painter, denied him admission on the ground that the Texas State Constitution prohibited integrated education. Painter acknowledged Sweatt "was duly qualified" for admission to the UT Law School, except, as Painter put it, "for the fact that Sweatt was a negro." He was offered admission to a Black-only state law school in Houston, obviously inferior to the one in Austin. Sweatt refused the offer.

Clearly this was a case of separate *and* unequal education. Sweatt saw his denial of admission as racist segregation and, taking his complaint to the highest court—represented by lawyers provided by the NAACP Legal

Defense Fund, including Thurgood Marshall—won in the case of Sweatt vs. Painter, paving the way for desegregation in education across the country—something that happened four years later in the 1954 landmark case of Brown vs. the Board of Education.

This is just one example of what's possible if one individual refuses to accept unequal treatment. Clearly, Sweatt did not achieve success by himself, but his refusal to accept racial discrimination got the ball rolling. To repeat: hope for radical change has to be married to collective action—in many cases requiring a lot of money and the best lawyers one can find who are committed to arguing for a cause that some might see as hopeless. For example, following a lengthy series of appeals of lower court rulings, the issue of the fundamental right to marry ended up in several circuit courts where a split led to an inevitable Supreme Court review. Just a decade prior, who would have predicted that in 2015 the Supreme Court of the United States would approve Same-Sex marriage, concluding that a fundamental constitutional right to marry is guaranteed to Same-Sex couples. Quite frankly, I would not have, even as God with all the knowledge I possessed on high. I think it's just a matter of time, and not a long time, before Houston passes an equal rights ordinance. This is one of my projects as I work with progressives, liberals, independents, and libertarians. This is the ethical work I do in God's stead.

So, you, claiming to be an ex-deity who can finally act in the world, want to work toward the transformation of the world, starting with Houston. You are committed to a number of progressive and human rights causes that require practical, often frustrating work, including the pursuit of legal remedies—working with diverse allies to bring about fundamental, indeed radical, social change. Is that a fair description your politics?

Yes, that's a good statement.

So God is a progressive?

God is dead. God chose to incarnate as a Same-Gender-Loving-Woman with Very Black Skin. I, as a human being, now experience prejudice and hatred firsthand; sometimes, as is now clear to me personally, it can be life-threatening. This affects my politics. I find liberals and progressives more supportive of the pride I take in who I am. Nevertheless, my views on some issues will not appear progressive. For example, I see abortion as the destruction of a human life and believe every attempt should be made to find an alternative. I'm in a deep sense pro-life, as was God. As the One who created all life, God valued human life within as well as outside the womb.

I have not changed my position now that I am a human being. Is discovering an imperfection in a fetus—or simply not wanting it—reason to abort it? Many liberals and progressives would say yes. As someone involved in the disability rights movement, I object to those who believe, for example, that discovery of Down syndrome is sufficient reason to abort a fetus. Are these human beings less valuable than so-called normal human beings? As the Creator who gave birth to a world where chromosomal abnormalities occur, I feel a special responsibility.

Those who see a pro-choice position as the only correct feminist position, and a test of being truly progressive, might want to look at what a writer with a disability, who is also a Feminist and Same-Gender-Loving Woman, says about this: Alison Kafer in her book *Feminist Queer Crip*. As she observes, a decision to abort can reflect the prejudice of Ableism, devaluing fetuses judged to be defective in some sense, making the termination of the life of these in utero human beings morally unproblematic.

Prenatal testing provides a method of eliminating from the population those who are perceived by many abortion proponents to be an undesirable class of human beings. George Will, the anti-Trump conservative columnist—and proud father of a son who happens to have Down syndrome—points out that in Iceland the ability to detect this condition in a fetus has been used as this country's final solution to the Down syndrome problem. In that country, Will points out, prenatal testing has become part of a "systematic attempt to erase a category of people." This troubles me. I'm of course aware that where abortion is legally prohibited many women who seek an abortion find a way, often endangering their health and lives, to end their pregnancy. So, I am not sure re-criminalizing abortion will solve the problem. I cannot provide an easy solution to this question, but you should be aware that my position on this issue is not what many would call progressive.

That surprises me. I have been pro-choice for as long as I can remember. I remain so. Still, I do understand your position on abortion, given your conviction that you feel ultimate responsibility for how life turned out and in particular for chromosomal abnormalities that have lead to the devaluation and termination of certain in utero lives. Despite my firm position, I know, as someone who taught ethics for three decades, that there are good arguments and good people on both sides of this issue.

16

Audre Lorde

Creation in the Image of a Woman

When I dare to be powerful, to use my strength in the service of my vision, then it becomes less and less important whether I am afraid.

—AUDRE LORDE

Is there someone who you see as your ethical model, providing an example of how to live as a human being in what you now claim is a God-forsaken world in which, as you are now very much aware, death can come at any moment?

As you may have guessed, I remain inspired by the life of Audre Lorde: by her poetry, prose, intersectional social activism, response to the amputation of part of her body, and the way she came to terms with mortality before liver cancer took her life. She shows us what is humanly possible. Lorde was a model of courageous speech, of the need to speak out in defense of people who have been treated with contempt—and to especially speak out when silence is expected. She was an early Silence Breaker when it came to People of Color, Same-Gender-Loving Women and Men, Older Adults, and the Medically Disenfranchised. Today, Audre Lorde—who was born in New York to Caribbean Immigrants—would also be speaking out loudly on behalf of Immigrants, people who have been demonized, abused, and violated of late.

Do you think Lorde would agree with the Jewish idea that the heart of a truly good life, ethically speaking, is what we are commanded to do in Leviticus 19: namely loving other as self, a love that needs to take the form of caring and compassionate behavior?

I think she might agree that it is hard to improve on the imperative to love others as we should love ourselves. There is, however, also much to reject in Leviticus where this love commandment is found. We should not forget Leviticus also attributes to God the commandment that a man should not have sexual relations with a man as with a woman because it is an abomination, and if he does, they both should be killed (Leviticus 20). This is a "commandment" that I know you reject. This so-called divine law has been interpreted, over the centuries, as a blanket prohibition of Same-Sex relationships and as justification for violence against violators. It has been used as a religious justification for the criminalization of Same-Gender-Loving behavior—and in some cases, for the murder of those who engage in such relationships.

Let's not forget that Texas and a number of other states had anti-sodomy laws until the Supreme Court declared them unconstitutional in 2003—a relatively recent decision. In 1998, a Houstonian, John Lawrence, who at that time was one of two men charged in Houston with sodomy, refused to accept this injustice and successfully fought to overthrow the law that prohibited him from being who he was. Again progress toward the abolition of an unjust law started with a lone Houstonian and ended in success at the Supreme Court. Houston's past has something to teach us about what is possible in the future. Of course, I cannot repeat too often that good lawyers are also needed as we work to eliminate unjust laws in Texas and the nation. With Trump in power, we have our work cut out for us as the Court becomes increasingly conservative.

I want to return to what you recognize as a genuine ethical imperative in Leviticus 19: the love commandment. Would you agree that this is the heart of ethical living? Many Jews and Christians would assert this.

Yes, but we should not ignore the *mitzvah* that precedes the commandment to love neighbor as self, also found in Leviticus 19—namely the commandment never to hate another in your heart, seek vengeance, or hold a grudge. This prohibition recognizes that there is toxicity in the emotions of hate, vengeance, and grudge-holding. Obviously, if I hate another in my heart, it will be difficult for me to treat this person in a loving way. And, as you know, there is a second very important love commandment at the end of Leviticus 19, one we have already discussed: the commandment to love the stranger—the outsider—as we love ourselves, and to treat her or him as our equal.

Yes, the Torah reminds those of us who are Jews that "we were strangers in the land of Egypt and thus should know what it feels like to be a stranger." Given how Jews have been treated as the hated other in too many societies to count, Jews clearly know what it feels like to be a stranger in a strange land. And let's not forget that in the Torah the Hebrew word for stranger, ger, meant immigrant, refugee, foreigner, or resident alien. It would be good at this time, when anti-immigrant sentiment is strong among Trumpites, to remind those among Trump's followers who are Jews and Christians that they have a higher law to follow. I think it may be difficult for White Nationalist followers of Trump, who regularly demonize immigrants, to overcome the resentment, indeed hatred, they feel for people they see as a threat to the "White Race." Asking them to love immigrants and refugees—to treat these strangers in a loving way—may be asking for the impossible. And of course, as I pointed out earlier, White Nationalists blame Jews for bringing immigrants here, a charge that I think is accurate if you take into consideration that for over a century the Jewish organization HIAS (Hebrew Immigrant Aid Society), mentioned already, has been in the forefront of helping refugees from all over the world. This is something Jews are divinely called to do. It will be a long time before those who hate Jews and Immigrants soften their hearts toward either. But I shall never give up trying to change their hearts from hate to love.

This is the difficult part: that is, changing people's hearts, especially if their hearts have become hardened against certain groups. One needs to be able to cultivate love as an emotion, whether for neighbors or strangers, before one can behave lovingly toward them. Ethical calls to change one's heart—from a feeling of hate to a feeling of love—are important because without this change, laws that eliminate discrimination and inequality of legal rights will leave people with the same toxic souls. But the project of changing people's feelings toward each other is, I agree, no easy task.

The emergence of laws that protect the rights of historically oppressed and despised groups is an important achievement, but it doesn't necessarily eliminate the feeling of contempt of one-time oppressors for the people they once dominated or the resentment of those who were once oppressed toward a group that historically treated them as inferior. Those in different racial groups who were once in a relationship of master and slave must work on themselves to overcome residual feelings of hostility they may still feel toward each other—if they are to live up to the imperative to love other as self.

And even if members of previously antagonistic groups could overcome the hatred they have, for a long historical period, felt toward each other—a big if but still a real possibility—the imperative to love neighbor and stranger as self may still be impossible to realize if those who were maltreated have internalized this hatred and thus suffer from self-loathing. This brings us to one of Lorde's important insights, namely that loving neighbor as self assumes that you are able to love yourself. The Torah doesn't really develop a notion of healthy self-love, but it's necessary to do so if the love commandment is to be meaningful. Persons who have been treated with contempt, people who have suffered through a long period of subordination and degradation, may lack a capacity for self-respect. Indeed, to be motivated to overthrow an oppressor, to see their cause as justified, the oppressed need to see themselves as equal in worth to their oppressors.

William Lloyd Garrison, the White founder of the New England Anti-Slavery Society, a proponent of immediate emancipation of slaves in the United States and publisher of abolitionist newspaper *The Liberator*, writing to Black subscribers in 1831, pressed for free Blacks to challenge "every law which infringes on your rights as free native citizens" and to "respect yourself if you desire the respect of others." And Delores Huerta (another hero of mine), co-founder in 1962 with Caesar Chavez of the United Farm Workers of America, argued that a social revolution must start with self-love on the part of victims of injustice.

So, if people who have been treated with disdain are to love other as self, they must overcome not only their hatred of those who have treated them as inferior, but also must often overcome doubts they have about their own worth. This is something Lorde recognizes as a serious problem: that those who have been denigrated since birth may have internalized this contempt. Often ignored in discussions of the ethical imperative to love other as self is how difficult it is for those who have been treated with disrespect, or even as worthless, to see themselves as love-worthy. I saw this from above.

Audre Lorde puts it this way: "I have to learn to love myself before I can love you or accept your loving." Notice the last part of that sentence: "before I can accept your loving." How can I believe that you should love me if I don't believe I am worthy of it? If I am to love another as I love myself, but I cannot love myself, I'm stuck. And feeling love for yourself may not come easily if all of your life you have been, as long as you can remember, regarded by the larger society as less than fully human, as deserving belittlement.

Jim, you belong to the community that gave us the love commandment. The Leviticus commandment to love neighbor and stranger as self was, although attributed to God, invented by the Jews. For centuries, however, Jews, as you have repeatedly reminded us, have been the most hated people in the world. They have, as you observed, been expelled from almost every society they lived in. They have been universally treated with contempt. They are the original Other. Anti-Semitism has been described as the longest hatred. Over the centuries, as you know, many Jews internalized this hatred and came to loathe themselves. Other Jews came to deny they were Jews, trying to pass as gentile. Of course, many did this simply to survive, but I can tell that others viscerally despised their Jewishness, especially if they looked stereotypically Jewish.

Christianity of course contributed to Jewish self-hatred. How must Jewish children have felt about themselves in Christian societies where they were frequently called Christ killers by their Christian playmates? Jews were literally demonized by Christianity, even thought to have horns! This demonization has a New Testament basis: readers should look at the Gospel of John (8:44) where Jesus is quoted as saying to Jews, "Your father is the devil." And totally apart from the long history of anti-Judaism and the charge of deicide, Jews have been in many societies treated as essentially dirty, dishonest, and untrustworthy simply because they were Jews, as if there is something both criminal and diseased about being a Jew. This is the myth of a mongrel Jewish race. "Jew" was and still is in many places a dirty word, a pejorative term. I have a Jewish friend who, because of this, feels uneasy about the use of the word "Jew." The view that made "Jew" a term of derision became part of the ideology of anti-Semitism that was adopted by the Nazis, who held that Jewish blood was different from the blood of others, as if it were somehow contaminated.

The Nazis exploited both hatred based on stereotypes of Jews as filthy, diseased creatures, comparable to vermin, and the centuries-old religious hatred based on the long-held irrational Christian belief that all Jews were guilty for the crucifixion of Jesus, a view officially held by the Catholic Church until 1965 (repudiated at Vatican II). So there emerged in Germany a popular view that Jews were both religious criminals and a contaminated race. This prepared the ground for the Shoah. As I have already remarked, this made it easy for "Christians" in different communities during the Holocaust, in places like Poland as well as Germany, to let Jews be taken away from their homes, to be removed from their sight. A Jewless world was for many Germans, Poles, and others something to be celebrated. And there is now a resurgence of anti-Semitism in Europe and the United States—and it is very much a part of many Muslim cultures where Jews are called "descendants of apes and pigs." We are now attacked by both the extreme right (White Nationalists who think we want to eradicate the White Race) and the extreme left (so-called progressives who identify all Jews with what they perceive to be the oppressive, genocidal state of Israel). I agree: demonization takes its toll.

My point is that this centuries-long hatred has had an impact on how Jews see themselves and has, over the centuries, made self-love a challenge for some. The identity we call "Jew" is, as noted before, a social construction, but it, like other constructs—such as gender or race—can generate contempt that has devastating results. Of course many Jews with strong egos and confidence in their self-worth—perhaps you're one of them—may have been unaffected by the centuries-old contempt others have felt for Jews, but over this long history, I can tell you, there were countless Jews who interiorized this hatred and despised themselves, even how they looked. You can be sure that in the Nazi death camps where Jews were deliberately kept filthy by the Nazis overseeing them, often covered in their own shit, self-contempt was difficult to resist.

I, who remember every form of hatred that has ever existed, am personally experiencing firsthand several forms of disdain. I'm a person whose multiple identities have been and still are despised and treated with contempt: such as being Female, Black, Same-Gender-Loving, and One-Legged. Just consider the long history of the disparagement of women, how it encourages women to devalue themselves. We have already talked about the pandemic of sexual abuse. Think about how, for centuries, women have been perceived as essentially inferior, less than fully human. Treated with contempt for so long by the dominant male culture to the point that, even today, when their husbands or partners beat them—many women, internalizing this devaluation, believe they deserve abuse. And many women stay with abusive men until, in too many cases, they are beaten to death. To beat someone to death you have to profoundly hate that person. I see victims of misogyny every day at the Bayou Women's Center, and it has taken a toll on me in a personal way. Every time I enter the shelter I breathe the air of disrespected, abused, and permanently damaged women—and, to repeat a paradoxical fact: many of these women actually blame themselves for their abuse and degradation.

Countless women over time came to think they were undeserving of the same respect as men because that is what males in authority told them. In Rabbinic literature we find Woman being referred to as a bag of filth, and Rabbi Eliezer in the Talmud asserts that the Torah should be burned rather than taught to women; blaming Eve for bringing evil into the world, asserting that all women share in her guilt, second-century Christian church father Tertullian calls Woman a gateway to the devil; in Buddhist literature we find a long history of many Buddhists saying that a Woman needs to be reborn as a man in order to achieve enlightenment, and Buddhist nuns have historically been, and still are in many places, subordinated to Buddhist monks.

Most major world religions, as they were and are practiced, contain teachings that disrespect women or, at the very least, call for the religious and marital subordination of women to men. This age-old degradation and hateful mistreatment of women has led many women, internalizing misogyny, to have a profoundly negative view of themselves, to see themselves as hate-worthy—and worthless. Thus, learning to love themselves has become for many women, all over the world, a struggle, something that requires ongoing work and radical changes in society, including a reeducation of women in the need for self-respect and a reeducation of men to see women as their equals, worthy of equal respect.

It is same with hatred of Black Human Beings who, for too long in this country, were described as naturally inferior, subhuman, smelly, and dirty—whose Black Skin, as we have seen, was taken to be a sign they were cursed by God. And Blackness was in many majority White societies identified with both evil and ugliness: the Blacker, the uglier and less valuable. We have seen that as an enslaved people in the United States, Blacks were, in many places, at the mercy of masters who could beat them at will, and sometimes beat them to death. As we have already observed, many owners of female slaves felt free to rape them, something that was a guilty pleasure for these masters because they knew that many Whites who discovered this would see such a sexual relationship as dirty as well as sinful. And, as we have also seen, many Black men who were husbands to these enslaved women felt contempt for themselves because they could do nothing to stop the repeated rape of their wives.

After slavery ended, during the Jim Crow era—a period when demeaning "Whites Only" signs appeared, when Blacks could not drink from the same water cooler or drinking fountain, swim in the same water, go to the same schools, stay in the same hotels, sit in the same sections of public transportation as Whites—and even after civil rights laws were passed, Blacks continued to be treated with contempt, as inferior human beings. And we should never forget that in the United States, between 1882 and 1968 there were, if my residual divine memory is reliable, over 4500 lynchings of Blacks—a number higher than the NAACP official figure (3446) because not every act of lynching was recorded. In a song made famous by Billie Holiday, "Strange Fruit" (lyrics and music by Abel Meerpool, 1937), we hear lyrics that describe Black bodies like fruit swinging in the southern wind, hanging from ropes tied to poplar trees. Some lynchings were actually the occasion for celebrations and picnics, even announced in the local newspaper—and photographs of Black Men and Black Women hanging from trees appear on postcards that were sent to relatives by those who enjoyed the festivities.

Given this long and shameful history, and the stubborn persistence of anti-Black attitudes to this very day, self-hatred among Blacks in the twenty-first century continues to be a problem. In *Breach*, her coming-of-age play about race, Antoinette Nwandu, the young Black playwright I mentioned earlier, creates as her central character a young pregnant Black Woman

who dramatically illustrates Lorde's thesis. The subtitle of the play is revealing: "*a manifesto of race in America through the eyes of a black girl suffering
from self-hate.*" The play illustrates how hard it is to love others when, in
Nwandu's words, "it's you that you loathe most of all." By the end the play,
her redemptive message is that Black Females *can* come to love themselves.
Nwandu calls the play "a love letter to Black Women."

And Women who love Women have been and continue to be treated,
like Men who love Men, as sinful and perverted. There have been and are
right-wing extremists who believe that those of us who refuse to conform
to heterosexist standards deserve to be treated with disdain and even killed.
Again, they have the Torah on their side. And from time to time, Women
who love Women have in different places and times been murdered. In Troy,
New York, last December a Lesbian couple and their two kids were viciously
killed in their apartment, a quadruple homicide clearly motivated by hatred.
Is it any surprise that many young women called "dykes," as I was today,
by those who hate them, come to hate themselves? Is it any surprise that
Same-Gender-Loving young people, because they have been taught to be
ashamed of who they are, frequently kill themselves? This is one of the tragic
consequences of scripture that can be interpreted as condemning Same-Sex
relations as disordered and sinful behavior. It has encouraged and legiti-
mated hatred of "Queers" and inculcated in these young people feelings of
self-loathing. Of course in many cases condemnation in scripture simply
provides an excuse for those who are homophobic to practice hateful speech
and behavior—to try to theologically justify what they feel in their viscera.

Finally, I have, as I mentioned earlier, experienced disdain directed
toward my One-Legged Body. A person who suffers loss of a body part may
come to see her changed body as deformed and ugly. She may hate her altered body and experience shame at her loss, sometimes called disability
shame. Those whose bodies don't fit the ideal of Abelism are often made to
feel they are less human and less valuable than the so-called Able-Bodied.
Given the emphasis our culture places on physical perfection, it's not surprising that many of us who are dismissed as "cripples" come to dislike
ourselves and feel inherently unlovable. I struggled for a number of months
with embarrassment at how I looked, feeling that I had become a very ugly
human being because of my physical loss. For a long time, I couldn't bear
to look at my stump. I was in fact ashamed of my appearance. I should have
known better. After all, I had been God, damn it!

Many people who have any one of my four identities take to heart the
contempt directed toward them, feeling a contempt for themselves that may
be hard, sometimes impossible, to shake off. If they believe what the dominant culture is saying about them, if they believe the negative judgments of

this culture, often intensified on hateful social media, they naturally come to despise themselves and, as a result, may want to destroy themselves. Lorde saw that such self-hatred is not easily transcended. She recognized that those looked down upon by others because of how they appear or who they sexually desire or the gender they identify with have a challenge as they struggle to see themselves as worthy of anyone's love. Society has an obligation to do everything it can to mitigate this self-hatred and show those who suffer from self-loathing how to overcome it. Schools at all levels have a responsibility in this matter.

Those of us who have succeeded in coming to love ourselves despite the contempt of others, who have overcome self-hatred, have an obligation to help others do the same. At the shelter I have an opportunity every day to help abused women see themselves in a new way, as persons who have worth, and to discredit those who have treated them with disdain. That's why I'm a volunteer for the Montrose Center's Empowering Houston's LGBT Youth (ages seven to twelve) on certain Sundays. That's why I've volunteered to work with amputees at the Sugar Land Medical Center. Based on our own experience of self-transformation, those of us who have learned to love ourselves can show others who suffer from culturally or religiously induced self-hatred that it is possible to come to truly value oneself.

Returning to the love commandment: the point is that there are many people who desperately need to learn to love themselves before they can begin to love others and work for the good of a larger community. It is of course important to work for the good of others, but one must begin by putting one's own house in order, by becoming convinced of one's own worth, by coming to genuinely respect oneself. We should never minimize the danger of the sickness of self-hatred that, if untreated, can lead to self-destruction.

Hillel, the great Jewish sage, captured this idea when he said: "If I am not for myself, who will be for me?"

Female, Black, Same-Gender-Loving, and One-Legged, I'm now comfortable with my multiple selves and committed to the promotion of self-respect for all human beings who possess an identity that others look down upon. Like Audre Lorde, I am proud of my often disdained multiple identities, seeking to build coalitions of like-minded people while not asking anyone to give up a particular identity. Like Lorde, I sometimes feel that I'm expected by different movements to which I belong to pick out one aspect of myself and make it my whole self, ignoring the other dimensions. I have to say with Lorde: "My fullest concentration of energy is available to me only when I integrate all the parts of who I am, openly, allowing power from particular sources of living to flow back and forth freely through all my different selves, without the restrictions of externally imposed definition." And I must add what she adds: "Only then can I bring myself and my energy to the service of those struggles which I embrace as part of my living."

You really are taken with the voice and life of Audre Lorde.

To be honest, she is the kind of person I had in mind as a model when I made my decision to incarnate, to become a human being. You could say that, since I exited heaven, I have been creating my human self in the image of Audre Lorde: Black, Lesbian, Feminist, Egalitarian, Revolutionary. When I lost my leg, I, paradoxically, found another piece of my self, just as being one-breasted became part of Lorde's identity after her mastectomy. Just as Lorde gained a new way of seeing herself and the world after her surgery, so did I. That's why she refused the offer of a prosthetic breast: she felt she had nothing to hide or be ashamed of. She was my inspiration when I chose not to hide my stump. Being one-legged no more completely defines me than being one-breasted defined Lorde—but it is a dimension of my identity.

When I was God, I witnessed suffering from afar without being able to do anything to relieve it. I experienced from on high the pain and loss—both physical and mental—that cancer causes human beings, especially terminal cancers, but I was unable to offer help. I was somewhat consoled and greatly inspired by how some individuals handled terminal illness, pain, and loss. Lorde was one of them. The pain she experienced after her mastectomy was all too familiar to me when I was God, as I had helplessly witnessed countless such cases. I observed untold numbers of people with cancer who suffered both from the pain of their disease and from the sometimes equally horrible pain that occurs immediately following surgery.

Lorde also experiences what I reported to you earlier: pain in a missing part, so-called phantom pain. Lorde says in *The Cancer Journals*: "My breast which was no longer there would hurt as if it were being squeezed in a vise." And as she also says: "that was perhaps the worst pain of all, because it would come with a full complement of horror that I was to be forever reminded of my loss by suffering in the a part of me which was no longer there." Lorde's physical pain is accompanied by a profound sadness at what she lost, a combination that brought with it deep despair. I felt something similar about my missing leg in terms of both physical pain and emotional loss.

Although there are traditional believers who, to justify an omnipotent God's nonintervention, argue that pain can ennoble the soul, make the sufferer a stronger person, Lorde, rightly, would have none of this. As she put it: "Pain does not mellow you, nor does it ennoble, in my experience." And let me add that children who die in pain from a terminal disease are not ennobled: they have no future, no opportunity to show they have been ennobled. Also, as God, I could not stand the often repeated, patronizing, false bit of theological comfort naïve true believers seek to give those suffering:

"God will not give you more pain than you can handle." Tell that to the children, or adults for that matter, who scream in agony before they die.

Lorde's battle with cancer—and her effort to rebuild her life and affirm her altered body after the amputation of her right breast—provides a model for all women who face coming to terms with bodies that society deems less than ideal, indeed as abnormal or shameful, a deviation from how the culture tells us women should look. "Growing up Fat Black Female," Lorde writes, "and almost blind in america requires so much strength that you have to learn from it or die." Die from suicide is what she means. And Lorde encounters, after her mastectomy, a strong prejudice against a woman with only one breast who refuses to hide or disguise this. She challenges this prejudice.

Lorde lives out the ideas developed in her important 1977 talk "The Transformation of Silence into Language and Action." An example of such transformation is how she handles breast cancer and the amputation of a breast. Let me repeat: she never denies the emotional loss she feels. She tells us in *The Cancer Journals* that the emotional pain caused by the amputation of her breast is at least as sharp as the pain of separating from her mother. Lorde does not want to judge other women for responding differently than she did to the loss of a breast or both breasts—by for example, keeping silent about it or choosing to wear a prosthesis.

What she does want to assert is this: if she is going to be true to herself and her need to affirm her new one-breasted body, she must transform silence about this into language and action. Lorde wants to decide for herself how she will appear after her surgery: she wants to define herself instead of being defined by others. She creates an example of what women can be in this situation, by simply refusing to make any effort to conceal what she has lost through surgery, never trying to make it appear she does not have a missing breast.

As she is leaving the hospital after her surgery, she is reprimanded by a woman from Reach for Recovery—an organization that helped women after breast surgery—for not wearing the prosthesis she was given. The woman even says: "You will feel so much better with it on. Otherwise it's bad for the morale of the office." Lorde is so outraged she cannot speak. So, she responds with silence, all the while furious inside. She is thinking: what every woman who has lost a breast actually needs is a healthy reminder that having one breast does not mean her life is over, rather than the message she is receiving from the medical establishment—namely that her life is over unless she uses an artificial breast to make her feel good about herself and the way she looks, mainly to make others feel more at ease.

Let me return to something I said in the beginning of our conversation, when I defended Lorde's insistence on physically appearing as she really is:

a woman with only one breast. I want to argue that her decision has nothing to do with the fact that she lives in a time that has not yet experienced the wisdom of postmodern and post-human thinking. For example, in her critique of Lorde's decision to refuse a prosthesis, Diane Price Herdl says of *The Cancer Journals*: "While in 1979 Lorde chose to love her one-breasted body as an alternative to remaining alien to herself," the emergence of post-human and postmodern art and theory "challenge the idea that any of us are ever alien to ourselves; in fact, we need to celebrate the alien to ourselves." Since Lorde wrote *The Cancer Journals*, according to Herdl, we have come to see bodies differently: "to see bodies as produced, as, in fact, forever alien to ourselves." I think this misses Lorde's point that a woman who chooses to appear as she is—in her case, with only one breast—is demonstrating that she has nothing to hide and is affirming that her body can be as human and attractive as female bodies that have two breasts.

Given Lorde's notion that it is important to be who you are and not try to satisfy a particular culture's expectations of how you should look, she would have accepted the decision of Trans Persons to change their bodies to match their personal perception of their gender identity. Whether that means a person who was born in a male body who identifies as female getting hormone therapy to grow breasts and having surgery that creates an artificial vagina, or the opposite in the case of a person born female changing an inherited body so it corresponds to a felt male identity, including the creation of a prosthetic penis and getting hormone therapy to make the chest look more masculine—to create in each case a body that corresponds with this Trans Person's self-perceived gender identity—I cannot see Lorde objecting to implanting "alien" parts into these bodies.

Lorde never says that there is something inherently wrong with the use of prostheses—artificial limbs, body parts, or technologies that are not part of one's natural body—if they can be chosen freely, for whatever reason: for example, even a prosthetic breast after a mastectomy as long as the woman has not been pressured and discouraged from accepting her changed body. Lorde observes that prostheses usually serve a real function. She even mentions artificial legs as an example of prostheses that enable otherwise disabled people to walk. Prostheses for Transgender people—and not all want them—may achieve a sexual function that enables them to have the sexual life they prefer and/or to appear to themselves, as well as others, as the persons they believe they are. It depends on a person's felt gender identity: who they believe they really are. And there are of course those who refuse the either/or of Female/Male and describe themselves as Non-binary, an umbrella term that can refer to a wide range of identities on the gender spectrum.

Lorde moved from silence to outspokenness in announcing what was at that time a transgressive position: refusing to wear a prosthetic breast. She then moves from speech to action by never trying to conceal her altered body. She shows us a prideful way to live in the absence of a body part, a way that says to onlookers that she has nothing to be ashamed of. Lorde's public announcement of her refusal to wear a prosthesis and her decision to dress in a way that revealed her actual shape paves the way for women to do this without being transgressive, thereby creating a new normal for women who undergo a mastectomy.

Lorde not only accepts the loss of her breast and her new body, but takes lessons from her mastectomy and terminal cancer that enable her to live in full awareness of her mortality—in fact seeing this as providing her a path to a new feeling of power and a new appreciation for life. There were times that Lorde thought she would die from breast cancer. As I already mentioned, she later died of liver cancer. Here is how she eloquently put this in *The Cancer Journals* (*and now Shekhinah appears to be mimicking Lorde's voice*):

> I mourn women who limit their loss to the physical loss alone, who do not move into the whole terrible meaning of mortality as both weapon and power. For once we accept the actual existence of our dying, who can ever have power over us again? I am writing across a gap so filled with death—real death, the fact of it—that it is hard to believe that I am still very much alive and writing this. The fact of all these other deaths heightens and sharpens my living, makes the demand upon it more particular, and each decision even more critical.

Lorde's words keep me aware of my own mortality and the importance of using time wisely. You might think that I should not need this reminder. But even though now lodged in a fragile human body, even after the life-threatening accident that took my leg, I sometimes forget I'm no longer a timeless being—so entrenched, after eons, is my assumption that I will live forever. I can still easily forget that I'm now mortal. So I'm indebted to Lorde for her example and her emphasis on the need to stay aware of the reality of death, something very much in the spirit of secular Buddhism. My near-death experience earlier today woke me up again.

Is there anything else you found in her life or writings you want to share before we're finished? This has to be one of my last questions before I depart. I have a wife with a serious disability who needs me to return.

I appreciate your patience. Yes, I want to share with you and your readers one of Lorde's unique contributions to living a meaningful human life. When earlier I spoke about Jesus, I attributed to him what I take to be the essence of divine love, something worthy of imitation: namely love that is self-giving and totally generous in character—love as *agape*. This is a transcendent form of love we should aspire to live out. I also mentioned the importance of *philia*, the love characteristic of friendship, something also to be cultivated and cherished. These forms of love contribute to a truly meaningful life. In addition, Audre Lorde recognizes the importance of another kind of love that is usually mistakenly thought to be reducible to sexual love, namely *eros*, a form of love we encountered earlier in discussing Cohen's "Halleujah."

In an important talk—titled "Uses of the Erotic: The Erotic as Power" (1978)—Lorde takes issue with a narrow view of the erotic that identifies it with sexual love. Although for Lorde, *eros* includes, but is not exhausted by, sexual love, it excludes something it is sometimes associated with: namely pornography—sexual desire that has nothing to do with love. According to Lorde, pornography focuses on sensation without feeling—for example the sensation of sexual pleasure, apart from a feeling of affection for another person. *Eros*, as Lorde uses the term, is the domain of feelings that may or may not involve a sexual relationship. The whole world of feeling, with the exception of anger, has historically been devalued by men who see it as the opposite of something they highly value: reason. Lorde is not arguing for women to abandon reason; rather her contention is that there is no need to be embarrassed by, or apologetic about, feelings. She argues that feelings, contrary to a common view, can be rational and cognitive: they can in fact be a source of knowledge and insight.

The erotic for Lorde is that which helps us connect with our deepest feelings—and our deepest wisdom. Sexual love—which, if it is truly love, does include affectionate feeling as well as sexual desire—is, I repeat, too narrow a category to capture what Lorde means by the term "erotic." Women were taught for centuries to separate the erotic from most vital areas of their lives other than sex. This has both limited women and impoverished the idea of the erotic. In its broadest meaning, the erotic for women, according to Lorde, is an assertion of their *life-force*: it is the creative energy that women, with the emergence of a more mature feminist movement, were, Lord thought, beginning to reclaim in their language, their history, their dancing, their loving, their work, and their lives as a whole. For Lorde the erotic is something that empowers women by legitimating *their* feelings and their right to express them. Women so empowered are, according to Lorde, dangerous: dangerous from the perspective of those who wish to keep them subordinated to men.

Is Lorde only concerned with women?

In her writings and speeches on the erotic that's her focus, but what she says is also relevant to men. For the erotic, understood in the broad sense, to play a role in the lives of men, they must be able to connect with their deepest feelings rather than devaluing this part of themselves. The erotic, according to Lorde, enables one to have a profound feeling of satisfaction and completion about one's life, the kind of fulfillment that is not at the expense of other persons. It is connected with the wish for a life well-lived. *Eros* is that which draws us toward excellence and toward a celebration of our lives. The erotic is, as she puts it beautifully, "a longed-for bed which I enter gratefully and from which I rise up empowered."

The erotic, according to Lorde, is about action as well as feeling: it is about how acutely and fully we can feel who we are in what we are doing. Being attuned to the erotic involves the deepest understanding and knowledge of our desires and emotions, of ourselves. It is the power to feel deeply everything we do and everything we experience. Thus, the erotic involves both feeling and action in an experience of being fully alive. It transcends what Freud labels "the pleasure principle." And it is the opposite of what Freud calls *thanatos*, the death drive. We can, however, experience the erotic even when death is imminent. Lorde experiences it as she is dying of liver cancer. The erotic, as she uses the term, cannot be separated from the spiritual—and the spiritual, in the deepest sense, cannot be separated from liberating social and political action: radical praxis.

Lorde sees herself as a poetic revolutionary and a revolutionary poet as well as a deeply spiritual person, as long as one does not reduce the spiritual to God or the afterlife, to a supernatural dimension. I consider myself a deeply spiritual person in my life as a secular Buddhist, even though I obviously don't believe that there is any longer a supernatural world. A socially engaged Buddhism, as I understand it, is about being fully alive and completely in touch with our feelings while striving for radical social change—and thus also feeling the need to connect with others in cooperative social action oriented toward the liberation of all human beings from suffering and oppression. It also means that you want others to be in touch with their deepest emotions, to feel fully alive, and to move toward excellence in all that they do. We should want all individuals to fully realize the erotic in their lives.

I still find Lorde's use of the term "erotic" elusive. Can you tell me what specific difference it made in Lorde's life?

The erotic functioned in Lorde's life in a variety of ways. One manifestation of the erotic for her was in the human-to-human connections she enjoyed, the sense of strength that comes from fully and intimately sharing one's life with other persons. This included her Same-Gender-Loving relationship with a professor of psychology, Frances Louise Clayton, her partner, and their relationship with the two children they raised. Unlike *agape* love, which is directed toward all persons, erotic love is directed toward particular individuals. More broadly, the erotic can also be found in participation in a particular community of people committed to the same goal: for example, equal respect for women. This shared aspiration forms a bridge between individuals who may be very different from each other in significant ways—for example, women of different races and sexual orientations. Women who are racially and sexually different can passionately share the same objective—namely, the creation of a society that guarantees women equal rights and equal respect. This common commitment never means denying their differences.

Black and White Women can erotically share a common commitment to freedom from oppression and a passionate desire to create a society where they are recognized as having the same worth as men. But of course Black and White Women, while sharing the same commitment to equality, have significant differences that set them apart. A Black Woman in the United States is very different, by virtue of her heritage, including slavery, and her daily struggle against racism, from a White Woman. And an Other-Gender-Loving Woman and a Same-Gender-Loving Woman can share a common cause—for example, reaching the goal of full equality for all Women—while never denying that their difference in sexual orientation sets them apart in an important way. Sexually, they inhabit different worlds. Women should never deny their differences even as they are erotically (not to be confused with the term "sexually") drawn together for a common cause: the freedom of women from all forms of discrimination and the achievement of full legal equality with men. So, while the erotic is that which enables an individual to celebrate her unique self and pursue personal excellence, it is also the power that binds different individuals together as they build coalitions to correct all forms of injustice and create a better society and world. *Eros* generates passion suffused with knowledge about how to connect with allies.

Sometimes, according to my reading of Lorde, the erotic feeling that provides the power and energy necessary for transformative social action—for instance, the fight against inequality and racism—is *anger*. This is an emotion that women have often been discouraged from feeling or showing, as if it's an emotion that men rightly and exclusively own, as if it is inappropriate for women to express anger. Anger may seem socially unattractive if expressed by a Woman, maybe especially a Black Woman. In fact, anger can be a life-affirming and power-giving erotic feeling if we understand *eros* in the broad sense that Lorde uses the term. It is difficult to feel weak when feeling anger, especially justified anger: for instance, anger directed against racial prejudice and belittlement. Earlier when we discussed God's emotional life, we never talked about the anger of God. The God of the Torah of course gets angry, but, as you know, often the anger of this mythical God is directed indiscriminately, as if God were an explosive that could be easily triggered, resulting in the death of the innocent well as the guilty.

The anger of the mythical God of the Torah after the golden calf incident is a good example: He was ready to destroy the entire Israelite community and would have done so if Moses had not dissuaded him, appealing to divine vanity ("What would the Egyptians say?"). Obviously this is not the kind of anger Lorde has in mind.

The uncontrolled rage the God of the Torah sometimes displays is different from the anger Lorde is discussing. The anger she has in mind is similar to the anger I felt as God: namely anger at injustice of all kinds: truly holy anger. Addressing a Women's Studies Association meeting in Connecticut in 1982—in a talk titled "The Uses of Anger: Women Responding to Racism"—Lorde tells her audience that every woman has a well-stocked arsenal of anger, potentially useful against various forms of oppression, personal and institutional, that arouse her anger. She does not endorse anger that is indiscriminately expressed and out of control: irrational anger, blind rage that cannot see straight. She recognizes that anger is only useful if it is intelligently directed at a legitimate target. We might call this controlled rage. As Lorde puts it: "Focused with precision, anger can become a powerful source of energy, serving progress and change." Lorde sees anger as justifiable and rational in particular situations; to borrow Buddhist language, it can become a "skillful means" to achieve one's justified ends. Lorde's approach transcends the binary of reason vs. feeling. Anger, rather than being essentially irrational, *can* become, if thoughtfully practiced, a wisely directed emotion.

For Lorde, legitimate anger can be both a motivation to and an instrument of radical social change: justified anger can be translated into action in the service of a vision of equal respect for, and liberation of, those who are oppressed. Anger against injustice can be cognitively valuable, bringing with it painful clarity about what needs to be done. Lorde's anger brought her suffering—anger does not usually feel good—but she became convinced that it also made it possible for her to survive as a Black Same-Gender-Loving Feminist. She was not about to give up anger unless she could find something just as powerful to replace it on the road to clarity. Anger rightly focused can give Black Human Beings and other disrespected communities the confidence to redefine the terms according to which they live and work. We can construct, as she eloquently says, "anger by painful anger, stone upon heavy stone, a future of pollinating difference and the earth to support our choices." As God, I too was angry about injustice everywhere and angry at my transcendent impotence. I'm angry now, and Lorde provides me with inspiration and guidance about how to use this anger—and of course now, as a human being, I *can* act on my anger, working with others who are equally angry about injustice, to actually help make changes in the world.

Antoinette Nwandu—who describes herself as a "*cisgender Black writer*" whose work, as we have seen, focuses on the themes of self-loathing and self-definition in the Black Community—finds, as I do, in Lorde's talk "The Uses of Anger" reassurance that her anger as a young Black Woman gives her the potential to transform insight into power. She feels, as I do, that Lorde's acknowledgment of her anger as a Black Woman helps her and other Black Women *own* their rage. Anger in the name of justice can be both socially subversive and powerful. Working together to change their condition, the justice-inspired anger of Black Women is loaded with information and energy.

So Lorde construes the feeling of justified anger as a rational emotion that, if properly harnessed, can drive us forward and give us a sense of control over our lives. Those who have been victims of bigotry and disrespect can take away from Lorde's analysis of anger this message: we must continually appropriate and transform the energy of fury into a creative life force whose power instructs us to respect ourselves and to demand equal respect from others. For a contemporary defense of the value of Female anger, your readers might want to take a look at Rebecca Traister's *Good and Mad: The Revolutionary Power of Women's Anger.*

You don't see anger as inconsistent with Buddhist practice? Doesn't Buddhism view anger as one of the three poisons, along with greed and ignorance?

On my interpretation, Buddhism warns us against hatred, not anger: hatred is the real poison because it often blinds us and does not allow us to see the one we hate as a human being. I can feel anger toward you while recognizing your humanity. Buddhism never tells us to deny our emotions. On the contrary, it encourages us to befriend even negative emotions to see what we can learn from them and to transform negative feelings into positive action. Remember, Lorde is not sanctioning blind rage or hatred, but construes anger as an emotion that *can* have cognitive content: it can teach us to become clear about how the values we believe in, such as justice and human dignity, are being violated. If not out of control, anger provides us with the energy we need to fight Sexism, Racism, Homophobia, Transphobia, Ableism, Ageism, Anti-Semitism, Islamophobia, and other forms of prejudice.

Recall also what I said about the Buddhist idea of skillful means: emotions, if used mindfully, can help us achieve important goals. Remember,

anger can motivate us to join with allies who are equally angry about being treated unfairly and to collectively channel our anger toward the end of
constructive social change. The *eros* of anger can thus be a creative social
force, justified indignation in service of a social good. For example, Lorde
was angry about the discrimination and sexism she encountered as a Black
Woman with cancer, and she used her fury at the medical establishment to
move from silence to speech to action. By the way, widespread racial bias
in the medical treatment of Black compared to White patients remains a
serious problem in the United States. The National Cancer Institute reports
that African Americans and other minorities receive a lower quality of care
and do less well after receiving a cancer diagnosis. And Lorde was ahead of
her time in warning about environmental causes of cancer and demanding
that the offending corporations be held responsible.

But anger is only one of the feelings that Lorde construes as having the
transformative potential to generate energy in the service of an empowered
life oriented toward liberation and personal excellence. The erotic, according to Lorde, can also be found in our capacity to experience joy, a positive
feeling that Buddhism encourages us to cultivate. Joy is one of the most
uplifting emotions a person can experience, and it is essentially connected
with the celebration of one's life. It is something one should wish for all others. Buddhism calls us to work at creating joy in our lives while also striving
to bring joy to others: indeed, learning to take joy in the joy of others is considered by Buddhism a good beyond measure, a sublime emotional state. I
think Lorde would agree with this. She tells us that she found joy in the way
she stretched her body in moving to music. Lorde liked to quote the American Feminist-Anarchist Emma Goldman: "If I cannot dance, I don't want to
be part of your revolution." Of course Lorde found some of her greatest joy
in the creative core of her life: writing poetry. Recall that she saw herself as a
poet revolutionary and a revolutionary poet. We might even describe her as
an erotic radical poet. And if she were alive today, as I acknowledged earlier,
Lorde would probably recognize the need to put poetry to music in order to
reach the widest possible audience.

For Lorde, the erotic can become the lens through which we scrutinize
all aspects of our existence, forcing us to honestly evaluate every dimension
of our life, to discover whether we are living a truly meaningful life. Lorde
believes that the assessment of one's life is "a grave responsibility"—if we
truly "want to move toward excellence instead of settling for the shoddy, the
conventionally expected, or the merely safe."

Lorde affirms the importance of pursuing a form of personal excellence
that can never be separated from cooperative action for the social good and
the liberation of all human beings. To be in touch with the erotic dimension

of life, to be in touch with our most powerful emotions—for example, anger and joy—means refusing to allow an external authority to tell us how we should feel or how we should live; it means being self-directed. For Lorde, if we are living a truly authentic life, working against all forms of oppression is one with affirmation of self. Motivated and empowered from within, we not only refuse to accept personal powerlessness, but also the powerlessness of others that society has historically disenfranchised. You should note that none of this requires belief in God or religion in any sense.

Is there anything missing in Lorde's vision? Briefly, if possible.

In a time when many people of a progressive persuasion are feeling despair about the world, what I think is implicit in Lorde's vision, but not fully developed by her, is the need for hope. If I who once lived as God have any message for people fighting injustice, it is that they cultivate hope, hope connected to collective action. Don't waste time petitioning God for help or praying for a messiah to show up. Instead, take matters into your own hands, continue to do the hard work of fighting bigotry of all kinds, create a world in which every human being is treated with dignity, and make every effort to minimize the suffering of nonhuman sentient beings and ecological destruction as you seek, with others, to save a wounded planet from the damage humans do to it daily. That would truly be the work of God, work in service to God.

Let me just say one more thing about hope, something you can find in the writings of the remarkable and wise Rebecca Solnit, someone you mentioned earlier as the author of *Paradise Built in Hell*. In an article in *The Guardian* in 2016 entitled "Hope is an Embrace of the Unknown," Solnit recognizes that with worsening climate change, unprecedented ecological damage, hideous economic inequality, the resurgence of racism, continuing misogyny, an uptick in anti-Semitism and Islamophobia, and a spike in attacks on members of LGBPTTQQIA+2 communities, many people who call themselves progressives are reduced to a mood of defeatism, cynicism, and hopelessness. Solnit tells us that practicing hope doesn't mean denying the reality of terrible things. Rather, she believes, realistic hope needs to be based on four things: critical thinking, the acceptance of grief, recognition that the future is unknown, and overcoming amnesia.

I applaud Solnit, a member of the White elite, for recognizing that a strategy for realistic hope is best expressed in the words of Patrisse Cullors, one of the founders of Black Lives Matter: "Provide hope and inspiration for collective action to build collective power to achieve collective transformation, rooted in grief and rage but pointed towards vision and dreams." What Solnit wants us to see is that failure can happen alongside success. While not denying defeats and worsening conditions, we have also to recognize important achievements.

Let's focus on the United States. Despite Trump, the Paris Accords are still supported by almost every other nation in the world, and many U.S. governors and mayors, even in red states, are doing what they can to confront and reduce the effects of climate deterioration, independent of the federal government. Younger Republicans are beginning to demand action to slow climate collapse. Despite continuing homophobia, marriage equality remains, even with a conservative court, a constitutional right. Despite an increase in anti-Semitism, we have a PEW research study that tells us that among a majority of Americans, one of the religious communities they feel the warmest toward is the Jewish, something we can expect to happen with respect to the Muslim community as people get to know their Muslim neighbors better. Despite the rise of White Nationalists who now openly and boldly march in cities for their cause, we have the presence of anti-racist counter-demonstrators in greater numbers at these rallies. Despite the continuing abuse of women in this country, there is now a new boldness shown by an increasing number of American women willing to name their abusers, women who have started a revolution. While we grieve negative realities and see them as tragic, we need also to celebrate successes, even if they are only partial victories.

For Solnit, genuine hope is always based on memory of past achievements—this is what she means by overcoming amnesia. Our knowledge that the future is uncertain, unknown, means that how things turn out will depend on what we do individually and collectively. As God, I built uncertainty into the universe, a universe that still includes, even if on a single fragile planet, self-conscious free beings. The positive meaning of uncertainty in the human world is that we have the power, the free choice, to transform things for the better. Buddhism teaches us to live in full awareness of impermanence: this means that what seem like solid forces of oppression and injustice are not. But accepting impermanence and uncertainty also means that a good future is not guaranteed, and the good we've achieved is not necessarily a permanent achievement. Impermanence means that our successes are not like solid things that are unalterable: we will have to work to maintain victories and, when our victories seem to be slipping away, we may have to fight new battles we did not anticipate.

So, while I left heaven because I couldn't bear to watch useless and unjust suffering occurring on earth, keep in mind that I did so in order to work as a human being, with other human beings, to diminish suffering in the world and fight for a more joyful future. Despair and cynicism are states of mind we cannot afford. Radical, informed, and realistic hope—hope based on both memories of successes and the acceptance that a good future is not certain—is what we need. That's the understanding of hope I would like to see spread. Again, a better future will not come automatically, the earth will not save itself, and God will not intervene to redeem humankind and the planet. It's up to us, as it has always been. God is no longer beyond us: She has become a human being, working for a new world, partnering with others to save the planet.

Just for the record: I don't believe God is dead. I continue to have faith, on the days I can believe, that there is still a God. I naturally have my doubts about the existence of God, as any thoughtful human being must. And there are many different views of God: they are of course all speculation. When I can, I believe in a God Who is limited in power but perfect in goodness: like the God you said you were. But I don't believe such a God would commit suicide. The God of my understanding—to borrow AA language—has the perspective of eternity. This cosmos is, on my view, one of many that contain intelligent life, and, despite what you say, I believe there is intelligent life in other parts of this universe. I believe in a truly wise God, One Who knows how to appreciate what is valuable in every universe that has so far existed—Who will bring into existence other universes in the future and will preserve in divine memory what is valuable in all of them. So, according to my theology, God has brought, and will continue to bring, into existence other worlds: Multiverses if you will, some with less suffering and more joy than the one we inhabit. God, on my view, has a larger vision of things and can lovingly and patiently handle whatever is thrown at Her. I imagine a God Who suffers with us—but Who can also give us strength while moving us to compassionate action. I imagine God inspiring the radical hope you just described. When I can believe, I believe in a God Who appreciates and remembers even the failures of those of us working to create a more just world and acting to save a damaged planet, a God Who will keep in perfect divine memory all of our ethical efforts, all of our unique lives, long after this universe is cold and dead. Since I imagine a God Who is related to countless universes the nature of which we can only guess, this is a God Who is always related in love to some world. And the God of my faith is always related to a world that includes intelligent, free subjects capable of reciprocal loving relationships with each other and with God. This God creates in every universe conditions necessary for the emergence of intelligent life, and within this form of life the inner urge and inner voice that inspires intelligent beings to a life of kindness and generosity. Although this God suffers with all sentient life, She is not overwhelmed by the suffering that occurs in this or any other cosmos. She also makes possible joy and takes joy in every creature's joy. In sum, I imagine a God Who is able to maintain equanimity because of Her transcendent, eternal perspective and capacity to preserve in perfect eternal memory all the good that happens in every universe. Eternally hopeful, this God knows how to begin anew, eternally. But that is only my take on God.

Thanks for sharing your view. As you have insisted, any view of God is only speculation. May those who have a need to believe, drawing from countless visions of the divine, find a view of the Transcendent (God, Nirvana, etc.) that enriches and gives meaning to their lives. And of course there are secular humanists who find meaning without recourse to the supernatural. I of course see my vision of God as more plausible than yours or any other view because I'm convinced I lived it. It is what I remember, although I have admitted that I could be mistaken—that I could have a false memory.

Even if what I have told you is a queer tale, it is for me a true tale. Of course that's what every true believer says. You of course think I've made up my strange story. From the beginning, I made it clear that, although I hoped that you would, I did not expect you to believe me. I wanted a sympathetic ear and a way to communicate my message to the world. You provided that. I hope we will have other conversations.

I do too. I'm sorry. I have go. My sitter has been patient. Maybe we can continue the conversation another Saturday or Sunday, during one of your long Sabbaths. Please, please, when you walk home, watch for traffic! Or better yet, since it's late, let me drive you home.

Thank you, with great appreciation. I remain rattled by what happened this morning. The darkness of night may bring out more haters. I know, however, that despite our theological differences, you will join with me and people of many faiths and those of no faith to try to change the minds and hearts of the haters, if not from hate to love, as least to self-doubt. And we must work on ourselves so that we don't also become haters, demonizing those with whom we disagree, no longer seeing them as human beings.

Acknowledgments

The author would like to acknowledge the following sources referred to by characters in various places in this novel.

Baker, Katie J. M. "What Do We Do with These Men?" *The New York Times*, April 27, 2018.

Batchelor, Stephen. *Secular Buddhism: Imagining the Dharma in an Uncertain World*. New Haven: Yale University Press, 2017.

Berdyaev, Nicolas. *The Destiny of Man*. Brooklyn: Semantron, 2009.

Bichell, Rae Ellen. "Scientists Start to Tease Out the Subtler Ways Racism Hurts Health." (Weathering) January 14, 2018. NPR transcript. http://www.npr.org.

Bonhoeffer, Dietrich. *Letters & Papers from Prison*. Translated and edited by Eberhard Bethge. New York: Macmillan, 1972.

Bowie, Herb. "Appreciation (Cohen's *Hallelujah*)." Blog: *Reason to Rock: Rock Music as an Art Form*. 2016. http://www.reasontorock.com.

Brinkley, Douglas. "After the Hurricane Winds Die Down, Larry McMurtry's Houston Trilogy Lives On." *The New York Times*, September 14, 2017.

Brooks, Gwendolyn. "The Preacher: Ruminates Behind the Sermon." In *The Essential Gwendolyn Brooks*, edited by Elizabeth Alexander, 6. New York: The Library of America, 2005.

Brushoff, Alan. "Review of play: *Breach: A Manifesto on Race in America through the Eyes of a Black Girl Recovering from Self-Hate* by Antoinette Nwandu." *Around the Town Chicago*, March 14, 2018.

Caramanica, Jon. "In Rap, Little Reckoning for Misconduct." *The New York Times*, June 6, 2018.

Ceballos, Gerado, Paul Erlich, and Rodolfo Dirzo. "Biological Annihilation Via the Ongoing Sixth Mass Extinction Signaled by Vertebrate Population Losses and Declines." *Proceedings of the American Academy of Sciences*, July 10, 2017.

Chan, Francis. *Crazy Love: Overwhelmed by a Relentless God*. Colorado Springs: David. C. Cook, 2013.

Coetzee, J. M. *Slow Man: A Novel*. New York: Penguin, 2005.

Craig, William Lane. "Theism and Big Bang Cosmology." *Australasian Journal of Philosophy* 69 (2006) 492–503.

Cuthbert, Lori, and Douglas Main. "Orca Mother Drops Her Calf, after Unprecedented 17 Days of Mourning." *National Geographic*, August 13, 2018.

Davies, Paul. "The Cosmos Might Be Mostly Devoid of Life." *Scientific American*. September 1, 2016.

Diamond, James Arthur. "S.Y. Agnon's Kaddish: Mourning for God." *Shofar: An Interdisciplinary Journal of Jewish Studies* 22 (2004) 22–42.

Dostoevsky, Fyodor. *The Brothers Karamazov*. Translated by David McDuff. New York: Penguin, 2003.

Douglass, Frederick. *Narrative of the Life of Frederick Douglass, an American Slave*. Mineola, New York: Dover, 2016.

Empire, Kitty. "Janelle Monae: Dirty Computer Review—from Dystopian Android to R&B Party Girl." *The Guardian*, September 28, 2018.

Ewer, William. "How Odd of God to Choose the Jews." In *Week-End Book*, edited by Francis Meynel. London: Nonesuch, 1924.

Fleming, Pippa. "Black Lesbians and Gender Fluidity." *The Economist*, July 3, 2018.

Foer, Jonathan Safran. *Extremely Loud and Incredibly Close*. Boston: Houghton Mifflin, 2005.

Gates, Henry Louis, Jr. "Ending the Slavery Blame-Game." *The New York Times*, April 22, 2010.

Hartshorne, Charles. *Omnipotence and Other Theological Mistakes*. New York: State University of New York Press, 1984.

Herndl, Diane Price. "Reconstructing the Posthuman Feminist Body Twenty Years after Audre Lorde's *Cancer Journals*." In *Feminisms Redux: An Anthology of Literary Theory and Criticism*, edited by Robyn Warhol and Diane Price Herndl, 144–55. New Brunswick, NJ: Rutgers University Press, 2009.

Heschel, Abraham Joshua. *God in Search of Man*. New York: Farrar, Straus, and Giroux, 1976.

———. *Man Is Not Alone*. New York: Farrar, Straus, and Giroux, 1976.

Hillesum, Etty. *An Interrupted Life and Letters from Westerbork*. Translated by Arnold J. Pomerans. New York: Holt, 1996.

Hubbard, Shanita. "Black Women Love Hip Hop, But It Doesn't Love Us Back." *HuffPost*, January 28, 2018.

Jacobs, Harriet, and Mary Prince. *The Classic Slave Narratives*. Edited and with an Introduction by Henry Louis Gates, Jr. New York: Mentor, 1987.

Jonas, Hans. "The Concept of God After Auschwitz: A Jewish Voice." In *Echoes from the Holocaust: Philosophical Reflections on a Dark Time*, edited by Alan Rosenberg and Gerald E. Myers, 292–305. Philadelphia: Temple University Press, 1988.

Kafer, Alison. *Feminist, Queer, Crip*. Bloomington: Indiana University, 2013.

Kazantzakis, Nicolas. *The Last Temptation of Christ*. Translated by Peter A. Bien. New York: Simon & Shuster, 1998.

Kent, Clarikisha. "*Blank Panther* is Ready to Take Dark-Skinned Actresses (and Colorism) Seriously." *HuffPost*, February 7, 2018.

Kendler, Maureen, quoted in D. Nyairo's "Celebrating Leonard Cohen with another 'Hallelujah' Moment." *The Daily Nation*, November 29, 2016. http://www.mobile.nation.co.ke.

Jenkins, Aric. "Stephen Hawking and Fellow Scientists Dismiss 'Big Bounce' Theory in Letter." *Time Magazine*, May 13, 2017.

Kantor, Jodi, and Megan Twohey. "Harvey Weinstein Paid Off Sexual Harassment Accusers for Decades." *The New York Times*, October 5, 2017.

Kimmerer, Robin Wall. *Braiding Sweetgrass*. Minneapolis: Milkweed Editions, 2013.

Kolasinki, Owen. "Kelly Marie Trans Speaks Out about Online Harassment: 'I Won't Be Marginalized.'" *Variety*, August 21, 2018.

Kurzweil, Arthur. "I *Am* the Little Jew Who Wrote the Bible." In *Leonard Cohen on Leonard Cohen: Interviews and Encounters*, edited by Jeff Burger, 369–93. Chicago: Chicago Review, 2014.

Kushner, Harold. *When Bad Things Happen to Good People*. New York: Random House, 1981. Interviewed by Jeremy Caplan: "Q & A: Harold Kushner." *Time Magazine*. October 12, 2006.

Lartey, Jamiles. "Black Lives Matter Movement: 'We Ignited a New Generation': Patrisse Khan-Cullors on the Resurgence of Black Activism." *The Guardian*. January 28, 2018.

Leibovitz, Liel. *A Broken Hallelujah: Rock and Roll, Redemption, and the Life of Leonard Cohen*. New York: Norton, 2014.

Levinas, Emmanuel. *Entre Nous: Thinking of the Other*. Translated by Michael B. Smith and Barbara Harshav. New York: Columbia University Press, 1998.

Levitin, Daniel J. *The World in Six Songs: How the Musical Brain Created Human Nature*. New York: Dutton, 2009.

Light, Alan. *The Holy or the Broken*. New York: Atria, 2012.

Lindsay-Abaire, David. *Rabbit Hole: A Play*. New York: Theatre Productions Group, 2011.

Lorde, Audre. *The Cancer Journals*. San Francisco: Aunt Lute Books, 1997.

———. *The Collected Poems of Audre Lorde*. New York: Norton, 1997. (Her poem "Power" can be found in this collection on p. 319.)

———. *Sister Outsider*. Berkeley: Crossing Press, 2007. ("Poetry Is Not a Luxury," "The Transformation of Silence into Language and Action," "Uses of the Erotic: The Erotic as Power," and "The Uses of Anger: Women Responding to Racism" can be found in this collection of essays and speeches.)

Lowry, Rick. "After Weinstein: A Cultural Revolution." *National Review*, November 24, 2017.

Manuel, Zenju Earthlyn. "The Hunger for Home." *Tricycle*, Spring 2018.

Michaelson, Jay. "So Long Leonard Cohen—Holy Sinner, Poet, Friend." *The Daily Beast*, November 11, 2016.

Milgram, Goldie. *Reclaiming Judaism as a Spiritual Practice*. Woodstock: Jewish Lights, 2004.

Moltmann, Jurgen. "God's Kenosis in the Creation and Consummation of the World." In *The Work of Love: Creation as Kenosis*, edited by John Polkinghorne, 137–51. Grand Rapids: Eerdmans, 2001.

Molodowsky, Kadya. "Merciful God." In *Judaism: The Norton Anthology of World Religions*, edited by David Biale, 705. New York: Norton, 2015.

Moore, Darnell L. *No Ashes in the Fire: Coming of Age Black and Free in America*. New York: National Books, 2018.

Murray, Nick. "How Pop Culture Wore Out Leonard Cohen's 'Hallelujah.'" *New York Times*, September 19, 2016.

Nietzsche, Friedrich. *Thus Spoke Zarathustra: A Book for None and All*. Translated by Walter Kaufmann. New York: Penguin, 2014.

Northup, Solomon. *Twelve Years a Slave*. New York: Barnes & Noble, 2007.

Norwood, Kimberly Jade. "Stories about Colorism in America." *Washington University Global Studies Law Review* 585 (2015) 585–607.

Nwandu, Antoinette. "Reading Audre Lorde's *Sister Outsider* after Charlottesville." *Los Angeles Review of Books*, October 30, 2017.

Pareles, Jon. "Pop Music in 2017: Glum and Glummer." *The New York Times*, December 22, 2017.

Popper, Karl. *Unended Quest: An Intellectual Autobiography*. Philadelphia: Routledge, 2005.

Prum, Richard. *The Evolution of Beauty: How Darwin's Forgotten Theory of Mate Choice Shapes the Animal World—and Us*. New York: Doubleday, 2017.

Ransby, Barbara. *Making All Black Lives Matter: Reimagining Freedom in the 21st Century*. Berkeley: University of California Press, 2018.

Reggente, Melissa. "Nurturant Behavior Toward Dead Conspecifics in Free-Ranging Mammals." *Journal of Mammalogy* 97 (2016) 1428–34.

Ricard, Matthieu. *Altruism: The Power of Compassion to Change Yourself and the World*. New York: Back Bay, 2016.

Sacks, Jonathan. *Essays on Ethics: A Weekly Reading of the Jewish Bible*. New Milford, CT: Maggid, 2016.

Segal, Benjamin J. *The Song of Songs: A Woman in Love*. Translated and Commentary by Benjamin J. Segal. New York: Gefen, 2009.

Solnit, Rebecca. "Hope Is an Embrace of the Unknown." *The Guardian*, July 15, 2016.

———. *Paradise Built in Hell: The Extraordinary Communities that Arise in Disaster*. New York: Penguin, 2010.

Sullivan, Andrew. "The Nature of Sex." *New York Magazine*, February 1, 2019.

Thanissara. *Time to Stand Up: An Engaged Buddhism Manifesto for Our Earth—The Buddha's Life and Message through Feminine Eyes*. Berkeley: North Atlantic, 2015.

Traister, Rebecca. *Good and Mad: The Revolutionary Power of Women's Anger*. New York: Simon & Schuster, 2018.

Villarosa, Linda. "Why Are Black Mothers and Babies in the United States Dying at Double the Rate of White Mothers and Babies?" *The New York Times Magazine*, April 15, 2018.

Wenig, Margaret. "God Is a Woman and God Is Growing Older." In *The Many Faces of God: A Reader in Modern Jewish Theologies*, edited by Rifat Sonsino, 240–48. New York: URJ Press, 2004.

Wiesel, Elie. "Letter to the Master of the Universe." *The New York Times*. October 2, 1997.

———. *The Trial of God*. New York: Schocken, 1979.

Will, George F. "The Real Down Syndrome Problem: Accepting Genocide." *The Washington* Post, March 14, 2018.

williams, angel Kyodo, and Lama Rod Owens. *Radical Dharma: Talking Race, Love, and Liberation*. Berkeley: North Atlantic, 2016.

Wilson, Edward O. "The 8 Million Species We Don't Know." *The New York Times*, March 3, 2018.

Wortham, Jenna. "How Janelle Monae Found Her Voice." *The New York Times Magazine*, April 19, 2018.

Zacharek, Stephanie, Eliana Doctermann, and Haley Sweetland Edwards. "Person of the Year: #MeToo: The Silence Breakers." *Time Magazine*, December 18, 2017.